Their Right to Vengeance

James Fisher Series
Book 2

G J Stevens

This is a work of fiction. Names, characters, businesses, places, events, locales, and incidents are either the products of the author's imagination or used in a fictitious manner. Any resemblance to actual persons, living or dead, or actual events is purely coincidental.

Copyright © GJ Stevens 2012-2023

The moral right of GJ Stevens to be identified as the author of this work has been asserted by him in accordance with the Copyright, Designs, and Patents Act 1998.

All rights reserved.

Copyright under the Berne Convention

British Library Cataloguing-in-Publication Data
A catalogue record for this book is available from the British Library

ISBN: 9798863169125

Other Books by GJ Stevens

James Fisher Series

Fate's Ambition

Post-apocalyptic Thrillers

IN THE END
BEFORE THE END
AFTER THE END
BEGINNING OF THE END (Novella)

SURVIVOR
Your Guide to Surviving the Apocalypse

Agent Carrie Harris Series

OPERATION DAWN WOLF
LESSON LEARNED
THE GEMINI ASSIGNMENT
CAPITAL ACTION (Novella)

Agent Carrie Harris – Undead Thrillers

STOPPING POWER – SEASON ONE

1

London

21st October

"Now," Farid screamed from the back seat of the hulking Range Rover, the metal leviathan lurching forward, its engine roaring towards the tiny gap between the two black BMW X5s blocking the deserted inner London artery.

In the plush leather beside him, Fisher pulled on his seatbelt before leaning to the side, staring at the eight dark-clothed figures with assault rifles draped over their shoulders, strolling as if without concern, to the side of the road.

Just as he pushed his arms out, locking them straight against the front seat, metal slammed against metal, the seatbelt pre-tensioners firing, snatching him into the leather. An airbag burst open at the side of his head, its shockwave gone in an instant as they rushed to a stop.

Opening his eyes, Fisher stared through the settling powder at their crumpled white bonnet filling half the distorted, shattered windscreen. At his side, Farid lay slumped against the door, his olive-tanned face paler than he'd ever seen before. Looking past the headrest, the driver lay with his head on the steering wheel as the front passenger moaned.

Glancing to his right with muffled pops burning his ears, everything seemed to float in his vision. The view only clarified when he saw one of Farid's men, his name forgotten, run past their wreck with a pistol held high. Recalling the second car that formed their convoy, Fisher watched the gun jerk, the sound sending pain through his head.

Before he could draw a much needed deep breath, Fisher coughed, holding his hand against his mouth at the stench of acrid smoke. Seeing thick, grey wisps seeping through the vents, he marvelled as it swirled, then twisted and turned its way toward him.

A sudden, spluttering cough jolted him back into the moment.

As his fingers found the seatbelt's release, the tension across his chest was replaced with a sudden ache, but the thickening air gave him no time to take stock. Pulling at the handle to his right, the door didn't open. His bones felt as if they ground together with each shove against the unmoving steel.

Heaving with a third push, Fisher stifled a yelp when it felt as if his chest ripped open, the door giving way just as its glass shattered, showering over him as he fell to the cold road.

Rising to his hands and knees, despite the stabs in his palms and his head seeming as if full of cotton wool, he crouched whilst doing his best to swipe the glass from his hands.

Not surprised to find their ride embedded in an X5 as he looked up, steam, or smoke, or both rose from the crush of metal and plastic. With his vision settling, he found the other Range Rover behind and a man raising from its bulk before he fired three gunshots, sending Fisher for cover.

Following where the man had aimed, Fisher spotted a line of figures, some of which he recognised, the sight reminding him what he should do. Reaching inside his pocket, he pulled out his Glock and levelled his aim at the furthest in the line and the one he knew as Hotwire.

Taking more care than usual, he fired a single round, congratulating himself on a perfect hit as Hotwire fell backwards and out of sight. Then feeling the car rock against his back, Fisher glanced over his shoulder to the passenger door as Farid stumbled across the road, the air lighting up with a chaos of gunfire seeming to come from everywhere.

Still with his door open, Fisher felt the hits against the metal as he raised his pistol to add to the barrage.

In a momentary lull, an engine started up and he watched the other Range Rover, its body peppered with holes, stutter forward as the horn rang out. The hail of bullets seemed to hold back as Farid and his companion dove in through an open door.

Fisher got to his feet whilst bending to keep low, but standing to run, gunfire sent him back down.

With a deep, slow breath, he felt his mind clear and raised his gun, firing toward those aiming his way before jumping to his feet, diving back through the rear door and across the leather strewn with glass. Not stopping to recover his breath, he was out the other side.

Despite the gunshots, he didn't halt; instead, running across the width of the road before rushing through a gap in the thick hedge, his arms flailed as he steadied in the wide open expanse of grass.

Leaving behind a roaring engine, Fisher took off across the deserted park towards the tallest building on the other side.

Still holding his gun, his gaze snatched left then right as he tried to get his bearings, whilst doing his best to fight the sense his lungs could give up at any moment. Somehow keeping up the sprint with a glance over his shoulder, his eyes went wide when he caught sight of two men in dark combat gear running behind.

Knowing their names, he took comfort they were two of their slowest.

Traffic rushed across the road ahead as he drew close. Pushing the Glock back inside his jacket, he jumped over the short metal railings, dodging the cars in both directions. Not noticing the flurry of horns and screech of rubber, he focused on the wide entrance of the high-rise hospital.

After a quick glance behind, he paused inside at a tall sign, his gaze rushing from side to side as he scanned the colour-coded list of departments. Finding what he'd hoped for, he was soon back on his heels, rushing down a corridor and following a red line painted on the floor.

Slowing only enough to slip between trolleys and hobbling patients, annoyed nurses and round security guards, the corridor soon split with the left-hand side blocked with a single section of rigid yellow barrier.

Without a pause, he vaulted into the unlit corridor beyond, where he dodged paint pots and brushes strewn against the bare plaster walls that swept around the corner. Steadying his pace, he caught his breath, stopping only as a door on the left opened.

With a glance over his shoulder when he heard what sounded like a paint pot skittering along the floor, but finding the corridor behind empty, he turned back to see Agent Harris in her grey suit, her strawberry blonde hair hanging at her shoulders, and a silenced Glock pointed at the floor.

Her steps made no noise against the bare concrete; or perhaps they did, his senses instead overwhelmed. Showing no emotion, she raised the gun, and unable to move he watched her lips slowly part.

"It's time to end this game," she said as a round spat from her gun.

***

London

10th October

Wearing a single-breasted waistcoat sandwiched by an expensive grey suit, a packet-fresh white shirt and black skinny tie, Fisher shuffled for comfort. With the leather chair creaking beneath him, he stared out of the small room's window, the tang of polish and dust hanging in the air.

From the dark mahogany table older than anything he owned, his crisp white Samsung chimed as it sat beside the modern black desk phone. Knowing without checking what the message would say, he looked at the empty identical leather chair opposite before turning back through the triple-glazed windows, each pane the thickness of his thumb, to the tower of mirrors reaching towards the sky.

Scraping back the seat, he stood as the door opened and pushed out his hand to greet the man wearing round, delicate spectacles. Bald from forehead to crown, with a thick bush of black hair growing on either side, in his pinstripe suit he seemed in every way the perfect stereotype of his profession.

"Mr James," the man said, his voice monotone as he reached out. In his other hand, his stubby fingers held a thin cardboard folder.

"I'm so sorry I'm late, Mr Martin," Fisher said with a wide toothy smile, unable to stop himself from grinning as he felt the man's shiver.

"That's no problem, Mr James. No problem at all," Mr Martin replied, shaking his head.

"I've had a complete nightmare setting up the transfer," Fisher replied, still holding the man's hand and watching him nod. "Did you know they've changed the contact number?"

"No," Mr Martin said, cocking his head to the side. "That is unexpected."

"I had a call this morning. They have a glitch in their system. No matter. I have the right number with me," Fisher said, releasing his grip and retaking his seat.

Mr Martin sat opposite before opening the folder and spreading out two single pages of white paper, taking his time to straighten them against the table's edge.

"Can I get you a drink, Mr James?"

"No, thank you," Fisher replied, glancing at the golden Rolex only half covered by his crisp cuff. "I have another meeting."

Mr Martin nodded, making microscopic adjustments to the paper's angle as he scanned their contents. "We have four hundred and sixty-eight kilos, made up of four hundred and forty-eight one kilo bars and six hundred and forty Britannias," he said, before looking at Fisher over the rim of his glasses.

"Yes. As agreed," replied Fisher, and the banker picked up the desk phone's receiver when it gave a single quiet ring, then listened for a short time before thanking the caller and replacing the handset.

"The transport has arrived. Let us conclude the transfer," he said with a nod.

Fisher pulled a square of paper from his inside pocket, before opening out its folds and placing it on to the table. Apart from two handwritten numbers on the top half, the page was blank. The first was the length of a telephone number, separated into the five-digit area code and six-digit subscriber number. The second was a string of ten digits. Fisher turned the page around and pushed it across the table.

"The new number," he said, and Mr Martin straightened his glasses. Then, without pulling up the handset, tapped at the keypad. A young female voice with a light Eastern European accent came from the speaker after two rings.

"Coutts transfer services. Can I have the transfer request number, please?"

Mr Martin pushed his glasses up his nose with his index finger before reading from the first page. "One, four, five, seven, five, three, oblique one."

"Thank you," the woman replied. "Can I have the originator reference, please?"

Fisher read his own ten digit number. "Eight, seven, five, three, four, six, eight, eight, eight."

"The receiver reference?"

"Eight, seven, four, two, three, six, eight, four, one," Mr Martin confirmed.

"And, finally, the transaction passwords."

"Ultima," Fisher said, looking right at Mr Martin, who stared down at the page.

"Rex, nine, eight, nine, nine, eight."

"Thank you," the voice replied. "To confirm, transaction one, four, five, seven, five, three, oblique one for twelve point five million pounds sterling completed at ten fifty-six. Thank you for using Coutts transfer services. Is there anything else I can help you with?"

85 Albert Embankment, London

1st September

The call of muffled sirens had grown as Fisher regained consciousness, but by the time he'd opened his eyes the frantic activity had died down, only leaving him with guilt in the pit of his stomach whilst knowing his life had changed forever. Only a few hours had passed since then, and he waited, sitting in an unfamiliar corridor, his gaze roving over the blank white walls dotted with many doors, then to the clean-shaven man in a black suit and tie who stood statue-straight in front of him.

But this time, the guard wasn't for him, instead for the man behind the door he stood next to. The man who'd led Fisher into a trap. The man who'd betrayed him in the worst way possible. The man whose actions meant death for his best friend.

Twenty-four hours ago, Fisher had sat in a first-class cabin on the way home, with Andrew waiting in the arrivals lounge. Twenty-four hours earlier, Fisher had just killed the man who'd kidnapped Susie, his beautiful friend. Fisher had put a permanent stop to the man exporting women like cattle.

Rewind even further and it was Fisher waiting with the armed guard on the other side of the door. He was the prisoner, held until he'd spilled all about his ability to convince anyone he was telling the truth, all with a simple touch.

A week before that and he'd just met Agent Carrie Harris. Barely a few hours had passed before he fell for her hard. Before today, she was in his every thought. He'd been ready and willing to follow her into the agency; ready to overlook the things he'd seen her do and the rest he didn't even want to think about.

Now she was his every second thought.

He couldn't help going over the moment he'd turned up at Alan's new flat to find the place empty, despite expecting a party to celebrate his return. He remembered the surprise on Alan's face when Andrew stood at Fisher's side, the look only giving him a brief pause. The reason became clear a few moments later.

Pulling him back into the present, a door opened and Fisher turned to the right, peering along the windowless corridor as a group of three middle-aged suits near-silently shuffled away. Once they'd disappeared through the far double doors, Fisher glanced up at the guard who he'd not seen move.

He thought back to the phone call, recalling his anger when he'd found out Harris hadn't gone back to her headquarters; instead she'd been watching him, but he'd had no time to cling to the thought when three men walked into the house behind Alan, whose outstretched finger pointed straight at him.

She'd burst in a moment later, sending bullets flying and carrying a rush of optimism. But Andrew had stepped out to protect his friend just as Fisher's nerve endings fired all at once, his muscles jerking with the voltage that sent him to the floor where he stared at the bullet hole in Andrew's forehead.

He knew he'd carry those memories forever.

By the time he'd woken, Alan had slipped from the house, only for the MET police to pick him up an hour later as he stepped onto a train.

Men in dark suits had already whisked Fisher away. They'd wanted to take him back to the Beacons, but he refused; not until he'd confronted Alan. And here he sat, waiting for Harris and Franklin, their boss, to finish their interrogation.

He waited to speak with someone he'd known as a friend. He waited in hope for the reason.

Fisher held his breath as the door opened and Harris stepped out, her eyes a little red with fatigue, her strawberry-blonde hair tied up as she looked back. Her brow lowered as if with a question.

Harris offered a weak smile as their gazes met and Fisher

stood when the door closed behind Franklin, whose expression remained blank.

"He's not talking," said Franklin, his voice drier than Fisher had expected.

"I'll make him talk," Fisher said, taking a step.

Franklin and Harris glanced at each other, then in his direction. Franklin nodded and held out his hand.

"Your weapon."

Fisher reached inside his jacket, pulled the Glock from its holster before handing it over, then took a deep breath and walked up to the door. Harris stepped in behind, but Fisher turned to block her way.

"I need to do this alone."

She halted, lifting her chin. "Don't hurt him," she said, reaching to put a hand on his arm.

"He's just killed my best friend. Why are you worried about him?" he snarled.

"I'm not, but he can't talk if he's dead."

2

London

10th October

Without the white armoured van slowing, Fisher let go of the large steel side mirror's support and hopped off the footplate, before giving an index finger salute in the driver's direction as it laboured up the last of the steep exit ramp. The van sat low on its rear suspension as it joined the busy London traffic, whilst Fisher weaved his way through the fumes and between the impatient cars.

A background of sirens grew louder in the distance as he bobbed around the flow of the lunchtime crowd, before slipping into a busy department store. Passing pretty perfume girls, pushchairs and baby clothes, he was soon out of the opposite entrance and back amongst the day-trippers and shoplifters, then into the passenger seat of a waiting Range Rover.

With the car worth more than most people earned in years pulling away from the curb, Fisher stared ahead.

"It's done."

"I know," came the response from behind the driver's mirrored glasses. "Your cut will be in your account tonight."

Fisher nodded. "What's next?"

With his leather jacket zipped to his chin, the driver turned his head to look through the rear-view mirror.

"We party," he replied, and a smile crept across his olive skin, wrinkling the stubble as he pressed his foot on the accelerator.

85 Albert Embankment, London

1st September

Alan sat behind the battered wooden table, his head in his hands whilst Fisher did his best to ignore the room so much like the one in South Wales.

Lifting his head as the door closed, Alan swept away a lank clump of hair from across his forehead. His bloodshot eyes widened and he sat up straight, the beginnings of a smile blossoming as he wiped his bare arm across his puffy face.

"James. Thank fuck it's you."

It wasn't the reaction Fisher had been expecting.

"You need to tell them they've got this all wrong," Alan said, leaning across the table. "It's nothing to do with me. You know that. Don't you?"

Fisher squinted, holding his breath. He wanted it to be true, but having seen it with his own eyes, he knew it wasn't possible. "You're lying."

"What d'ya mean?" Alan said, his eyes widening as Fisher stepped closer.

"Easy way or the hard way? You choose," Fisher said, as he fought to stop himself screaming the words. Alan's mouth fell open, and he stood, waving his hands in front of him.

"Hey. Don't do that spooky shit on me."

"Sit down," Fisher bellowed, watching as Alan froze, then lowered down to the plastic chair where he placed his forehead on the table.

Fisher remained standing.

"I was told to," Alan replied, his voice almost a whisper as he lifted his head.

"By whom?"

"Paul, but he only wanted to help," Alan said, his eyes widening as he sat up straight.

"Who the hell is Paul?" Fisher replied with a glare.

"I've known him since I was at school."

"Why have you never mentioned him before? Where is he?" Fisher took a step closer and Alan looked down at his clasped hands, rubbing his thumbs together.

"Where is he?" Fisher shouted.

"I don't know. He... He... He moved away. I only speak to him on the phone now."

Fisher looked at the ceiling and drew a long, deep breath.

"He only wanted to help," Alan added, his voice quiet again.

"Help who?"

"You, of course. He called yesterday and told me you were coming home and you had Susie with you. He said I should throw a party and some of your work friends wanted to come."

Fisher took another step forward as Alan's voice sped.

"Okay, okay. He wanted to offer you an... an... an opportunity. He said he knew what you could do, and wanted to help you make the most of it. You know, with money and stuff." Alan's lips turned up in a cautious smile.

"Why didn't he talk to me? Why did they try to abduct me?" Fisher replied, his jaw clenching.

"Hey, I didn't know they would do that. Honest, I wouldn't lie to you. There'd be no point."

Surging forward, Fisher picked up the empty chair and threw it, just missing Alan's shoulder before it hit the wall, crashing to the floor in a fog of plaster.

"You're a liar," Fisher shouted. "Why the fuck did they try to kidnap me?"

Alan's expression hardened, his eyebrows lowered. "Cos you're such a fucking goody two shoes. They knew you'd need convincing," he said, shouting back, but before Fisher could react, the door flung open and hands grabbed him by the arm.

As Harris pulled him from the room, Fisher saw the mirror covering the opposite wall, barely recognising his face distorted by anger as she slammed the door behind them.

Landing hard against the wall, she pushed her face right in his, her chest against him.

"Don't let him get to you. He's lying," she said, keeping her voice level.

"He can't lie to me," Fisher said, sliding out from her grip and striding back into the room. When no one stopped him, Alan bolted to his feet as Fisher rushed over with Harris following. He grabbed Alan's collar and pushed him up against the cracked wall, squeezing his hand around Alan's wrist.

"If you don't tell me the truth, I'm going to fucking inflict so much pain you'll beg to die," Fisher screamed into Alan's face, spraying him with spit.

Harris pulled at Fisher's arm and he let her drag him backward, releasing his grip as Alan slid down the wall, shaking his head as he hit the floor.

"It's true," Alan said as tears rolled down his cheeks. "I'm telling the truth."

3

Eight Walworth Road, London

10th October

The brown leather creaked as Fisher sat back on the sofa, which, other than the matching couch opposite, the stout table in between and the dining set, was one of only a handful of furnishings in the paint-fresh penthouse apartment on the thirty-eighth floor. With his suit jacket unbuttoned and tie hanging loose around his neck, he'd torn himself away from marvelling at the capital's enchanting evening light show.

The apartment door burst open and in walked Farid with a drink-soaked smile and his arms around two beaming beautiful women, each with hair to their shoulders. One blonde. One brunette. He held a bottle of clear spirit in each hand, his holstered pistol on show as his shirt rode up when he released the women.

Dropping onto the sofa opposite, Farid slammed the two bottles onto the glass table, flashing his sparkling white teeth as the brunette disappeared through the door to the kitchen. She returned holding a tower of four shot glasses, which she soon spread out across the table, then stood to Farid's right whilst the blonde waited on his other side.

Farid's smile broadened.

"Vodka," he said, gesturing his open palm to the blonde. "Or Tequila?" he added, swapping hands to point to the brunette as all three of them grinned with raised eyebrows.

"I'm a vodka man, as you should know by now," Fisher replied, expressionless. Without hesitation, the blonde grabbed two glasses from the table and poured from the bottle before she slid one in front of Fisher, then came around the table and perched beside him, landing so close he could feel her warmth through her clothes.

Her hand crept up his thigh. "And I'm a lucky girl. I've

heard great things about you."

Gripping his thigh, she ran her tongue across her lips and leaned in close to his ear. "I can't wait for you to fuck my brains out," she whispered, her Slavic accent thick.

Fisher leaned forward, upending the glass into his mouth before turning to look her in the eye. "Soon, but first I need to talk to Mr Farid alone." The blonde narrowed her eyes, peering across at the Arab, who nodded, his smile gone. The two women stood, clasping each other's hands before walking to the hallway leading to the bedrooms.

"We'll try not to have too much fun without you," the blonde said over her shoulder, before turning to the brunette and planting a kiss on her full red lips. They ran, giggling as one chased the other through the doorway.

"Keep it short," Farid said, not hiding the edge of impatience in his tone as he refilled his glass.

Fisher's phone chirped, and he pulled it from his pocket, then slipped the jacket off his shoulders to reveal the fourth generation Glock 17 in its black leather holster.

Farid's expression hadn't changed.

After laying his jacket on the sofa beside him, Fisher picked up his white, slim Samsung and glanced at the banking app's notification, showing the new deposit of two point four million pounds, which more than tripled the existing balance. Slipping the phone into his trouser pocket, he leaned forward.

"What's the next job? Another bank?" Fisher said.

Farid flashed his teeth with a smile. "This one's a little more interesting, but the same deal. Two point four on successful retrieval of a package."

"Where's the package?" Fisher asked, his eyes narrowing.

"Belmarsh Prison."

The words brought a smile to Fisher's lips. Then he watched Farid pull out a brown A5 envelope from inside his jacket pocket and push it across the table.

"Who's the customer?" Fisher asked. They both turned to the giggles coming from the corridor.

"You don't need to know," Farid said, shaking his head.

"I don't need to know," he added, pointing at his chest.

Fisher's attention moved to his right as the kitchen door opened and out walked a man who he'd seen in the apartment before. A thick, jagged white line on each side of his face ran from the corner of his mouth to his ear, the horrific scar highlighted by stubble.

Turning back, Fisher spoke again. "When do I get to meet them?" he said, but as he finished, the front door burst open and in walked two of Farid's men, both Eastern Europeans, each with two girls in their arms. The blonde and brunette appeared from the corridor, both wearing only matching black bras and tiny knickers.

Fisher stuffed the envelope into his jacket pocket as Farid stood.

"Enough questions. Time to party," he said as he jumped over the back of the sofa before pressing his lips hard to the brunette's mouth and pawing at her breasts.

The blonde swaggered over, taking Fisher's hand, and led him to the bedroom.

85 Albert Embankment, London

1st September

"You're either losing your touch or he's telling the truth," Harris said as they walked into the darkened room on the other side of the one-way glass.

Fisher shook his head. "He's lying, but he believes it's the truth."

"So there's no chance your influence just didn't work?" Harris said, raising an eyebrow.

He didn't answer; instead, he stared at Alan, who held his head in his hands.

"We need to find Paul," Fisher said when Alan hadn't moved.

"We're already on it. We'll get him picked up. In the meantime, I think you should come to his flat with me."

"I'm not travelling all the way to Nottingham," Fisher said, shaking his head. "I need to get the truth out of him."

"Nottingham?" Harris said, her brow furrowed. "His flat's in Potters Bar, not Nottingham."

Fisher turned to look her in the eye before shaking his head. "He's lived in Nottingham for ten years. That's where he went to Uni. It's where he works."

"We've already confirmed with the electoral roll, electricity provider and water company. He's lived in Potters Bar for the last four years."

Fisher peered back through the glass. "In that case, I better come along."

4

Eight Walworth Road, London

11th October

Fisher sat bolt upright, his eyelids bursting open as the image of Andrew's face with a bullet hole in the centre of his forehead flashed into his semi-conscious mind. Wincing, he squinted at the bright sunlight streaming through the plate-glass windows, the curtains hanging on each side.

Shielding his alcohol-weary eyes with his hand, Fisher glanced to his side and the naked blonde beauty sprawled on top of the white silk covers.

He shook his head, intensifying the pain as he tried to remember her name, despite knowing it was unimportant.

He picked himself up from underneath the smooth sheet, adjusted the waist of his black Calvin Klein's and stepped into the en-suite bathroom, where he stared in the mirror at the cut on his cheek which had almost healed.

After a glance at the bedroom's reflection as the Slavic beauty stirred, unaware of her surroundings, Fisher rubbed his chin with his thumb and forefinger. Feeling the stab of black stubble, he took a step back, opened the mirror to reveal a can of shaving foam next to a bumper pack of Gillette disposable razors. He grabbed the first razor and the can of foam before running the water.

With the stubble dealt with and face clean, he threw the razor into the bin, just as the naked woman, her body a picture of perfection, eased the bathroom door open.

"Do you mind if I pee?" she said in a low tone, her face showing the signs of sleep broken by alcohol.

Fisher smiled, then stepping to the side, he left the room.

Potter's Bar, London

1st September

Pushing his Glock back into its holster, Fisher followed Harris to the underground car park and towards the blinking lights of a BMW One Series, before speeding through the bomb-proof doors and out into the orange glow of Albert Embankment.

Not speaking throughout the hour-long journey, his mind rolled with questions he was desperate to know the answers to, their amplitude growing as they slipped from the M25, passing by dim streetlights. Fisher sat up, taking note of the trees lining the streets and the gleaming cars parked in front of wooden garage doors, each house spaced well away from their neighbours. A pleasant area to live.

As they slowed and made a turn, he saw the three-storey building beyond the closed iron gate that blocked the road between two tall houses looking crisp and unweathered, as if untouched by time. The gate slid at a snail's pace to the side to reveal a spacious car park and a row of expensive cars on the dark blacktop.

Harris parked in a bay marked with bright wide letters, the visitor's space between a year old black Jaguar and a white Audi TT about the same age. Without words, they slipped from the car and headed toward the communal entrance, where Harris pulled a set of keys from her suit jacket.

"Only six flats," she said as she searched through the keys.

Fisher raised his eyebrows, watching when she presented a slim black fob up at a key symbol on the door entry system. A loud chime sounded before the mechanism clicked, the door opening as Harris pushed against the hand plate.

"Which number?" Fisher muttered, his voice a little dry as they headed into the well-lit hall.

"That one," Harris replied, pointing to a burgundy wooden door past the carpeted stairs to the right. "Number two," she added, looking at the keys before holding out a long straight silver Chubb and pushing it into the lock.

Fisher shook his head, knowing it wouldn't work, then held his breath as it turned.

The upper latch twisted as Harris tried the fourth key and he watched in silence as, with care, she pushed the door open, following her across the threshold, the smell hitting him as the door closed behind him.

The odour didn't surprise him. Everyone's home smells to outsiders. Most times it is neither pleasant nor foul, but it tells you a lot. Did they have pets, or smoke? Were they fastidious cleaners?

Fisher felt a glimmer of relief as he breathed the stench of rotting food, dust, and stale smoke. Alan didn't smoke. It was the wrong flat and a small smile rose on his lips as Harris clicked on the lights before heading along the corridor.

The decor was as modern as he'd expected from the outside, but the fresh sheen had long faded, replaced instead with a grubby film. Light fittings hung lank from the ceiling, their shades crisscrossed with cobwebs trapping dust. Beside the door, a set of four holes gaped in the wall with a line of coat hooks lying on the floor below, the coats covered with a fine dusting of plaster.

This wasn't the Alan he'd known since university and it wouldn't take long for Harris to figure out they were in the wrong place.

Raising his hand, Fisher pushed a door to the left ajar, but stepped back at a fresh wave of the foul odour. Every countertop in the kitchen was piled high with dirty plates, pots, fast food containers and ashtrays overflowing with cigarette ends.

Whoever lived here was an animal. It wasn't Alan's home, he was sure.

5

Eight Walworth Road, London

11th October

Back in a pressed suit, and with a coffee in hand, Fisher sat alone on the edge of the black leather sofa surrounded by the hedonistic debris of last night's party. Placing the steaming cup on the thick pile carpet, he picked up a discarded black cushion and wiped powder residue from the tabletop before spreading the contents of the envelope across the glass.

He recognised the man in the first glossy seven by five. His name was Daryl Diamond; or to use his tabloid title, The Coffer Killer.

Most people in the country would know his name after hearing the infamous story retold in countless documentaries, news articles and a Hollywood film. A safe cracker by trade, he ran as part of a small crew, gaining notoriety and had their own police task force whose sole purpose was to hunt them down in hope of justice for a growing list of violent bank robberies.

But the crimes were soon eclipsed when Daryl added his own signature to the acts by changing the combinations, then locking staff and customers in the vaults after they'd emptied the money. Without Daryl's skills to defeat the locks, the police found only bodies when they finally opened the vaults.

It took four such killings, and sixteen dead, before his crew grassed him up; it led to sixteen consecutive life terms.

The Coffer Killer was one of those few they'd had in mind when the government conceived HMP Belmarsh, a prison built to hold the worst of the worst in the early nineties. Although young when the murders took place, Fisher, along with the rest of the world, could never forget the stark black-and-white image of Daryl staring wide-eyed toward the lens, because it appeared in the papers or on TV every few years.

The faded colour photos spread across the glass were different to that famous shot, and were instead a series of distant pictures taken of a young, already balding man not looking at the camera.

Fisher peered up from the table as he tried to figure out what Farid's boss could want with one of Britain's most notorious murderers. When the answer didn't come, he took a sip of the rich coffee and, staring at the photos, he shrugged, reminding himself the reason didn't matter. If the boss wanted The Coffer Killer, then Fisher would deliver him with a bow around his middle.

The front door opened, but without glancing up he knew it was the maid. Nine o'clock on the dot and here to turn the apartment back to luxury before Farid awoke from his drug-prolonged sleep.

Fisher shuffled the paper back into the envelope.

***

Potter's Bar, London

1st September

With reluctant breaths of thick air, Fisher stood at the doorway staring at dust-covered junk piled on a bed almost up to the ceiling.

Games consoles, electronic gadgets, magazines and empty boxes once filled with expensive consumer electronics lay like an abandoned exhibition of a frivolous adolescent's life.

Opening the next door to a bathroom, he lingered only long enough to confirm the squalid, stained porcelain wasn't fit for much anymore. A second bedroom was worse than the first, with stacked electronics and rubbish ready to collapse.

Putting his head around the last door, he found a king-sized bed covered with a stained duvet he didn't care to linger on. Uncapped pill bottles and towering ashtrays littered both bedside units, whilst foil condom wrappers, some split in half and some yet to be called for, lay scattered across the floor. On the wall toward the foot of the bed, a giant sixty-inch flat screen TV hung, but the scratches and long dried splashes across its face would have ruined any popcorn night in.

Among the scattered debris, Fisher's gaze fell on the tight blue check of a shirt half covered with a tattered porn mag. With a tentative step, he bent over, casting the magazine to the side and pinched the fabric between his fingers.

Shaking his head, he remembered the store where Alan was the assistant manager, sure they didn't wear the same uniform as those on the shop floor.

"Gloves please," Harris said, her words at his back making him jump. Turning, he found her holding out a blue latex pair. "We've got to get you into training soon," she added with a raised eyebrow.

Fisher thanked her with a nod and pulled them on, picking up the shirt again and turning it around, where he stared at a plastic badge the shape of a rosette pinned to the left breast pocket.

Alan
Customer Assistant
Here to Help

A dried, dark orange stain ran from the top of the rosette and down the front. Letting go, he shook his head, all doubt gone.

6

Eight Walworth Road, London

11th October

The cleaner said goodbye in something that resembled his language as she dragged heavy rubbish bags behind her and stepped past the leather-embossed front door. As the wood slid into the gap, like clockwork, a door opened down the hall. Moments later, Farid walked bare chested across the lounge, his bottom half covered with black jeans before he disappeared through the door to the kitchen, only to reappear moments later with an espresso cup in hand, slumping down onto the sofa opposite.

Fisher took a swig of his drink, poured moments earlier by the maid.

"Good night?" he asked, making no attempt to hide his survey of the mottled scars lining the olive skin of Farid's upper body.

"It was okay. You?" Farid said, raising a brow.

"Likewise," he said with a shrug. "What's-her-name seemed to have a good time," he added, waggling his finger towards the corridor.

Farid sniggered. "You have a talent in that area. I have girls begging for an invite to my parties. What's the secret?"

"Sorry, Farid, if I told you we could no longer be friends."

Farid laughed, fidgeting in the seat.

"So when's the job?" Fisher asked, cradling the hot cup in his hands.

"As soon as you're ready," Farid replied, sipping his drink.

"Can I ask what we want with a psycho serial killer?"

Farid laughed again and rubbed the bare skin along his ribs.

"He's not a serial killer. He just got carried away and is a genius in his area of expertise. Plus, I'm told he's changed. Age does that."

Fisher nodded as he sipped, his eyebrows raised. "Are you expecting me to just walk in there and bring him out?"

"Pretty much," Farid said with a slow nod.

It was Fisher's turn to smile. "It won't be quite that simple."

***

Potter's Bar, London

1st September

Curling his lips, Fisher felt the heat building under his collar, no longer able to deny he was standing in Alan's home and that Alan had lied to him for such a long time.

Taking care with his steps, Fisher headed into the hallway, distracted with questions rolling through his head. Before long, he stood in the lounge with a sofa to his right which angled toward the biggest TV he'd ever seen.

The room swept left to a dining space where a grand table stood piled with more junk. Heavy curtains covered the far wall and when Harris switched on the lights, the blanket of dust told him no one had opened them in a while.

Barely paying attention, Fisher found the room filled with expensive furniture and gadgets, each covered with a thick layer of dust. Below the TV, he spotted the latest version of Xbox, PlayStation and Wii, finger marks tracking their surfaces.

Beside the sofa, the leather on the arms worn through, were several coffee tables, the tops of each covered with smoking debris, empty junk food wrappers and twisted beer cans. A laptop sat on the floor beside a well-worn spot on the carpet with the lid closed, resting on a metal Christmas sweet tin. Cigarette burns potted the laptop's gloss.

A green canvas bag he recognised sat on the floor to his left, bulging at the seams, which thrust forward an image of Alan carrying it on his back. Fisher imagined Andrew standing at his side, weighed down with his own hiking kit and his mouth wide with laughter. Fisher could almost feel his legs ache with the memory of their bag's weight.

"He was going somewhere," he declared as he shook the image away and knelt on the carpet, unsurprised to find its pile speckled with burns.

Unclipping the bag's twin buckles, he pulled up the hood and tugged at the drawstring toggle, before picking it up and upending the contents, watching laundered clothes spill onto the filthy floor. An A4 transparent wallet was the last to fall.

After sliding the nylon zip across, he emptied the contents onto the pile. Two bundles of sterling, each wrapped in banker's straps marked as five hundred pounds, were followed by a pouch printed with the British Airways livery. Then a long, oddly-shaped key dropped out. Harris picked up the BA sleeve and pulled open the flap.

"A one-way ticket to Venezuela," she said, raising her brow. "First class and travelling tomorrow." Pinching the opening, she peered inside and shook her head. "There's no return."

Fisher's expression didn't change as he picked up the key, the shape of which he'd never seen before.

Where a standard key would be the reverse of the lock's profile cut into one or two edges, this had four profiles mounted as a cross. He handed it to Harris after she pushed the ticket back into its wallet.

"His passport should be here somewhere," Fisher said as he peered around the room. Harris nodded, watching as he delved through the rucksack's side pockets, only to drop the bag after coming up empty-handed. Instead, he joined Harris, scouring the rest of the living room, then retracing his steps to search the rest of the flat before meeting in the hallway an hour later.

"Hi. We're there now," said Harris and it took Fisher a

moment to realise she was on a call, talking into thin air to her operational assistant, Clark, back at headquarters in the Brecon Beacons, using her communicator's direct link embedded in her skull to allow, amongst other things, hands-free calling.

"Can you give me a list of what they found on Mr Bullard?" she said, then waited, nodding every few moments. "And in the car?" She waited again, turning towards Fisher as she shook her head. "Can you run a check on a key? Yes. It's got four edges. I'll send a photo."

Harris pointed toward the plastic pouch and he reached inside, pulled out the key, and held it out. Instead of taking it from him, she took out her device that looked like a thick version of an iPhone, pointing it at the key.

"Oh, okay," she said, her voice rising a few seconds later. "Yes. Call me back."

"No passport?" Fisher asked.

"No," she replied with a shake of her head. "Clark thinks it's for a safe deposit box." Fisher nodded and moved back to the sofa. "He'll call me back with the addresses of local vaults."

"I found something," Fisher said after a moment and peered inside the open sweet tin he'd taken the laptop from. Inside were bags of dried green buds, blue extra-large cigarette papers and a pouch of rolling tobacco.

"You don't want to know what I found in his bedroom," Harris said. "We should get some rest. I'll get someone to turn this place over."

7

Eight Walworth Road, London

12th October

Fisher woke with a sharp intake of breath.

Shaking his head, he tried in vain to clear the image away, the same scene he'd woken to since he'd witnessed the death of his dearest friend. Pain pounded at his temples as he opened his eyes to overcast light spilling through the plate-glass windows, the curtains hanging neatly to each side.

Fisher's hand shielded his alcohol-weary eyes as he glanced across the bed at the naked brunette beauty next to him, her pert breasts exposed as the silk white cover came to just below their curves. He didn't bother trying to remember her name. He knew it didn't matter.

Picking himself from underneath the smooth material, he adjusted the waist of his black Calvin Klein boxer shorts and stepped into the en-suite bathroom.

Staring at himself in the mirror, he rubbed his chin with his thumb and forefinger. Feeling the stab of stubble he took a step back, opened the mirror and pulled out shaving foam and the first razor to hand.

With the stubble dealt with and his face clean of foam, he chucked the razor into the open bin just as he heard the front door slam closed.

Like clockwork, he thought to himself.

Vauxhall, London

1st September

It was late as they arrived in the car park underneath the St George's Wharf Hotel, where Harris led Fisher to the lift and reception on the ground floor. She checked them both in, requesting two rooms under the names Seymour and Bennett. Fisher wasn't sure which one she meant him to be.

For a moment he'd hoped they'd share a room; he wasn't sure why, they'd barely kissed, but he could do with the company. Tonight of all nights.

Not saying anything as she handed him the fob, at Harris's insistence they grabbed food and ate in the lounge bar. Neither felt like drinking, wanting to keep a clear head for tomorrow.

Within an hour they were on the tenth floor, parting to their neighbouring rooms. On the bed Fisher found a holdall, the same type as the one Harris had handed him as he'd stood in his pants almost two weeks ago. Inside were two white t-shirts, a pair of black jeans, underwear and a fabric black coat. All his size. He sent Clark a text message thanking him and received a reply in short order.

Check the false bottom.

Intrigued, he pulled up the cardboard layer at the bottom of the bag, under which he found a padded compartment. Unzipping the base, he took out a thin box of twenty-five 9mm rounds and a brown envelope. Inside were five hundred pounds in twenties and a brand new passport. Flicking through the pages, he found, other than his photo, it was blank.

Unsure how much use it would be, on autopilot he stripped naked, folding his clothes and placing the gun and holster by the side of the bed, careful to cover them with his ultra-thin armoured vest before he jumped in the shower.

Cleaned and refreshed, he slid into bed, closing his eyes

as he hoped for sleep.

8

HMP Belmarsh, London

18th October

A shrill tone rang out as Fisher pressed the intercom on the side of the austere brick wall. Waiting in silence, his gaze drifted up to a weathered Royal crest high above his head until a woman's monotone voice sprung from the tinny speaker.

"Control Room."

"Mr James to see Mr Bragg," he replied, leaning toward the box. Without delay, a sharp ring leapt from the speaker and the door lock buzzed.

Fisher stepped through the battered frame and into a dirty white rectangular room where four bright-red upholstered chairs waited to his left, underneath curled information posters advertising security procedures in washed-out colours.

Ahead, a flaking blue-painted steel barred gate marked the entrance to the prison proper. To the right stood a normal white door, then a long reinforced misted glass window, half of which waited to the side. An age-weathered woman in a prison officer's uniform looked out from the space.

On the shoulders of her plain white blouse, silvered letters hung on black lapels with the name of the prison. Around her neck hung an ID badge and behind her, the office staff busied their fingers on keyboards as they stared at their screens and chatted.

"Do you have an appointment?" the woman said in a rasping smoker's voice, whilst narrowing her eyes and pointing at the visitor's book in front of her.

Fisher smiled, nodded and picked up a chewed Biro, filling out fictitious details as she pushed a phone handset against her creased face.

With the pen replaced, the woman turned the book around.

"Do you have ID, Mr James?"

Fisher pulled out a brown leather wallet, sliding out a blank white plastic rectangle the size of a credit card. Holding it between three fingers across the long edge, he positioned it in front of the woman.

As she moved her wrinkled fingers to take the card, he turned his hand and made contact.

"You've already seen my ID."

She looked up, and with the briefest of nods, she signed against his entry before tearing off the top section and pushing it into a clear plastic wallet.

"Someone will be down to collect you."

***

Alone at the desk in his plush bedroom with a laptop, a quick search of the internet found the governor's name, but with no details of where he lived or photos of his face, a handful of news articles covering failed kidnap plots confirmed he'd be well protected.

With no time to find a high-ranking police officer in the know, or a journalist with a cache of information ready for a scandal to break, despite knowing Clark could get all he needed in seconds, his career change meant he was flying solo.

He'd mulled the idea of watching the prison, perhaps following the governor home, but first he'd have to find out what he looked like. In the short time he'd been in the service, he'd learned only the most basic of skills; not enough to stay hidden from protection officers whose job it was to keep their charge safe.

Fisher had thought about going to the local tax office. Everyone had a tax record, each with reams of information filed away with their returns. All he'd needed was to shake a hand, and he'd have access to vast data. But he needed some information to start with.

Then again, there were hundreds of organisations who'd

also hold what he needed. Phone companies. Banks. Schools too, if he had kids. But he needed someone he could sit down with. Someone he could touch.

This stuff was much easier if he'd kept the backing of a government-sponsored intelligence agency.

He'd thought about walking into the prison and shaking hands with as many people as he found. But without an appointment, who would step from their office to see him?

Shaking his head, he knew he had no other choice but to find the governor outside the prison. After that, the rest would be easy.

His mind drifted to his friend George, who he'd barely spoken to since finding out he worked for SIS. He'd be glad to help, but knowing Farid monitored his mobile phone and the computer, he wouldn't do anything to lead them to his friend.

With the postcode for the prison tapped into Google maps, he'd brought up an aerial view of the site. His gaze soon headed north, finding a symbol of a wine glass besides the Prince Albert, soon imagining the place full of off-duty prison staff relaxing after a hard day's work.

They'd have a social club in the prison somewhere, but how many of the seven hundred staff would prefer to be away from their bosses when they let loose, free of what he didn't doubt were strict rules.

Half an hour later and Fisher had changed, and along with his two bulky minders, he'd left the flat for Thamesmead. Within four hours he had the name and shift pattern of a lovely young lady called Grace who worked in the prison's HR department, someone who was very keen to impress her boss by helping to organise a surprise birthday party for the governor's wife at his house.

The very next morning, the text message came through with an address only twenty miles away. A day of discrete surveillance along the street was all it took to confirm she'd come up trumps, and the following weekend he followed the governor's car to a local supermarket.

His security was easy to spot, and in a public space he could get very close. A quick smile and a shake of his hand was all it took for the governor to wave off the pair before Fisher planted the seed. A phone call to his office on the following Monday confirmed the appointment.

9

Vauxhall, London

2nd September

Sleep didn't come.

Every time Fisher closed his eyes, the round bullet hole torn into Andrew's skull came instead. Concentrating on his breath, he tried to think about anything else. There'd been no time to process any of what had happened in the last three weeks, let alone the death of his best friend. His mind wandered back to the time spent worrying over Susie, reminding himself of his determination to find her, his near-death accident and brief stay in hospital, then meeting Trinity. Her allure intoxicating him even more when she'd became Harris.

He remembered how he'd felt and how those feelings had intensified, culminating in the near kiss before Susie opened the door when their flight was ready. He'd wanted nothing more than to hold Harris since then. He'd wanted to breakdown in her arms, knowing it wouldn't change how she thought of him. He wanted her reassurance that everything would be okay.

His thoughts turned to Harris lying on the other side of the wall, but rather than taking comfort in her proximity, he couldn't help but wonder why they were in separate rooms. They'd slept in the same space before, but was that before she'd realised where they were heading? Before she realised what a mistake it would be?

Perhaps their chance had passed. Rolling on his side, he forced the thought away.

Andrew's motionless wide eyes flashed into his head as a drop of blood rolled from the bullet wound, whilst Alan stood at the edge of his vision. Watching. Directing.

But why?

So many questions fought for his attention as he stirred under the covers.

Why had Alan lied about where he lived?

How could he afford the flat and all the expensive things inside?

He'd been lying about the job, but had a steady stream of cash. The flat alone would cost a couple of thousand a month.

Fisher sat up, shaking his head. "Had he done it for money? If so, who would pay him?" he said, speaking out loud.

Throwing off the cover, Fisher dressed in his new clothes before slipping from the room.

The bar to the right of the darkened hotel reception area stood empty. Seeing Fisher arrive, the lone receptionist moved from behind the counter, smiling as she walked over and poured rum over ice. After leaving a large tip, Fisher found a shadowed corner in the lounge where he sat by a window facing out into the night.

His appreciation for the bartender grew when he noticed the clock above the reception counter showing three AM.

With shallow sips of his drink and breathing in the sharp oak aroma, he felt an inner calm as he stared out at the dark street, the view reminding him of what he'd seen through the plate glass of the coffee shop back when he hadn't realised he was staring at the headquarters of the Secret Intelligence Service and the country's last line of defence.

At least that's what he'd believed those few weeks ago. Back when he'd not known about his new employer.

Fisher didn't know what the organisation was called, but Harris had explained in the nineties SIS had become too public and the government created a new secret organisation to operate without the same scrutiny.

They pushed SIS further into the public eye, but whilst leaving it with a significant operational remit, they transferred much of what they had done in the shadows, and more, to a new secret organisation.

They'd slashed the SIS's budget in the name of reform,

whilst diverting funds to the new structure they'd also given the power to generate its own revenue, as long as the activities didn't contradict those of its primary task to safeguard the UK and her allies.

In 2005, the organisation became self-sufficient, drawing no direct budget from the UK government, which allowed it to stay out of the view of all but a handful of trusted ministers.

A car door's slam broke into Fisher's thoughts, but it was only as a boot lid closed he saw the car outside the main entrance. With a sip of his drink, he watched the hotel's front double doors open as in walked two wide men dressed in black, one carrying a dark holdall, the other reaching inside his coat.

Despite looking around as they strode to the desk, they failed to see Fisher shrouded in darkness where he watched, his breath halting as the closest man pulled out a suppressed black pistol and pushed it up to the face of the shocked receptionist. Giving her no time to react, a bullet ripped through her skull before smashing into the wall behind.

Unable to breathe, Fisher stared in horror as the pair headed to the lift and walked through the opening doors.

10

HMP Belmarsh, London

18th October

After ten minutes of boredom scanning the posters, a middle-aged woman in a blue skirt and cream blouse appeared from the door beside the reception counter. Confirming who he was, she led Fisher down a corridor with tired magnolia walls, stepping along a dark carpet worn in the centre as they passed offices at regular intervals to his right.

Soon, through a wooden door with a reinforced glass porthole, a dulled brass plaque announced the offices of senior management. Decorated in the same drab shade, it was less worn and with black and white photos hanging on the wall, each a headshot and chronicling the short twenty-year history of the jail's governors.

Their journey ended as the secretary pushed through a door into a reception office. With an unoccupied desk to the right, two upholstered red chairs rested against the wall opposite, besides which stood another door with the words Governor Bragg printed on a polished brass plate. The scene reminded him of waiting outside the headteacher's office.

"Please take a seat, Mr James. Governor Bragg will be with you shortly," she said, offering her hand toward the chairs as she moved behind the desk and tapped on the keyboard.

Sitting, Fisher couldn't help but focus on the muffled voices coming from the office, but as the door to his left opened, he sat up straight when a tall, uniformed police officer complete with body armour and utility belt walked out, talking as the governor followed.

For the first time since he'd been at the prison, Fisher felt his heart rate rising, despite telling himself to calm, knowing there was no chance the officer was here for him.

Fisher looked away, not wanting to make eye contact as the governor led the officer outside.

When Bragg returned alone, Fisher stood, watching the man's eyes narrow as he turned his head to the side. His silver hair showed little evidence of its former colour, aside from deep black bushy eyebrows refusing to give up their pigment. Between his white, short sleeve shirt and the top of his trousers, he wore a belt holding a black leather pouch and a pager clipped at his side. Clean-shaven, stress had leathered his skin and for a fleeting moment, Fisher felt sorry for what the next few weeks would bring.

Sensing the governor's reaction, the secretary introduced Fisher, who watched as a glint of recognition appeared with a flicker in the man's expression before he offered a sturdy handshake and led Fisher into his inner office.

"How can I assist you, Mr James?" the governor said, his accent spotted with his Scottish upbringing.

"You agreed to give me a tour of the Category A facilities," Fisher replied, his eyebrows raised.

"Did I? Why would I do that?" he said, narrowing his eyes.

"Let me get you my card," Fisher said, and he reached inside his trouser pocket before pulling out the credit card-sized rectangle of plastic.

***

Vauxhall, London

2nd September

In the shadows, Fisher slowly stood, his mouth hanging open as he felt for his gun just as a vision of his thin bullet-proof vest laying over his Glock in his room upstairs jumped into his head.

Closing his mouth, panic raced in his chest until his hand found the communicator. Pulling it from his pocket, he jogged around the chairs and tables as he tapped to dial Harris. When she hadn't answered by the time he'd arrived at the reception desk, he grabbed the phone from its wooden surface and held the receiver to his ear with a finger poised over the buttons, unable to remember the number for either of their rooms.

When a sequence came to mind, he dialled, but with no answer after four rings, he jabbed a second set of digits.

Urging Harris to answer, his gaze settled on the body slumped over the reception desk before straying to the thick blood pooling around the keyboard.

"Hello?" she answered, her voice slow.

"Dead receptionist. Two men coming for you," Fisher said, doing his best to make himself clear. "Or for me, I guess."

"Where are you?" she replied, much quicker this time.

"Reception."

As if unsure which of the many questions coming to mind to ask next, Harris spoke only at the knocking against wood in the background.

"Get out of here," she said before slamming down the phone.

11

HMP Belmarsh, London

18th October

Despite walking beside the man in charge, Fisher couldn't help but feel the atmosphere of the place weighing him down as their feet tapped out a rhythm. The governor's narrative pointing out the names of the wings and their purpose did nothing to ease the tension he felt with each glimpse of men in baggy grey tracksuits, as he forced himself to focus along the corridor and not toward those cleaning or walking in the opposite direction in step with a prison officer.

Each of the fifteen battered steel gates he followed through took them closer to the place described as a prison within a prison. Belmarsh's notorious High Security Unit.

Arriving at a checkpoint manned by four officers in short-sleeved shirts who stood beside an array of detection equipment, Fisher felt his heart pounding in his chest.

Coming to a stop, they waited as an inmate dressed in a bright yellow and green jumpsuit, the word 'Prisoner' emblazoned across the shoulders, submitted himself to the guards just as Governor Bragg spoke again.

"You have to remove outer clothing, then take off any jewellery, putting it along with the contents of your pockets and any bags in the grey containers, ready to go through the x-ray machine. The team will then search through your hair and ask you to shake your head and run your fingers through. Next is your mouth, nose and ears. If you have a collar, they'll lift it before feeling around the tops of your shoulders, along your arms and into your armpits, between your fingers, your palms and the backs of your hands.

"They'll search your torso, neck to waist, then your waistband on one side. Your abdomen's next, then legs and crotch and your shoes, whilst removed, before finally checking your feet. They'll repeat the process on the other side of your body."

As the prisoner turned with the officer's palms running over his back, Fisher felt sure he'd seen the guy's weathered face in the papers before.

"Then if we miss anything metallic, the scanner will pick it up," the governor added, as the prisoner headed through the archway. To Fisher's surprise, they applied the same strict process to the escorting officer who'd waited at the side.

Only half listening as the governor continued to talk, Fisher thought better of the choices he'd made before he'd committed himself to his audacious plan. Fearing the governor could hear his pounding heart, he watched as the lone operator sitting behind the x-ray machine scanned the screen, with the prison officer's coat disappearing into the metal tunnel.

As the officer collected his jacket and the other man beckoned Fisher forward, he knew it was already too late to change his mind.

With a step, and taking great care, he pulled off his jacket to reveal his crisp white shirt. Placing the jacket at the mouth of the x-ray machine, he took another step forward, but just as he submitted himself, his right leg moved across his left and he stumbled. Pushing his hands out, the officer about to pat him down caught him and Fisher gripped the man's wrist, looking him in the eye with a thin smile.

"I've got nothing on me," Fisher whispered close to the officer's face, then stood and raised his hands for the search.

Without delay, the officer stepped forward, running his purple gloves along Fisher's hand and down to his armpits. His gloves ran along his body, Fisher twitching as they travelled over the lump in his navel, but the officer didn't pause or ask for an explanation.

Hoping his dread stayed from his expression, Fisher turned to his right as the conveyor began rolling his jacket forward and watched for the inevitable wide-eyed alarm that appeared only seconds later, the machine operator's expression falling as the silhouette of the handgun appeared on the screen.

***

Vauxhall, London

2ⁿᵈ September

Even though only two weeks had passed since a surly Miller, the military liaison for his employer, had thrust the protective vest and Glock at him, standing at the darkened reception desk, Fisher felt almost naked without them.

Sensing the familiar metallic hint in the air, he knew he shouldn't hesitate to follow Harris's advice to the letter, but the thought of leaving her to deal with the men who hadn't paused before shooting the receptionist never entered his mind. Despite knowing what Harris was capable of, he pushed through the door beside the lift and ran, taking two steps at a time.

The intense physical training he'd received on the four-day voyage across the Atlantic had stood him in good stead and he arrived barely out of breath, the orange light leaking into the stairwell as he eased the door on the tenth floor landing open.

Peering through the crack, his gaze landed on the backs of the two murderers. With silenced handguns at their sides, Fisher watched as the taller of the pair ran up to the wood and smashed his shoulders against the barrier before it burst open from a ferocious kick.

"Oi," Fisher called as he pushed the landing door wide, only realising what he'd done as both men paused their assault and turned their close-cropped heads his way. With a brief glance at each other, they both raised their weapons and ran towards him, ignoring the bleary-eyed man who appeared at a door before quickly closing it when he saw the pair.

Grabbing the handle, Fisher pulled the door shut before launching himself up the stairs as he wrestled his phone from his trouser pocket. Without slowing, he tapped at the screen, with Harris picking up before the first ring completed.

"I'll bring them back down soon. Be ready," he said between breaths.

"You should have listened to me," she replied, her voice calm and showing no surprise at his words. "I'll be ready."

"Grab my gun from my room," Fisher blurted out, then ended the call before she could finish her expletive.

With the slam of the door below, he burst out onto the twelfth floor and ran.

Finding the layout of the floor identical to where he'd just come from, he rushed along the curved corridor, taking little notice of the gold numbered doors either side. Soon reaching the opposite staircase, he pushed through into the stairwell, but rather than racing along the other side, he held the door ajar and peered back.

Each passing second brought doubt. Were these men too unfit to climb so many steps, or had they figured out his plan and doubled back?

With his impatience at standing still close to getting the better of him, the door across the hall burst open and the two heavyset men appeared around the curve, both panting, their brows reflecting the glow from the overhead lights.

The guy in the lead lifted his head, strain written across his expression as he snarled between breaths. His gaze locked with Fisher's, the sight seeming to renew his energy, leaving his partner trailing behind clutching his chest.

Just before the door closed, Fisher saw the straggler turn around, but not pausing on the sight, Fisher rushed up the concrete stairs.

After two more floors, he slowed for breath and steadied himself with his hand on the banister, pleased he'd split the pair up whilst knowing he was in the most dangerous phase of his plan. If they followed him onto the right floor, they'd trap him.

Grabbing his communicator, he double pressed the home button to show the hidden applications, and he tapped the green circular icon to the sound of a door slamming a few floors below. Tentatively pushing the door, he found the corridor empty. Forcing shallow breaths, he listened to heavy footsteps getting closer.

Swapping his gaze between the corridor and the stairwell below, Fisher smiled at the growing effort echoing up. Knowing he could pause no more, he eased out into the corridor just as the far door burst open at the end of the passageway.

Instinct took over and he changed direction, his muscles soaking up the fresh burst of adrenaline as he bounded up the stairs again before rushing out onto the next landing, where he slowed to a walk and held his phone out in front, watching the hundreds of stationary red dots from the other guests filling the green background either side of a dark green corridor.

When he saw a faint green spot showing Harris many floors below and two lone red markers pulsing along the corridor, he smiled and ran on past the many rooms before heading down the four flights of stairs on the opposite staircase.

12

HMP Belmarsh, London

18th October

It took less than a second for the officer's eyes to narrow and his chin to raise as he spoke without taking his eyes from the screen.

"Sir," he said, his voice calm. An officer standing at the side looked over, an eyebrow raised as if the tone meant only one thing. With a glance back to where the governor stood, the officer looked at the x-ray operator as he walked behind the machine.

Fisher barely saw the man's hand move before he unclipped his radio from his shirt pocket. With his stare locked onto the screen, he leaned into the receiver and pushed the talk button.

"Gate Hotel Alpha. We have a code bravo. I repeat. This is Gate Hotel Alpha. We have a confirmed code bravo."

With his hand still on the receiver, the supervisor looked up, staring, narrow-eyed at Fisher.

Seconds passed with no response, while Fisher held the man's gaze in the hope he was managing not to show his growing panic. He knew full well the coded message should trigger an immediate response. A reply should at least have confirmed receipt before they issued a network-wide call to all and sundry, which would then provoke a flurry of activity, sending officers rushing to help.

None of the officers expected the silence, and one by one they turned to the governor. As the supervisor leaned into his radio again, he relaxed at the voice through the speaker.

"Uh, that's a negative Gate Hotel Alpha. Cancel code bravo and let them through."

At least three officers held their breath and questioned each other with sideways looks. The supervisor looked back at the screen, his eyes narrowing further as he tried to reconcile the response with their training. When he eventually looked at the unconcerned governor, he shrugged. With a final look at the screen, he pressed a red button and the conveyor belt rolled again.

The jacket passed out through the hanging plastic strips within a few seconds and no one complained, stunned as Fisher stepped up and pushed his arms back into the material.

***

Vauxhall, London

2nd September

Fisher's gaze went straight to their doors as he arrived back on the tenth floor. The splintered wooden surrounds were an unwelcome signpost along the empty, softly-lit corridor. His door stood open, sagging on its hinges, and the other remained closed with Harris nowhere to be seen.

Creeping across the carpet, Fisher poked his head inside the entrance but found his gun and vest gone.

Just as he stepped over the threshold, he heard a footstep behind, but before he could turn, an overwhelming force rushed him backwards as two firm hands clamped around his upper arms, dragging him across the corridor and into a darkened room.

13

The door slammed closed, blocking out the light with a sharp click of the latch and a soft hand clamped around his mouth, a delicate perfume surrounding him.

"Light!" Harris said, snapping out the command and before her word had barely faded, the room lit with a soft glow.

Fisher twisted around as much as the grip would allow to find a bare chested man withdrawing from a bedside lamp. A blonde woman sat up in bed beside him, her eyes wide with the cover drawn up to her neck.

Harris's hand fell from his face and as she pushed him gently out of her grip, he turned, their eyes meeting. It was all he could do to stop his mouth falling open when he found her wearing the scarlet silk nightdress from the first night they'd met, the lace edging still funnelling his gaze to the fullness of her breasts in stark contrast to the jet black Glock in her right hand.

"I would have dealt with them," she whispered, leaning forward, but before Fisher could protest, he turned to the sound of a door slamming along the corridor.

"Take this," Harris said, and Fisher turned to find her offering his gun by the barrel. Unsure where she'd secreted it, but soon revelling in its weight, he grabbed his communicator from his pocket and found two bright red dots heading towards their position along the corridor on the screen.

Tipping the display for Harris to look, she nodded before Fisher took soft steps towards the door, where he looked through the spyhole, finding nothing but the battered doors of their rooms opposite.

With a glance back down at the phone, he watched the red dots arrive from the right of their position, and peering back through the spyhole, he heard mumbled broken English laced with a strong Eastern European accent as the men filled the view.

Harris took his place, then backed away as their voices

faded, her eyes going wide when a woman's shrill voice replaced their noise.

Refocusing on his phone, his eyes did the same when another red dot moved a few rooms down and he watched, transfixed, when it arrived in the corridor.

Before he could show Harris, a deep Slavic shout called from the corridor, followed by a high pitch scream replying from just outside their door.

With no delay, Harris lunged forward, pulling the door open before she swung out into the corridor. Fisher raised his Glock and followed.

***

HMP Belmarsh, London

18th October

Despite not knowing what to expect, Fisher found the High Security Unit smaller than he'd imagined for a place so infamous. The four spurs of the building branched out from a central hub, and the governor explained they could each hold a maximum of twelve inmates, although often accommodated less. It wasn't uncommon for a single ultra-high security prisoner to be housed alone on one spur.

Arriving at the central control room filled with banks of CCTV monitors across two walls, a tall shaven-haired officer greeted them, his eyes narrowed, doing little to hide his surprise at the unannounced visit.

At the governor's request, Officer Smith, according to his name badge, left his two colleagues sharing sideways looks as he accompanied them to Block Three.

"You'll have twenty minutes before they're back from the gym," he said, as he led the way with a bunch of keys jangling at his side.

Passing through another double set of iron gates, Fisher held his tongue, not voicing his surprise that despite accommodating the country's most dangerous and socially unacceptable prisoners, the wing wasn't too much different from those he'd already seen in the main prison. A pool table, its metal legs pinned to the bright red concrete floor with bolts thicker than his finger sat in the centre of a small common area, with six cells facing each other from opposite walls.

With Fisher's head throbbing more with each footstep, he struggled to keep from turning toward each unaccustomed noise. Instead, as he peered in through the cell doors, listening to the governor reciting the inmate's daily regime, he forced himself to stare at the details. The stainless steel toilet, the family photos amongst full page spreads of naked women tacked to the walls and the kettle resting on a small metal sink. The monotone script did nothing to stop the rising fear.

After five minutes of mindless description, a gate slammed somewhere at the other end of the room and the governor stopped short.

"They've finished early," he said, looking in the sound's direction. "So that's where we'll conclude the tour."

"I want to see the place occupied," Fisher said, only just able to get the words out.

The governor's eyebrows lowered, his shoulders slumping as he turned to face Smith, but seemed to stop himself from complaining before leading Fisher to the nearest cell and describing the differences between those on the HSU and the main prison.

Fisher heard none of it, instead focusing on the rabble of deep voices echoing from down the corridor. Governor Bragg soon stopped talking and spread his arm across Fisher's front as if to shuffle him from the room. Despite his screaming instincts to follow the instruction, and the pounding pressure inside his head, Fisher at first ignored the gesture before relenting a few breaths later.

Stepping from the cell, he found six inmates all dressed in baggy maroon tracksuit bottoms, four in matching tops while the others wore sweat-marked grey T-shirts, each heading through the open door at the end of the wing, followed by three stone-faced officers. Fisher feared his eyes could stop working at any moment, the pain in his head compounding when he realised none of them were his target.

It didn't take long for the governor to grab Fisher's arm, pulling him to one side, but Fisher could already see a skin-headed man, muscles straining at his shirt, separating from the others as he scowled in Fisher's direction, quickly running toward him.

"That's mine," he growled, his face blotched red as he rushed. Before the governor could open his mouth, the govenor fell to the side, pushed out of the way as a balled fist flew at Fisher.

With no time to react, Fisher fell to the concrete, unable to get up as boots pounded his side. Before he pushed his eyes closed, he saw the inmate drop to his knees to pound at Fisher's stomach.

With his mind reeling from the unprovoked attack, Fisher's instinct pushed him to lash out, contacting something soft and fleshy until a heavy hit in the navel knocked the wind out of him. Only then did the commotion draw away and a shrill alarm sounded, its noise seeming as if coming out of every wall, with boots pounding the floor to drag the attackers away, then rushing Fisher to his feet as officers and inmates traded punches.

Five minutes later Fisher sat on the same reception chair, sipping a cup of weak coffee as a plump prison nurse reassured him he'd broken nothing, but perhaps he should get checked out at the hospital.

With the pressure in his head just a dull ache, the pain instead trumped by that in his stomach and the bruises feeling as if they blossomed all over his legs, he stood with care at the sight of the cab pulling up in the visitor's car park.

14

Vauxhall, London

2nd September

The first shot went off before he'd stepped from the room, the thug's bulk falling into a heap before Fisher had his gun level. With a wisp of smoke from the end of Harris's Glock, the thud of a silenced round seemed to zip past Fisher's ear and he pulled the trigger, only knowing he'd hit when the man clutched his chest as he fell backwards, thumping his head on the carpet.

Harris rushed forward, still with her gun aimed, sliding the pistol from the closest guy's grip with her bare foot before rushing to the other to do the same, then prodding his face with her big toe.

A sound from behind caused Fisher to turn, where he found a middle-aged woman swaddled in a pink dressing gown laying on the carpet, surrounded by a dark halo soaking into the carpet.

He'd slowed from a run before he'd arrived at her side, but as the hole in her forehead told him that not even the best doctor could save her, the clicking of locks pulled his attention away.

"Everyone stay in your room," Harris called out, somehow keeping her voice calm. "The police are on their way."

As doors pushed back into place, she stepped to Fisher's side and leaned in close.

"Grab your things. We're leaving," she said, but he couldn't move; despite all that had happened, his gaze transfixed on the sway of her nightdress as she walked to her door and presented the key-card.

After closing the door behind her, Fisher's feet remained fixed to the spot as he looked at each of the three bodies, closing his eyes and biting his lower lip.

More dead, he thought to himself as he shook his head, then opened his eyes to stare at the man he'd shot. His third kill.

"Now!" Harris snapped, already back in her grey suit and pointing to the battered wooden opening.

***

Queen Elizabeth Hospital, London

18th October

With his arm wrapped guarding his stomach, Fisher watched a group of children run in and around the lines of packed chairs whilst parents tried to shout them down. Elderly couples shook their heads in silence and dusty workers held limbs in the air, strapped with loose, blood-soaked bandages.

Couples and others with their friends and relatives clustered together, whilst many waited alone, all gazing now and then to a red LED sign scrolling from right to left despite the four hour waiting time having not changed since he'd arrived.

The rhythmic hum of the empty vending machine helped drown out the squeals of play and the drunken singing as he watched the almost constant stream of stretchers wheeled in by those dressed in green.

Glad of the thinking time, Fisher didn't care that he'd already been there for longer than the sign suggested.

His past had taught him to be content when alone. Before Susie had disappeared, he spent his days up trees or watching the TV, on his own more often than not. Solitude gave him the security he'd craved. Whilst alone, no one could discover what he could do and force him into a lab so they could probe the freak for answers.

Sometimes he thought perhaps he should have stayed at home rather than let his friends convince him to go on that trip to Snowdon. Andrew would still be alive, but if they'd gone without him, Susie would have still gone missing and he knew all too well what would have happened to her.

He wouldn't have met Carrie.

He wouldn't have met the woman who'd become the sunshine peering through the clouds. He wouldn't feel the glow in his heart, even though a storm had rolled in and blotted out her brightness.

Shifting his weight in the plastic chair, he welcomed the stab of pain in his chest, daring not to think about what would have happened if the skin-headed man hadn't held back.

Watching a young Asian couple who'd arrived at the same time as him stand when a middle-aged nurse in light blue scrubs called out a name, he rose from his seat despite the stiffness of his joints as he longed for painkillers.

Instead, finding a spot by the main entrance, he leaned against the wall, watching patients and visitors passing the drawn out moments with cigarettes and chat, then ignoring the call of his alias three times, he concentrated on the new ambulances arriving as others flashed their blue lights and raced back off into traffic.

With a glance down the long road to his right, he stood up straight when he saw a police car racing towards the hospital with an ambulance following. It wasn't long before the panda car tucked itself out of the way and two police officers jumped out with a third and fourth uniformed pair leaping out of the back of the ambulance, flanking a stretcher.

Fisher headed to the reception desk and, as the wrinkled receptionist tapped on her keyboard, his name rang out over the PA system again.

15

London

2nd September

Waking with light through the curtains highlighting the unfamiliar room, bleary-eyed, it took Fisher a moment to remember they were at a safe house arranged by Clark.

Checking his phone, it was already eight as he pulled out of the bed and stretched his tight leg muscles, but it was only as he slid the thick curtains to the side that he remembered they were high in a tower block; although he hadn't paid attention to exactly where.

Sure that to many, the towers and the distant over-sized Ferris wheel was recognisable in an instant, they had little meaning to Fisher. Rather than lingering in the hope the sight would bring recollection, he slipped on his protective vest, white t-shirt, black jeans and unfolded his coat before holstering his Glock 17.

Leaving the covers straightened and gripping his bag, he left the room in search of the kitchen. Settling for a coffee without milk, the fridge and cupboards bare of anything fresh, he made himself comfortable at the small kitchen table where he pulled out the pistol and slid a replacement round into the magazine just as Harris appeared in her wrinkle-free grey suit.

"Coffee?" Fisher asked, pointing to an empty mug he'd left on the counter.

"Thank you," she replied with a smile and, no matter how hard he looked, he saw no sign of fatigue.

"But there's no milk," he added as he stood.

"It's the maid's day off," she replied, flashing her brow whilst reaching high into the furthest cupboard and placing a can of powdered whitener on the side. "I can't stand the stuff myself."

Fisher shook his head, spooning coffee, then adding

water to the mug.

"Thank you," she said after taking a seat opposite him as she sipped. Pulling her lips from the mug, she caught his gaze. "Let's clear something up."

Fisher nodded, his blood going cold as he prepared himself for what she might say.

"If you disobey my orders one more time, then I can't work with you," she said, her gaze not flinching.

Fisher's expression fell, surprised at her choice of words. "I came back to help you."

"I told you to leave. It's arrogant that you think after less than a few weeks your help would do anything but add to the danger," she said, her expression unchanged.

Although his head shifted to the side, he remained silent.

"You've not had a single day of training," she added, raising her chin. "My job is to protect you. I can look after myself." Despite seeming as if she had more to say, Harris stopped herself.

"But... But..." Fisher stuttered.

"If you're blinded by any feelings you have for me and insist on putting yourself in unnecessary danger, then I'll step aside and let someone else take my place," Harris said, before standing and walking out of the room.

***

Queen Elizabeth Hospital, London

18th October

It took two minutes for the shaven-haired nurse to confirm all Fisher's injuries were superficial. After issuing a script for ibuprofen, and taking care not to draw attention to the weight of his jacket, Fisher slung it over his shoulder before heading with a slight limp from the calm of the minors area to the bustle of activity around the corner.

Beyond the automatic doors were eight bays bordered with blue paper curtains. Whilst some were drawn, the rest were left open at the centre, not hiding a motionless patient whilst men and women in multi-coloured scrubs busied themselves like worker bees around a hive. Much of the activity focused on two patients, the others left to rest flat on their beds, their faces covered in masks as a tangle of cables disappeared beneath their gowns to a symphony of monitors pinging coded messages across the room.

Some had relatives holding hands, their grave expressions mirroring one another. Others were alone, leaving those they cared about not knowing their danger. Pushing away the thought of who would turn up for him, Fisher's gaze found two prison officers flanking the furthest bay.

He didn't know where the other uniforms were.

Stepping towards the bay, with a bald head and face heavy with wrinkles, his skin pale and lips blue, the man laying on the bed looked a shadow of the black and white mugshot burned into the nation's memory.

Unsurprised when the officer to the left stood tall, his round face and protruding belly reminded Fisher of an eighties wrestler, despite the bleak uniform.

Fisher reached out to the man in the bed.

"Can I help you, sir?" the officer said, stepping into Fisher's path as his East London accent curled his lips.

Taking little notice of the guard, Fisher pushed his hand to his mouth as he peered to the side. "Dad?"

When the patient didn't respond, he glanced at the two men, their raised brows betraying their surprise.

"I'm sorry, sir," the other officer said, his stature a little less pronounced than his colleague's, but his belly just as round. "You can't see him right now. They're transferring him to a secure room. Perhaps then we can start the paperwork."

The purr of a phone nearby added to the tones surrounding them.

Fisher nodded, letting his body shrink as he looked at

each of them. "I understand, but please, can you tell me what's wrong with him? All I know is they found him unconscious."

Both men exchanged looks then shook their heads. Fisher took a step back.

"I'm afraid we can't say anything. It's more than our jobs are worth," said the officer, still blocking the view.

"Okay," Fisher replied after a pause, then swapped glances between the pair, holding his gaze with each until they looked away.

"He's..." the man to the right said, his voice soft before he paused with a look from his colleague. "Look, he's had a once over. The doctor said he's not in immediate danger. Try not to worry."

Fisher was about to speak when a loud tone sounded from the PA system, followed by a woman's voice.

"Multiple adult trauma, five minutes. Multiple adult trauma, five minutes."

"Thank you," Fisher said, looking at each of them and offering out his hand. "Thank you for looking after my dad."

The officer standing at Fisher's front looked down at his hand, then over to his colleague before he leaned forward, taking the grip.

As their skin met, Fisher smiled.

"The doctor will be a while. I *can* wait here and you want a coffee," he said, watching the other officer's brow lower, until, with a clasp of his hand in Fisher's as he spoke, his expression melted.

16

London

2nd September

Looking up from the long cold contents at the bottom of his mug, Fisher found Harris leaning beside the intercom at the doorway, her brow raised with the unanswered question.

"We're fine as we are," he replied. When all she did was stare back, her expression unchanging, he raised his chin. "How did they know where to find us?"

"There must be a mole in SIS," she said, her expression softening as she placed her mug in the sink and took the seat opposite him.

"Are you sure?" Fisher replied, leaning back.

"The hotel was an SIS arrangement. They have five rooms reserved each day, chosen at random before they're swept for bugs. We just took advantage of what they already had in place."

Fisher sat up a little straighter. "Did SIS know about Alan? Could *they* be the ones who set me up?"

Harris shook her head. "If it was an official order, then we'd have known."

Fisher looked down at his empty cup as he forced the tension in his shoulders to relax.

"What now?" he said without looking up.

"Whilst we look for the mole, we'll avoid contact with SIS. We'll use only our resources. I've also arranged some protection."

The intercom buzzed with a high tone and beside the door, Fisher found a familiar face lighting up the small screen.

A few seconds after Harris pushed the door release, the screen came alive again, but instead of showing the communal front door, there was a picture of the hallway just outside the entrance to the flat where Biggy and Lucky, two of the Royal

Navy Special Forces operatives that helped them save Susie less than seventy-two hours ago, stood.

Harris pushed the door release for a second time and Biggy, the squad leader, bounded into the room in jeans and an unzipped three-quarter length leather coat, showing off a blue t-shirt. Wearing almost the same clothes, Lucky followed behind.

"Where's the damsel in distress?" Biggy said, his beaming smile not faltering at Harris's withering look.

***

Queen Elizabeth Hospital, London

18th October

With a pair of silver coins pushed into the vending machine in the adjacent hallway, one after the other, two black coffees chugged from the hidden spout and as Fisher picked up the second of the hot cardboard cups, he spotted his cue for the next stage of his plan about to walk past.

Balancing the scalding liquid with care, he followed the woman in the dark blue tunic past a tall police officer slouched and uninterested in the corridor's intersection. As moments later she arrived at a side room, a metal sign clung to the door.

Matron.

After fumbling the lock open with a large bunch of keys, the woman headed in, leaving the door ajar. Fisher slowed, counting to ten before pushing the door open with his shoulder and finding her with her back to him. She settled into a seat at a desk along the furthest end of the small room, reading from a stack of white papers.

The desk along the wall was not only piled high with multi-coloured forms, but was also home to racks of freestanding shelves loaded with boxed medical supplies. To its left, more shelves filled the space while the tall wide doors of a white cabinet stood the other side.

As Fisher edged in through the door nursing the paper cups, the woman turned in her seat.

"I'm sorry, sir. This is a private room," she said, her delicate voice not hiding an edge of authority. Ignoring her words, Fisher stepped up to the table and settled the cups on what he guessed were a tall pile of patient notes in tatty beige cardboard jackets before turning and offering out his hand.

With widening eyes, the matron backed out of her chair.

"I'm here for the audit," Fisher said, watching her eyes narrow before she tentatively reached out. "Didn't you get the memo?" he added, gripping her hand as she shook her head. "I'm here to audit the medicine cab…," he said, his sentence tailing off as she sighed and eased herself back into the chair, her initial concern gone as her gaze went to his chest as if in search of an ID badge matching her own.

"I'm the Trust's auditor," he said, still gripping her hand and she met his eyes with a nod. "I need the keys to the medicine cabinet," he added, releasing his light grip.

"Is there a problem?" she replied as she delved her hand into her tunic pocket.

"It's a random check, that's all," he said, watching her fumble before handing over a small bunch of keys.

"We check it every shift change," she replied, her gaze darting across the desk as if searching for something.

"It's okay. There's no issue. It'll take minutes and then I'll be out of your hair," he said, doing his best to keep his tone soft. Finding what she'd searched for, the matron leaned across the desk and pulled a clipboard from under a pile of pink forms.

"The controlled drugs register," she said, passing over a notepad clipped to a wooden board.

"Thank you. That was my next request," he lied, before turning and pushing the key the woman had pointed out into the silver lock of the white steel cabinet. Leaving the bunch hanging in the lock whilst pretending to glance over the register, he held her in his peripheral vision until she turned in her seat and returned to her paperwork.

Pulling the thin metal doors open, Fisher stared at the Aladdin's Cave of white and brown bottles and boxes of all shapes and sizes. Not knowing where to start, he scanned the register. Soon finding Valium on the list, he glanced up to the corresponding space in the cabinet and there it was. Trying not to smile, he checked back to the nurse without moving his head before scouring the list again.

Although he'd memorised each of the trade names for everything he sought, after looking over the list twice, he hadn't found what he wanted. With a shake of his head, he looked again with his heart pumping hard in his chest, slowing only when he found the name Flumazenil. Unsure why he hadn't seen it the last time he'd checked, he looked up to find a glass jar where he'd been expecting to find a box of tablets.

After another glance to the nurse, he picked up the bottle, but before he pushed it into his pocket, he noticed the words *BY INJECTION* on the side.

17

London

2nd September

"We have half the troop assigned. Four on, four off for twenty-four-hour coverage," Biggy said, answering Harris's question and still grinning as he looked around the kitchen. "They've cleaned this place up since we were last here," he added with a playful jab on Fisher's shoulder, who replied with an unsure smile. As if remembering why they were at the flat, Biggy's tone stiffened as he ran his hand across his short afro hair. "We'll have two outside watching and two inside. When you want to travel, the outside team will provide advance clearance. Does that sound alright?" he said, looking between them, despite everyone knowing it was Harris he was asking.

As the squad leader of Four Troop, X Squadron of the Special Boat Service, standing at five foot eleven, Biggy's height had somehow gained him the moniker a long time ago. Despite his lively nature and ability to make those around him laugh, he'd proven to Fisher he was all business when he needed to be.

"Isn't that overkill?" Fisher said, glancing between the pair.

Harris shook her head. "Do you like the alternative?" she said, but didn't wait for an answer before turning back to Biggy. "It wasn't just a paint job. I'll fill you in on some upgrades later. Who knows your whereabouts?"

"Just Miller. As far as everyone else is concerned, we're on exercise, putting some new weapon system through its paces in the middle of Dartmoor with the rest of the guys."

Harris nodded at the mention of Miller, the military liaison to the agency and Biggy's commanding officer.

"So, what's the plan for today?" Fisher said, turning to Harris.

"We've got three safe deposit locations to try the key," she replied.

"And I want to talk to Alan," Fisher said, but Harris shook her head.

"They transferred him to the Beacons this morning. Like I said, we need to avoid Vauxhall."

Fisher bit his bottom lip.

***

Queen Elizabeth Hospital, London

18th October

After delivering the coffee to the grateful guards, Fisher dragged an extra chair from the waiting area, but not before snatching at the top of an unaccompanied trolley brimming with supplies just outside the cubicle. Despite pushing the plastic seat over to the nearest officer, the burly guard ignored the gesture and remained standing.

In the short time he'd been away, the amount of people rushing between the bays had increased and it wasn't long before a woman voiced her annoyance at the prisoner taking up space.

Moving to the head of the bed, Fisher stared down at the monitor's screen where coloured graphics displayed the patient's vitals and traced his relaxed heart rhythm.

Pulling the thick white sheet tight around the waterproof mattress, Fisher smartened up the bed before leaning in to stroke the hairless head of the stranger. The cubicle felt like a pocket of calm amongst the life and death in balance for those outside the curtain.

In his peripheral vision, Fisher sensed the guards look his way, only for them to turn as he glanced over, both pulling their cups up to their mouths as if to hide their guilt at the intrusion.

"Ah. Sweet coffee. You can't beat it," the shorter guard said to his wrestler colleague.

As Fisher continued to stroke Daryl's head, he let his eyelids droop just a little as he tuned into the rhythmic trills and beeps of the surrounding monitors.

It didn't take long for the guard's first wobble and after a few moments both their heads bowed, the movement shallow at first, growing deeper with every new note as the Valium took hold.

The wrestler was the first to give into the chair whilst he sipped from the cup, his colleague following soon after. After glancing at the patient almost in unison, one after the other they closed their eyes.

Knowing the opportunity could be short-lived if the other guards they'd arrived with turned up to relieve their colleagues, Fisher didn't hesitate. After taking care to push them back into their seats to prevent them toppling, he pulled on purple gloves and a disposable yellow plastic apron plucked from dispensers on the wall, then shoved the bulk of the prisoner onto his side, ripping open his gown to expose a freckled back.

Laying a scalpel and plaster wrapped in sterile plastic packaging on the bed before pulling out the Glock, he flicked the magazine-release just behind the trigger and with his thumb, emptied sixteen rounds one by one into his pocket before laying the seventeenth on the bed.

After hastily refilling five of the rounds, not wanting to waste time on pushing any more home, Fisher slipped the weapon inside his jacket. With a tight grip, he took the round he'd placed on the bed and unscrewed the bullet from the cartridge. As the hollow bullet came away, he pulled out a thick, black plastic tablet from the space.

The wrestler's long snore drew Fisher's attention, and he leapt to the man's side, grabbing his round nose before the guard spluttered, his breathing returning to normal.

Back at the patient's side, Fisher twisted a freckled arm

and pulled it around to his hairless back, tugging it to its extremes before drawing a bold black line at its furthest reach. Ripping the scalpel from its sterile packaging, he made a precise nick high up the skin just below the black line and the two sides separated, letting out a few drops of blood before he forced the black capsule inside the wound and pushed the bulge up along the skin. Contorting the arm back around, he double-checked the placement. With the wound swabbed, he closed the two sides together with Steri-Strips and plasters before rolling Daryl onto his back.

Taking the clear bottle from his pocket, Fisher squinted at its tiny writing but drew back, his eyes going wide when he found no instructions. Shaking his head, he tapped the underside of the pale, freckled forearm with two fingers, because that's what he'd seen on TV. Although he didn't know what was meant to happen, he wondered for a moment if his employers would consider Daryl's death a failure.

Shaking his head again, he pulled out his phone before tapping his fingers on the screen's keyboard, his alarm growing when he found there were three types of injections. Unable to find what he needed on the bottle, he glanced at the curtain before turning back to the screen, knowing he had little choice than to put his trust in Wikipedia's reporting that Flumazenil was delivered intravenously.

Following the link, he clicked on the first page, which led him to a website giving advice to drug users on how to inject safely. After scanning past the warnings and disclaimers, slowing at the bold writing titled *Arterial hits*, he held his breath at the thought of what might happen if he got this wrong. With infection being the least of his concerns, his prognosis already poor, he skipped the section and read on.

Step one: Prepare the dose.

The information on the bottle helped, and clipping the needle onto the small syringe he'd found on the trolley outside, he drew up three millilitres and tapped the end. Daryl didn't flinch as the excess sprayed over his face.

With the task seeming a little simpler than he'd first

thought, Fisher looked up, holding his breath when the note from a neighbouring monitor changed from a rhythmic beep to a loud bong. A moment later, the curtain swayed as the sounds of activity crowded the next cubicle along.

When no one pulled the curtains wide, he continued reading.

Step Two: Replace the needle cap and find the site. Use the forearm if available. Clean the injection site.

With a shake of his head, he tapped the arm hard, watching as a blue vein rose below the pale skin, then removing the cap and taking great care, he pushed the needle into the skin at what he guessed was twenty degrees, the syringe facing towards the armpit, then stopped and read on.

Step Three: Test the insertion.

Pulling back the plunger just a little, Fisher smiled when a crimson cloud plumed into the syringe before he eased the plunger down until it was empty. Pulling out the syringe, he dropped it into a yellow sharps box mounted on the wall, then placing a plaster over the pinhole, he ripped off his remaining glove and apron.

The guards were still out cold as he glanced over, then he leaned past the monitor, pulling the plug from the socket before, one by one, he ripped the soft, sticky pads from the chest.

Dropping the cables onto the floor, Fisher grabbed a clear plastic bag tucked against the wall and found it filled with a plain grey tracksuit. Rubbing his knuckles on Daryl's pale sternum, it took just a matter of seconds before he squirmed and opened his eyes. Fisher held his gaze for a long moment before smiles bloomed on both of their faces.

Trying to sit, the clatter of metal at Daryl's side drew their attention to the handcuff tied against the bed's low rail, but before they could do more than share a wide-eyed look, they heard a deep voice asking which bay the prisoner was in.

Pulling away from the bed, Fisher grabbed the scalpel he'd set by the monitor before bounding over to the furthest of the two officers, his gaze fixed on a bulge in his black trouser pocket. Slashing the material open, he found a small set of keys.

The curtain edge slid open and there stood a young male Asian doctor looking down at the clipboard just as Daryl pulled on the jogging bottoms.

Closing the curtain behind him, the doctor looked up, his gaze going to the sleeping guards before landing on the muzzle of a black Glock 17 pointed at him.

A minute later, Fisher and Daryl, dressed in the doctor's white coat, were in the back of a stolen white transit van heading away from the hospital.

18

London

2nd September

Within half an hour, they were back in the traffic, immersed in the new car smell of a black BMW X5. With Fisher in the back beside Harris, Lucky sat next to Biggy, who guided the four by four through the clogged streets.

Unable to take his gaze from the iComm communicator mounted on a flexible gooseneck stuck to the windscreen, Fisher stared at what at first glance seemed to show any normal GPS display, but although a car icon hovered in the centre of the bottom quarter, a second car ran ahead with a thick green line linking the pair.

As their X5 wound down the streets, Fisher watched the connecting line occasionally turn red before the route between the two would update, with Biggy guiding them along its course.

"It's linked to the lead car," Harris said, and Fisher glanced her way before turning back to the screen. "The advance team is a few miles ahead, following a route the computer selects based on various risk factors. As they travel, they'll carry out their own assessment for pinch points or possible surveillance locations. If they disagree with the set route, they can overwrite the computer, which updates our screen."

"That's pretty cool," Fisher said, unable to stop himself from smiling.

"When the advance team arrives at our destination, they'll make sure it's safe, checking for ambush or other compromise and then determine the best approach, or of course, call an abort."

"Like air traffic control?" Fisher said, glancing to his side.

"Yes. I guess so," Harris replied with a nod. "It allows for more than one lead car for high-risk convoys and it's possible to use for just a single car too, just taking advantage of the risk database."

Fisher's smile broadened.

"I thought you'd like it," she added. "It's part of your iComm's standard package."

Fisher glanced down at his trouser pocket where the communicator's bulk bulged the fabric.

"One minute," Biggy called out and Fisher sat up straight, peering out of the windscreen and then past Harris to a small shop on the high street. With the pavement busy with pedestrians and cars parked along the kerb, Fisher glanced over the faces of those ambling by.

"I'll give you a hundred quid if you can pick out the forward team," Lucky said, twisting around in his seat, the scar above his eye tightening as he laughed.

Fisher turned, peering along the street, but he shook his head, looking over to Lucky. Biggy's laugh boomed out as he pulled into a bus stop a few cars down from the shop.

The four doors opened as the BMW relaxed on its handbrake, with Lucky coming around to take Biggy's place in the driver's seat whilst he followed at the rear, sandwiching Fisher with Harris walking in front, as they headed to the shop's front door. After the briefest of enquiries, they rejoined the traffic.

With the sun blazing through a light haze, they arrived on a trading estate another mile or so from the squalid flat, driving past small business units with either To Let signs up high, or bright banners showing off company logos. Within a minute, the units had grown in size, with car parks full of vans and big estate cars as the distance between each building grew wider.

Soon finding themselves down a secluded cul-de-sac where a lonely silver ten-year-old Mercedes Benz saloon sat in the car park in front of a half brick, half metal-sided unit, the sign above the front door read *Barr Securities*, the text next to a picture of a golden four-sided key.

Finding a space by the entrance, the three jumped out, leaving Lucky in the driver's seat, just as a high-speed train rushed past, high on the embankment close by.

With Fisher taking the lead, he pushed open the fingerprint-marked glass door, stepping into a small but empty reception area. A thick glass partition rising to the ceiling split the room in two, with one side separated by a countertop whilst the other held a thick, golden door in place, the paint worn along the handle running along its length to reveal the grey metal beneath. A white plastic card reader waited by its side. Above the counter, just below head height, a circle of drilled holes waited in the glass. Below the counter, a letterbox sat.

Peering around the door at the small space beyond, apart from a solid looking entrance, it held no interest.

The door didn't budge as Fisher pulled then pushed, but glancing back at Harris, he spotted a slim red phone mounted on the wall beside the main entrance. A dog-eared piece of paper held a faded handwritten scrawl. *Dial 100 for assistance.*

Pulling the phone from its cradle, Fisher exposed the keypad, finding the buttons for one and zero rubbed clean of their text. Three rings later, a young man asked how he could assist, his voice devoid of sincerity.

"I've lost my swipe," Fisher said.

"Name?" the voice replied, sharp and impatient.

"Alan Bullard."

"Give me a moment," the voice said after a delay.

"Wait in the car," Harris said and with a nod, Biggy left them alone to scour the room for the five minutes it took for the door beyond the glass partition to open and for a young south Asian man in t-shirt and jeans to appear, wiping his mouth with a handkerchief.

"I can't find your record," he said, shaking his head, his voice a little muffled from beyond the glass. "What was the name again?"

Fisher glanced at Harris, but her expression didn't change as she stepped forward.

"I don't know what you mean," she said, shaking her head. "We're here to rent a box?"

Squinting, the young man peered back. "I'm sure you said you lost your card?"

"We've just arrived," Fisher replied, shaking his head. "Some guy left as we came in."

Looking at the main entrance before wiping his mouth, the man turned to Fisher. "Do you have two documents to prove your ID and address?"

Fisher nodded.

"Okay. Come through," he said, reaching forward. The door clicked and Fisher grasped the handle. With the door closing at their backs, the young man pulled a card from his pocket and swiped at a reader beside the second door before ushering the pair into a dim corridor.

The man then squeezed past the pair, guiding them to the right, where they found another sturdy metal door with an illuminated keypad at its side. Further to their right were three plain white wooden doors. The first had no sign but a brass plaque on the rightmost showed it was for *Staff Only*, whilst the other was a toilet.

The man didn't falter, opening the unmarked door and beckoning them into a simple square room with three chairs around a table. Moving to the space in front of a dusty, antiquated Dell monitor with its cables disappearing through the centre of the table, he offered his hand towards the opposite chair. Rather than sitting, Harris stepped forward and took his hand.

"I'm Claire, and you are?" she said.

Lowering his brow, he nodded. "Sanjay," he said, pushing on a smile that didn't reach his eyes.

Harris soon let go, taking a seat as Fisher stepped up and gripped the hand.

"I'm from the Financial Services Authority," Fisher said, watching as Sanjay's smile sank, his shoulders raising as he pulled out the stained handkerchief to wipe his brow. "I'm here to perform an audit on your Know Your Customer verification data."

Fisher sat next to Harris, watching as Sanjay's shoulders seemed to relax, although he still hadn't spoken.

"Is this your first audit?" Harris said.

Sanjay nodded.

"It's straight forward," she replied, looking over to Fisher.

"In preparation, the office opened an account and all we need to do is check how you have stored the details," he added.

Sanjay's eyes narrowed, then he stepped to the side to give Fisher space as he brought his chair around to sit beside the young man.

"We used a few names and details for the account. I need to go through each one," Fisher said as he settled into the seat. With a curt nod, Sanjay reached for the mouse when an application appeared on the screen showing an empty search box. He looked back at Fisher with expectation.

"Alan Bullard," Fisher said, watching the word appear in the box as Sanjay typed.

No matching results, came the message as he pressed return.

Sanjay cleared the message and his fingers hovered over the keys again.

Fisher glanced at Harris. "They must have given us the wrong paperwork," he said with a shake of his head. "It happens. Have you got some of the other details they've used in the past?" Fisher added, watching straight-faced as Harris nodded, then pulled out her communicator before dictating Alan's address.

No matching results.

"Try George Cooper," Fisher asked, using the name of the mutual friend who'd introduced Alan to Fisher and the rest of their group at university.

No matching results.

Fisher fumbled in his pocket and pulled out the unique key. "This is one of yours, isn't it?" he asked, knowing the answer when Sanjay's eyes widened before he nodded. "How can you be so sure?"

"We had these made when we opened. They were our unique selling point back when they were the cutting edge of lock technology. Can I see?" Sanjay said, reaching out and taking the key. Turning it over in his hand, he stared at a tiny number, then turned back to the computer and tapped in the digits. Alan's image appeared on the screen, nestled in amongst a series of text fields.

"The box is registered to a James Fisher."

19

Eight Walworth Road, London

19th October

Fisher sat bolt upright, pushing the heel of his hand against his eyes as he tried to push away what had forced him awake.

After a long moment, his hands slid down his face as the pressure behind his eyes abated. To the sound of sideways rain battering the huge pane of glass, the curtains hung neatly on each side. Rubbing his temples, he glanced across the bed to the naked brunette beauty, her curvaceous contours accentuated by the black silk sheet hugging her body. He knew names were unimportant and picked himself from underneath the smooth material, adjusting the waist of his black Calvin Klein boxer shorts as he stepped into the en-suite bathroom.

Staring in the mirror, he rubbed his chin with his thumb and forefinger and feeling stubble, he took a step back, opened the cabinet door and pulled out the can of shaving foam and the first razor to hand.

With the growth dealt with and his face clean of foam, he chucked the razor into the open bin as he heard the front door close.

***

London

2nd September

"Is everything alright?" Sanjay said as Fisher stared at the photocopy that, if it weren't for Alan's expressionless face staring back, could have been of his own passport and driving licence.

"Yes. All seems in order," Fisher replied, taking time to form the words, hoping to hide his surprise whilst he peered at each photo's edge. Unable to find any evidence of a join or imperfection, he leaned back. "You've passed the audit. I just need a printout of these for the file?"

"Sure," Sanjay replied with a nod before tapping at the keyboard.

"Once we've collected the contents of the box, we can file our report," Fisher said as he stood.

Sanjay shook his head as he got to his feet. "I'm sorry. I can only open the box to Mr Fisher," he said, glancing over with an apologetic smile.

Fisher laughed, his face consumed by a wide smile as he looked at Harris. Seeing her expression hadn't changed, his smile fell and anger tightened his chest. Stepping up to Sanjay, he touched his bare forearm.

"I'm James Fisher, and it's my photo on the database. Cut the crap and get the box open."

"Fisher!" Harris snapped, taking a step toward him, but seeming oblivious, Sanjay handed back the key.

"Follow me," he said, stepping to the door. Fisher followed whilst doing his best to avoid Harris's glare.

Reminding Fisher of a swimming pool changing room he'd often visited as a kid, the vault walls were lined with deposit boxes, and clustered like lockers in the centre of the room. At each end of the island, a wooden frame held frosted glass which formed a small enclosure.

Leading them to the far end, Sanjay held his hand out for the key before examining the serial number for a second time, then pushed it into the lock set in the top left-hand corner of a dinner-plate-sized metal door. With the key inserted at eye level, he reached inside his pocket and pulled out a similar key before sliding it into a second lock in the top right hand corner. Turning the key, he motioned for Fisher to do the same.

With both rotated, Sanjay pulled out a metal box, sliding

it halfway out before withdrawing his key. Fisher tried to do the same, but it wouldn't budge.

"Your key stays in the lock until you push the box back. I'll be in my office if you need me," he said, before handing over an empty envelope with Fisher's name on the front. "When you're done, pop the key in here and post it in the letterbox in reception."

Fisher nodded before Sanjay turned and left the vault, then clasping the box with both hands, its weight came as a surprise when he pulled out the steel container. Its depth was about double its height and after guiding it into the glass room with Harris squeezing in behind and closing the door, he sat in the solo seat.

"Go on," she said, nodding to the box resting on the table as she peered over his shoulder.

With a deep breath, Fisher pulled up the stainless steel lid to find the box full and a yellowed sheet of paper resting on the top. The nearest edge appeared to have been ripped from a pad and had numbers scrawled across the length. Stopping himself from touching the page, he rummaged in his trouser pocket and pulled on a pair of latex gloves.

Taking care as if the page could fall apart at any moment, he placed it on the table before his attention went to a dark blue Nokia mobile phone, the type he'd owned ten or more years ago.

Moving it to the side with as much care as he'd given the paper, he drew out five identical brown leather-bound books, but found nothing on the outside to show what they were. All but one were worn, with the leather spines discoloured and cracked. A handgun rested under the fifth. Its sleek black finish filed back to grey just above the trigger guard.

Harris's hand appeared from over his shoulder, taking the weapon as Fisher stared at a passport; he confirmed with a flick through the pages it was Alan's actual document. It nestled on top of four crisp bundles of American Dollars.

With barely a word, Harris left whilst Fisher went back to the scribblings on the page, but unable to make any sense of the faded pen marks, he took hold of the first book, opening it to the middle where he recognised Alan's cursive writing. Thumbing back to the start, it didn't take him long to realise it was a journal of sorts, each entry undated. Closing the leather, he turned back to the spine and found each numbered with faint ink at the bottom.

Taking the first volume, he opened it at the beginning.

20

London

19th October

Vehicles on the opposite side of the orbital motorway stood stationary and from the front passenger seat, Fisher imagined each frustrated driver cursing as they watched Farid cruise their white two-year-old Range Rover toward them before rushing by.

Behind Farid, a bulky shaven-haired passenger sat, his expression transfixed on the traffic disappearing over the horizon. Fisher hadn't met him before, or maybe he'd just forgotten his face, having met so many people recently. Most weren't big on introductions, apart from the women, who were always keen.

"What happened when they found the gun?" Farid said, his lips parting with a smile. "How on earth did you get out of that?"

"I'm not going to lie," Fisher said, a smile taking over his face. "Even though I'd put the hours in before, I was shitting myself."

"How the fuck did you prepare for that?" Farid said, glancing over, his smile waning.

"It was easy enough to find the security foreman in the pub near the prison," Fisher said, raising his brow as he glanced at Farid's renewed smile. "And he seemed happy enough to tell me everything I wanted."

The car swerved to the right as Farid's laugh boomed, bringing with it a grumble from the guy in the back.

"I told him the governor was testing the procedures the foreman had just told me about, and in order that they wouldn't disrupt the rest of the prison, the governor wanted any radio calls for backup cancelled."

"And they bought it?" Farid said, screwing up his face.

"What about the governor? He was right there with you."

"What can I say?" Fisher replied, smiling wider. "I'm good at what I do."

"You've got balls," Farid said, laughing again. "How did you know it would work?"

Fisher shrugged, his gaze falling on a sea of red lights, pulling out his Glock as Farid reached to the centre console and turned the radio to the last gasps of a breakfast show. With a glance to his left, Fisher wasn't surprised to see a black Range Rover filling the wing mirror, reminding him that whilst no one ever spoke about it, there was always at least one other car following.

Examining the gun, Fisher released the magazine before pulling back the slide, then peering into the chamber, the brass round glinting in the sun, he let the magazine home and slid the pistol back into his holster.

"So, what am I getting this time?" Fisher said, staring along the road.

"It's a key, or a set of keys, I'm not sure. Just take everything on the peg," Farid said, slowing the car to join the queue.

Fisher looked down at the square of folded paper resting on his lap and the code he'd scribbled in the corner back at the apartment, which Farid had assured him would come in useful.

"Are we having a night off tonight?" Fisher said. The guy in the back laughed as Farid caught his eye.

"If you're not up to the job, then sure, but I'm not turning down the ladies," Farid said with a smile. "There'll be complaints if they have to settle for Benny."

"Oi," the guy in the back mumbled before thumping his fist into Farid's seat.

"Okay. One more night, just to keep them happy," Fisher said as he forced a smile.

Within half an hour they'd left the motorway, pulling up at double yellow lines outside an industrial revolution era building with its five storeys towering over them. Peering to the signs pointing towards the university reception, Fisher jumped out, stretched his legs and disappeared across the road.

Ten minutes later and he was back in his seat as they sped off.

21

London

2nd September

Wednesday

So here goes.

Jackie said it might help me control my issues if I wrote what I'm thinking, rather than bottle it all up. It makes sense, I guess. I can't go on like I have been, so I'll give it a go. I'm not sure what to write, though. She says it doesn't need to be all formal or anything, or need any dates, but it might help if I put the day of the week, so if I read it back, it makes some sense.

I'll start tomorrow.

Thursday

She looked at me across the hall today. I think she smiled back, but it might have been someone standing behind me. She's so beautiful, especially when she sings on the stage. I could listen for hours.

After lunchtime rehearsal, I helped Marshy set up today's lesson. Stuart gave me a funny look when he saw me. I need to keep out of his way or there'll be trouble for both of us.

I just watched an excellent documentary on Channel Four with my mum about the history of the NASA space programme. She got excited when I talked about wanting to do something scientific as a job, but she reminded me I need to work on my grades.

Goodnight. Why am I saying goodnight? It's a diary! Why am I...

Friday

No rehearsals today, but I saw Shelley in maths. She left early, something to do with the play. Paul said she was going to the clap clinic to get herself checked out, but I told him she wasn't like that.

I had a near miss with Stuart and his idiot flunkies on the way home from school, and I had to go down an alley on Forbes Street to avoid them. Paul said I should let them do what they wanted, then they'd find out the mistake they'd made.

"They appear to be some kind of therapeutic diaries," Fisher said to Harris as she opened the viewing room door holding a small cardboard box.

"Alan's, I presume?" she said as she helped load the contents into the box with the handgun nowhere to be seen.

"It doesn't say," Fisher said, shaking his head. "I'll go through them," he added as he thumbed through the pages.

"Are you okay with that?" Harris asked as Fisher stood, holding still as if deep in thought.

"If they go halfway to telling me why he betrayed me, then yes, I'm okay with that."

Replacing the stainless steel container back in its slot, Fisher turned around to find the cardboard box at her feet as Harris examined the handgun.

"It's loaded," she said, holding his gaze for what felt like a long moment.

Hurrying through the streets back in the X5, Fisher looked at the sheet of paper whilst Harris leaned over and took a photo with her iComm.

"Clark," she said into the air. "We've got three long numbers, each twelve digits." A tone rang in Fisher's head and he pulled out his communicator, reading the message on the screen.

Accept encrypted incoming conference call from Night Watch?

"Morning Night Watch," he said, holding back a smile at Clark's call sign.

"Good morning. I'll start checking numbered bank accounts and that sort of thing first, then I'll pass it over to the Doughnuts. What else did you find?"

"A mobile phone," Fisher said, his hand moving around the contents of the box.

"Can you get me the SIM number and IMEI, please?"

Harris took the phone from Fisher and turned it around

in her hands as if checking its weight. Seeming satisfied with what she felt, she pulled off the back cover and recited the details to Clark.

"There are five diaries, too. Well, one's empty. I'll go through them as quickly as I can, and oh, there's a handgun," Fisher said.

"A Bersa Thunder-mini 9mm with the serial numbers removed," Harris added, glancing at Fisher. "It's Argentinian."

Fisher raised his brow, unsure how he should react to the detail, then turned his attention back to the contents of the box. "And two thousand dollars in fresh bills, his passport, and the scrap of paper."

"Plus, we have a picture of a possible fake passport," Harris added.

"Leave it with me and I'll see what I can do with the numbers," Clark replied. Without a farewell, the call ended.

"*Possible* fake?" Fisher said.

"It could be a legitimate print," Harris replied. "I could get you one in about an hour and that means other people can, too."

Squinting, he looked back at her.

"I understand, but it would have to be from the good guys, not the bad ones, right?" Fisher said, moving his head to the side.

Harris laughed, her cheeks dimpling until just the rush of the traffic surrounded them for a long moment.

"He means GCHQ," Harris said. "Their building looks like a doughnut, so that's what we call them."

Fisher nodded and picked up the first diary.

Chelmsford

19th October

Turning the executive four by four onto a long narrow street lined with stone houses built up to the pavement edge, Farid straightened the wheel as just ahead a bright blue Subaru leaned on its stiff suspension to race around the corner, soon shaking their bulk as it rushed by their side with its beacons flashing and siren wailing.

He kept the car straight, keeping his speed even as five white police cars followed with three ambulances and a police van in their wake.

With the sirens fading, Fisher stepped from the tall car, striding along the street toward a building with an oversized three-storey bulk that appeared perilously balanced on the much smaller ground floor. A blue rain canopy covered the entrance like the peak of a cap, whilst high on the building's front, white letters announced Chelmsford Police Station.

Climbing the steps to the raised forecourt, Fisher turned to his right as a sixth police car, packed with four figures dressed in yellow and black, pulled out from a gate to the side.

Soon in the building, he walked up to a raised enquiry desk, behind which a middle-aged woman with blonde hair down to her shoulders and no insignia on her uniform welcomed him with a smile. Their eyes soon met and he gave a brief grin; within moments he was through the secure door with a visitor's badge around his neck.

22

London

2nd September

Monday

Everyone is going to be there to see the delivery of the car. At least then we can get on with building the set and then it will be time to put together the lighting plans. I can't wait!

Tuesday

That idiot was hanging around the stage at lunchtime. Shelley was there, of course, and I spilt water down my trousers. She hadn't noticed, but Stuart shouted that I'd pissed myself. I saw her laughing and soon so was everyone else. Paul told me to lamp him, but I just ran.

Wednesday

Mum just got a phone call from the school. They were looking for me. She told them I wasn't well. Good on ya Mum.

She asked if everything was all right. I don't think she was convinced when I said I was okay. She made my favourite dinner, bless her.

I hope I don't see Stuart tomorrow. I want to stay calm and I am, in the most part, at least. I guess this writing is working!

"It's got a pin lock on it. Let's see what Clark comes up with," Harris said, holding the phone as Fisher turned back to the pages in his lap.

Saturday

Mum's dead.

It seems odd writing it down and I want to rub it out. The words on the page seem to make it final.

Monday

I've just read through the last entries from three weeks ago. All that crap is unimportant now, but as the days go on, I can feel myself getting angrier. Hopefully writing will help again.

She got hit by a car whilst minding her own business. The driver didn't see her because he was going too fast.

They said she died instantly.

They said she felt no pain. I'm not sure if it's true. I think they say that just to make relatives feel better. They're not going to say it was a long, painful end. Anyway, it doesn't make me feel any better. Should it?

They've told me I have to move in with my grandma in Nottingham. I don't even know her, but I've got no choice. It's that or I have to go into care until I'm eighteen.

Friday

Today is the last day of this school so it's time to make a move on Shelley. Paul agrees. It's now or never!

It was a mixed day in the end. I found out Shelley was seeing Stuart. Paul told me. I didn't believe him, but when I saw them together, it was obvious. I wonder how long they've been going out?

I surprised myself at how calm I was about it all, even when I saw him on his own on the way home from school. Paul was angrier than me, so angry he ran up to him and pushed him around. I wish I had the words to describe the intense surprise on Stuart's face. I bet he thought it was a dream.

When he fell, I kept control and just watched Paul kick the shit out of him. I didn't join in. I wasn't angry anymore. I just watched as his blood pooled on the ground and his teeth sprayed across the path. I got a bit of blood on me, but I won't be needing this uniform anymore anyway.

There's another NASA documentary on tomorrow night. I'll be watching it on my own in my new bedroom, I suppose.

Fisher looked up from the page, peering at the street flashing by the window at Clark's calling tone.

"Vigilem," Clark said without a greeting.

"Watcher," Harris replied. Her eyes narrowed and her brow lowered as she glanced over.

"Yes. Latin," Clark confirmed. "We got it from the last set of numbers on the page. It was a very simple indexed alphabetic code that took ninety-six seconds for our software to crack."

"But what does it mean?" Fisher asked, looking over at Harris.

"I'm afraid that's for you two to figure out," he said and hung up.

Monday

I started the new school today, and it seems like a friendly crowd with not too many dickheads. The headteacher seems alright as well. He said they're putting on Oliver this year and he'll add my name for lighting crew if I want, which I said I would.

Wednesday

Grandma had a call from the police today while I was at school. They want to ask me some questions. They're going to come to the school tomorrow. I guess they want to ask me about what Paul did. He said to run away, but I told him that would be stupid. Anyway, all I did was watch. Paul was the one doing all the work.

Thursday

I found the Stuart character in my new school. I guess there's one everywhere. I'll keep an eye on him. If need be, I'm sure Paul can sort him out.

The Police were no problem. I told them I'd just walked home that day. At least Stuart's not able to tell them what Paul did.

Friday

Stuart mark two seems like a carbon copy of the original. I think his name is Greg, same profile. He picks on the weak or the intelligent, or anyone who isn't average. I almost showed him who was the boss today, but this time it was Paul who kept me under control.

Fisher's phone rang again. It was Clark.

"I've forwarded your old mobile. You've got George Cooper on the line. Do you want to speak to him?"

George was one of James' close friends. He'd known him since university and had helped James connect with MI6, leading him to meet Harris and to save Susie from the white trafficking gang. But there was a problem. Talking to SIS was off the table.

"Yes, please," Fisher replied before hearing a slight click on the line. "George?"

"I've just heard," George said, his voice slow and calm. Fisher closed his eyes, then turned to look at Harris, shaking her head. "Are you okay?"

"Just about," Fisher replied. "If I'm honest, I'm not sure it's sunk in yet."

"Do you know what happened?"

"No details. I just got a call as well," Fisher said, taking a deep breath.

"I've tried calling Alan, but I can't get through. Have you spoken to him? Does Susie know?"

Fisher shook his head even though George couldn't see. He'd been thinking about Susie a lot and wanted to be the person to tell her, but held back, knowing that meeting any of his friends could mean more of their blood on his hands.

"Can you tell her? I can't do it," Fisher finally said.

"Of course. Are you sure you're okay?" George replied, not hiding his concern.

"I think so, but I've got to go." Clicking off the call, he turned to Harris and shook his head. "They're going to think I'm a shit friend."

Harris leaned across the back seat and he felt her warm hand on top of his.

"I promise you we'll deal with this as quickly as we can," she replied.

Fisher nodded before turning to stare out of the dark tinted window as outside people got on with their lives as if nothing had happened.

Monday

I met this guy today. He's part of the stage crew. He seems like a nice enough bloke and didn't take offence when I talked to him. Paul doesn't like him, but he doesn't get on with unfamiliar faces. We hung around together for most of the day and I don't think he minded. At one point, Greg came over and had a go at me. I stayed quiet, but George put him in his place. No fists, just words. I was pretty impressed.

Monday

I haven't written for a while and I almost feel like saying sorry, but that would be stupid. I've stayed away from the diary because everything seems as if it's going well. I've been around to George's house loads and he's been here. I really like the guy and now Paul doesn't mind him anymore, plus Greg steers clear of us, too.

Thursday

I got my GCSE results today and I've done great. Five B's and three C's. George got almost the same results.

I feel like my head's in a good place now, and if he's telling the truth, my key worker thinks so too. I guess he can't be lying, unless he's just trying to get rid of me, because they've discharged me from supervision. Now I only have to visit with him every six months.

I think it's the writing, and George, of course. He said I should keep up the diary for as long as I can, but if I need support, then I've got the number.

Paul popped up and told me to throw the diary away. It's been a while since I've seen him, but I told him to piss off.

Friday

We're going on a camping trip for a week to the Isle of Wight in the summer holidays. It will be just me and George, and I know it'll be awesome. Gran gave me some cash, so we're going to a camping shop to stock up on supplies.

Monday

The camping trip was ace and something quite amazing happened. We got served in a pub just outside the campsite, probably because we were in the middle of nowhere. Anyway, we had a few pints and were pretty pissed. A group of lads came up to us and started causing trouble. I just walked away! I couldn't believe it. I just got off my stool and walked away. Six months ago, Paul would have turned up and I know what would have happened. In fact, I can't remember the last time I spoke to Paul...

Wednesday

We've all been told it's time to apply for uni courses. George is going to do law or economics at either Cardiff or right here in Nottingham. Science is out of the window because of my grades, so I'm going to apply to do a business course in both cities. We agreed to pick the one we both get a place on, then we can get a flat together and live it up. It's going to be amazing. Beer and girls for three straight years.

I'd prefer Cardiff to here, but it will be a massive laugh either way.

Monday

A-levels going okay, but maybe not as well as I'd hoped. The second year is turning out to be much harder than the first. I got my letter from UCAS through today, and I got a provisional place at Nottingham, subject to pretty low grades, so it should all be fine. The best news is that George was accepted, too. On the beers to celebrate tonight.

Saturday

What a night! We both pulled, but I must admit George's bird was a damn sight better than mine. Let's just say we didn't exchange numbers!

As Fisher turned the last page, they pulled into the underground garage.

***

Chelmsford Police Station

19th October

The corridors were silent as Fisher strolled along the deserted first floor, passing open doors to canteens and offices, past noticeboards crammed with mug shots and grainy images plucked from CCTV. Between checking for his likeness and scanning the grey nameplates stuck to the doors, he soon found what he was looking for.

After twisting the round handle and confirming the door wouldn't open, he held his breath and listened to the rising volume of footsteps along the corridor before a tall police officer came around the corner. Staring at the Glock's muzzle, he came to a stop, his eyes wide.

"Good morning, Sergeant," Fisher said, with a glance at the three down-pointing chevrons on the man's shoulders. The grey-haired sergeant remained silent, his gaze moving from the end of the gun to look Fisher in the eye. "What's your name?"

"Uh… Sergeant… Sergeant Benton," the officer stuttered.

"Your first name?" Fisher replied.

"Greg."

"Don't worry about this," Fisher said, waving the gun

around before pointing it at the floor. Almost instantly the officer's demeanour changed, his expression hardening as he puffed up his chest, seeming as if he was about to pounce.

Fisher lifted the gun back up and waved it at his centre mass, but the sergeant took a step forward, reaching for the baton hanging from his belt.

Looking on in disbelief as he held the gun up, Fisher realised that without a touch the sergeant believed his words and was anything but concerned about the weapon.

"Stop," Fisher shouted as the man got closer. "I'll use this," he added, centring his aim.

As if Fisher had flicked a switch, the aggression fell from the man's expression and he slowed, dropping the baton as if only just noticing the gun.

Despite what he'd just seen, it wasn't the time to do anything but find what he'd been sent for.

"Where are the keys to this door?" Fisher called out, motioning to his right.

"In my pocket," the officer replied, raising his palms without being asked.

"Open it," Fisher barked, and the sergeant's eyes narrowed toward the gun before fishing out a set of keys as he walked the remaining few paces and had the door open within a moment.

Beyond the door was a storeroom about the size of a large bathroom, but rather than full of soaps and towels, it held an array of expensive police toys.

"In," Fisher said, motioning for the sergeant to step inside, then doing as he asked and leaving the keys in the door, Fisher marvelled at the rack of shelves stacked with equipment, much of which was still in its packaging. There were first aid pouches, boxes of purple surgical gloves and so much more, whilst spare uniform and stab vests hung on hangers to one side. To Fisher's left stood a wire cage door, bolted together with thick rounds of steel encompassed with a padlock.

Beyond the cage doors were menacing dark riot gear,

including helmets and wooden sticks, along with a smaller cage housing TAZER stun guns and bright red canisters of CS spray. At his front, battery charging banks crammed side by side on a countertop with their cables running off to a series of sockets. Three radios sat on charge, whilst around twenty slots remained unoccupied. Above the counter stood a shallow metal cabinet. Despite having nothing to describe what it held, with its shape and location just as Farid had described, including the heavy-duty lock, Fisher smiled.

"Turn and face the wall," Fisher said, motioning towards the cage with his Glock, then watched as the sergeant followed his instructions without saying a word.

With his attention back on the charging points, he pressed the red power button on the nearest radio, watching as a red LED beside a stubby aerial flashed for a few seconds then went off as a low, tinny voice came from the tiny speaker.

"In place, Alpha-Charlie-Fife-Four. Out."

A second voice replied. "Received Alpha-Charlie-Fife-Four. Out."

Taking the keys from the door, and after making sure the sergeant faced away, Fisher searched the bunch, glancing back and forth between the lock.

"VG. Area one secure. Alpha-Tango-Seven-Zero. Over."

"Received Alpha-Tango-Seven-Zero, please hold position. Out."

Despite checking almost half the keys, he'd still not found the right size.

"VG. Urgent. We've got a second witness saying they spotted an IC6 male wearing Arab white dress carrying a black handgun. Alpha-Charlie-Three-Four. Over."

Fisher listened.

"Received Alpha-Charlie-Three-Four. Proceed to Command Post with witness. Can you confirm which area you are in? Over."

"Area four, and witness describes suspect heading into Area Five. Alpha-Charlie-Three-Four. Out."

"Received, Alpha-Charlie-Three-Four. Out."

"All Zulu call-signs proceed to Area Fife with caution. Control out."

Fisher went back to his search.

"VG. Received, Zulu-Alpha-One-Zero. Out."

"VG. We've got University liaison with me, Alpha-One. Out."

"Received, Alpha-One. Out."

Fearing the distraction was playing out quicker than he liked, Fisher pushed his hand inside his jacket pocket and pulled out a silver foil-wrapped package the size and shape of his thumb. Beneath the foil was a brown playdough-like substance.

"VG. Area Three secure, Alpha-Tango-Three-Three. Out."

"Received, Alpha-Tango-Three-Three. Out."

Taking care, Fisher moulded the putty between his palms until he'd fashioned a long sausage, which he joined at the ends to make a small circle he pushed against the cabinet door. With the keyhole in the centre of his creation, he pushed his hand in his pocket, pulling out a small black cube with a red button on the front face. After pressing it into the plastic explosive, he pushed the red button, then turned and walked through the doorway.

"I'd get out of there if I were you," Fisher called from the corridor.

As the officer ran out, Fisher slammed the door shut and crouched against the wall, pressing his fingers into his ears. Without asking, the sergeant did the same, just before a loud pop from behind the door spat dust and smoke from the gap at the floor. Not waiting long for the debris to clear, Fisher ushered the officer back inside.

"Resume the position," he said to the sergeant, who complied without question.

"Zulu-Alpha-One-Zero, please confirm your eta to Area Five, Control. Over."

As Fisher fanned the air with his hand, he was pleased to find the radios had survived, and that a jagged metal hole had taken the place of the lock. The small door stood open.

"VG, standby, Zulu-Alpha-One-One. Over."

"Received, Zulu-Alpha-One-One. Over."

Fisher checked the sergeant still faced the cage then, covering his hand with his jacket sleeve, he pulled the cabinet open. Inside were five rows of six key hooks and on all but two were bunches of keys accompanied by a white plastic tag.

"VG, Area Two secure, Alpha-Tango-Three-Two. Out."

"Received, Alpha-Tango-Three-Two. Out."

"Zulu-Alpha-One-Zero, repeat transmission, over."

Pulling the folded page from his pocket and starting from the top left corner, he turned each set of keys around, checking the code against his note.

"Zulu-Alpha-One-Zero, repeat transmission, over."

Fisher moved to the second row.

"Zulu-Alpha-One-Zero, repeat transmission, over."

Finding what he wanted on the third row, a single key for a mortice lock and a small transparent plastic bag containing an access card, he lifted the key before peeling the label off, whilst continuing to search through the rest of the cabinet's contents. Finding a set that was almost the same, Fisher lifted a second set from another hook on the row below before swapping the labels and hanging them back in the space he'd earlier emptied. He then grabbed another four keys at random and stuffed them into his jacket pocket.

"VG, Area Fife clear, Zulu-Alpha-O..." The voice cut out before he could finish the sign off, replaced by a shrill two-tone alarm ringing out from the radio. Wheeling around, Fisher looked at the sergeant crouching, huddled and facing the cage, then turned his attention back to the radios.

"Emergency panic alarm activation," the voice said. "Code Zero on an unassigned handset." The man's voice, whose tone carried a question, halted. "And it's at Chelmsford nick."

Fisher's stare lingered on the radios before turning to the sergeant, then to the radios once more, watching the two screens flash. With another turn, he launched toward the uniformed man, spinning him around by his right shoulder where he clutched the missing radio.

23

London

2nd September

"What have we got so far?" Fisher said to Harris, sitting opposite her at the table in the safe house with two mugs of black coffee between them.

"Sorry?" she replied, her eyebrows raised as she looked away from staring out of the window to the quiet sunlit street below.

"Are you okay?" Fisher asked, reaching over the table, but before he touched her hand, she pulled away.

"I'm fine..." she said, stopping herself as if she'd had more to say, but then continued when Fisher replied with a weak smile. "I'm struggling with this whole situation. I just hope I'm not too close to the investigation."

"You've said that before. In Wales," Fisher said, nodding. "And that ended well."

"Until it didn't," Harris replied, picking up her cup as she looked back down to the road.

"I refuse to work with anyone else," Fisher added.

Looking back up, her eyebrows raised and she sat up straight, placing the mug back on the table. "Be careful saying things like that. You're important to the agency, but they won't put up with you trying to run the show."

They sat in silence for a long moment before she sipped from her mug. "Let's review."

Fisher nodded, leaning down to his side and pulling his overnight bag from the floor and placing it on his lap, then slipping on a pair of gloves. Lifting his clothes out of the way, he found the two suppressed handguns and the set of keys they'd taken from the thugs who'd attacked them at the hotel. Placing everything on the table, he dropped the bag on the floor and drew out a scrap of paper they'd taken from one of the dead guys and placed it next to the guns.

Standing, Fisher leaned over to the kitchen counter and grabbed the box before laying out the contents. When he'd finished, he took a step back and stared at the stack of diaries, the bundle of American cash, the passport, phone, scraps of paper and the Argentinian handgun, beside which he placed the airline ticket and the sterling from Alan's flat.

"So what does it add up to?" Fisher said, staring at the haul.

"Don't forget what we took from the scene…" Harris said, cutting herself off. Fisher could already guess she was talking about where Andrew had died.

"The two handguns and the stun baton," Fisher replied, hoping she wouldn't feel she'd have to mention it again. "Was there anything else recovered?"

"No," Harris said, not meeting his gaze.

"Are the handguns linked?" Fisher said as he picked up one of the black weapons fitted with a silencer they'd taken from the two thugs the previous night.

Harris nodded.

"They've all had the serial numbers filed off, but I wouldn't have expected anything else. Plus, they're all South American. Obviously," she said, waving her hands over four of the pistols. "These are Taurus PT92 pistols from Brazil."

With the weapons lined up, it was only the one taken from the safe deposit box that was noticeably different.

"What about the car keys?" Fisher asked.

"Let's see what Clark thinks," she said, pulling out her phone. Seconds later, Fisher accepted the conference call. "Clark, can you confirm the details of the car at the hotel last night?"

"It came back to a Mr Randell. I've emailed you the address." A short tone rang from Fisher's phone and as he pulled it from his pocket, he noticed the new email icon. "I've told the police to leave it with us."

"Thank you," Harris replied. "Did you get anything from the phone?"

"It's pay as you go and all we see is one call a month, along with a weekly data burst. It rings the same number, but the trace comes back negative. I think it's turned off the rest of the time."

"So the car's our only lead?" Fisher asked.

"It looks that way," replied Harris. "Any luck on the mole?"

"We've set up some honey. Now we wait to see what happens."

***

Chelmsford Police Station

19th October

Grasping three radios in his hand, Fisher locked the storeroom's door before retracing his route through the corridor to the stairwell. About to push against the fire exit's bar, hearing boots rushing from somewhere close, he turned the way he'd come, dropping the radios when he glanced back to find another police officer holding a baton and running towards him.

"Stop there," the copper called, but pulling the pistol from inside his jacket, the officer ducked into a side room.

Fisher turned and ran, dropping the sergeant's keys as he slapped the fire door's push bar down.

24

London

2nd September

Saturday

I haven't seen so much of George over the last couple of weeks, he's either around her house or they're out together. He keeps saying sorry, but it makes no difference.

Saturday

George finally came around and it must have been two weeks since I last saw him. I was happy he came of course, but he only had half an hour to spare. We watched a documentary but he was constantly texting her. What's the point in being here when his attention is elsewhere?

Sunday

I finally got out on the beers with George last night, but he was so preoccupied with her even though she wasn't there. He was either texting her or talking about the fucking bitch. I tried getting him to pull some bird but he wasn't having it. In the end I, er, chucked a few vodkas in his beers, got him well pissed up, then Paul turned up. He only went and paid some bird to get off with him. Somehow he then paid someone else to send a picture of them snogging to his bitch's phone.

   I think I'll be seeing a lot more of George now!

Monday

I feel a little guilty.
   She dumped him.
   To be fair it wasn't a surprise, but it seems to have hit him quite hard.

He went around to her house but her dad threatened to beat him up if he turned up again. It's probably for the best.

Paul says I'm soft for feeling guilty, but I told him I'd changed whilst he's been out of the picture. He didn't pay much attention. Oh and I didn't get into Cardiff Uni, but at least we both got a place here in Nottingham, so who cares if they didn't see anything in me.

<u>*Wednesday*</u>

George is gutted. She told him that she'd loved him but she could never forgive him for what he'd done. He can't understand why he did it. He can't forgive himself for fucking it up. He told me he got a place in Cardiff and said he might go there to get away from everything that reminded him of her.

All he wants to do is forget about her.

I told him I didn't get a place there but he didn't seem to take any notice.

He'll change his mind. I'm sure.

***

Eight Walworth Road, London

20th October

Head throbbing and mouth dry, the same image greeted Fisher as he woke. Pushing it away with ease for the first time, he opened an eye then closed it again, catching sunlight streaming in through the open curtains. As the bed moved, he forced his eye open and stared at the South American beauty stirring next to him.

Luana. That was her name. She'd just turned eighteen and now he couldn't stop thinking about her. He knew she was different the moment she'd come through the front door. As their eyes met, the fascination was instant.

Farid had wanted him to try one of his special girls, pointing to a blonde Latvian whilst two of his guys salivated over Luana. Grabbing her by the wrists whilst cursing and taunting her with what they'd do, Fisher had no choice but to come to her rescue.

The men's eyes lit up when Farid explained to Fisher it was her first night, so she'd be no good, but their reaction stoked his resolve and he knew he'd do anything to protect her from what they had planned.

Farid didn't put up a fight, telling him it was his loss as he followed the three remaining women towards the bedroom.

She was from Brazil, just one of the many things he'd learned as they talked late into the night. She'd arrived in the UK with her mother, but on her sixteenth birthday, her mother didn't return from work and the police showed little interest.

Rather than going into care, she ran, travelling to one place, then another with decisions made on a whim. When she could no longer get by on the kindness of strangers alone, she knew the price of survival meant difficult choices.

Something drew her to this place and last week she found herself knocking at the door.

As the memory of their conversation kept coming, he couldn't help but stare at her beautiful naked body and her light brown hair streaked with blonde as it lay flat against her tanned skin, smooth to perfection.

When she stirred in her sleep, he shook his head, but with his brain seeming to travel slower than his skull, it knocked him out of the trance. Tearing himself away from her beauty, he picked himself from underneath the smooth material, adjusted the waist of his black Calvin Klein boxer shorts and stepped into the en-suite bathroom.

Staring into the mirror, he rubbed his chin with his thumb and forefinger. Feeling stubble, he took a step back, opened the mirror and pulled out the can of shaving foam and the first razor to hand.

With the stubble dealt with and his face clean of foam, he

took a deep breath, then looked at the razor in his hand.

Luana stirred again and, after a glance over, he chucked the razor into the open bin. Tearing a piece of toilet paper from the roll, he heard the front door slam closed as he left the bathroom.

Fisher dressed, then plucked a pen from the bedside drawer and scribbled on the toilet paper, pushing the message into Luana's brown leather bag sitting on the wooden dressing table.

25

London

2nd September

Dropping Fisher and Harris at the kerb and around the corner from their destination, at Harris's command Biggy drove the car away whilst the pair continued their journey on foot, walking side by side along the suburban street lined with detached houses set back from the road. The wide distance between the houses, the neat green verges and the gleaming four by fours and sports coupes confirmed the affluence of the neighbourhood.

The house was simple enough to find, helped by the brass lettering on the wrought-iron gate as Fisher pushed at its smaller pedestrian neighbour. After it opened without a fuss, they headed up the block paved path alongside the empty driveway and toward the large, detached house surrounded by a garden marked out by fir trees tall enough to give the owners plenty of privacy.

Harris pushed a simple white button nestled in a swirling moulding mounted to the stone wall and as the chime's echo died, she tapped the Glock resting in her shoulder holster through her lightweight jacket as if to remind Fisher to be on his guard.

It wasn't long before a middle-aged man opened the door, standing a little shorter than the both of them, his balding head set off by a blue polo shirt covered with a sleeveless diamond patterned jumper. He raised an eyebrow before tilting his head as if he'd expected someone else.

"Can I help you?"

"Mr Randell?" Harris asked, her tone bare of any enthusiasm.

"Yes, and you are?" he replied, keeping his eyebrow raised.

"Can I ask about the whereabouts of your BMW X3?" she said, not answering his question.

"It's in for repair. Who are you and why are you asking about my car?"

Harris forced a smile. "We believe your car has been used to commit a crime. Can you tell me the name of the garage and we'll leave you to your business?"

"Oh shit. I knew something like this would happen," he said, his face reddening. "You try to save a bit by avoiding the main dealer and it gets fucked." The man stepped into the house before returning with a business card. "Is my car alright?"

"It's fine. Someone will be in touch soon, Mr Randell," Harris replied, taking the offered card. "Thank you for your help. Please don't contact the garage whilst we continue our enquiries," she added.

Without waiting for his reply, she turned with Fisher following as they walked back down the driveway.

***

Eight Walworth Road, London

20th October

Alone on the sofa with a mug of hot coffee encircled in his hand, Fisher stared out at the bright day glinting from the tall buildings blocking the horizon. Farid had risen moments earlier, but after a quick hello, he'd wandered off to the kitchen from where the first smell of cooking bacon came.

Breakfast, Fisher thought to himself. *That's a first.*

To the sound of feet soft on the floor, and having drained his cup, Fisher turned to see Farid carrying a steaming mug, followed by a young woman he'd seen a few times in the background. In her late teens or early twenties, she wore loose fitting shorts with a vest top that seemed a little too tight to be comfortable, but served well to highlight her pert C cup.

Smiling over as she came through the kitchen door, she carried sandwiches on a tray with bacon poking out from the middle. Her smile seemed a little forced, perhaps hiding some inner uncertainty of what the meeting would bring.

With her brown hair tied up behind her head and her skin still marked with the faint signs of makeup, as Farid sat down in his accustomed space opposite Fisher, she placed the tray with care on the glass table before heading back to the kitchen, only to reappear moments later with plates. Setting them down beside the sandwiches, as she turned to leave, Farid shot her a glance.

"Where are you going?"

Turning back around, her smiled had disappeared, then without talking she perched on the edge of the sofa next to him, biting her lip as she watched them eat.

"Aren't you hungry?" Fisher asked, but when she didn't reply he glanced to Farid, shaking his head.

"She's watching her weight," he said. "The nights of excess are taking their toll."

Fisher knew that couldn't be true and made a point of thanking her as she took the empty plates before she disappeared behind the kitchen door.

Finding a toothpick from somewhere, Farid leaned back into the sofa as he let out gas.

"So what's on today's agenda?" Fisher said when he could no longer stomach the silence.

"Nothing," Farid replied with a shake of his head.

"Nothing?" Fisher asked, not hiding his surprise.

"We're preparing, but you don't need to be involved. So until it's ready, we wait."

"How long?" Fisher replied, squinting.

"I don't know," Farid said, pulling out a lump of something with the pick.

"I have to warn you," Fisher said, watching as Farid's brow raised. "I don't wait well. You should keep me busy."

Farid was the first to break the stare. "Okay," he said, raising his chin. "What do you want to do?"

"Give me another job?" Fisher said.

"I'm giving you the chance to relax, but I have plenty of menial things you can do. Wouldn't you rather chill out?"

"I'll relax when I'm dead. Keep me busy. Please," Fisher said, keeping his voice low.

Farid regarded him for a long moment before nodding.

"I'll make a call," he said, as he pulled out his iPhone and slid his finger across the screen.

"Who are you calling?" Fisher said, nodding toward the phone.

"The boss," Farid replied as he tilted his head to the side.

"Why don't we go and see him?"

"Not yet," Farid said before he stood and shook his head.

"Why not?"

"He's not in the country," Farid replied, squinting.

"Where is he?"

"Mr Fisher," Farid said, pushing on a smile. "You're asking a lot of questions."

"This is what I'm like when I'm bored," Fisher replied, grinning, only for his expression to fall, a pulse of electricity rushing along his spine when the man with the long scar down his face came into the living room.

Although he'd grown used to the comings and goings of some downright odd and unpleasant people in the flat, every time he saw this guy, he still felt repulsed. Despite wearing a business suit, he'd never seen him leave the apartment. He'd never seen him speak, and this time was no different. After a brief stop in the kitchen with Farid staring at his phone, the guy headed back along the corridor.

"I'll make the call," Farid said, interrupting his thoughts.

26

London

2nd September

"Nothing on Falcon," Clark said as Fisher walked back to the car with Harris. Falcon, according to her earlier explanation, was the name for the database used by GCHQ, MI5 and MI6, and was much like the Police National Computer. "But intel on PNC shows the business is connected to a local crime syndicate," Clark added. "It's low level, but headed by someone we used to have an interest in. Along with the garage, they're also linked to various other businesses around Fulham Road, Southwest London."

"A good place to hire muscle," Fisher said, jumping back into the X5 waiting around the corner.

"I think the men that came after you were subcontracted, and that's been good news so far. They clearly weren't capable," Harris said as Fisher frowned. "But it means there's some separation from the person paying the bills."

"Let's pay them a visit," Fisher said.

"We will. Tonight. He frequents one of his clubs, and there'll be lots of witnesses," Harris replied as the car pulled away from the kerb.

<u>*Thursday*</u>

I haven't seen much of George lately. Again!

There's a spot in the woods behind his street where you can see his bedroom window, so I know he's not left his house for a few days, other than to go to college. Our exams are next week and I hope this doesn't put him off his stride.

<u>*Wednesday*</u>

George seems to have perked up now the exams are over and I'm seeing him a bit more often. I think we're back to how we used to be, but he's not quite there yet. We haven't talked about uni for a while, but I'm sure we'll both go to Nottingham.

Thursday

Our results are out today, crossed fingers.

Shit. Shit. Shit-ity-shit.
   I didn't get into Nottingham Uni. What are we going to do? I need to speak to George.

Fuck.
   Fuck.
   We spoke, and he seemed sad, but then he said it made him feel better about deciding to go to Cardiff now because wherever he chose, we wouldn't be going together.
   Fuck. I don't know what's going on. Everything seemed to be going so well. Now this.
   Fuck.
   I didn't realise he'd decided already, and without speaking to me.

I've been on the phone all day, none of the Welsh unis want me, but I got a place through clearing in Nottingham Trent. I checked with George, but he said it was too late. He's already accepted the course in Cardiff.
   Fuck.
   It means we've only got the summer to look forward to now.
   Fuck.

Saturday

It seems the thought of going off to Cardiff makes George feel better, and he certainly seems back on form.
   I was devastated at first, of course, but I've been looking at jobs and training programmes in Cardiff. Although there's nothing I fancy yet, I'm hopeful. George says of course I can visit, but it won't be the same. He's

suggested another camping trip. We can think of something then.

Wednesday

I've let this go again. Silly I know. But I've been spending so much time with George, making the most of him, and now he's gone off to taff-land and I start my course tomorrow. He told me he'd call me this weekend to let me know if it's okay to come up soon, like I'd asked. I need to check the train timetable when I get time.

Thursday

Nottingham Trent is full of knobs. Paul punched a lecturer in the face and now they've kicked me out. I lasted a day, but they said they wouldn't press charges as long as I stay away from the campus.
    I need to speak with George. Hopefully, he'll answer his phone soon.

Monday

George didn't call. I tried him again, and he picked up on the third or fourth try. He apologised but said he knew I'd understand how busy he'd been. I asked if he'd made any new friends, but he said it was too early to tell. I thought it best not to mention my situation. I'll leave it until we can speak face to face.
    He says I can't go up for two weeks. They have some flatmate bonding thing going on. I'm not sure what that means.

Saturday

I got a job in a supermarket. I'm only a shelf stacker but I'll be running the place before long. The first thing I'm going to save up for is driving lessons. I've booked the coach for Cardiff for next weekend and I'm thankful that so far Paul has stayed away from work. At least these first few days, anyway.

Eight Walworth Road, London

20th October

"Do you still want to keep busy?" Farid said as he walked from his bedroom holding a scrap of paper.

"Yes," Fisher replied without delay. Farid nodded, then as he stood in front of Fisher sitting on the sofa, he held the torn page out.

"One condition," Farid said. "If I tell you what the job is, you've got to take it. Do you understand?" he added, his eyes pinched.

"No problem," Fisher replied, hoping he sounded more confident than he did in his head.

"Good. Have you ever killed someone?" Farid said as he stepped closer.

"Yes," Fisher replied, his blood going cold, knowing with Farid looking him right in the eyes, he'd see a lie. The first had been an act of self-defence on the Rashana. The second was the architect of his friend's kidnap and the head of the cartel trading in young women. There was no time to think of the third.

"Who is it?" Fisher said, trying to halt the train of thought.

Farid handed over the paper. "Someone whose usefulness has expired."

Glancing at the scribbled name and address, Fisher couldn't stop his eyes from widening as he let go. Scooping the page from the floor, he looked up at Farid. "When?"

"There's no time like the present," Farid said, raising an eyebrow.

Fisher lifted his chin, telling himself that another wouldn't matter.

"You'll have Joel and Samir with you, but I've got other business to attend to," Farid said as he glanced over his shoulder.

Fisher smiled. They were the pair he'd saved Luana from

the previous night and he couldn't have wished for better company. About to speak, he realised Farid had turned, then grabbing his leather jacket from a chair, the Arab disappeared through the front door without another word just as Joel and Samir came from the corridor.

He'd worked with the pair once before. Both were also of Arab descent, but with a light Birmingham accent, Joel was raised in the UK. With a wiry frame and of average height, he was in his late twenties with jet black shoulder-length hair and always wore cropped stubble that contrasted with his olive skin. He walked with a very slight limp and Fisher knew his hair covered a long scar on the back of his neck that he'd seen when he was over-indulging at a nightly party.

Samir was the opposite. Tall, but well built. With his hair cropped to cover his well progressing journey to baldness, he spoke little English. At least Fisher had never heard him speak the language.

Pulling out his phone, Fisher typed a message and sent it to Farid.

"I want the same girl again tonight."

The smiley face reply was almost instant.

27

In the oldest of the substantial Range Rover fleet, of which Fisher knew there to be at least five, none of which were over ten years old and each a different colour, the trio set off over the river to Southwest London.

Despite already knowing the target's place of work, Fisher programmed the sat nav with his home address and with five minutes left showing on the screen, the brummy, Joel, pulled out a pistol Fisher knew to be Argentinian, with a long suppressor fitted to the end.

"It's untraceable," he said, handing it over. "Dump it at the house," he added before turning to stare back out of the windscreen.

Fisher turned the cold metal around in his hands. In so many ways, it seemed so different to his Glock. Despite being made from light silvered metal, aluminium he guessed, it was much heavier than the larger fourth generation Glock 17 holstered to his chest.

With its surface peppered with buttons and little switches, it more closely resembled the British Army Browning High Power than the composite pistol warmed from his body heat. After checking the safety was in the right position, he removed the magazine, counting the rounds before pulling the slide back to chamber the first.

The writing stamped on the slide confirmed the calibre as .380, incompatible with his NATO rounds. Above the trigger guard where the serial number should have been were deep scratches.

Feeling the car slow, Fisher watched as they pulled up to the kerb before pushing the weapon inside his jacket pocket. No cars parked along the wide road where houses lined only one side, the other bordered by a sprawling green space with the bright paint of climbing frames and tall swings in the furthest corner.

"Wait here until I call," Fisher said, not waiting for a reply, closing the heavy door as softly as he dared before striding along the well-maintained path, passing four houses, each different from the next other than being set far back behind long manicured driveways.

Number Twenty-One stood out in no way at all. It was the same as the others because each house was different from its neighbours. Parked in the driveway of the bare brick three-story was a six-month-old Volvo four by four, facing towards the road like a dog guarding its territory.

With his feet crunching gravel as he slipped through the side gate, he scoured for signs of movement. Finding nothing but the white wooden front door underneath a tall canopy, he pressed the large brass doorbell set into a wooden surround.

***

London

2nd September

With a brief check of the names Fisher had fought to say over the pounding bass, the stout bouncer in black looked up from the list and motioned for his two colleagues standing at the side to let them pass. As they moved, the man to the right, who was almost indistinguishable from both his colleagues, motioned away from the downward heading stairs toward a padded door on the left with the letters VIP embossed in leather above.

Somehow the music seemed to quieten as a rainbow of lights from the main club to the right flashed over the comfortable-looking red leather armchairs and sofas dotted around the wide room. A bar took up much of the far wall with row after row of backlit bottles. After taking only a handful of steps, Fisher realised the room was suspended over the side of a packed dance floor with a glass barrier keeping much of the noise at bay.

Turning back, a blonde hostess in a short dark skirt and tight white blouse stepped toward them, introducing herself as Lenka as she led them to a sofa facing the bar.

"What would you like to drink?" she said in a thick Russian accent as they took their seats, then leaned over towards Fisher, the material across her chest tightening as it pulled at the buttons.

"A bottle of Dom Perignon," Harris said. "Your best vintage."

Standing tall, Lenka turned her way and smiled before walking back toward the bar.

Fisher forced himself to look away, glancing instead over to Harris as she straightened her short skirt and crossed her legs with care.

After questioning Mr Randell about his car, Harris had Biggy drop her off in Soho whilst he took Fisher back to the safe house where she met them a couple of hours later, laden with supplies including the two-piece cream suit and black tie he wore, and the skirt and tight bright pink top that almost made his eyes pop from their sockets, hardly recognising her when she'd come out from the bedroom along with glasses and a blonde wig.

With only four tables in the VIP area occupied, three by middle-aged men with women young enough to be their daughters, and another by the balcony populated with three men, each looking anywhere other than at each other with half-empty tall glasses of something fizzy.

Their bottle arrived within less than a minute, their glasses half full a moment later, then as Lenka stood up tall, Fisher peeled three fifties from a thick wad along with a crisp twenty for her trouble.

Her eyes narrowed as she smiled, leaving Fisher unsure if she seemed to sway her hips a little more on her way back to the bar.

Clinking their glasses and taking their first sips, the music's volume grew. Relaxing back into their seats, they both spotted a crowd of scantily clad young women entering the room, each dressed like their own version of a dominatrix, complete with whips.

Met by another hostess almost identical to theirs, she smiled as she pointed with her open palm to the opposite side of the room.

Before they could move, Fisher called over.

"Come and sit next to us, ladies. Free champagne."

Sharing wide-eyed looks, the girls all giggled, nodding as the hostess led them to the neighbouring table.

"Two more bottles of your finest," Fisher added as they rounded on their seats and with the tempo of the music speeding, he stood and introduced himself, shaking hands with each of them, only breaking off to unfold cash from his roll along with another healthy tip.

"You're enjoying this, aren't you?" Harris said with a raise of her brow as Fisher rejoined her, craning in close to hear her.

"Who wouldn't?" he said, beaming as he looked into her hazel eyes, already feeling the effects of the alcohol on his confidence. "Do you know which part I'm enjoying the most?" he asked, leaning closer still, his mouth a mere breath from hers.

"I think I can guess," she replied as she swapped over her crossed legs and took a tiny sip from her tall glass. Fisher tore himself away and thought better of drinking much more. Instead, he looked around the room and took in the music between the high laughter from the table beside them.

Within half an hour and not much more of the champagne gone from their glasses, Lenka sauntered over, bending as she arrived and put her mouth so close to his ear he could feel her breath on his cheek.

"Is there anything I can do to increase your enjoyment tonight, sir?"

Fisher turned his head and their noses almost touched, but she didn't move away.

"There is something," he replied, watching her smile.

"But I don't think this is the place I can get it."

"You'll be surprised. For a man of your means we can do, I mean, we can get you anything," she said with a lick of her lips.

Fisher turned his head to the side, putting his lips so close and as he did he found her hands, then placing a folded twenty in her palm, he pressed gently against her soft skin.

"I want to speak to your boss," he whispered, then pulled away.

Lenka stood up straight, sliding her palm into her pocket for just a moment as she gave an over-the-top smile before heading over to the table by the balcony where its three occupants were already peering back.

Two of the men were significantly larger than the third, but despite their black suit jackets, the bulging fat rolling over their eyes and neck told it wasn't from muscle. The third was much smaller and wiry, his skin darker as if weathered from the outdoors, or years of smoking.

As she arrived, Lenka leaned into the thinner guy, who nodded, and within a few seconds, she'd stood and headed back toward the bar. The man she'd spoken to picked up his drink and took a sip, then placing it back on the table he walked over, his gold front teeth shining as he smiled.

"May I?" he said, his accent almost matching Lenka's as he pushed his open hand out towards the stool. Fisher nodded. "Lenka tells me you want to speak to the boss?"

"Lenka said I could get what I wanted," Fisher replied, watching as the man's eyes narrowed, looking Harris up and down.

"We can be very accommodating," he said, not turning away. "But I just need to find out why you want to speak with him. I'm sure you understand."

"I do. Can I get you a drink, Mr…?" Fisher said.

"Platonov," he replied, turning back to Fisher as he pushed his hand out.

Fisher couldn't help but smile.

28

Southwest London

20th October

Fisher stood back as the bell rang, counting ten seconds before a shadow appeared through the frosted glass followed by the fresh face of a girl with jet black hair as she opened the door.

"Hello?" the teenager said, peering around the edge.

"Hi. Is your mum there?" Fisher replied with a gentle smile.

Without hesitation, the girl disappeared, leaving the door ajar.

"Muuuum," she called out as the shadow disappeared.

Moments later, the door opened to a mid-fifties woman, her face thick with foundation and a muffin top stomach spilling over the top of her pink house suit bottoms, a matching top zipped over her substantial bosom.

Fisher raised a smile as the woman spoke.

"Can I help you?" she said, her Russian accent softened from years away from her homeland.

Within seconds she'd invited him in, convinced they had an appointment and before she'd offered coffee, she was on the phone to her husband, demanding he come home straight away to deal with some unspecified household emergency.

Moments later, Fisher packed the pair off in the Volvo, without their mobile phones.

London

2nd September

Platonov held the heavy wooden door open, making way for Fisher to walk into the large office with stale cigar smoke hanging in the air. In front of him sat a large, grey-faced man behind a dark wooden desk, its edges inlaid with green-stained leather. Almost bald and with thin glasses balanced on the end of his nose, he wore a white shirt with dark blue braces tight against his shoulders.

Holding a hardback book with golden Cyrillic writing peppering the spine, the man didn't look up, but as the door closed, he held a finger in the air, his lips twitching with delight. A short crystal glass tumbler rested on his left, half filled with a thin brown liquid, whilst the rest of the vast tabletop was bare.

Fisher didn't speak; instead, he looked at the shelves laden with books filling most of the four walls, apart from where a dark wooden unit stood on the left with a crystal decanter three quarters full of the same brown liquid. Three upturned glasses surrounded it.

The booming bass was now only a memory, replaced by Platonov's gentle breathing.

With a satisfied grin, the man behind the desk closed his book, placed it with great care on the table before he picked off his delicate glasses and laid them on top. Fisher stepped forward and offered his hand. The guy extended his large, pudgy mitt and leaned slightly forward.

"You trust me," Fisher said as their hands touched.

The guy's hairless brow furrowed. "I don't even know who..." he said, his English clear but laced with a heavy Russian accent before he paused and the skin on his forehead relaxed. "I'm sorry, Mr Fisher, I didn't recognise you."

Unable to keep his eyes from widening, Fisher hoped the man behind the desk couldn't hear the pounding of his heart as the Russian waved his hand to dismiss Platonov. Using the same hand, he gestured for Fisher to sit. "Can I get you a drink?"

"No, thank you, Mr...?" Fisher said as he welcomed the chance to take the weight from his legs, fearing they might go from under him at the realisation that not only did this man know who he was, it was the second time his ability had failed in as many days.

"Bukin. Viktor Bukin."

Fisher nodded and lifted his chin. "You know who I am, so perhaps you know why I'm here?" he said, turning his head to the side.

"I can only imagine you're trying to find out who is sending those incompetents after you," he said, raising an eyebrow. "Am I right?"

"Yes," Fisher replied, trying his best to stop his rapid blinking at the man's candid answer.

"Firstly, let me apologise for dragging this out," Viktor said, sinking back into his seat, the words sounding dulled through the pounding of Fisher's heart in his ears. "It's my fault entirely. I underestimated you and your colleagues." Despite what he'd expected, Fisher felt the panic ebbing and after a moment he had enough control to reply.

"Can you do me the courtesy of telling me what this is all about?" Fisher said, surprised when his mixture of emotions hadn't tainted his tone.

Viktor's smile bunched his cheeks, but rather than seeming smug, it appeared sympathetic.

"It is a business transaction. My organisation's services were secured by a customer to provide you to them, preferably unharmed, but certainly alive," he said, then opened his hands out. "That is the completeness of the transaction."

None of this was a surprise.

"We'll pay you double," Fisher said, hoping it didn't sound like he'd blurted the words out.

"Mr Fisher. I am an honest businessman and I can't do that. It would go against my moral code," he said, then laughed before taking a short sip of his drink. "Are you sure I can't get you something?"

"I could shoot you," Fisher said, ignoring the question.

"I could shoot you, Mr Fisher. There are lots of things that can be done, but the problem you have is that I'm just a service provider. There are lots of organisations like mine that would happily take over the contract. You wouldn't believe the competition I face. My suggestion is to give up hiding and get this over with."

Before he could continue, the shrill call of a fire alarm echoed from the corridor. "Well, it would seem you didn't come alone today," he said, his posture deflating. "Let's call this one a draw. I'll give you five minutes to get out, then the game is back on."

Fisher stood and offered his hand. Viktor pushed his out and their palms touched.

"I'm not Mr Fisher," Fisher said, but a roar of a laugh erupted from Viktor's belly.

"I suggest you don't waste this opportunity."

29

Southwest London

20th October

Standing in the kitchen, Fisher didn't need to strain to hear the clatter of the front door opening then shutting a moment later as quietened voices chatted in a harsh language he didn't recognise. Their volume soon increased and the door to the kitchen opened, with Viktor Bukin showing little surprise when he saw Fisher standing in the far corner of the room leaning against the granite kitchen counter. The bulky minder who followed him in didn't double take at the sight of Fisher's borrowed gun raised toward him. Instead, he made to reach inside his grey suit jacket just as Fisher pushed out his palm and spoke.

"That would be the worst decision of your life."

Seeing the minder withdraw his empty hand from his suit jacket, Viktor's frown didn't last long before it was replaced with a smile, his eyes narrowing as he looked back at Fisher, who hoped he hadn't betrayed his own surprise.

"Where's my family?" Viktor said.

"They're fine, Mr Bukin. This is not about them," Fisher replied, ushering the pair deeper into the room. Viktor nodded and together they edged away from the door.

After moving two paces forward, Fisher pulled out a set of steel handcuffs and threw them at the minder who looked like an old Russian mobster. "Cuff your man's hands behind his back," Fisher said, turning the gun on Bukin.

Viktor nodded to his employee, who then turned away to make it easy for his boss. With the cuffs in place and his weapon removed from his holster, Fisher pushed the employee into the larder before securing him with a second pair of cuffs to a pipe sprouting from a yellow bulky gas meter.

"Thank you for waiting," Fisher said, finding Viktor

hadn't moved as he closed the larder door.

"Is this revenge, or are you showing off your new trick?" Viktor said, lowering his eyebrows.

Fisher shook his head, both to answer the question and in the hope it would push away his own search for answers. Was it the gun pointed at the Russian's companion, or his developing ability that had stopped the minder from taking out his weapon?

"Just business," Fisher said, reminding himself of the conversation they'd had a few weeks earlier. "I work for your former customer now and I've rendered you surplus to requirements."

Viktor shrugged. "It's a cycle. So what happens now?"

"I'm here to kill you."

"I don't think you have it in you. Are you a killer, Mr Fisher?" Viktor said.

Before Fisher replied, the sound of the front door opening and closing drained the colour from Viktor's face.

"You're right. It's not something I want to become a habit," Fisher said with a smile. "Whereas these two, I don't think they're bothered," he added, nodding at Joel and Samir as they walked through the kitchen doorway.

"Where's the other one?" Joel said, and Fisher motioned to the larder before turning back to Viktor.

"Hold him still," Fisher said, waving the pistol at the old man.

Samir moved to the Russian's left as Joel stationed himself the other side, each placing a hand on his shoulder and another around a wrist. Fisher raised the gun and fired before moving his aim and pulling the trigger a second time.

The two Arabs fell to the floor whilst Viktor still stood, his eyes wide and mouth hanging open.

Fisher reached inside his pocket, drawing out a third set of cuffs and throwing them. Viktor didn't react as they clattered against his chest, splashing his trousers with the Arab's pooling blood as they landed on the floor.

London

2nd September

Stark, bright light greeted Fisher as he walked back into the VIP lounge to find the red leather grubby and faded in the harsh glow of the fluorescents. With the shrieking alarm having replaced the beat, apart from Harris and Biggy, the place was deserted. Walking into the corridor and passing a fire call point with its safety glass cracked, a leggy blonde in a high-visibility yellow jacket over her black suit ushered them toward the entrance.

About to step out into the cool night air, a large bouncer Fisher recognised from their arrival stepped into their path, but soon stumbled backwards with blood flowing from his misaligned nose.

"Sometimes I don't know my strength," Biggy said, his tone deadpan as he climbed aboard the X5.

"Did you hear what he said?" Fisher asked, turning to Harris as Lucky drove them from the kerb, passing between the parting crowd of dazed revellers.

She nodded, confirming the comm link had worked and she'd heard both sides of the conversation.

"What now?"

"I'll have a team keep him busy night and day. They won't have time to come after you," Harris said, pulling on the tan suit jacket she'd left on the rear seat.

Doing his best to push away the disappointment of her covering up, Fisher looked out at the streets lit with neon. "Others will step in."

"But it will give us a couple of days perhaps," she said, placing her hand on his. Closing his eyes at her touch, he kept his head turned as he relaxed. "We'll figure this out," she added, moving her hand.

Feeling vacant with her warmth gone, Fisher blocked out her conversation with Clark as his mind drifted back to

Viktor's reaction when he'd become the second person on which his influence had failed, both of which had a hand in Andrew's death.

"I need to see Alan," Fisher said, unable to think of anything else as Harris ended the call.

30

Southwest London

20th October

Fisher watched as Joel writhed on the kitchen floor, slipping in his blood, his hands slick as he pressed them against his chest. Samir hadn't moved since he'd slumped.

Unsure how he felt about another death by his hand, Fisher couldn't stop himself from remembering those he'd killed, but feeling as if he'd left someone out, panic tightened his chest. Had this become the new normal?

With a deep breath, the feeling ebbed, replaced by a numbness that clouded his brain as he looked at Viktor staring back with his mouth hanging open. Unable to hold the look for long, his gaze fell to Joel, watching his bloodshot eyes flash wide, and he stared up as Fisher pushed his hand inside the blood drenched denim jacket, pulling out a warm handgun.

With the old Russian quiet, through the sticky liquid, Fisher checked the empty chamber, released the magazine and threw the gun across the room, sending blood splattering along the skirting.

"Why?" Joel moaned as he met Fisher's gaze, sending blood spraying from his mouth as he coughed.

Fisher leaned down and tapped Joel's clammy cheek with his open palm.

"I'm saving the taxpayer money," he said, "and keeping women everywhere safe from you."

Joel's expression dropped, his face almost as grey as Harris's favourite suit.

"I told you to stay in the car, but you gave me an opportunity I couldn't pass up," Fisher said, taking a step back just as blood made it to his polished black leather shoes.

Unscrewing the suppressor from his own Argentinian gun, Fisher pocketed the weapon before peering down over

Samir's lifeless body where he plucked up his jacket and pulled out the dead man's pistol. Screwing in the suppressor, he took a step towards the rear door, then without pause he cocked the gun, lifted his arm and spat a round between the dead man's eyes.

Pleased with his aim, he unscrewed the suppressor and threw the weapon underarm into the man's blood-covered lap and turned to the larder, opening the door.

The minder stared out, sharing the same gaping-mouth expression as Viktor when Fisher motioned the old Russian into the larder. They both watched as Fisher pulled a chewing gum-sized tab of plastic explosive from his pocket before pushing it against a joint between the gas meter and the pipe, then added a small black box at its side.

"If you want to savour your last moments, don't touch that," Fisher said, watching the pair staring at the black box and the slowly flashing LED as he closed the door and pushed a chair under the handle.

Walking past the car tyre swings, Fisher barely flinched when the trees rustled and car alarms sang with the plume of smoke and flames reflecting from their windows.

***

10,000 ft above the England / Wales Border

3rd September

Monday

I just got back from Cardiff. Wow, that was a fun weekend. I would have stayed longer, but I have a shift in a couple of hours.

George certainly seems to be settling in alright up there. A couple of his flat mates are dicks, but they know how to drink. I was so close to banging one of the women. Susie, I think she's called. At least until I found out she was frigid. Next time I'm up, I'll see if I can have one of the others!

Tuesday

I spoke to George a few minutes ago, and he says I can't go back until next month because he needs to concentrate on his studies. I'm learning to drive now, so when I have my car I'll just show up. It'll be fine. He'll love the surprise.

Monday

Things are on the up! I've got an interview for a fast track management position in a couple of weeks' time. It turns out it's the day I come back from Cardiff, but I'm sure everything will be okay. I'll just take it easy on the beers.

It looks like those fucks who decided university was the best way to start their career might have got it all wrong!

Sunday

What a rocking weekend! Everyone had a good time and I'm warming up to the crowd up there, but I definitely think that Susie is a lezza. It looked like she was going to punch me when I moved in for the kill.

That James is a bit of an oddball as well. They all seem to be licking his ass all the time. I can't see it myself. Anyway, interview tomorrow. Best I get an early night.

Monday

Tossers, the lot of them.

"You're not quite ready yet, Mr Bullard. You need a few more months' experience on the shop floor."

Fuck it!

George rang me to see how the interview went and I couldn't quite bring myself to tell him I didn't get it, so I told him they're giving me a trial for a few months. By the time that's done, I'll have the job anyway. It's not really a lie.

Friday

Whoop, whoop.
I just passed my test and now all I need is a car.
Perhaps I'll have enough dough in two hundred years or so, but in the meantime, it's the train for me. Cardiff, here we come.

Fisher looked up from the leather-bound diary as the sleek black chartered chopper's wheels touched the familiar hard standing. Looking out of the darkened windows, the sun was rising over the dull concrete building and the entrance to their hidden subterranean state-of-the-art headquarters.

Clark had arranged the flight within two hours of taking Harris's call, and an hour later they left Biggy at City Airport with his team for the night off. In the Brecons, with enough military nearby to retake a small African nation, protection wasn't an issue.

The doors slid open as the aircraft settled on its wheels, then lifted off when the pair reached the safety of the concrete wall with Fisher's thoughts already turning to the only other time he'd been at this place before he was part of the team. Before he'd found Susie, and when Andrew was alive.

So much had happened since he'd left the isolated building, and now he was back, this time calling the shots to find out why his influence hadn't worked.

He wanted to know much more, of course, like what had driven Alan to hand him over to those after him, certain it was the key to keeping his friends safe so everyone could get on with their lives.

Once through the multitude of guarded security doors and down the unending series of floors, arriving at one of the lowest levels, he stepped from the stairwell, the walls no longer fresh with satin white paint; instead, bare concrete greeted them as the lighting went from ornate high level long fluorescent lamps suspended on thin chains, to galvanised steel strips encased in tough wire mesh fixed to the ceiling as the temperature felt just a little too cool.

Out from the stairwell, a tall security desk stood beside a large red painted metal door, to the side of which a thick glass panel recessed into the wall. Two men with enormous necks stood beyond, both dressed in black, with their uniform showing no designation.

The guard to the right tipped his shaven head at Harris as a small metal drawer scraped toward them. Harris pulled off her ID badge from her black jacket and took out the Glock 17 from her shoulder holster before placing them in the rubber-lined drawer. Turning to Fisher, he did the same. With his gun and ID alongside hers, the drawer slammed shut before the guard removed the contents and his colleague stepped forward.

"Number Five," the guard said, leaving Fisher unable to detect any accent.

Harris nodded as the heavy door to their side swung open to a long corridor, with the identical lighting and steel ventilation grills fixed to the ceiling as a second red steel door waited closed in the distance.

With a metallic click echoing out, the door opened to two men standing on the other side, only one of which Fisher recognised.

Franklin stood on the left, wearing his usual black suit, whilst the man on the right wore a doctor's overcoat, both of them watching their approach with Styrofoam cups in hand, their expressions blank, nodding as the pair arrived.

"Agent Harris," Franklin said, then turned to her side. "Mr Fisher, this is Doctor Devlin. He has been assessing Mr Bullard."

"Carrie," Devlin said with a nod, then turned to Fisher, lips curling with a smile.

"Have you injured him?" Fisher replied.

"No," Franklin said. "Doctor Devlin is a psychologist."

"I've assessed his mental state, and it's not good news,"

Devlin replied, his tone warm.

"In what way?" Fisher asked as he looked past the two men to the four sets of metal security doors, each painted bright yellow further along.

"He's deluded," the doctor replied. "And exhibiting the symptoms of paranoia and schizophrenia. He's certain someone called Paul told him to do those things, but just talks about him as a friend. Someone who is always with him. I understand that you're close to Mr Bullard?"

Fisher turned his attention away from the corridor, locking his gaze with the doctor.

"I used to think so," Fisher replied in a low voice.

"Did he ever mention someone called Paul to you?" the doctor said, turning his head to the side.

"No," Fisher replied with a shake of his head. "But he mentions him in his diaries."

Dr Devlin raised his brow as he spoke. "Did he ever mention about being treated for any mental health issues? We're having issues finding his medical files."

Fisher shook his head. "Although he had anger issues when he was younger."

"The diaries will help my diagnosis," the doctor said.

"I haven't finished reading them yet. Why are we interested in a diagnosis? All we need is to find out why he got my friend killed," Fisher said, his tone rising.

"With a diagnosis we can stabilise Mr Bullard in order to help us question him. Any questioning at this point would be useless," the doctor said, turning to Franklin. "You will have my report on your desk by nine o'clock. If you can provide the diaries, it may aid my determination of a treatment programme."

"Thank you, Doctor Devlin," Franklin said, just as the doctor moved past Harris and headed away.

Franklin turned to Fisher. "We've all got the same goals here, Mr Fisher. Please remember that."

"Can I see him?" Fisher asked, turning to Harris who looked between them before nodding almost imperceptibly.

Without another word, Franklin stepped between the pair, following the doctor through the main door.

31

Eight Walworth Road, London

20th October

"Don't do that to me again," Fisher said, doing his best to keep calm.

"What happened?" Farid said. Sitting across the glass table, the Arab's eyes were wide as he leaned forward.

"The two idiots you gave me screwed up," Fisher replied. "I told them to stay in the fucking car, but halfway through, they barged right in."

Farid sat back in the seat, clasping his fingers tight together as Fisher continued.

"Bukin must have had someone watching the house. It was like the Wild West after they arrived, but don't worry, I contained it."

"Apart from the car," Farid said, his voice calm as he raised his chin.

"Apart from the car," Fisher repeated with a nod. "At least no one can identify the bodies."

"Why did you leave the car?" Farid said, his eyes narrowing as he took shallow breaths.

"Your men had the keys and there was no going back once I'd set the charge," Fisher replied. Farid stared over, leaning his head to the side until, after a long pause, he nodded.

"At least the job is done. The car's untraceable anyway," Farid said, relaxing further into his seat. "Next time, don't make the evening news. Four bodies in a gas explosion attracts the wrong attention."

Fisher nodded, doing his best to ignore the man's greater concern over the loss of the car rather than his two employees.

"Yasmin," Farid called towards the kitchen, where a few seconds later the girl from breakfast appeared at the door wearing the same clothes she'd had on this morning, along with a familiar limp smile. "Tea," Farid snapped, both turning to Fisher who nodded then watched as she disappeared back behind the door, leaving the pair in silence with Farid thumbing through his phone.

Within a few minutes, Yasmin laid out a bright metal teapot and bone china cups in front of the two men before scurrying back to the kitchen.

"Tomorrow is the big day," Farid said, breaking the silence as he poured from the pot. Fisher nodded. "There's a building I need you to visit. It's just down the road from that police station and it's a research facility," Farid added, reaching inside his jacket and pulling out an A5 brown envelope.

"What do you need?" Fisher said, leaning to take the envelope.

"An item," Farid said, watching as Fisher pulled open the unsealed flap to spread the paper contents across the table. "And tonight you get your night off."

"What, no party?" Fisher said, knowing that with Farid's laughter he'd sounded just as disappointed as he had in his head.

"You wanted the young one again. Have I found your thing?" he said between booming laughter. "Not tonight."

He couldn't deny it. He wanted to see Luana again, but for different reasons.

"You've got it bad, my friend," Farid said, laughing again, but rather than catch his eye, Fisher poured over the papers from the envelope. The first showed a printed address, a BAE Systems building in Great Baddow, recognising the company name as a defence contractor who built ships and planes and all manner of kit for the military.

On the other was a crudely drawn schematic of what looked like a bullet, below which an exploded diagram showed electronics and wires where he'd expected gunpowder.

"What is it?" Fisher said, holding up the page.

"Fuck knows, but it's five million quid to you."

Underneath the last sheet, he found the keys and swipe card he'd retrieved from the police station a couple of days ago. Next to it, his face stared back from a security pass.

"So where does Daryl fit?" Fisher said, looking up from the spread.

Farid lifted the page with the address, turning it over to a floor plan with sections highlighted with a range of vibrant colours.

"The facility has five zones. You'll have a cover story to get you into Zone Five," Farid said, tapping on the ID badge on the table. "You'll have to deal with Four," he added, then pointed to the keys and key card. "These will get you through sections Three and Two. Zone One is the most difficult and will be up to Daryl. Once you're inside Zone Two you'll need his speed."

"How long do we have?" Fisher asked.

"Twenty minutes because after that the security system goes to the next level," Farid replied.

"What's the next level?" Fisher replied.

"We couldn't find out, but in that sort of place it could be anything."

Fisher nodded as he picked up the plan.

"Once we're done, I want to meet the boss," Fisher said, looking him in the eye.

Farid nodded just as Benny, another of Farid's many guys, came from the corridor and coughed into his cuff.

Farid stood. "Please excuse me. I have an appointment," he said before leaving.

Brecon Beacons

3rd September

The heavy metal door clanking against its battered stops revealed a short corridor with more unfinished concrete walls. A metal drain ran along the edge of each wall, whilst a blue vinyl coated the floor. Both doors on either side of the corridor were of the same construction as the rest, but painted a bright green.

Waiting until the door closed at their backs, Harris led them to the green door on the right where she pressed her phone up against the faint outline beside the metal and, without delay, the door opened inwards.

Fisher didn't wait, stepping through the widening gap, then stopped and turned, looking Harris in the eye.

"Can you give me a moment?"

She didn't speak, her brow lowering as he held eye contact.

"Just a few minutes," he added.

After a pause, she stepped back, letting the door close.

Surprised when the room was nothing like the place he'd been interrogated in those weeks ago, he found Alan sitting behind a stainless steel table with its legs bolted to the concrete, the nuts bright orange. He perched on the edge of a metal seat. The floor had the same bright covering as the corridor. A single fluorescent lamp in an enclosed wire guard clung to the high ceiling.

Alan stared at the table, paying no attention to Fisher's arrival. Dressed in an all-white cotton jumpsuit with a long zip up the front, he sat with his hands at his side.

"Alan?" Fisher said, still standing at the door, watching as his former friend lifted his head to reveal a pale complexion highlighted by red eyes as if he'd not slept in some time.

"James?" Alan said, squinting as if unsure.

Fisher stifled a flicker of guilt at the sight, but reminded himself that Alan looked much healthier than Andrew had with a bullet between his eyes. Doing his best to keep the contempt from his expression, Fisher took a step and raised his hand.

Alan stood, chains rattling and drawing Fisher's gaze to the silver cuff around his right wrist.

Taking another step, Fisher reached out, holding back the crawl of his skin as he clenched the man's arm in a tight grip.

"I can stop this," he said, watching Alan nod with tears forming in the corner of his eyes.

"Please," he replied.

"You're going to be okay," Fisher added, a slow smile rising on Alan's lips as he blinked. "You can trust me," he continued. "Andrew is fine."

Fisher swallowed down a lump in his throat as Alan's expression slackened, his head slowly moving from side to side.

"You're lying," he said, drawing away as he tried to pull his arm back. "I saw him."

Fisher's brow tightened as he kept his grip, his lips bunching as he tried to push away the image of his dead friend.

"He's alive," Fisher said, squeezing harder as his breathing raced. "He's fucking alive."

"Andrew's dead," Alan said, not able to get out of the grip. "You're hurting me."

Fisher let go as the door opened. Before she could say anything, he glared at Alan as Harris pulled him into the corridor.

32

Eight Walworth Road, London

21st October

Reaching for his bedside to silence the incessant alarm, Fisher sat bolt upright from a vision of Luana, an older version at least, still haunting his thoughts as he stared at the closed curtains and the hint of sun from the windows beyond.

With wrinkles lining her face and her dark hair flecked with grey, the dream's remains faded as his thoughts drifted to his task for the day.

Almost surprised to find his bed empty for the first time since this place had become his home, dismissing the thought, he picked himself from underneath the deep red silk covers, adjusted the waist of his black Calvin Klein boxer shorts and stepped into the en-suite bathroom.

Staring at the mirror, he rubbed at his chin with his thumb and forefinger and feeling stubble, he took a step back, opened the mirror and pulled out the can of shaving foam and the first razor to hand.

With the stubble dealt with and his face clean of foam, he nodded to his reflection. Hearing the front door slam, with a deft move of his arm, he smashed the head of the razor clean from the handle and threw the remains into the bin.

***

Brecon Beacons

3rd September

Not putting up a fight as the door clicked back, then following

Harris along the bare concrete walls in silence, Fisher shook his head as he tried to process how Alan could be immune to his suggestion.

Collecting their belongings from the security checkpoint and striding in her wake, taking the steps two at a time, he couldn't help but wonder what made Alan so special. By the time they'd levelled out three floors up, with Harris reaching for the door handle, he still couldn't understand how his gift hadn't worked.

"Where are we going?" he asked, stepping through the doorway after Harris unlocked it with a press of her phone.

"To see Clark," Harris replied, not turning back, instead unlocking a second door only a few steps beyond to reveal a dark, cavernous room.

With no lights hanging from the high ceiling, Fisher peered along lines of desks arranged in rows, each mounted with multiple large monitors whilst on the far right of the room an array of massive screens filled the wall, showing bright maps, graphs, pie charts, along with digital counters and TV news feeds from around the world.

Along the wall in front and to the left, side offices were partitioned with tall glass. Some partitions were transparent, showing off chairs and long tables inside, whilst others were obscured as if with black curtains.

"Welcome to the operations nerve centre. One of them at least," Harris said, her pace increasing.

Fisher nodded even though she wouldn't have seen, unable to think of anything to say as he looked over at the many men and women. Some were dressed in suits, others more casual in t-shirt and jeans whilst they either sat at desks wearing wireless headsets, or otherwise strode around the room with purpose.

It took a long moment before he saw Clark in the centre, a smile bunching his cheeks as he raised his hand to beckon them over.

Fisher followed Harris as she strode between the desks, taking Clark's embrace as they met. Letting go of Fisher's handshake a short while after, Clark took a tablet from his desk, then guided them to a side office. With a rush of air, Clark pushed the door wide, and Fisher exercised his jaw before his ears popped when Clark pushed it closed.

As Fisher and Harris took seats beside each other at the far end of a dark wooden table, Clark's fingers played over a bank of switches beside the door, each marked with a different coloured sticker. The door sucked against its frame as the glass walls turned black. Without being told, Fisher realised he'd sealed them off from the rest of the world.

Sitting at the side of them both, Clark opened the tablet's cover and the screen lit.

"We've identified four out of five of the men you've encountered and all trace back to Bukin," Clark said as he turned the tablet around, scrolling through four black and white mug shots with notes underneath neither of them had a chance to read. "And Bukin confirmed as much in your conversation."

Fisher nodded, watching as Clark turned the tablet around before tapping at the screen.

"Alan's plane tickets were paid with cash from Heathrow the morning of the incident." Harris nodded along as Clark spoke, but Fisher stared at the wall, tapping the desk with his fingers.

"Did you want to say something?" Clark asked, looking Fisher in the eye.

"We can't let him get away with this just because he's sick in the head," Fisher said, balling his fist. Clark shot Harris a look.

"That won't happen," he said.

"Any more on the mole?" Harris asked, changing the subject.

"We've made progress, but it could take time to narrow down our findings. We need to see what gets leaked."

"Send me in," Fisher said, his voice raised. "I'll find out who's keeping secrets."

Harris turned, looking Fisher over.

"There's not enough security clearance in the world that would allow you to find out the secrets they're keeping," she said, somehow keeping her voice light and a thin smile on her lips.

Fisher stood, scraping back his seat. "We're going," he said and strode towards the door. When Clark arrived at his side, the press of the button revealed Franklin striding over, glaring in their direction.

33

Eight Walworth Road, London

21st October

Clean from the shower, Fisher headed into the lounge, finding Farid sat in his usual place with a coffee in hand and staring at his watch. Darryl Grant sat on the floor in the room's corner by a tall rubber plant, his attention focused on a large-scale schematic spread over the tiles.

Fisher shuddered when he saw the scar-faced man sitting on the sofa next to Farid. With most of the henchmen he'd met dotted around the room, there was no doubt they were all waiting for him.

Watching the cleaner step from the kitchen wearing yellow marigolds, his gaze followed as she headed down the corridor. With no party last night, she'd be finished soon. Surprised that those waiting didn't seem refreshed, instead of heading to the sofa, Fisher wandered into the kitchen where he found the largest mug and filled the kettle to the top.

With the fridge stacked with beer, cider and mixers, he took his time to scour each cupboard, drawing out beans and a loaf of bread. Seconds later, with a pan on the cooker top and scraping tomato sauce from the can, Farid appeared from around the doorway, his eyebrows raised.

"What are you doing?"

"Making breakfast. It's a big day. Do you want some?" Fisher replied with a smile.

Farid rolled his eyes, disappearing out of sight without replying.

Ten minutes later and Fisher took a seat at the dining table, inhaling the steam from the beans piled high on toast. Chewing each mouthful to savour each bite, he sat with his back to the tall floor-to-ceiling windows and listened to the rustle of a newspaper. Paying only little attention when the cleaner placed a small bin bag by the front door, he couldn't see where she headed. Taking another mouthful, he paused when Farid appeared on the other side of the table.

"We're going," Farid said, glancing at his watch before grabbing the plate from in front of Fisher and striding to the kitchen where it clattered into the bin.

Before Farid returned, Fisher strode to his bedroom, returning a moment later with the bag from his ensuite bin before dropping it on the growing pile by the front door.

"What are you waiting for?" Fisher said, turning to Farid.

***

10,000 feet over Gloucestershire

3rd September

<u>*Monday*</u>

What a cracking weekend again. I got a night out with just George. It was great. We set the world to rights as we always used to. I felt a little guilty not telling him the truth about the whole job thing, but it's not like I'm lying. I'm just a little ahead of myself.

Anyway, when I came home yesterday, there was a knock at my door and there was some fella who sounded like a fucking aristocrat. He said he was going door to door offering an opportunity.

He's a PhD student or something, studying Anthropology. I think that's what he said. They were offering money to people to take part in an experiment. It sounded pretty cool and thought perhaps it might mean some cool new drugs, but it turned out it was a social experiment. It's still easy money nonetheless and I have plenty I need to spend it on.

All they want me to do is keep a diary about my friends. I told him I didn't have any local friends, but he said it was okay if I wrote about friends that lived elsewhere. He said it didn't matter if I didn't see them that often, almost as if he knew my next question. Ha!

So anyway, they're going to pay me two hundred pounds if every time I go to Cardiff I write a set of observations. I told him I already write a diary, so he said I could just continue that. Before he left, he said that the terms of the experiment meant those I was writing about couldn't know what I was doing. He made it clear I couldn't tell them, otherwise they might change their behaviour. It's a blind trial, or something.

With this money I'll be getting my car much quicker!

Looking up from the diary, Fisher realised it wasn't the first time he'd heard this from one of his friends. Last time, it was Susie just before she'd vanished. With a deep breath, he punched in her number, unable to stop questioning if it could be a coincidence.

Greeted by her voicemail, he felt guilty at his relief and pushed the phone back into his pocket as he realised she probably wouldn't be able to hear him with the drone of the helicopter's engines anyway.

After closing his eyes, he tried to blank out the sound, but it wasn't long before he awoke to the door opening and he stepped into the fresh morning air, following Harris into the back of the waiting X5. Only as they passed between the airside gates did Fisher pull open the fourth of the leather-bound books and found where he'd curled over the page.

For ten more minutes, he scanned monotonous entries, until all he had were blank pages.

"He stopped," Fisher said, glancing to Harris, then back to the book.

"Perhaps he got bored," Harris replied, looking up from the pile of documents she'd brought with her.

"It was just getting interesting," Fisher replied. "I don't get it," he added, then pulled out his phone and searched for a number. "George. How are you doing?" he said after a single ring.

"I'm fine, mate. How are you holding up?" George replied, not hiding the concern in his tone.

"It's still a bit of a blur," Fisher said, blinking in hope that the image of the hole in Andrew's forehead wouldn't appear.

"I get it. How's the new job? You should take some time off," George replied.

"The job's fine, and I need to keep busy. Can I ask you an odd question about Alan?"

"Sure. Talking of Alan, I haven't spoken to him since, uh, Andrew," George replied, his voice tailing off.

"Did Alan have a friend called Paul?" Fisher said, ignoring the comment.

"No," George said without a pause.

"How are you so certain?"

"How can I put this in a good light?" George said, then paused. "Alan was a loner when I met him. He had no other friends until he met you guys."

"Thanks," Fisher replied, letting the conversation falter into silence until George murmured.

"Sorry to ask, mate, but do you know the funeral date?"

Fisher closed his eyes and drew a slow breath.

"No, I don't," he replied. "I've got to go."

George's voice rushed to fill the space before Fisher cancelled the call.

"Can you call Susie? She's been trying to get hold of you."

Fisher nodded to himself.

"Will do," he said, staring at the back of the seat.

34

London

21st October

In convoy, Farid sat next to Fisher in the back of Farid's least favourite car, the Evoke. Not for the first time, Farid reminding those who'd listen how it pandered to the urban driver too much and he wouldn't buy any more.

Bennett drove with Mo beside him. Like most of Farid's guys, both were tall and well built, employed for their appearance as much as for their individual skills. Mo's long black ponytail rested on the shoulder of his grey suit. Bennett had no hair to speak of.

The second car stuck behind them like glue, with Daryl and two more hefty employees inside as protectors or custodians. Which of the two, he wasn't sure.

The pair of Range Rovers weaved around the streets of London and, being ten o'clock in the morning, whilst the commuters were tucked up in offices it was shoppers and brightly-dressed sightseers heading off to fill their day with adventures.

"Are you okay?" Farid said, looking up from his copy of The Times to Fisher's fingers drumming on the centre armrest.

Fisher stopped tapping. "I've just got a bad feeling about today."

"If you're worried about Daryl, then don't. He's a professional," Farid replied, before engrossing himself back into the paper.

"How long was he inside?" Fisher said after a long moment.

Farid looked up, not hiding the irritation on his narrowed brow. "A long time. He'll be fine," Farid said, then paused for thought. "I'm sure," he added with a laugh when the tapping began again.

Within ten minutes, the traffic slowed to a crawl as the cars worked their way along a residential street with tall Victorian houses towering either side. They should have only been moments from a dual carriageway along the Thames' embankment, but were instead stuck in start-stop traffic.

Another ten later and they'd moved little, with Fisher watching agitated drivers turn off their engines and stepping onto the road where they stood on tiptoes, searching for the cause of the holdup. Pulling open the heavy door, Fisher did the same, but seeing nothing, he retook his seat.

It was another twenty minutes before they edged forward.

Coming around the slow corner, Bennett cursed the culprit, a set of temporary traffic lights controlling four lanes merging into a diversion to the left. Their frustration grew as despite being some fifty-car lengths back, the lights only let three cars through at a time.

"Typical," Fisher said as he peered along the vacant four lanes barred by cones and orange barrier after the lights.

Bennett growled in broken English. "I bet they won't even start working until tomorrow."

Despite the two in the front groaning with each red light cycle, it was another fifteen minutes before their slow crawl took them within a car's length of the amber light.

With an impatient right foot, Bennett committed to follow the sports coupe through the orange signal, but a moment of hesitation from the driver of the two-seater caused him to bunny hop to a stop as its engine faltered. Bennett slammed on the brakes, sending everyone but him lunging headfirst, much to Farid's annoyance.

Just as the amber changed to a definite stop, the lightweight coupe surged into the distance, leaving them next in line. Bennett called out in guttural Arabic Fisher had earlier learned the crude translation for, but the tension inside eased when the light turned green and the car followed the alternative route away from the dual carriageway and along a residential road with tall stone houses on either side.

The sports car was already long gone, with Bennett keeping them at the speed limit. The last thing he wanted was for a speeding ticket to blow the mission.

As Fisher glanced at the buildings, they soon gave way to a green expanse of open space with a park to their left and rows of tennis courts to their right. He couldn't help but note the empty road ahead with the pavements clear of pedestrians.

Only movement seen through the windscreen caused him to look ahead, focusing on a dark car pulling out from a side street.

"Boss," Bennett said, breaking the silence, then as Fisher looked in the mirror up front, he found the man's attention fixed behind. Twisting around in the seat, he saw a black X5 behind their rear car getting bigger in the view. Farid had seen it too, dropping the paper as he looked through the rear glass.

Bennett slowed the car, and those following did the same. Fisher, like Farid, looked to his left and then the other way, but with tall bushy hedgerows and wire fencing, they found nowhere for their convoy to go other than the road ahead.

Fisher looked at Farid and the Arab returned the look as together they reached inside their jackets to draw their pistols.

Farid pulled back the slide on his Bersa Thunder to chamber a round. Fisher checked his own weapon and confirmed it was ready. Pushing the guns back home, they both stared through the windscreen.

"Now," Farid screamed, and Bennett didn't need to be told what he'd meant as he jabbed his foot down on the accelerator, making micro adjustments to the steering wheel, guiding them toward the tiny gap between the two black BMW X5s parked nose to nose blocking the road.

Fisher scrambled to pull on his seat belt and braced as the Range Rover sped towards the roadblock.

He stared without panic or fear as eight armed men walked clear of their pristine vehicles, then he closed his eyes and hunkered down into a brace, ready for their two and a half tonne car to reach the four tonne blockage.

Opening his eyes to clouds of airbag powder, he found

the windscreen cracked and the bonnet of the white Range Rover crumpled into the black of the X5s. Fisher turned to his side and saw Farid out cold, a purple bruise already forming on the side of his light brown forehead. Bennett lay slumped with his face against the steering wheel, whilst Mo's indistinct noises made no sense.

With a loud pop from outside, his ears screamed with pain, his head feeling as if full of cotton wool. He glanced to his right and through the window he saw one of Farid's guys. His name had left him, but he was sure he was running from their other car and he pointed a black pistol. With another loud pop, his hand recoiled.

The air grew thick with smoke and Fisher pulled at the handle to his right, but found the door wouldn't move. He shoved against the heavy steelwork with his shoulder, bones crunching as the door held firm. Pushing through the pain, the door finally relented just as the window shattered into hundreds of fragments, showering him with glass as he fell to the hard Tarmac.

His head still woolly, Fisher sat on the glass-strewn road with his back against the door. To his left were the two damaged X5s and to his right, the other Range Rover stood undamaged. Crouched behind it, one of Farid's guys popped off shots to hold off the group of assailants.

Only in that moment remembering what he carried, Fisher reached inside his pocket, pulled out his Glock and levelled it at those who aimed in their direction. Taking his time, concentrating as he tried to blink away the fog clouding his head, he fired a single round. A perfect shot. Hotwire fell to the ground.

Behind him, he heard the passenger door open and Fisher looked up over the seat to Farid falling out of the car. Someone shouted, the call echoing from behind. Fisher added to the chaos, firing off another two rounds of covering fire, his lead smashing into the rear of the black cars.

Somewhere an engine started, and a horn sent him flinching until he peered back when the gunfire quietened.

The others were already in the second car. Fisher tried to stand, but as he did, gunfire rained in his direction.

By now his head had cleared and he fired off a shot at a high angle and jumped to his feet, scrabbling back through the rear seats of the crippled Range Rover. Once on the other side, shots rained out from the second car, pinning their attackers down as Fisher looked around for options. Finding the only choice was a small gap in the hedge, he scrambled across the width of the road, before rushing into the wide open park.

Running across the deserted grassland with his gun still in his hand, he looked left and right, his head darting from side to side as he tried to get his bearings. Still sprinting, Fisher risked a glance behind and pushed harder when he saw the two men on his tail.

Arriving at the road on the other side of the park, Fisher slipped his Glock inside his jacket before jumping the short metal railings and dodging cars from both directions at the front of a high-rise hospital. After a quick glance over his shoulder, he rushed into the main entrance, pausing in front of a tall sign as he looked along the colour-coded department listing.

Soon he was on his heels, heading down a corridor to his right, guided by the coloured flooring.

Rushing between trolleys and hobbling patients, annoyed nurses and security guards, he found the split in a corridor he searched for and a yellow rigid barrier blocking the way to the left. Not slowing, he launched himself up, lifting his legs as high as they would go, and was soon into a dusty corridor with paint pots and brushes strewn by a dusty wall.

As the corridor swept to his left, he slowed with his gaze fixing on a door at the apex.

Catching a noise from behind, a paint pot falling to the floor perhaps, he stopped and turned but found the corridor empty. Snapping back around, he found Harris in her grey suit with her strawberry blonde hair hanging at her shoulders, holding a silenced Glock pointing to the floor.

Her heels clicked against the bare concrete and he stood transfixed by her beauty, craving her touch. With no emotion, she raised the gun, and he watched, his feet fixed on the spot as her lips parted.

"It's time to end this game."

All he heard was a deep thud when a bullet jumped from her gun.

35

London

3rd September

The sun was already heating up the day as they returned to the safe house. With Hotwire bounding up the stairs, his heavy-set frame leading Harris and Fisher up the nine carpeted flights, Swiss, a member of Biggy's troop he'd only introduced five minutes ago, followed at the rear.

Fisher had got to know Hotwire, along with many other members of Biggy's troop, over their four-day journey across the Atlantic to rescue over twenty young women from the grasp of a white slavery ring.

Hotwire was a comedian, as were most of the other men to some degree, but along with the rest, he proved himself a reliable warrior in the field when it counted. Not that Fisher thought he was in any place to judge. Like all those in the SBS he'd met so far, he only knew him by his nickname, given by their comrades in arms. He'd started his career in the Fleet Air Arm of the Royal Navy, and for a reason which Fisher wasn't privy to, there was a long running joke he'd stashed a helicopter somewhere in South America, ready for his eventual retirement from the elite fighting force.

Swiss, much like the other members, wore jeans and a baggy leather jacket that no doubt concealed an arsenal of weapons. The cut of his shaggy hair was just outside of the strict British Military regulations that didn't apply to their community. Knowing Fisher's curiosity about each of the trooper's names, Biggy had already told him Swiss was an inter-service knife throwing champion.

Arriving at the flat, Fisher soon noticed two brown sealed cardboard boxes about the size of milk crates sitting on the kitchen table. On spotting them, Harris turned to Hotwire.

"We checked them over," he said with a nod.

Picking up her iComm, Harris selected an app, then held up the phone as if taking a picture. Watching over her shoulder, an image of the box appeared, then as she touched the screen at the side, a circular menu appeared at her fingertip. After moving her slender digit in a slow concentric circle, the menu cycled through colours of the rainbow whilst at the same time parts of the image highlighted with the corresponding colour. It wasn't until the menu turned deep orange that a rectangle in the centre of the box highlighted in the same iridescent hue.

Seeming happy with the results, she pushed the device back into her pocket and took Hotwire's six-inch blade he'd drawn from an ankle holster.

"It looks like a battery," she said as she sliced the centre of the brown packing tape with the over-sized combat knife.

Fisher moved up beside her, recognising the items from Alan's flat as she lifted them out and laid them on the table.

First came the battered quality street tin, followed by a car key and a spiral bound, hard-cover notepad Fisher hadn't seen before. Harris flicked open the pages of scrawled names and addresses and passed it over, but he kept his attention on the papers and business cards, the piles of takeaway menus dotted with penned phone numbers. Lastly, she placed Alan's laptop on the table.

"It's an address book," Fisher said, looking along the lined pages. "It's got my address. Our address at uni and my last address in Uxbridge." He paused for a moment as he continued to read. "And my parents' old address. George's, and Andrew's. Susie's," he said, narrowing his eyes as he read in silence. His brow furrowed, and he shook his head. "Weird," he added.

Harris lifted her head from the paperwork. "What?"

"There are only addresses of people I know and places I used to go. Even my old depot and a pub I've met Susie at. There's so many places."

"Did you ever meet Alan at any of them?" Harris said, stepping closer.

"A few, but not all," Fisher said, scanning the list with his finger.

"Some of this stuff makes little sense either," she said, pulling out a clean sheet of A4 paper. "The team compiled an inventory, along with interim analysis. There are lots of prostitute's calling cards, and I mean lots. He liked variety, it would seem," she said, raising her brows. "The numbers scribbled on the takeaway menus are all linked to drug dealers. There's a written warning from Tescos about a harassment incident."

"What about the laptop? Did they get access?" Fisher said, interrupting.

"No. It's password protected. We'll send it off soon, but if it's got anything more than standard encryption, it may take a while."

Fisher stepped close to the table and after placing the address book on the side, he repositioned the laptop and opened the screen. It stood out from the rest of the flat's contents because it was old, with two keys faded beyond recognition. Powdery ash filled the plastic seams and cracks at the side of the screen. The display came to life a moment later, bright with the Windows XP logo followed by the login screen and Alan's name pre-filled as it prompted for a password.

"What could the sick fuck have used?" Fisher said under his breath. He typed in his name and pressed enter. The prompt confirmed he'd guessed incorrectly. He tried a few more obvious choices. Alan's date of birth. Car registration number. First pet's name, but when none of them worked, he wondered if those were made up too.

Picking up the address book, he flicked through the pages, examining each one until he reached the end where he started at the beginning again. Harris pulled out her phone and thumbed across the screen.

"They also found binoculars, banks statements, an urn of ashes. Initial tests show they're human remains," Harris said at his side.

"His mother," he replied. "But then again, maybe not."

Harris nodded. "There's a radio scanner, empty cardboard boxes for GPS trackers, leather bound diaries, sealed and unused, an extensive collection of books, mostly about espionage and surveillance."

"Was he a professional?" Fisher said, picking up the fourth diary and rereading the last entry.

"Not in our line of work, no," Harris said as she played her teeth against her bottom lip.

"So where the fuck is the money to pay for all this coming from?"

Harris looked up from her phone. "The answer's in here."

Fisher picked up the address book and opened the first page.

"He's watching something," he said in a low voice.

"Or someone?"

As she spoke, Fisher looked up from the page, his gaze locking with hers as his eyes widened. Placing it beside the laptop, he tapped at the keys and hit return. The screen went black, replaced by a picture of a naked young woman laying on her back with her legs spreadeagled on a wooden floor and her hands beckoning towards the camera.

"Watcher," he said as he turned to Harris, who wore a wry smile.

He turned back to the computer. Aside from the graphic image, the desktop was bare with no icons or toolbars showing.

Fisher pressed the Windows key and the familiar toolbar appeared at the bottom of the screen. Clicking the Start menu to the left and using the trackpad, he found the recent documents link. There was only one entry on the list, a Word document titled *Vigilem*.

Double clicking the link, he caught a delicate waft of Harris's perfume as she moved closer.

Realising it was another journal, or a logbook but with dates against each entry, he scanned the document. The colour drained from his face as he read the entry at the end of the long document.

1st Sept 2010

This will be my last entry. The flat's all organised, and they'll be there from five, just in case he's early. All I have to do is let him in. By the time Andrew arrives it will be done. He'll discover the bodies and it's hello to South America and party central.

"They weren't planning a kidnap. They were going to kill me," he said, barely able to get the words out for the lump in his throat.

"You and someone else," Harris replied, her eyes narrowed.

Fisher shook his head and stood up tall. "But that makes little sense. Why the stun baton?"

Turning away, he stared at the blank kitchen wall, then after a moment he turned to Harris as a thought came to mind. "Andrew was meant to find my body."

Harris sucked in the side of her mouth. "I don't know," she said, shaking her head.

"So who was the other person meant to be?" Fisher asked as he reached up and absently pulled at his hair, turning to the door as Hotwire entered the room holding a small radio, his eyebrows low and not hiding his concern.

"I'm sorry to interrupt, but Biggy spotted two vehicles scoping out the building. We have to move."

Harris nodded, then turned to Fisher. "Grab what you can. We're going," she said just as Hotwire's radio came to life with Biggy's deep voice.

"Two cars. Multiple occupants. I count six and they just rammed through the barrier and into the parking garage. Execute plan Alpha."

36

"Received," Hotwire said, pushing the radio to his mouth as he watched Fisher dump the laptop into the box. "Let's go."

Harris picked up a black holdall from the corner of the room and, before swinging it onto her shoulder, she pulled out an iPad.

"What's escape plan Alpha?" Fisher said, following her out of the kitchen, holding the box.

"Just stick with me," she said, distracted as she tapped the tablet's screen.

Peering over her shoulder he saw the screen arranged with six CCTV images in two rows of three, his focus landing on the first, which showed a group of surly men jumping from two black Mercedes in the building's underground car park. His gaze soon switched to the next image, a small room with a bed in the centre. Moving to the next, he found a stairwell, and in the one after, the fuzzy black and white of a BMW X5. The last pair showed the outside of the apartment door from different angles.

As the last man in the car park slammed the car door shut, he walked around to the boot, where he pulled out a bright red enforcer battering ram.

After hurrying to keep pace with Harris, she stopped at a door, pulling it open to what he soon realised was the plain-looking room from the iPad's screen.

"Put the box down," Harris said, and he did as she asked, despite wondering why they weren't already rushing out of the front door. Taking the tablet as she passed it over, Fisher's eyes narrowed when he looked up from the screen to see Harris with the strap of her holdall across her chest, and Hotwire standing either side of the divan bed, reaching as if about to lift it up.

When movement caused him to glance back at the screen, not able to see the men, his gaze went instead to himself standing in the simple room. Despite looking where the camera must have been, he saw no sign, but the thought vanished when he saw Swiss running down the stairwell.

Looking up and finding the bed angled at forty-five degrees, Fisher drew back as Harris knelt in front of a circular stainless steel hatch with a checker plate surround beneath it. Two dust-covered grab handles stood either side of the hatch's centre.

Fisher stared, eyes wide as she pulled her iComm from her pocket, then pushed it against the centre of the hatch, which with a fluid motion, rose proud of its frame. Replacing the phone back in her combat trousers, the muscles in her arms tensed as she pivoted the circular hatch, lifting it open. With only a quick glance down to whatever was below, she sat, shuffling her legs into the opening before her feet touched metal and she shimmied out of sight.

"Go," Hotwire said, tipping his head toward the hole in the floor. After only a moment's pause as he realised he had to follow and, kicking the box towards the hatch, Fisher dropped to his rear, dangling his legs before he passed the iPad to Harris, who reached up. The room below was an undecorated version of where he sat, apart from the hole in the ceiling and the grey metal ladder reaching to the floor.

"Come on," she said, beckoning him down, but before he could move, he glanced back up, reaching for the box and pulling it toward him. After dropping it into Harris's hands, his feet found the first rung, and he lowered himself just as a loud thud echoed from above.

"They're here," Hotwire said.

"Come on," Harris bellowed. Realising he'd stopped, with a last glance up, Fisher rushed down the remaining rungs to find she'd discarded the box and was pushing Alan's laptop into her holdall.

Just as she'd pulled the zip across, Fisher's gaze landed back on the iPad and five scowling men in the lobby outside their door, whilst in the bottom right-hand picture Swiss lay on the floor clutching his stomach.

"No time," Harris shouted as she swung the holdall back

onto her shoulder, grabbing Fisher by the arm and, without looking back, pulled him into the corridor.

The rest of the walls were raw and unplastered, as he'd expected, the floor pristine chipboard as if the place hadn't been touched since the day it had been built. A clap of muffled thunder echoed in the space but he couldn't see the screen at the angle she held it.

"Hotwire. You there?" Harris called as they rushed through the corridor. Despite no reply, she didn't slow and instead of heading to the front door, she guided Fisher into what had been Fisher's room on the floor above. He'd expected the unpainted walls, but not the reinforced steel door she drew him towards.

Arriving just as the thud of the battering ram vibrated through the walls, Harris looked back for the first time. Reaching inside his jacket, Fisher paused with his hand on the butt of the Glock as he felt the warmth of her hand on his arm.

"You won't need that," she said, and he pulled his hand away just as footsteps rushed from the corridor.

"Sorry. I struggled to get the damn hatch to seal," Hotwire said, a little out of breath and with sweat sheening his forehead.

With no reply, Harris pushed her phone to the door's side where a moment later they heard a faint click, despite the racket coming from above. Grabbing the handle, her muscles tensed as she leaned back, pulling the door open to reveal a short windowless corridor, the walls concrete with a wide set of double doors beside an industrial lift and a red fire door emblazoned with health and safety stickers warning of so many dangers.

Harris urged him through and Fisher did as he was told, with Hotwire following behind. Fisher glanced back as the door slammed shut, his brow furrowing when he found the opening had almost disappeared, camouflaged by an expert's hand as unfinished concrete. The seams were invisible.

With an optimistic bong, the lift doors opened to reveal a

spacious but battered interior. With Fisher's stomach soon telling him they were on their way down, before long the doors opened to reveal an underground service area with a handful of white-lined parking spaces, each empty apart from a bright yellow mini skip overflowing with rubble.

Doors dotted the concrete walls, each plastered with yellow health and safety warning notices. A large red roller shutter dominated the length of the far wall. A second smaller roller door covered a section of wall to his right which Harris was already walking toward.

As she approached with her phone in her hand, Fisher heard the echo of a mechanism and the rollers jerked upward to reveal the bold headlights of the dark blue BMW X5 he guessed he'd seen in the CCTV. Hotwire jogged past Fisher before squeezing between the car and the garage wall and within a few moments, the hazard lights flashed a single blink and the engine roared to life.

After a second more, the car pulled out and stopped, the huge tyres squealing on the grey painted concrete. Harris opened the front passenger door and followed the bag inside as Fisher ran around to the other side. Before Fisher's door slammed closed, the engine roared, and they lurched forward, Fisher grabbing the door handle to brace himself as they raced towards the second set of closed roller doors. When they'd reached two car lengths away and the main rollers hadn't risen, Fisher gripped hard, his hand aching before the slatted metal rushed up and out of the way to reveal the bright daylight of an empty street.

Glancing back, Fisher let out a breath when he saw no one following, but his heart rate jumped when a moment later he heard the squeal of tyres and he span around in his seat to find a white Mercedes saloon rushing onto the road behind them.

"Hotwire," Fisher called with an urgency in his voice as he reached for the door handle.

"Seen it," he replied, his voice barely rising. With the engine screaming as they sped, Fisher fumbled on his seatbelt and watched Hotwire push his cuff to his mouth.

"Mobile hostile right behind. Looks like four up," he said, with Fisher watching Hotwire's expression pinch before relaxing as he spoke again. "Okay. Leave it with me," he replied as he gripped the wheel with both hands. "Biggy's a bit tied up. It looks like one of the X-Rays is determined not to stay down."

"Are they okay?" Fisher said.

Hotwire nodded. "I think so, but he didn't have time to chat," he said, flashing his brow before fumbling in his pocket. Looking through the windscreen, Fisher saw a woman step into the road, her belly round and protruding. With no time for Fisher to call out, Hotwire slammed on the brakes, sending them lurching against their restraints.

With a quick glance over his shoulder as they rushed back up to speed, Fisher stared at the three men scowling from the car, almost at their bumper. A chorus of car horns turned him around as Hotwire swung the car to the right, bullying his way through the thin traffic one handed as he fumbled in his pocket with the other.

"Got it," Hotwire called, grinning as he held up a black mobile phone, paying little attention to the cars scattering left and right. Harris made no effort to intervene as he fumbled with the handset, only looking up just in time to see the red light ahead. With enough space between the two lanes of traffic, Fisher pushed himself back into his seat, not wanting to see what would happen, but before he knew it they were through the lights, just as a double-decker bus shot across their view, leaving Hotwire making only the smallest of adjustments as he pushed the phone to his ear.

Fisher turned back around to find the Mercedes had slowed, but finding no traffic, they were soon bearing down again. He turned to face the front, his gaze falling on Harris reading text on her phone as the car jerked from side to side. About to say something, Hotwire spoke.

"Boss," he said, his voice calm as if he were laying on a lounger with a cocktail in hand. "How's the testing going?" he added, palming the steering wheel in a turn, sending the tyres squealing as they left the main road. "Great. I've got a bit of a sitch here and Biggy is otherwise disposed. Are there any assets nearby who can lend a hand?"

Fisher glanced over to Harris, still paying no attention.

"That's great. Thanks," Hotwire eventually said and, much to Fisher's relief, he tossed the phone into the centre console and took the steering wheel in both hands. His grip was short-lived, moving instead to tap at the built-in Sat Nav.

"Can one of you do me a favour?" Hotwire said, his voice still flat as the screen lit up.

Fisher nodded, catching Hotwire's eye in the mirror.

"Keep shouting out what they're doing back there?"

"Sure," Fisher said, rapidly nodding before he twisted in his seat for a better view. "He's getting fucking close."

"That's it. Keep it up."

Fisher's back pressed against his door as they sped through another sharp right turn, his eyes going wide when a dull pop came from behind. Relieved to find a puddle of white liquid in their wake and a flattened container against the road, he tried his best not to linger on the woman on the pavement, staring wide-eyed with her hand at her mouth.

"Still very close, but holding," Fisher shouted, reminding himself of his task.

"Are the occupants doing anything?" Hotwire said, as if they were chatting over a pint.

Fisher leaned closer to the rear window.

"No. They look a little bored," he finally replied, then glanced to the windscreen at a loud tone and found the app which had guided them to the safety deposit boxes on the screen. His gaze didn't linger long when a flurry of horns sounded from behind.

"They've hit a car," Fisher said, then paused. "It looks like they're alright and they're coming back on us. Fast."

Another tone came from the front and despite knowing he shouldn't, he looked at the map zooming out and rotating one hundred and eighty degrees, where a second car appeared with a green line strung between them. Peering along the street ahead, he found it blocked with stationary cars, the pavement on either side choked with pedestrians.

Fumbling for his gun, Fisher drew in a deep breath.

37

"Roger that, Highfall," Hotwire said into his cuff before he cocked his head toward his passengers. "We've got help. I just need to figure out how to reach them."

Fisher was about to question how long they could keep those chasing behind at bay, but before he had a chance, Hotwire slammed on the brakes.

"Hold on," he called out and about to stop, he jammed the gear stick into reverse, building their speed in the opposite direction. The chassis rocked as he came off the gas whilst at the same time yanking the wheel and pulling the handbrake, spinning the car.

Fearing Hotwire had lost control, Fisher pushed his arm out against the driver's seat as they lurched to the right. With his gaze falling on Harris, he double took when he saw her reading her phone, just bracing herself with a hand against the door.

Through a cacophony of complaining horns and somehow still with a decent head of speed, their car raced in the opposite direction to where they'd been heading.

"I vote for getting there in one piece," Fisher called out, his eyes wide as they faced down the white Mercedes rushing towards them. Glancing in the mirror, hoping for confidence in Hotwire's eyes, instead he found a smirk on his weathered face. Taking no comfort in the expression, he tore himself away, bracing himself against the front seat as he forced his eyes closed.

When the impact he'd expected hadn't come, Fisher pushed his eyes open to find only the normal traffic on the road, the back of the Mercedes instead getting smaller in the mirror as smoke rose from its tyres whilst swerving in a failed attempt to mirror Hotwire's J-Turn.

"You're losing them," Fisher called out, not hiding the joy from his voice.

"Shit," came Hotwire's reply as Fisher felt their speed

slow, then watched as the white car soon grew larger in the mirror.

Back up to a decent speed within a few moments, Hotwire guided them along the dual carriageway, slipping left and right amongst the thin traffic, their movement almost graceful despite his glances back and forth between the mirror and the windscreen.

With every change of lane, Fisher turned in his seat to find the Mercedes had grown closer, turning back many times just as Hotwire manoeuvred them out of a near miss, squeezing between the traffic or perilously close to the parked cars.

Their flowing dance soon took them around a tall London bus just as the traffic ahead slowed. With the bus in the way, Fisher was blind, his view filled with riveted red metal as he twisted around in every direction, willing the traffic to speed up. Eventually getting ahead, he caught sight of a rusting transit van double parked with men in dust-covered overalls throwing rubbish into the back.

Hotwire soon positioned the car in the inside lane, then, to the blaring of horns, bullied the drivers to move over as he somehow squeezed past on the right, mounting the curb and almost touching the barrier separating the two opposing lanes. Letting go of his breath once they'd passed the obstruction still in one piece, Fisher turned back to the traffic, which had almost stopped as fists shook with the distance between them growing.

The sharp grind of metal on metal announced the Mercedes had also passed the shocked drivers and was catching up with ease.

"They're gaining on us," Fisher called out, his tone high as he leaned over the back of his seat.

"That's the plan," Hotwire replied, unable to stop himself from laughing.

"No, I mean it. They're getting too close," Fisher said, adding an urgency to his voice.

Glancing the way they were heading, Hotwire's eyes went wide when he realised they were almost at their bumper.

"Shit," he said with the speedo needle rising, then dropping as they approached a junction, the road splitting left to an ever-narrowing street whilst the dual carriageway continued right.

Harris looked out of the windscreen before leaning forward and glancing in her side mirror.

"How long do they need to set up?" she said, her voice as calm as if asking what was for breakfast.

Hotwire shook his head and glanced at the dashboard. "About ten minutes."

"We can't be early," she replied and Fisher followed her gaze to the GPS screen Fisher hadn't realised Hotwire had programmed. The time to the destination showed two minutes.

"I guess we'll take the scenic route," Hotwire said, his voice tailing off when a sudden jolt from behind sent each of them looking backwards and the Mercedes lurching forward before the two cars connected.

Gripping the wheel, Hotwire pushed his foot down, building the gap before he chose the left-hand lane.

"Do another left," Fisher called out, concentrating on the screen. Harris sat up in her seat, as if taking notice for the first time.

"That leads into the town. We need to keep away from people. Go off road," Harris said, shaking her head and pointing to a sprawling expanse of green ahead.

Barely slowing, the twenty-inch wheels bumped up the kerb and a moment later Hotwire rotated a gloss black selector on the centre console as the car cruised across the undulating ground, pitching them up and down in their seats. Seeming not to have noticed the road bridge way off to their left, Hotwire guided them towards a stream criss-crossing the diagonal of the park. Fisher hoped it was shallow.

The tempo of their vertical motion slowed as Hotwire corrected their path to avoid dog walkers whilst Fisher watched the Mercedes bounce over ruts the X5 had no trouble with. Only moments before the BMW's wheels got wet did the driver of the other car realise it wouldn't end well if they tried to follow.

Only just able to correct their way out of a skid, the Mercedes changed course towards the gravel road leading to a bridge, whilst the BMW rolled through the stream with water fanning out either side and steam hissing from the brakes.

"This is our chance to get away," Fisher said, craning his neck to their pursuers before turning to find Harris shaking her head.

"They'll find us again," she said, looking down at her iComm. "Besides, we may get some useful intel."

Just as the ground beneath them became smooth after bouncing onto a road and turning right, slowing as the narrow park gates approached, Hotwire's foot hovered over the accelerator a little longer than Fisher wished to let the Mercedes close up.

About to press into a gap in the traffic, Hotwire slammed on the brakes, propelling Fisher into his belt when he spotted an elderly man crossing the road in front of them.

Glancing out of the rear again, Fisher's eyes went wide, finding the view almost completely white, apart from the blue of the passenger's narrowed eyes as he pushed his hand inside his jacket.

"Go," Fisher called, ducking low in the seat just as their car leapt forward before veering to the left, weaving amongst the traffic. Taking comfort in their renewed speed, Fisher lifted his head, watching the houses lining the road become the rising ramp for the motorway, his stomach only sinking when he saw the sea of red brake lights on the horizon.

When Hotwire made no complaint at the sight, Fisher looked back over his shoulder as their pursuers joined the wide road. Jerking the car to the right, then left and back again, Hotwire danced them between the building traffic, ignoring the hand gestures and horns.

Hearing the first call of sirens, it wasn't long before the flashing blue lights of the white Volvo XC70 cleared a route through the traffic. With the Mercedes nowhere to be seen, no one spoke as the two-tones grew louder, then without prompt Harris spoke, although by her demeanour Fisher realised she wasn't talking to either of them.

Hotwire slowed, placing them in the middle lane as they passed the first marker for the junction at what felt like a snail's pace.

Fisher watched the Volvo match their speed, hanging back a couple of car lengths from the BMW as they ate up the empty lane, then as Hotwire pulled them into the inside lane, the police car followed. Counting down the seconds until the junction, Fisher watched the blue lights reflecting from the inside of the car as they took the off-ramp whilst the XC70 continued on.

With a deep breath, he realised Harris must have called them off. Remembering their pursuers, Fisher whirled his head around to find the Mercedes racing past a tall van and gaining on them.

"They're still with us," Fisher shouted, turning back when he felt the car slow, only to find a short line of cars stopped at red lights. Gripping the seat back, they swerved to the left, their tyres crunching over the gravel-strewn hard shoulder as they shot past the queue and into the path of a seven and a half tonne lorry heading from the right and into the same space.

Not daring to look, Fisher gritted his teeth, but hearing the blast of an air horn, the impact didn't come.

"They're still there," Fisher said between his heavy breaths, whilst trying to hold tight with their car speeding around the roundabout before rising up the ramp and heading the way they'd just come. Somehow, the Mercedes soon appeared in the rearview with an arm reaching out of the passenger door and pointing something dark towards them.

"Gun," Fisher called, only to turn around to find the traffic ahead slowing to a crawl.

38

"Go," Harris said, her voice raised, but despite her command, the car didn't speed before an unmistakable gunshot lit their senses, followed in quick succession by a second.

Feeling the round's impact through the seat, Fisher looked for where it hit as pressing down the horn, Hotwire veered the car to the left despite the road blocked by slowing cars.

"Down there," Harris said, her words sharp as she pointed further left and a narrow gap between the cars and the verge. Without reply, Hotwire tugged the steering wheel, the cars parting a little more and within a moment they'd mounted the curb as they raced lopsidedly between the traffic and the Armco barrier. Dust and debris kicked into the air, obscuring Fisher's view.

"There," he shouted, pointing to a gap.

"Seen it," Hotwire said, cutting him off before slowing as he readied for the turn, but as the speed bled they were shunted from behind, forcing him to grapple with the wheel, knowing even the slightest touch with the barrier would send them ricocheting off into the traffic and it would all be over.

"Hold tight," Hotwire shouted, but leaving no time for Fisher to renew his grip, the car veered to the right, pushing him into his seat as he squeezed his eyes shut. When the impact he'd thought so inevitable didn't come, his eyes went wide as the road opened out in front of them.

With a shake of his head as he turned to find the Mercedes right behind somehow, Fisher had no time to linger on the gun pointing at him before they raced down the exit ramp and were swerving along a residential street to extend the gap between them.

Before long the houses and shops thinned, industrial units taking their place as the road narrowed and Hotwire slowed to a cautious pace, despite Fisher's constant reminders of their shadow. Soon their route headed between a pair of partially demolished buildings on either side, both sites surrounded by black hoarding.

Arriving between the two buildings, Hotwire slowed, shedding speed as if to let the Mercedes catch right up, until taking him by surprise, he sped, pinning Fisher back in his seat as he stared at the car behind.

Before the chasing car could follow between the buildings, a flatbed lorry rolled out from behind the hoarding, its air brakes hissing as it came to a stop, blocking the road.

Smoke billowed from the Mercedes' tyres as they squealed, just as four black silhouetted figures came from nowhere and surrounded the car.

Looking ahead, Fisher caught Hotwire's wry smile.

"Fuck," Fisher said after taking a long breath, not caring if the others heard.

"Are you okay?" Harris asked with a glance over her shoulder as they rejoined the motorway. Fisher eventually nodded, and slowing his breath, he watched as she reached into her footwell and drew up the laptop, handing it over. "Keep yourself busy."

With a flicker of excitement, he opened up the lid and scanned the document.

"There's over four hundred entries," Fisher said, looking up.

"You've got plenty of time," she replied. "We have a two-hour drive ahead."

"Where are we going?"

"The nearest thing I have to a home," Harris replied, looking at her phone.

"You have a house?" Fisher replied with a raise of his brow.

"Sort of. I don't get back as often as I like, but sometimes I need somewhere to switch off."

He knew there was no point in asking where it was. Instead, he stared at the fields and trees rushing by with a rising excitement at what her place might be like.

With a last glance over his shoulder and finding no cars

racing up behind them, he scrolled to the first entry.

39

3rd February 2002

I found the perfect car. I easily covered it with what I had left of the money the researchers gave me for taking copies of my old diaries, together with half of this month's wages. Its first journey will be to Cardiff after I pick it up tomorrow!

I can't wait!

4th February 2002

I surprised George at eight o'clock in the morning. It's like it was meant to be. His door was unlocked, but when I found his room empty, I panicked that he'd pulled the night before and was sleeping somewhere else. I sat in the chair in the corner of his room thinking about where he could be and a few minutes later, he walks in. He'd been in the toilet!

All bleary-eyed, he climbs back into bed, not noticing me until I called out his name, absolutely scaring the living crap out of him! It makes me laugh just thinking about it again.

Anyway, he must have been pretty shocked because he said some nasty things, although by the time I'd taken him out for a spin in my new wheels, then into town for breakfast, he'd got over it. He apologised for what he said and we got wasted with Susie and James, who joined us just after lunch.

Oh, and George seems to be over that girl. I can't even remember her name now.

Many more good times to come!

28th February 2002

I sent the first log over and I got an email back from Dave, the researcher, saying that I need to write more detail about each of the guys, otherwise there's nothing for them to analyse for the experiment. I'll do my best. I hope this isn't going to become a pain in the ass!

5th March 2002

I spoke to George a couple of times, but there's nothing really to report. He says things are going well. I told him I'm missing him but he said I can't come up every single month or I'd lose my job. He also told me not to surprise him again. I'm not sure why, we had the best time.

Who said making money was difficult? I bought some rad stuff this week, and I ended up staying awake all night playing on the Xbox. It was only when my alarm went off I realised. That shift was a real bitch!

I really want to tell George about all the cool things I've got now, but that would just be stupid because they'd stop paying me. I wonder if I keep this up, perhaps I could leave Tesco. They'd fight to keep me, of course, but they'd get over it, eventually.

31st March 2002

Okay. So ditching the day job is not an option. Dave thinks my friends will ask too many questions and it would ruin the experiment.

April 2002

Nothing to report. Spoke with George once. Going up to see them in May. Do I still get paid?

Apparently not!

8th May 2002

I spent the weekend in Cardiff. We got drunk like every other time.
I'm not really sure what I need to be writing here.
The only news was that James's friend Andrew couldn't make it because he was working. George came out, of course, and so did James, with Susie tagging along on the second night after she came back from a weekend at home with her parents.
I'm slowly working on her and playing the long game.
George was the same as usual. James somehow managed to get us

all free tickets to the cinema, and we watched The Bourne Identity. I'm guessing he knows the guy on the door. It was a cracking film. I love spies and shit.

2nd June 2002

Nothing to report.
George said he was desperately trying to make up for not going to his lectures all year. I think he must be exaggerating. Who doesn't go to any lectures?
Either way, he told me in no uncertain terms not to come up until he says it's okay.
Anyway, I upgraded the car today. It's going to be a surprise when I see him next!

July 2002

George is not around this month. He's been given a second chance for his exams and says some bullshit that he's really trying this time.

3rd August 2002

George came home for the summer and so I get him to myself for a couple of months. There are no plans for the others to come down.
He seems a little distant, like he's changed, but I think everything will be just fine after a couple of days back.

5th September 2002

What a great summer. We did loads of cool things together and had a really great time. The only thing that ruined it was some comment about wanting to get back to Cardiff.
Dave told me I need to step up my game or the money's going to stop. I need to write more. It's a drag, but the cash is awesome.

11th September 2002

I gave George a lift back to Cardiff in the A-Mobeel! It was nice to open her up on the motorway. Afterwards we had a quiet drink that evening in his new flat, just the two of us, because everyone else is back tomorrow. It's a shame I've got to get home for a shift. I can't miss another.

25th October 2002

George is coming home!!! He's just told me on the phone!

After a year of doing nothing, they've kicked him out!!

I'm going to head up, help him pack, and give him a lift back. The boys are going to be together again.

2nd November 2002

Fuck it.

Once again, something gets in the way. George has decided to stay up in fucking Cardiff with fucking James and Susie. He got offered some random job in a call centre, which he said he didn't even apply for. Sorry, I don't fucking believe him. No, actually, I'm not fucking sorry. Fuck you, George.

27th December 2002

He only came home for two days. Two days! I wish he'd stayed at uni now. His fucking job is getting right in the way. In fact, it's even worse than that. It's menial shit, but he loves it. Can this get any worse?

2nd January 2003

How depressing is spending New Year's Eve on your own? The answer is very depressing and I should know! At least I got a call from George asking me if I wanted to come up to Cardiff because he had the house to himself and a few days off. I'm jumping in the car now!

4th January 2003

That was a brilliant couple of days, but I forgot to ring in sick at work.

I was hammered when I got a phone call from my boss wondering where I was. If George wasn't there, I would have told him where to stick his job.

When I got home, I remembered I'd got myself a nice souvenir. Whilst George was having a dump, I went into Susie's room and pulled out a lacy pair of knickers from the top drawer. George almost caught me. It was a close-run thing.

<u>February 2003</u>

Nothing to report.

Fisher looked up from the screen, rubbing his eyes as he pulled the ringing phone from his pocket. It was Susie.

Drawing a deep breath, he forced a smile. "Hey you," he said.

"Your phone's been off. I've been trying to get you. Were you there? Are you okay? Sorry, stupid question," she said, her voice quietening.

"I'm okay. No, I wasn't there. Are you okay, Suse?"

"Yes. My parents are treating me like a princess, which is going to get annoying very quickly. They want to take me away to Norfolk for a couple of weeks to give me some space," she replied.

"You should go. I think it would do you some good to get away for a little while."

The line went quiet, but from her slow breath, he knew she was still on the line.

"You're working for them, aren't you?" Susie said slowly, as if considering her words. Fisher didn't know what to say, so he kept quiet. "I'll take that as a yes."

"I've got no choice," Fisher replied. "Take your parents' advice and get away."

"Okay," she replied, sounding distant.

"One more thing," Fisher said as a thought occurred to him.

"Yes?"

"The guy who wanted to you to tell him all about me, can you describe him?"

"Sure. He was tanned, fit, about mid-thirties, but hot with it. He had a foreign accent. Either Spanish or South American, I'm not sure which."

"Thanks, Suse, and I'll call you soon," Fisher said.

"James, be safe and I love you."

"I love you, too," Fisher replied, hanging up as the rolling motorway turned to an A road between empty ploughed fields.

1st March 2003

I've been told to look more closely at the trio. Apparently, they think it will work better if I just focus on George, Susie, and James. I'm heading up this weekend and at least I know they're not interested in Andrew. Not really sure what they mean when he said 'more information', but all I can do is my best.

13th March 2003

George is George. There's nothing I don't already know about him.

Susie, she was looking hot. We all ended up in the pub for the entire day, talking shit, drinking beer. I hope no one saw me staring at her. Sorry, but it's biology. It's not my fault, I'm programmed like this. The feminists have no idea of our struggle.

James. Now what can I say about him? He's an oddball. He's likeable though. Maybe that's it. Maybe he's just too nice. Come to think of it, every fucker seems to like him. They all seem to want to do stuff for him, but, get this, he never takes them up on it. He's a goody two shoes. Still, it's not in a boring way. He likes a good laugh, but I think I'm the only one who doesn't love him.

14th March 2003

I've finally figured out why Susie's so frigid. I think she's got it for James, although he can't see it.

They seem to be almost inseparable. Every time I go up, they're together. But they're not shagging and that's the weird bit. If I were fucking her, then I wouldn't leave her side. I wouldn't let her out of the bedroom. But they're not.

I reckon you take Susie out of the picture, he'll be a lot different. I reckon that's why he's so nice.

12th April 2003

An odd thing happened while we were in this club. Everyone was having a good time. I was standing on the balcony just checking everyone out and I happened to see James and Susie dancing all nicey, nicey before this really big guy comes up behind Susie and pinched her ass. That's what it looked like, anyway. She took exception to it, of course, but the guy thought it was hilarious. He was really drunk. That goes without saying.

He then tried to grab her tits. There was no one else on the dance floor paying any attention, but James just went up to him, grabbed his bare arm. I thought I was about to watch James having the shit kicked out of him, but the guy bent down as James talked into his ear. After a few seconds, he stood back up, then said something to Susie and headed off the dance floor toward the exit.

Susie turned around to James and seemed to be as surprised as I was, then hugged him. Bloody weird. I'm desperate to know what he said to the big guy, but when I asked him, he just shrugged and said he was so pissed he didn't remember any of it.

24th May 2003

I've just heard Susie's been mugged, and she's in hospital. I'm going to head up at the weekend. It's a good excuse for a visit.

26th May 2003

It turns out she had to have an op to fix the bad break, and she's also found out she has some issue with pain or something. I don't know exactly what, but she'll be bedridden for a few weeks. It'll be interesting to see how James is without her.

It's quite funny because he was meant to go with her to some afternoon casting for a crap play, but he got held up at uni. I guess she wouldn't have been mugged if he was there. Even funnier, turns out she got the wrong date for the casting anyway.

14th June 2003

Bored. George is busy with work. Susie is laid up in bed and James won't come out without his little princess. Maybe I better check next time I come up.

15th June 2003

Eventually, I managed to convince James to come out to the cinema whilst Susie was sleeping. He said he'd sort out the tickets and it was a great way to find out who it was he knows. Anyway, despite James asking me to get some popcorn, I followed him. It turns out he didn't know anyone. He told them he was the Area Manager's son and said he was allowed free tickets. The guy behind the desk fell for it and didn't even bat an eyelid. I think I might try that at our local multiplex.

We watched Kill Bill. It was a good film and I'm a little surprised, but I actually had a good time with James on his own. We even stopped off for a quick beer on the way home. I need to make sure I don't get infected with his niceness and become one of his sycophantic zombies!

1st July 2003

Susie and James have gone back to their parent's homes for summer and with George working all the time, there's nothing to report, although I got a bonus for the last one. I guess Dave likes the film reviews.

August 2003

Nothing to report. George is still in Cardiff. I guess that's his home now.

14th September 2003

The gang's back in town and I headed up the week uni started. Everyone was a little surprised to see me so quickly. Susie's all healed now. James is still loved by everyone and George seemed pleased enough to see me. Apparently, James and Susie spent some time together over the holidays, but when I asked him if he was shagging her yet, he told me he still wasn't. He seemed to take a bit of offence at what I said, so I guess I better be a bit more careful.

<u>8th December 2003</u>

I got a phone call today from Dave. Apparently, I'm not making enough effort and they want to stop paying me until I submit my next observation.

Not being funny, but I'm getting bored with this now. It doesn't feel right putting some of this shit down on paper and, to be honest, I don't really see the point. The money does come in handy, though.

<u>4th January 2004</u>

Back in Cardiff for New Years.

Andrew's up too and I found him having a go at James. It was kinda weird watching someone pissed off with him. I don't know what it was about, but they seemed to clear it up quickly enough. Something to do with not paying the rent money, I guess.

In the end, we all went out to a club, and we met up with loads of drama student friends of Susie's. Wow, she knows some fit girls. I had far too much to drink, so did George, and I ended up having a really strange drunken conversation with him. We were talking about James and some weird trick he can do.

When he wakes up, I'll ask George about it.

<u>5th January 2004</u>

George denies saying anything about James and shrugged it off as just pissed talk. I'm not so sure, but my head hurts too much to think about it now.

<u>6th January 2004</u>

We did have the conversation, I'm sure. My head's clear now and I remember everything. When I asked him again, he said he doesn't remember anything, but then he said if there was anything to say, then it should come from James. Not that there was anything to say that he knew of.

Does he think I'm stupid?

This secret thing they're all keeping from me is pissing me off. I gotta go home now, but I'll call James about this when I get back.

7th January 2004

I didn't call James despite it running through my head and not being able to think about anything else. If there's nothing to find out, then I'm going to look like a right prick. I'll talk to him when I go up next month. We're going to some beer festival at the uni or something.

16th February 2004

I talked to James today after a few sherbets and told him I knew they were all keeping something from me and I didn't like it. After a little while and a few more beers, he said he did have a secret, but rather than telling me, he got up and walked over to some German fella, shook his hand, and got two free pints.

We didn't speak again for the rest of the night, and I'm more confused than ever. What's the secret? Everyone wants to give him stuff?

1st March 2004

Dave called me. He sounded pretty excited and told me to concentrate on James. It must be something to do with his thing. But what is his thing?

2nd March 2004

I can't sleep. Why can't I see it?
He's a nice guy, everyone likes him. Everyone does what he wants. Is that it?

Does he have some paranormal power to make people like him... Like a hypnotist or something. I rang Dave. He wouldn't say much. He just said to ask him to do stuff for me, but I'm not sure what he means?

6th April 2004

When you know something's up and you just watch him, it's obvious. He does it all the time. Maybe it's his winning personality or maybe it's witchcraft, but everything changes when he touches someone. He'll shake someone's hand and their expression changes. They relax. He touches people a lot. He shakes a lot of hands. People he just meets.

He bought a TV at the weekend and George told me he got it half price. Bloody half price.

8th April 2004

It looks like it's all change at the university where they're doing the research. Dave's gone, replaced by some funny talking guy, Angelo. I think he's Spanish. Anyway, he says things are going to be different. The first thing to happen is I get more money!!

He also wants me to ask James if he keeps in touch with some woman from his childhood. That's all the detail he'd give me. Not sure how I'm going to slip that one into conversation!

30th April 2004

I'm moving to London. I've got no choice. Angelo says they want more observations, especially over the next few months, and now that James is coming back home soon, they want me to stick close to him. They've sorted out a flat and everything, but I'm keeping my place up here. It doesn't seem right, but I'm not supposed to tell anyone I've moved. What's really odd, though, is that he told me I have to get a new job at Tesco's, somewhere local. That's a pain because the university is now paying me double what I get there a month.

11th June 2004

The new place is nice, and it's bloody big. I've got a safe box which I've been told to keep some things in, including a phone. I can't see why that's necessary for the experiment, but it pays the bills. And then some.

<u>12th June 2004</u>

The stuff James can do is bloody amazing. I can't believe it's taken me so long to figure it out. Why the hell didn't he tell me? It's so obvious and all the other guys know.

He could get anything, but instead he's spent all this time just doing a boring IT course. If it was me, I'd be president of the world by now.

I asked how he does it, but even though he was pretty pissed, he didn't give anything away. He says he just can.

I had a little look around his room when he was out at uni the other day. I couldn't find anything out of the ordinary. No special rocks, or rings, or anything! I didn't even find any porn or naked pictures of Susie. Oh yeah, they're not shagging. Whatever!

<u>13th June 2004</u>

Their exams are over and we went clubbing in Cardiff. They wouldn't let us in the VIP lounge at first, but of course James convinced the bouncers he was loaded, and we got in. It was a reasonable night, and I managed to get off with some Russian bird.

I couldn't think how to get to speak to James about this woman, the one from his childhood. We don't really talk about that sort of shit. I thought it would sound well weird if it just came out of nowhere. Eventually I spoke about my family and stuff, and he says it was just him and his parents, no one else to talk of.

<u>21st June 2004</u>

George called me. James's parents have gone missing. I've got this niggling feeling that something ain't right here. I can't help thinking my employers have something to do with this, a bit like what happened with Susie.

I called James, and I was going to tell him everything, but he didn't answer. George told me he can't get hold of him either. Andrew had told us he wants to be left alone.

Fisher looked up from the keyboard, turning to look out of the car window, unable to read on as his head filled with memories of the time.

Shaking his head, he didn't want to believe Alan had been watching him all that while. Could it be a work of fiction, or an elaborate cover for something else he was doing?

As more questions rushed into his mind, Fisher did his best to dismiss the thoughts. Convincing himself Alan wasn't clever enough to make it all up. There had to be someone else in charge.

As the thought solidified in his head, Fisher slid the cursor down the side of the screen and scrolled past five years of entries.

3rd July 2010

They want me to see someone in London. He's a specialist. They think that based on my observations, they've figured out a way to stop James from using his influence. They want to try it out on me and have asked if it was okay. It's not invasive, they said, which I think means they don't need to cut me open, so I agreed and I'm heading down to a place in Harley Street next week.

11th July 2010

It was weird and I don't remember much, just this bright light. They told me it was some kind of hypnotherapy and he set up some defence against suggestions outside of my mind. I don't feel any different, though. I do, however, remember the guy's name because it was kinda weird. Dr Francis Norman Stein. He gave me a card just in case I get any side effects.

12th July 2010

I've been told things are changing and I need to step it up a gear, again.

Now it's not just casual observation.

They delivered a load of gear and there's some pretty cool stuff in there. They want me to follow him around, but I won't need to do too much because we're all going camping in Snowdon next month. I'll have three days to write about, so I upgraded my phone. It's got real keys, which means I can type away anywhere so I don't forget anything.

31st July 2010

He just goes to work, that's it. Apart from that, he'll have the odd beer with Andrew, but that's all. I haven't seen him doing anything with his influence over the last twenty days.

10th August 2010

God, Andrew and James don't half talk a load of old nonsense when they're together. James was saying that he wouldn't use his influence to get women. Ha, I'm with Andrew on that. I'd be like a rat up a drainpipe.

Now I'm knackered, what with listening to their drivel and trying to keep in range of the transmitter in their car, all without being seen. I just parked up somewhere in Llanberis and will give it five more minutes before I join them at the campsite.

Fisher looked up from the computer, the conversation with Andrew still as clear as if it were this morning.

He'd give anything to be back at that time again. He'd stop Susie from getting kidnapped and then deal with Alan.

Feeling anger growing in the pit of his stomach, he looked across at the rolling hills. Who the hell were these people Alan was working for?

When no answer sprang to mind, he took a deep breath and turned back to the screen.

10th August 2010

I'm sitting on the bog in a pub in Snowdon and I've just witnessed the full power of what James can do. This really scary bloke looked like he was going to batter us all. James tried to reason with him but got nowhere. Then he did it. It was so simple and so obvious. Never have I seen a clearer demonstration of the power of his talent. They touched, and the bruiser ran off like a scared little girl. He thought he was going to get creamed. Ha. By James. Ha. It was awesome!

I wouldn't like to be on the receiving end, that's for sure. Ah yes, and I managed to grab a quick squeeze from Susie too!

11th August 2010

This trip is turning out to be a gold mine. James explained all about the consequences of using his ability. He says he needs to be really careful and think about what people will do with their absolute belief in what he says. I think that's why it's been so hard to see him using it. He's scared of what could happen. He thinks he killed his parents. I'm not so sure.

12th August 2010

The fun ended early. Susie disappeared. I reckon she's pissed off somewhere because it's her time of the month or something. Bloody women. I was really getting somewhere. Fucking bitch. I hope she didn't see me staring at her!

17th August 2010

I haven't been able to get hold of James and so I spoke to Andrew, only to find out he's been in an accident. No one's saying anything else though. He's at the Royal London in Whitechapel, but I've been told I can't see him.

25th August 2010

Phone call from Andrew, James is out of the coma. I'll call him in a bit.

I spoke to James, and he said he was going away.
    He brushed me off and seemed preoccupied.

At least he's alright.

26th August 2010

I can't get hold of him. I even went over to his flat, but it's all locked up and his phone was on the table. I guess that's why he hasn't called me. I called Andrew, but he didn't know anything. At least that's what he said.

Angelo called; he wants to know where James is. I told him I didn't know. I told him he didn't sleep at his flat last night. How the hell does he know James has gone away?

I think they think I've stopped helping them. They told me they know about that kid, Stuart. They told me they know what I did and I need to find James or they're going to tell the police. I told them he's probably looking for her in bloody Snowdon, knowing him.

28th August 2010

I've still heard nothing and I've been told it's time to change what we're doing. The time for watching is over and they're moving to the next phase of the operation.

When we next find out where James is, I have to arrange to meet and then they will send some people to pick him up.

I'm not sure about that and I told Angelo. He told me I had no choice because I'd already gone too far. If I did it, they would get me settled in another country, South America maybe. It wasn't worth considering what would happen if I didn't go through with it, apparently. I kinda believe them. It's been a long while since I last thought the programme was still being run by a university. They're giving me too much money for that to be true.

I asked what would happen to him once they had him, but he said all I needed to do was to point him out. I asked if they would hurt him. He said of course not. They need him alive.

I thought about just telling James everything so he could get away, but then this last eight years would have been wasted. Anyway, would he be able to save me from these guys? Would he even want to help save me after everything I've done?

Andrew called. Susie's safe and James will be back soon.

"They weren't going to kill me," Fisher said into the silence.

"Sorry?" Harris replied, turning to face him.

"Call Clark and get them to search the building where Andrew was killed. They were going to plant two bodies to make it look like I died, and I guess Alan too?"

Harris shook her head. "We would have figured out it wasn't you," she said, staring back with such an intent.

"Maybe they were going to burn the place down, or they were just buying time," he replied.

Harris turned in her seat.

"I'll get it checked."

40

"They found two bodies," Harris said an hour later as Fisher stopped re-reading the diary. "One was about your height, the other Alan's. They were in a car a street away. It was the smell that drew them in. There were a load of plumbing tools in the car, so they checked around the house and found the gas was rigged to blow just before seven. Someone hadn't primed it."

"That was when Andrew was due to arrive," Fisher said, pushing the laptop closed just as his iComm beeped. A message from George confirmed Andrew's funeral would be in ten days' time.

Fisher looked out of the tinted window, but rather than taking in what he saw, he kept telling himself they shouldn't be running away to somewhere safe. He should be at home comforting his friends, and being comforted.

He wanted to see Andrew's parents. He wanted to talk it through and tell them how amazing Andrew was. He wanted them to know what their son had done for him and that he hadn't felt a thing at the end.

He wanted everyone to know what Alan put them through.

But it wasn't just Alan. He knew that now. Someone was manipulating him, just like the hired muscle that seemed to be everywhere Fisher went. Someone was directing their every move too.

"We should be looking for the mole, not running away," Fisher said.

"I know," Harris said, turning in the front passenger seat to look him in the eye. "But we're not the best people to do that."

"I should be with my friends, or what's left of them," Fisher replied, staring out the window.

"And they'd get to you within minutes, with your friends in the crossfire."

"I know all this," he snapped. "Sorry," he quickly added

as he looked over. "I thought we were all powerful. Our employer, I mean."

"They're just people, like..." she said. "Like me."

Fisher paused. She'd been right not to say they were people like him. They weren't. He wasn't like everyone else and it was those differences that caused the bad things to happen. When Susie went missing, he'd had to make the same choice. To run and hide for the rest of his life, hoping others would save the day. Or use his gift to control his destiny.

Even now, with Harris's help, he felt as if he could achieve anything.

Raising his chin as he looked at the countryside racing past the window, he'd decided. However high the pyramid rose, he'd make them pay for what they'd done and stop it from happening again.

Taking a deep breath, he felt himself calm and a thought sprang to mind.

"There's an easy way we can find the mole," he said, turning to Harris with a smile.

"No," she said, her voice firm even before she'd turned around.

"What...?" Fisher replied, sure she must have missed what he'd said.

"I already know what you're going to suggest," she said.

"How?" he said, sitting up in his seat.

"Despite the short time we've known each other, I can read you like a book," she said, turning to face ahead.

"And what a time we've had!" he said, laughing, unable to stop himself from remembering the adventures of the past fifteen days whilst hoping Harris was doing the same.

Replaying the near kiss whilst they sat together in the British High Commission in Barbados, their reducing speed and the delicate odour of freshly cut grass pulled him back into the moment as their tyres crunched against the gravel driveway winding its way to a white cottage criss-crossed with dark oak beams against a backdrop of the rolling countryside.

Manicured flowerbeds bordered each side of the house,

blooming with a rainbow of splendour. A striped lawn butted, ruler-straight, against the gravel drive.

"Home, sweet home?" Fisher said and Harris nodded with a grin, the likes of which he'd seldom seen as she jumped out of the car, almost skipping to the front door which stood ajar. Fisher, holding the laptop to his chest, followed.

The door opened all the way just as she arrived, and without hesitation or a backwards look, she flew into the arms of a wrinkled, grey-haired lady. Their hug lasted longer than Fisher had expected before they released and the woman turned toward Fisher.

Harris gestured in his direction. "Aunt May, this is James. He's a friend of mine. James, this is Aunt May."

Fisher extended his hand as the woman untied a bright floral pinafore from around her waist before stepping forward to offer her hand.

Her smile took over her weathered face and after the introductions were over, Aunt May seemed keen to leave, telling Harris she'd stocked the cupboards for a few days. Despite the offer of tea, she rushed away with little more than a glance at Hotwire, still sitting in the car.

"I don't know what I'd do without her," Harris said, watching from the doorway as the old woman headed away down the path. "Aunt May and her husband look after the place."

"I thought your family was dead," Fisher said.

"She's not an aunt by blood, but she's as good as. They look after me, and it's nice to let someone do that once in a while."

Fisher nodded, and they headed into the house.

After a small evening meal, Hotwire made himself scarce while Fisher and Harris retired to a cosy living room, both sitting on a three-seat sofa with a glass of Chardonnay. Much like the outside of the house, the room felt warming and comfortable, despite the unlit fire the sofa faced towards.

"Was this your parents' house?" Fisher asked as he

imagined cosy winter evenings with the family gathered around.

Harris shook her head.

"My family aren't dead. That was a lie," she said.

Fisher nodded, his eyes narrowing as he turned his head to the side.

"But they might as well be. I decided a long time ago not to see them, for their protection," she replied, and Fisher understood. "A bigwig mathematician working in the insurance industry who made companies a lot of money gave it to me about ten years ago. He was very grateful to be alive."

Fisher raised his brow and Harris smiled before she sipped her wine.

"Go on," she said, and Fisher held his expression firm. "What were you going to say in the car?"

"Why don't you tell me?" he replied, settling back into his seat, still convinced she'd got him wrong.

She nodded, setting the glass down on a coffee table.

"You want to let them capture you," she replied.

Fisher couldn't help but smile. "So why not let me? I can work my magic from the inside," he said, his expression firming as he spoke.

"I can give you a hundred reasons, but ultimately it's just too dangerous. You don't know why they want you," she said, picking up her glass.

"Money, probably. They'll want me to do stuff they can't and for that they'll need me alive and cooperative," he said.

"But how they make you cooperative is an issue. Anyway, the agency knows how dangerous you could be if you were on the wrong side. They'd never sign it off. You know that as well as I do."

"But I can control what I do and I can tip you off," Fisher replied, straightening up in his seat.

"What if they ask you to do something dangerous, or against our interests? What if you need rescuing?"

"We'll communicate somehow," he replied before she could ask more.

About to speak, Harris held back, the pause giving him the first sign she might consider how to make it work.

"It's still no," she said a moment later with a shake of her head. "There is no way we'd get clearance."

"So we don't ask. It would help us convince everyone. Don't you think?" he said. She looked him in the eye before turning away to stare into the empty fireplace and placed her glass on the table. After what felt like such a long time of silence, she turned back with a far off expression.

"We couldn't ask them anyway. Because of the mole," she said as her focus came back.

A broad smile spread across Fisher's face and he took their glasses from the table and handed Harris hers.

"We need to prepare," she said, not sharing his gesture. "It'll be dangerous and we won't be there to support you, but I've got a few things that may help."

Gulping down the last of her wine, she shuffled towards him.

"There's something I need to do first," she said, leaning and taking his almost empty wine glass. Settling it down on the table, she leaned close enough for her breasts to press against his chest before their lips touched, sending a warmth flooding between them. Moving his hand to her back, her phone vibrated on the table.

Pulling away, Harris sat up, then grabbing the phone, she disappeared into the kitchen.

41

London

21st October

Cocking his head to the side, Fisher turned just as one of Farid's goons thudded to the ground, with Lucky out of breath as he appeared from around the corner. The sailor nodded, looking at the blood leaking from where the dead man's right eye had been, before speaking quietly into his cuff and turning back the way he'd come.

Fisher turned to Harris as she unscrewed the suppressor, then pushed the Glock back into her jacket. Expressionless, she stepped forward. Fisher opened his arms, and she did the same, both leaning in to pull each other close.

Taking a deep breath, he drew back for a better look. Harris mirrored the gesture. Before long, they leaned back in, their lips touching. Harris was the first to pull away, stepping back and looking him in the eye.

"I missed you," she said as she wiped lipstick from his lips with her thumb.

"I missed you, too," Fisher replied, unable to relax his grin.

"Farid's circling the hospital. We haven't got long," she said.

Fisher nodded, pulling out a brown envelope from inside his jacket and handing it over. Sliding out the pages, she flicked through the photos of Daryl, the address in Great Baddow, the police station, the plans, and the description of what they were hunting. Within a minute, she pushed the envelope back into his hands.

"You've got to go," she said, taking him in a tight embrace.

"But what do I do?" he replied, holding her close.

"Carry on. We'll deal with this. You better go," Harris

said, pulling away as a door opened behind her. "Go," she said, raising her voice and pointing along the sweeping corridor when he hadn't moved.

With a nod, Fisher turned, but after walking a few steps, he twisted back around.

"There was something else…" he said, stopping himself when the door had already closed.

42

Farid laughed down the phone as Fisher sat in his usual spot back at Eight Walworth Road with a cup of strong coffee in his hand, listening to the one sided conversation as the Arab paced the room. After a moment, he held his step and with a raise of his eyebrows he smiled toward Fisher.

"Where did you find them?" Farid said, nodding. "Send over their details and we'll bring them in."

Clearing the call, he shouted for vodka at the top of his voice before sitting down in front of Fisher.

"How did they find us?" Farid said, all signs of joy gone.

"ANPR?" Fisher said with a shrug. "You can't go anywhere without them reading your number plate," he added, as Yasmin stepped from the kitchen with a tray holding two crystal tumblers filled with ice beside a bottle of vodka, its red and silver label frosted over. "A car was compromised?"

Farid raised his brow and turned side on, examining Fisher's blank expression.

"Not anymore. They're both smouldering on an industrial estate twenty miles away," Farid eventually replied, waving the girl away.

"We held our own, though," Fisher said with a nod. "I saw at least three of them go down hard," he added, pouring two fingers of the clear liquid into each glass. The corners of Farid's mouth raised as he nodded. "What about the job?"

"It's still on," Farid replied. "We go again tomorrow. The boss is impatient."

Fisher nodded as the alcohol stung at the back of his throat. "What next?"

"We party," Farid said, laughing and as if someone had heard, the main doors opened to Benny, pushing them wide with a trail of barely dressed women behind. Each of the eight swarmed like bees around a flower, encircling where they sat. Each of them stared at Fisher without speaking, their lips pouting as they flexed and swayed their scantily-dressed forms.

"Where's the Brazilian?" Fisher didn't look at the new arrivals as he spoke.

Farid grinned as giggles rose from the women and many raised their hands.

"She didn't turn up. That's whores for you."

Fighting the disappointment, Fisher turned to each of the girls, barely noticing them whilst hoping she'd read the note and that was the reason she wasn't here. Reassuring himself she was safe, he focused on the choice. There were blondes, brunettes, two south Asian, one French, a Pole or other Eastern European native. Two English. One short Welsh girl and an American.

It was the tanned American that caught his eye and, without thinking, he asked if she could dance. Not saying a word, and with the other girls unable to hide their jealous gazes, she gyrated as if around an imaginary pole, her hips thrusting forward as she blew him a kiss.

With his mind made up, the rest of the girls turned to Farid, who picked both Indians, leaving the remainder with forced smiles and dispersing to the other men.

Taking the ice-cold bottle and his glass in one hand, he held out the other for the American and led her into his bedroom.

Her name was Tyler and she perched on the edge of the neatly-made bed where Fisher topped up his glass and handed it over. She drank it in one and handed it back, but rather than refilling it, he turned and placed it on the wooden dresser. By the time he'd turned back, she'd already slipped off her tiny lace top and stood ready to pull down her matching knickers.

"Don't be so eager," Fisher said as he moved towards her, taking her hand in his whilst staring into her eyes, repeating the same words he'd whispered at the same time each night.

"Tonight we made love until the early hours of the morning and I was the best you've ever had. You need a good night's sleep," he said, then let go, watching her mouth open with a wide yawn.

"I am very sleepy," she said, laying down on top of the covers.

Out cold within minutes, Fisher emptied his trouser pockets, resting his watch next to the almost empty blister pack of Valium before he stripped to his Calvin Klein's, clicked on the TV and watched the news. With Tyler dribbling into the pillow next to him, Fisher drifted off to sleep.

***

The back of Fisher's head throbbed as he opened his eyes, peering at the grey light from the overcast sky. Taking care as he looked around, he found the velvet curtains tied neatly on each side and, rubbing his temples, he glanced across the bed at the naked beauty. He'd remembered her name this time and watched the slow rise and fall of her chest under the silk cover.

Picking himself up from underneath the smooth material, he adjusted the waist of his black Calvin Klein boxer shorts and stepped into the en-suite bathroom where he stared in the mirror.

With his thumb and forefinger, he rubbed his chin. Feeling stubble, he took a step back, opened the mirror and pulled out the shaving foam and bag of razors before throwing them into the bin.

43

"Mr James and Mr Franklin from Solid Security," Fisher said, holding up his fake pass in front of the overweight and heavily made up BAE receptionist. "We're here to investigate a door control unit on the Sec4 system."

Replying with a mundane smile, she flicked through a box of index cards to her side before pulling out two plastic badges. With a glance at each of them and after tapping on the keyboard and clicking the mouse, she handed the cards across the reception desk.

Fisher looked at the badge showing his cover name and the words 'CONTRACTOR. TO BE ESCORTED' across the bottom, along with a large red zero in the top right corner.

"Take a seat. Someone will collect you," the receptionist said, speaking for the first time.

Fisher nodded, picking up the heavy tool bag from where it rested at his side before stepping away from the counter and, followed by Daryl, moved to an adjacent row of six comfortable looking seats with their backs pushed up against a plain wall inlaid with glass cabinets. Beyond the glass were an array of unrecognisable objects made from a mixture of metal and plastic, each with a corresponding label.

After clipping his badge to the collar of his brown polo shirt with an embroidered logo of the fictitious firm, Fisher set a thirty-minute countdown on his Timex before staring in silence at the blank wall opposite. They didn't have to wait long before a lanky middle-aged man emerged from a double set of doors. Wearing loose blue dungarees streaked with grease and paint, a lanyard swung across his front in time with a blond ponytail. In the top right of the badge, Fisher spotted a bright orange number four just before their eyes met.

Ignoring the man's shudder, Fisher picked up his tool bag.

"Joe," the man said. "And you were meant to be here yesterday."

"Trouble on the roads," Fisher replied with a shrug,

recognising the Yorkshire accent.

With short, high-pitched laughter from his side, they both looked at Daryl's wide grin.

"What's up with him?" Joe said, his eyes narrowing as he leaned slightly toward Fisher's bald companion. "I know you, don't I?"

Of course he did. Everyone knew the younger version of Daryl, his youthful image imprinted on the nation's psyche. Fisher hoped the hard years inside had made enough of a difference.

"He's got one of those faces," Fisher said, leaning to Joe. "He looks like a celebrity," he added, gripping the man's hand. "But he's nobody."

Holding his gaze for a moment longer, Joe shrugged and looked back at Fisher.

"Anyway," Fisher said. "What's the problem with the system?"

Joe shrugged again and shook his head. "Damned if I know. We've had no reports, only the call from your office flagging a problem from the remote monitoring."

Fisher nodded. "Makes sense. I'll take a look, then we'll get out of your hair."

"Follow me," Joe said, before turning towards the white double doors he'd just come through.

Eyeing the discrete cameras high on each wall, they followed through the double doors only to be greeted by another set just ahead, besides which stood a large blue number five stencilled across half the height of the far wall.

Reminding himself of the plan he'd studied, Fisher told himself this was the first security zone.

Still following in the procession of three, Fisher watched as the maintenance technician pulled his ID card from the plastic holder hung around his neck, staring as he slid the edge of the card through the thin metal reader at the side of the door, below which waited a bright red fire alarm call point.

With no delay the doors pushed open, revealing a long white corridor with a thick blue line running just above the skirting, the marker interrupted by openings to new corridors and other doors either side with another double set in the distance and a large orange four stencilled to its right.

Without conversation, Joe led them halfway down the corridor before stopping at a door on the left marked *Maintenance Workshop*. Unlocking it with his pass and after a quick look over his shoulder, he stepped in and they followed.

The thick stench of grease and solvent greeted them whilst the sheer amount of clutter left Fisher in awe as his gaze wandered over every crammed surface. Hundreds of tools hung on every wall, each with their own painted red silhouette. Heavy wooden workbenches were everywhere, the surfaces covered with equipment, computers, vacuum cleaners and much more, each in a state of disassembly.

In the centre of the space stood two free-standing racks, with each shelf piled high with years of accumulations. Row upon row of glass jars filled with screws, nuts and bolts and all sorts of tiny bits and pieces, whilst cardboard boxes lay stacked across the floor. Just inside the door was a lone desk with a flat screen monitor rising above haphazard piles of dusty plastic files and papers covering every inch of the wooden surface.

Without delay, Joe turned to the same desk, picking up manuals and catalogues before dropping them with little care to the floor, revealing a keyboard and mouse covered in a blanket of dust. He then stepped to a workbench where he reached for a chair on wheels, and after removing a bag bulging with tools and patting the seat with his palm, he slid it to where he'd cleared a space.

Gesturing to the desk, Joe held out his palm for his guests and Fisher took the seat before pressing a button on the monitor in hope it would turn on, rewarded moments later with the Windows XP logo and a prompt for a username and password.

Before he could turn to ask, Joe spoke.

"The username is maintenance. Capital M, and the password is joe123! All lower case," he said, as he filled a grease-smothered kettle from a hand basin in the room's corner.

After holding down the right keys, Fisher fed in the details and a moment later, a sandy beach appeared on the screen. Leaning to his tool bag at his side, he pulled a memory stick from a side pocket and pushed it into a USB slot of the computer under the desk.

"I'm loading diagnostics. It'll take a minute or two," Fisher said over his shoulder, but Joe seemed to take little notice as he poured hot water into a chipped mug. With a glance up at Daryl, Fisher held his gaze when he didn't react, then raised his brow, watching as the man seemed oblivious to the prompt they'd agreed on the journey down.

"Tony!" Fisher snapped, regretting the sharpness of his voice as Daryl stared back wide-eyed, just as Joe looked up from stirring what smelled like coffee. "You said you were desperate for the toilet when we got here."

Daryl's mouth opened in realisation. Then he nodded with an urgency that reminded Fisher of a toddler. Fisher turned to Joe, leaning his head to the side with an apologetic smile before Joe set his mug down and walked to the door.

"It's down the corridor on the left," he said, pointing through the opening. "Then another left and a right."

Daryl stepped out and peered the way Joe pointed, then raised his hand, waving it from side to side as if tracing the journey in his head.

Sighing, Joe led Daryl down the corridor, leaving Fisher clicking the mouse in a flurry of motion, loading the contents of the USB stick to the machine before a schematic image appeared.

"There's your problem," Fisher said as Joe reappeared at the door a few moments later. Arriving at his side, the technician squinted at a schematic drawing showing part of the building. In the centre, a pictogram of a door highlighted red, next to which stood a large orange four.

"Can you take us here?" Fisher said, pointing to the screen.

As Joe moved away, distracted by Daryl's return, Fisher pulled the memory stick from the port and the image disappeared from the screen.

44

Standing outside the door with the orange stencilled number looming on the wall at its right, Joe snapped his ID card from the lanyard and slid it through the reader, which was identical to the last, along with the companion fire alarm call point. Together, the three watched as the double doors opened at pace, revealing a corridor with an orange stripe low on the wall as people in shirts and ties strode its length before it turned at a right angle.

After placing his tool bag at the base of the left-hand door to keep it open, Fisher leaned up to the frame as he examined its detail, or at least gave that impression.

"Excuse me," a commanding deep voice said at Fisher's back, quickening his heart rate as he glanced over his shoulder to a burly skinhead security guard manoeuvring himself through the gap. His gaze fell to a holstered yellow Taser by his side just as he stepped out of the way, making him want the Glock he wished he had strapped under his arm.

As the guard disappeared down the corridor, Fisher found the first and only sign of the near invisible embedded door technology before reaching inside his bag to pull out the first screwdriver to hand. Hunching over to obscure Joe's view, he made a screwing motion on the white metal plate he'd found on the frame low to the floor.

"All done," he declared as he stood, launching the screwdriver to land in the bag with a metallic clink. "Can I test it with your card?" Fisher said, holding out his hand as he stepped further into the corridor whilst sliding the tool bag to let the doors close.

Joe stepped in just in time, and for a moment, Fisher broke eye contact, his gaze instead falling on Daryl's grin.

Tearing himself away, he took the offered card, hoping Joe wouldn't glance toward Daryl standing on the other side of him.

With a swipe of the plastic against the reader, the doors

opened towards them. Fisher nodded as he forced a satisfied smile, watching as Joe moved back through the doors and replied in the same fashion, then reached out for the card.

Taking a single step forward, Fisher pushed out his hand, then as Joe went to take the card, Fisher followed with the other hand, placing the tip of his forefinger on Joe's palm. Spotting Daryl already walking further into the building, Joe looked up before Fisher could speak, then grabbed the card from him.

"It's this way," Joe called, causing a woman dressed in a sharp, bright blue suit to look up from her phone as she walked towards them. Daryl kept on moving. With his cheeks reddening, Joe mirrored the anger Fisher felt and headed after him.

Fisher shook his head, hoping to clear his frustration just as a thought sprang to mind. Uncertain if he could do what he hoped would save the moment, he closed his eyes and drew in a deep breath.

"It's past your tea break, Joe," Fisher said, projecting his voice.

Joe's stride slowed, then he came to a stop with his shoulders moving as if a shiver had run down his back. Lifting and then tilting his wrist, he glanced at his watch, holding the look as he shook his head. With a tap of his finger against the timepiece, Joe looked over at Fisher with his brow hooding his eyes.

"We'll make our own way out," Fisher quickly added as he arrived, forcing his hand into the other man's. "We'll leave straight away and no one will know."

Joe's eyes narrowed further for a long moment, then shaking off another shiver, he turned on his heels and headed off the way they'd come.

Shaking his head as Joe left through the Zone Four doors, with Daryl nowhere to be seen, Fisher rushed back to collect the tool bag and, walking quickly, followed the orange line as it swept around to the right where he found Daryl at the far end, heading along a series of short steps towards a red three and the next double set of doors.

"Are you trying to fuck this up?" Fisher said as he arrived, pushing his face close to the back of Daryl's head. Daryl slowly turned around, expressionless, as if he hadn't understood.

Resisting the urge to punch the man, knowing it wasn't the time, he instead stepped back and dug into the deep uniform trouser pockets to pull out the access card, along with the key he'd liberated from the police station a few days before.

With a swipe of the card through the machine, which also had an attached keypad, Fisher stood back when it didn't respond. Finding the corridor empty as he glanced over his shoulder, Fisher pushed against the finger plate. Realising it wouldn't move, he heard squeaking wheels from behind. Turning, his gaze fell on a tea lady pushing a trolley as she disappeared to the right and along another corridor.

Staring at the doors, Fisher shook his head, then looked at the plain plastic card. Turning it over, he noticed for the first time the words *Emergency Use Only* in red across the bottom.

Standing at the door, Fisher stared along the plain white corridor, finding the plasterboard ceiling behind him peppered with smoke detectors, sensors and fluorescent lights inlaid at the edges, spraying light against the walls.

A protective vinyl covered the floor and rose to meet the orange line a short distance up the wall. Halfway down the corridor, a green euro legend illuminated sign hung from the ceiling and depicted a white stick man running out of a door.

Fisher turned back to the keypad; he eyed the emergency call point above.

"Smash the glass," Fisher said, nodding to the red box on the wall, then turned to Daryl when he didn't move, finding him with his arms across his chest and scowling. "What are you fucking doing?"

Daryl shifted on his feet. "Do you know who I am?" he said, his voice high pitched. Fisher raised a brow as Daryl spoke again. "You need to give me some respect."

As his feminine tone resounded from the man's mouth, Fisher realised it was the first time he'd heard him speak.

"We don't have time for this bollocks," he replied, his adrenaline pushing away any thought of how funny he found him. "I thought you were a psychopath, but based on what I've seen, you're just a child. Do I respect you? No. Do I want to put you down? Yes. Now please push the fucking fire alarm so we can get the hell out of here."

Daryl's eyes narrowed and he held Fisher's stare for a long moment before he turned to the call point.

As the klaxon wailed, Fisher realised his breath raced and his heart pumped hard. Knowing he couldn't operate in this state, he closed his eyes, forcing himself to calm. After a couple of seconds, he pressed a button on his digital watch for the seconds to subtract, then, swiping the card, the doors opened, doubling the insistent sound.

Fisher took the lead, marching along the red-striped corridor as people appeared from offices and around the two corners, the flow increasing with every moment as more people poured past them to follow the green signs above their heads.

Secondary alarms added to the urgency with emergency exits complaining someone had opened them.

No one panicked. Instead, they chatted to their neighbours striding at their sides, not paying any attention to the pair walking in the opposite direction and it wasn't long before Fisher saw the calm of the Zone Two doors above the traffic.

With the high-pitched squeal pulsing in his ears, as the flow subsided he wished the same could be said for the intense volume urging them to flee. Then, almost able to touch their goal, a slender bare arm pushed out from the crowd, blocking Fisher's way.

45

Daryl bumped against Fisher's back as he came to an abrupt stop, the crowd giving way to the owner of the arm, a short blonde woman wearing a high-visibility yellow vest. A couple of sizes too large, one side hung loose on her shoulder, swamping the frills of a white blouse underneath and dropping almost below a short black skirt. Her child-like features glared up as she held a black clipboard against her chest.

"That way," she said, her voice high-pitched, cutting through the squeal ringing in their ears.

When they didn't turn, she moved her hand from the wall and pointed along the flow of pedestrians. Fisher looked over his shoulder, then back toward the Zone Two doors before their eyes met.

"It's this way," he said, raising his voice over the alarm.

With a shiver, the woman's expression softened and she looked away, her attention catching on the thinning flow of administrators and scientists. Dropping her arm, her eyes narrowed as she shook her head.

"This is the right way," Fisher repeated. Not staying to watch her confusion deepen, he headed against the traffic again.

"So what do you do when you're saving people's lives?"

Turning at the sound of Daryl's high voice so close behind, with a double take at finding the blonde walking at his side, Fisher blocked their path, leaving the woman looking up wide-eyed as he cupped her hand. "No," he said, looking at each of them. "This isn't the right way for *you*. Do you understand?"

After a moment's pause, she pulled her hand from his light grip, glanced at the near empty corridor behind before scurrying away without looking back.

"I'm going to fucking shoot you if you don't stop," Fisher barked over the siren, glaring at Daryl's toothy smile.

"Come on. I've got a lot of time to make up for," Daryl said, not bothering to hide the creepy edge to his voice.

Shaking away the thought and standing beside the large painted two, with just the incessant alarm for company, they stared at where the reader and keypad had been on each of the other doors. Instead, a small sign waited on the wall. A yellow triangle with a black exclamation in the centre and the words, *Caution. Automatic Security System.*

Looking up from his watch, he spotted the keyhole on the right-hand side of the door. Finding the police station key from his pocket was the perfect match, his jaw dropped when he pushed into the vast warehouse.

Feeling dizzy as he looked up to the high roof, he turned back, locking the door behind them before returning to the grid of individual rooms spread out across the vast expanse. He counted five to his left, right, and front. The glass walls resembled the operations centre. Most were opaque, leaving only a handful obscured in darkness.

Strip lights hung down in those he could see into, lighting desks and chairs, many with workbenches at the side, and boxy machines covered in yellow warning labels. The matt black floor felt rubber-like, but with no lights between the rooms, their darkness contrasted to where they'd just left.

With no sign anyone had ignored the klaxon's complaint, the thought fell away when at the far end of the corridor of glass offices reaching out in front of him, he spotted the purple doors of their final destination, flanked by pairs of red fire extinguishers.

Hearing a second, quieter alarm, Daryl strode between the rooms stretching ahead, with Fisher following, peering either side into each space and the multitude of bright, red-dotted electronics standing by for action.

As if to mark their arrival at the far end of the room, and the only reason Daryl had come along, the main klaxon halted its incessant scream, leaving behind its quieter sibling chirping to his right. His gaze followed to find an open fire exit.

Glancing at his watch, Daryl stepped to the right of the

double doors where he moved the fire extinguishers a few steps away, before taking the tool bag from Fisher and kneeling in front of the wall with the purple number. Fisher watched the man's demeanour change, overcome by an air of calm enthusiasm as he took precision tools from the dusty bag, laying each out in what seemed to be a specific sequence.

After half a minute, Daryl placed his palms on the wall beside the door before running them slowly over the surface, as if he could sense what was on the other side. With a quick look around, Fisher moved to the nearest office, where he leaned against the glass wall. Whilst Daryl tapped his index finger in a circular motion along the wall, Fisher glanced at his watch.

"Twenty minutes," he said, as Daryl reached over everything he'd laid out, pulling a claw hammer from the bag before attacking the wall with fevered blows.

The master at work.

Pushing away his disappointment at the show, Fisher stared into the cloud of plaster dust almost obscuring the man before the hammer sailed out from the fog, clattering into the tool bag. The metallic scrape and clink of tools took over as the dust settled, leaving Fisher to glance back and forth between his watch and Daryl's hands in the cavity he'd opened up, where every so often he caught a glint of tarnished grey metal and thick riveted seams.

"It's been troubling me," Fisher said as he stepped behind the dust-covered safe breaker, who swapped a pair of pliers for a bright red box with an LCD display connected to probes via spiral cables. "Why you? Everyone knows how good you are, but you've been inside for years."

Daryl's motion stopped and twisting around, he ran the back of his sleeve across his forehead.

"Behind this modern facade," Daryl said, tapping a knuckle on the plasterboard, "is an antique. But it's still the strongest strongroom ever made. They've only ever recorded three successful break-ins in under thirty minutes. All were by me."

Holding his hands out, he shook them side-to-side as if he were in some sort of jazz ensemble.

Fisher leaned in toward the hole, watching as Daryl removed a thick plate exposing where faded coloured wires and bulky electronic components hid. Daryl turned, squinting up.

"You're in my light."

Fisher stood back and looked at his watch, but barely registering ten minutes remained, a mechanism creaked and the doors parted, opening outward.

Lights flickered on between the doors that from the outside looked like wood but soon revealed glinting steel as thick as Fisher's arms as they levered wide, leaving him to stare at lines of metal shelving rising from the floor to the ceiling as row after row of lights illuminated.

Unsure what he'd expected, the sight of boxes, some plastic, others cardboard, filling the shelves left Fisher a little underwhelmed. Only as a heavy clunk felt through his feet signifying the doors had stopped moving did he step inside, his movement slow at first, followed by Daryl holding a screwdriver in his powder-coated hand.

Peering around the shelves, each container was labelled with a large white paper sticker. Some peeled at the edges and yellowed with age, whilst others were bright enough that they could have been stuck in place that very day. Counting around twenty boxes on each shelf and with five shelves per row in lines of six, there were six hundred to search, and all he had was the picture of what he was hunting for, along with a cryptic name.

Despite regretting a glance at his watch to find their time was fast running out, rather than give rise to panic, Fisher racked his brain for the best way to approach, but before he could come up with a plan, he spun around to the clang of the metal and fire exit alarm silencing.

The doors had closed.

Feeling the temperature already rising, shaking his head, the penny dropped that by his own free will he'd stepped into a vault opened by the Coffer Killer, who'd chosen the same claustrophobic death for his other victims.

46

Only just able to keep the panic at bay, Fisher turned, surprised to find Daryl looking at him from along the aisle. The relief was only short-lived when Daryl's wide-eyed alarm told him no matter the cause, he was still stuck inside a vault.

Breaking the stare, Daryl leapt forward, rushing the door with his shoulder but when he yelped and they were still locked in, he jumped to the side, crouching as he jabbed the screwdriver into the plaster.

The renewed hope soon ebbed away as Fisher watched, listening to the clang of metal against metal before Daryl sagged, settling on the floor as he dropped the screwdriver.

Watching the bald man staring at the wall, Fisher noticed the seconds ticking by just as Daryl animated, picking up the screwdriver and pushing the blade through the plaster skin to open up an ever-increasing circle. Deciding he couldn't bear to watch on helpless and doing his best to ignore the rising heat, Fisher drew hope that inside the Aladdin's cave of a room there might be something that could get them out.

Scanning across the labels of the nearest boxes and their technical abbreviations, each held a slip of paper peppered with signatures he guessed were updated whenever the contents were removed from the space. Some boxes were stuck with drawings, helping to discount them from his search, whilst those without left him speed-reading text before he could move on to the next.

Many of the contents were familiar tech, or other things he recognised, like miniature robots, or their components, thin flying mechanical devices and many phones, from an eighties brick to the type of handsets he'd carried around for years.

Trying not to let the intrigue at what he saw slow him once he'd ruled it out, his gaze passed over what looked like a pair of army boots, then to a bright yellow shotgun before forcing himself to scan past a respirator and rolls of unassuming fabric, instead looking at an older version of his communicator much like a bulky version of the first generation iPhone with round edging.

He couldn't help but pause when on the side of the next box the label read *iComm6A Multiverse*, the picture depicting a longer and thinner version of the device he'd had to give up.

Daryl's insistent probing of the wall reminded him of what he was there to do. Only a moment later, his gaze fell on what he hoped he'd been looking for. Recognising the picture of the bullet on the side, Fisher checked the abbreviation against the folded notes from his pocket, peering at the name and finding the E-round v0.165.123 rev. 56 hadn't been checked out for five years. It was old technology.

Realising now wasn't the time for reflection, leaving lines in the dust, Fisher pulled the blue plastic container from the shelf and placed it at his feet. Hearing a huff of breath from the door, he glanced to Daryl, who stared at the pot-marked wall, shaking his head.

Not wanting the sight to dampen his excitement, Fisher turned back and pulled off the plastic lid to find four small but identical attaché-style cases sitting upon yellowed papers. The cases weren't much larger than a packet of cigarettes.

With care, he took each out, stuffing all but the last one in his pockets. Self-conscious, he glanced to find Daryl staring from the door before going back to hacking at the wall.

How long he'd been watching, Fisher didn't know, but dismissing the thought, he unclipped the catches of the last case. Pulling open the lid with care, he stared at ten rounds of ammunition sitting in a bed of black foam. Other than a dull grey finish, there seemed no difference to the rounds he was used to.

"It's no good," Daryl roared, then gritting his teeth he clasped his dust-covered hands over his bald head, sending the screwdriver clattering to the floor. "There's fucking steel skin everywhere. I can't get to the controls. We're fucked."

"I'm not giving up," Fisher said, before turning back and placing the attaché case on to the floor, then pulling an adjacent box from the shelf and ripping off the lid.

"What are you looking for?" Daryl said, rubbing his head.

"There must be something we can use."

Daryl turned away. "On this?" he said, his voice going high as he pointed over his shoulder. "If you find an acetylene torch, I'll get right to it," he added, his tone flattening as he shook his head.

Ignoring the comment, Fisher noticed two bright-red handguns stacked on each other inside the box he'd just pulled down. Narrowing his eyes, he took hold of the first, and although light, it felt familiar enough. With his attention landing on the case by his feet, raising his brow he looked at the wall, wondering how thick the steel could be.

Despite not knowing if it would work, with nothing else to try, he pulled two cartridges from the attaché case, then after rolling the warm metal in his fingers and finding nothing that might halt his plan, he slid them into the empty magazine before pulling back the slide.

"Stand back," Fisher said, motioning with the weapon for Daryl to move.

Wide-eyed, Daryl shook his head. "No chance," he said, but seeing the determination in Fisher's aim, he did as asked.

Despite his pressure on the trigger, the striker's release took him by surprise, squeezing his eyes closed as its point smashed into the primer at the base of the bullet, igniting the propellant in the cartridge, where the confined explosion accelerated the dull projectile to seven hundred and thirty miles per hour as it rotated along the rifled chamber and out from the muzzle, hitting the wall quicker than a blink of an eye and pushing through the thin plasterboard with ease.

As the soft round compressed against the steel buried behind, leaving only an unseen scratch, the miniature electromechanical engine converted the kinetic energy to a devastating electromagnetic pulse which surged through the steel divider.

With not enough time to get his hands to his ears, a high-pitched squeal sent them both reeling.

His mouth dry with plaster dust and the air thick with the stench of propellant, Fisher opened his eyes to darkness, his ears ringing as he pushed the warm gun into his pocket.

"What the fuck?" Daryl exclaimed before he seemed to slip, skidding across the floor on a discarded container lid, sending him crashing into the door.

Despite blinking furiously to clear the dust from his eyes, Fisher thought he saw a dull light from the doors. Forcing his eyes to stay open to get a better look, he stepped around the box with his hand on the shelf as a guide. Nodding, he realised it wasn't a trick when, above the ringing in his ears, he heard the call of the emergency door alarm.

Kneeling, he found the container at his feet and quickly grabbed the second weapon, pushing it into his waistband, along with the remaining case.

Pressing his shoulder against the door, he was still surprised to find it moved under his weight and stepped from the vault, relieved to feel the conditioned cool air washing over him. Although brighter than the stifling vault, as he looked across the view he found the lights inside the nearest few rooms were dark, along with the LEDs of the equipment.

Turning back to the vault doors, he watched Daryl stumble out, his expression blank until his gaze fell to Fisher's pockets bulging with the small attaché cases.

"We did it?" he said, tilting his head to the side.

"We..." Fisher replied, but stopped himself when a new klaxon formed of two high-pitched calls, each more urgent than the last, wailed. "That's our cue to leave."

Ignoring Fisher's words, Daryl looked to his left just as a rush of air, like that of an opening airlock, came from the same direction, followed by the whine of motors and hiss of servos before a clank of metal vibrated the floor.

Almost by instinct, Fisher pulled the warmth of the red gun from his pocket, readying his finger on the trigger as the sequence repeated. *Whine. Hiss. Clank.*

He hadn't moved before the cycle came again, the timings seeming so precise as a white light grew brighter from the same direction.

Unsure whether to move to get a better look or to stay hidden, Fisher stared at Daryl looking toward the sound, his eyes wide until the rhythm stopped and the light remained stationary then extinguished, replaced with a thin red band of laser that moved sideways from the floor to ceiling. Before the beam could reach him, Daryl rushed beside Fisher.

"What is it?" Fisher said in a whisper, but Daryl didn't reply before the bright light came back with the sequence starting again, this time faster and rising in volume.

Whine. Hiss. Clank.

Gripping the red gun in his hand, Fisher puffed up his chest and stepped out from the shadow of the glass office, distracted by Daryl rushing to grab a fire extinguisher and wield it above his head.

Turning, the air went from his lungs when he saw where the noises were coming from.

47

Fisher stared at a long, yellow metallic strut, a leg with cables and metal pipes running up its length to a yellow and black bevel-edged cube resting on another two which were identical, but before he could take in the detail, a blinding light obscured his view, forcing him to turn away.

With a *whine, hiss, clank,* Fisher shielded his eyes as he watched Daryl standing at his side, raising the fire extinguisher a little higher, but sagging at a high-pitched electronic voice.

"IDENTIFICATION CODE!"

Unable to look at the thing he'd not yet put a name to, Fisher glanced at Daryl as the bald man opened his mouth. "What the fuck is that?"

Giving Fisher no time to reply, with a hiss of servos, the mechanical creature spoke again.

"VOICE PRINT FAILED. IDENTIFICATION CODE FAILED. INTRUDER. INTRUDER."

A *whine, hiss, clank* followed, then repeated in quick succession, too fast for the pair to react before high pressured air rushed from behind the intense light, pluming towards them.

Remembering what he'd done to the door with the gun he still held, he pointed the weapon in its general direction and pulled the trigger, but when the explosion didn't rush the air, a click of the striker being the only reply, Fisher's heart sank.

Grappling with the slide in hope he could free the jammed round, when it wouldn't move he pressed to release the magazine, but still nothing happened. Looking up from the useless gun, he found Daryl staring back wide-eyed, gritting his teeth and raising the extinguisher higher before rushing at the beast and sending the cylinder into the air.

The light went out as the heavy canister clanged against the centre of the cube, but when the thing gave no reaction, Fisher peered through the slowly dissipating vapour.

The robot was formed of a metallic yellow cube the size

of a pallet of bricks with a round light in the centre, its glass shattered. Four legs held it up, not three as he'd first thought, the metal struts sprouting from a compact grey platform. Behind the platform were two large green gas canisters with pipes snaking across its body to nozzles on the front. The renewed hiss of the thick vapour rushing out snapped Fisher from the inspection.

"Keep it occupied," he shouted as he turned, rushing past Daryl and back into the vault. "Stay away from the gas," he called over his shoulder, as he pulled boxes from the shelves and tried to remember where he'd seen what he looked for.

"Shotgun," he said out loud as he ripped the lid from a clear plastic box, taking the weight of the yellow weapon.

He'd never handled such a thing before, but having watched enough films, he found a catch at the side and it snapped open, pivoting in the middle. Peering into the box in search of ammunition, his heart raced when he found an attaché case about double the size of those with the E-bullets in. One-handed, he unclipped the catches and flipped the lid open as a heavy metallic thud echoed from the outside of the room, Fisher imagining the other extinguisher bouncing from the robot's metal as the hiss of servos followed.

"Are you okay?" Fisher called.

"Yeah. I knocked a foot out, but it's back..." Daryl called, his last words drowned out by a coughing fit, but Fisher had no time for concern when rather than finding long red cylinders with brass one end, the cartridges were transparent and showed a jumble of electronics inside with three sharp pins mounted at the business end.

"Shit," Fisher spat, but despite his uncertainty, he pulled three shells from their protective foam and pushed them one by one into the chamber. With a quick glance around, he snapped the metal together, pumped the slide underneath the barrel, then strode toward the doorway with the hiss beyond intensifying each moment.

Pulling in a deep breath and about to squeeze his lips tight, his gaze fell on a box he'd knocked to the floor, besides which was the alien-like face of a rubber respirator staring back at him.

With the mask clinging tight to his face, he found Daryl doubled over, his head bright red as he struggled for breath. A large fire extinguisher lay by his feet.

Turning to face the source of the smoke, Fisher pushed the stock into his shoulder, and squinting, took aim and pulled the trigger.

With recoil biting into his shoulder, the bullet hit the joint between the over-sized square head and the platform, sending a shower of sparks falling to the floor. The box head moved from side to side, and despite gas still pouring out, Fisher spotted a panel on the front open and a black tube emerge in his direction.

48

Pushing the shotgun forward, Fisher glanced at the weapon and despite the sweat streaming from his forehead and the clear front of the mask steaming up, he noticed blank writing on the side of the stock. TASER. With a shake of his head, he realised he held a larger version of the stun gun, which was excellent for taking out people but useless against the metal beast.

At his side, Daryl wretched before the colourful contents of his stomach piled beside the red cylinder. About to look away, the stark white letters on the extinguisher sparked a renewed rush of adrenaline as Fisher realised it was full of water.

Despite the moisture running down his face, Fisher couldn't help but smile.

"Spray the bastard," he shouted, pumping the gun for the second time.

Daryl looked over, wiping his mouth on the back of his sleeve, but rather than standing, he squinted at his feet and doubled over. Yanking the mask up, Fisher was about to speak but with a breath, he felt a chemical bite inside his throat. The relief was almost instant as he pulled it back down.

Shaking his head, Fisher kicked Daryl in the side, pointing to the extinguisher and then to the robot whilst miming pulling the trigger.

"Spray it," he shouted, before coughing the last of the stinging chemicals from his lungs.

Forcing himself to stand up straight, Daryl struggled to find purchase on the pin keeping the two halves of the trigger apart as Fisher aimed the shotgun back at the robotic creature, watching as a second black tube sprung from the other side of its head.

As the cuboid rotated to face Fisher, a jet of water sprayed from his side, the liquid drenching the metal skin, stopping only as a projectile launched from the tube before landing unseen with a thud. Fisher turned to find Daryl on his back on the floor with his hand reaching toward the extinguisher as he held his shoulder.

A spurt of water came from the hose, but stopped almost as it started when another projectile hit the bald man square in the chest and he fell backwards. Knowing he would be next for what he guessed were non-lethal baton rounds, Fisher swung the gun back to its target and fired, sending fifty thousand volts arcing around the soaked metal creature, its servos and motors whirling all at once, causing its legs to spasm in different directions in a brief dance before acrid smoke billowed from its joints. With a final stuttering move, the platform crashed to the wet floor.

Smiling to himself, Fisher turned to check on Daryl, but finding the spot empty and with the vapour all but gone, he pulled off the mask before spinning around on his heels as he revelled in the cool air's relief.

Dismissing the flash of concern that he hadn't found the murderer, after placing the shotgun on the ground, Fisher ran toward the emergency exit. Shielding his eyes against the bright sun and drawing deep breaths of the crisp air, using his fingers, he patted his short hair flat then pressed his hands against his face, hoping to remove any creases left by the snug-fitting respirator.

Outside and to his far right, hundreds of people huddled in groups around bright-yellow jacketed fire wardens calling out names. Fire fighters milled around their red engines whilst two police cars sat empty in the car park.

Excited by the interruption to their day, no one seemed to notice as he slipped around the long barrier blocking the road, and Benny didn't turn in the driver's seat as Fisher slammed the waiting mini-cab's door closed.

"It's just me," Fisher said, turning his head to the knocking sound from the boot, but the slow roll of the car ambling along the quiet roads was the only reply he received.

After ten minutes or so, the clatter behind him slowed, going altogether when they left the car behind in a petrol station car park, swapping instead to a small hatchback that soon sped down the motorway. At Thurrock services they climbed into one of Farid's Range Rovers and within ten minutes they raced along the M25 until the road narrowed with a single track either side, and they were in through a gap in a wooden demolition hoarding in a quiet industrial estate somewhere near Tilbury. The dusty rough concrete was the only sign of the building that had once towered over the area.

Fisher spotted Farid with his arms open and beaming like a Cheshire cat as he peered out from one of his cars, then parking nose to nose, Farid took him in a tight embrace before craning to see if anyone would follow.

"Daryl?" Farid said, not letting any concern reach his smile.

Fisher shook his head. "He did his job, then vanished."

Farid nodded, his smile growing wider.

"He must have realised what was next to come. But we were successful, weren't we?" For the first time Fisher heard doubt in his voice.

"Of course," Fisher replied whilst reaching into his pocket, but as his fingers curled around the curved form of the crimson gun, he realised he'd meant to hide it. With no other choice, he fumbled in his pocket and withdrew the handgun and the three attaché cases, then held them tight in his hands.

Farid leaned forward, but Fisher stepped back. "I want to give them to the boss myself. Seeing as we're going to meet him."

Farid's thick eyebrows lowered. "I advise against playing the game this way, Mr Fisher. The boss doesn't take kindly to these childish ways."

Fisher's expression didn't change and he raised his chin, turning his head to the side. Eventually Farid picked out his phone and turned his back before speaking in hushed tones. Standing in silence, he ended the call. When he turned around, he held his gun out, pointing it at Fisher's chest. Benny stepped from the car with his pistol raised in the same direction.

Doing his best to hide his surprise, Fisher concentrated on his breath as he tried to figure out his next move.

"I warned you against this course of action, didn't I, Mr Fisher? Now give me the bullets and we'll talk about what happens next," Farid said, motioning to the front of the car.

Fisher steeled himself as he moved up to the bonnet and, with care, placed the boxes and the pistol on the polished metal, then backed away with his palms raised.

Farid nodded and the driver stepped out, walking around the front before taking what Fisher had placed and headed around to the back of the car.

"Now, Mr Fisher, you have a life-changing choice. Cooperate and be part of something special, or behave like a child and it will be the last anyone sees of your particular talent." As Farid spoke the last word, a squeal of tires caught his attention, turning his head and shoulders through ninety degrees to a convoy of three black X5s racing through the gap in the wooden hoarding.

Fisher lunged forward, knocking the pistol from Farid's hand before diving into the small gap between the cars. Hitting the ground, he lost his grip and as he searched for the gun, he heard both engines either side roar to life before, with a crunch of gears, they both shot backwards, leaving him out in the open.

Looking up to Farid's car, he made eye contact for a split second, but as he held his gaze, he disappeared into the dust of a turn to the roar of the other car racing back towards him.

Gunfire burst into the air, but from Fisher's vantage, he couldn't be sure of the source. Looking up, all he could see was the front of the Range Rover filling his view before he squeezed his eyes closed.

49

Thinking better of burying his head in the sand, he opened his eyes just in time for the X5 to smash into the Range Rover about to hit him. Despite the collision sending the heavy car veering out of the way, Fisher scrabbled up on his hands and knees, propelling himself away enough only to feel the rush of air as the two joined cars sailed past, tyres screeching.

Staring wide-eyed, the doors pushed open from another X5, with familiar faces pointing automatic weapons jumping out to surround the wrecked Range Rover. Only with the rattle of automatic gunfire from behind him could he tear himself away, watching the passengers of the two other X5s send a hail of shots towards Farid's car as it headed between the gap in the wooden hoardings.

In a blink of an eye, the car was gone, leaving behind the decaying sound of its roaring engine.

With a lull descending, a large hand filled Fisher's view and he looked up to find Biggy standing over him. As he pulled Fisher to his feet, they turned to the blue horizon and the sound of a Merlin's powerful rotor blades cutting through the air.

Clouded in dust as it touched down, Fisher could just about see the side door slide open with Hotwire and Lucky jumping to the ground, crouching on their haunches to cover their arcs of fire with powerful HKs.

Smiling, Fisher took heart at seeing Hotwire and couldn't help but nod to himself at the confirmation that his well-aimed shot hit his armour in the right place, but the thought swept away when he spotted Harris sitting in the aircraft's belly, her slender hand beckoning him over.

Climbing up the steps, Fisher wanted to take her in his arms, but as Biggy, Hotwire, Lucky and Boots joined them, they lifted off in a swirl of demolition dust.

With a deep breath, Fisher flopped down into the seat and closed his eyes, taking in the roar of the engines, the chatter of those on board and the airframe's unmistakable mechanical scent. For the first time in a long while, he felt safe.

Despite relaxing into the motion of the helicopter as every second passed, it wasn't long before his legs shook and he lay his hands on top, hoping to calm the tremor.

Feeling Harris's soft hand on his, he felt she knew only too well what he'd gone through. The culmination of weeks undercover in constant fear of your life, or those depending on your success.

From the combat-hardened elite heroes to the theatre fresh aircrew, all on board knew too well what it was like when the adrenaline dissipated to leave an emotional vacuum.

"Are you okay?" Harris mouthed as he opened his eyes, but despite having thought so much about this moment over the past few weeks, he couldn't answer. He'd pictured her striking hazel eyes in his dreams, able to bring them to mind whenever he wanted.

Despite eventually nodding, from her expression he knew he hadn't convinced her.

"We'll pick him up. If we don't get him now, he'll be easy to find. It's something SIS are good at," she said, squeezing the top of his hand still resting on his knee.

"What about the problem?" Fisher replied, looking around the faces sitting opposite before he turned back to Harris, who raised her brow.

"That problem is resolved."

"You found them? Who was it? And what about the project?" Fisher said, tilting his head.

"It's fine. Relax. We'll be touching down in five minutes and we'll give you all the details."

As she moved her hand and sat back against the fuselage, her expression changed. Pulling out an iComm, she handed it to Fisher.

"Did she call?" he said, his eyes going wide, then his brow furrowing as Harris looked back with a blank expression.

"Did who call?"

After dismissing the reply, within five minutes, their

wheels touched down on the retractable helipad on top of 85 Vauxhall Cross, and flanked by those they'd travelled with, Harris led Fisher down the stairs.

"When did you tell Franklin?" he said, taking two steps at a time.

"After our meeting at the hospital," she replied, not looking back.

"How'd he take it?" Fisher said, his voice rising over the clamour of their feet on the concrete.

"Let's just say he was happier that you hadn't gone rogue than he was pissed off about the unauthorised operation," she said, then slowed and turned to look him in the eye. "And he knows about how things have developed, with, uh…" she added and waved her hand in the air toward him. "With your influence," she finally said, before turning back to speed down the steps.

Fisher spoke only as they arrived on the lowest level, following as she headed along a white walled corridor.

"How'd he find out?" he said as he walked alongside her, the others hanging back.

"Bukin. We've debriefed him, and on that note…" Harris said as she slowed and turned with her eyes narrowed. "Next time you want someone extracted from a building you're about to blow up, a little more notice would be helpful," she said, raising her eyebrows.

Fisher's cheeks bunched as he drew his lips back to show his clenched teeth. "Yeah. Sorry about that, but where did you leave it with Franklin?"

"He wants to understand the changes and train you before any further operations."

Fisher shrugged, following her into a large white room dominated by an oval wooden table surrounded by chairs. With no windows and the lights down low, Franklin stood as they entered the room. Not surprised to find him without a smile, Fisher found no reluctance to shake his offered hand before he followed Harris around the table's curve to take seats facing Clark's image projected on a white wall. Clark nodded as they sat down.

"To business," Franklin said, his voice gruffer than usual. "It's good to hear you haven't left the fold, Mr Fisher."

Fisher pushed on a smile as he nodded, the expression falling as Franklin continued to speak.

"But a word of note. That is not how we do things here. All operations must be authorised," Franklin said, then took a deep breath. "As you are new, I'm not blaming you," he added, then glanced at Harris, then at Clark. "I've already spoken with your colleagues about this. Now we need to get you into training ASAP. After the funeral next week, it's straight off to the Brecons. In the meantime, you're staying here for class work in preparation."

Fisher held himself from speaking. Instead, narrowing his eyes, he looked towards Franklin, unable to understand why he was talking so much about his training when they were still in the middle of the operation.

"I'm looking forward to my training," he said with a nod and watched as Franklin replied with the same gesture. "But aren't there other priorities?"

Franklin glanced at Harris before returning his gaze to Fisher.

"Such as?" he said as he lowered his brow.

"Finding the man behind the murder of my best friend," Fisher said, not stopping even though he saw Franklin about to interrupt. "And getting the E-Bullet back."

Franklin shook his head and placed his palms on the table as if he were about to stand. "We have competent investigators dealing with who was behind the killing, I assure you," he said, standing. "And the weapon you gave them was a fake," he added with confidence in his voice.

"No, it's not," Fisher said, shaking his head.

Franklin stopped himself from pushing the chair underneath the table as he held Fisher's gaze. "On what basis do you believe that is the case, Mr Fisher?"

"I used it to escape the locked vault."

50

Still standing, Franklin couldn't stop staring at Clark's image as Fisher described in great detail what had happened when he used the weapon, the older man's eyes going wide when he described the high-pitched squeal as it detonated.

Not waiting for the report to finish, Clark picked up the phone before hanging up after a few moments.

"The order to swap the weapon out for a dummy is still sitting on someone's desk. Apparently, they had a major event this morning and didn't have a chance to execute it," Clark said, trying not to react to Franklin's narrowing eyes. "There are six items missing from inventory, the details of which are on the way over."

Lifting his hands from his sides, Franklin covered his eyes with his palms and held his breath for a long while until he turned to Fisher, then Clark.

"You mean to say that everything that happened this morning was real, and that Mr Fisher breached the secure facility rather than being let through?" Franklin said as he lifted his chin.

Clark nodded, as if unwilling to speak.

"What are they missing?" Franklin said, his words considered. Clark shook his head.

Fisher pushed his hand inside his coat and pulled out the red handgun, placing it on the table before taking out the small metal case and resting it alongside. With all eyes on him, they each watched as he opened the case, then took out a single round and passed it over to Franklin.

"Farid has thirty of these and a gun to fire them with," Fisher said.

Taking the round, Franklin rolled it between his thumb and forefinger before looking at Clark. "What do I need to know?"

Before Clark had the chance, Fisher spoke. "It's a low radius EMP weapon."

Franklin turned his head and nodded.

"It's very effective," he added, watching a scowl crawl onto Franklin's expression at the sound of Clark tapping on his keyboard.

"The data files have arrived," Clark said without looking up at the screen and they all turned, watching his image shrink to a smaller window in the top right-hand corner of the projection, the left replaced by rows of text marked TOP SECRET (ORCON) in bold red letters.

"The weapon appears to utilise the principle of EMP," Clark said. "Or Electromagnetic Pulse. It is the same type of discharge which emanates from a detonated nuclear weapon. Some years ago, the bods at BAE created a way of generating the pulse with a lightning-fast decay rate, therefore localising the effect."

"That doesn't sound so bad," Fisher said as he continued to read down the screen.

"You're wrong," Franklin replied, closing his eyes and rubbing his forefinger at his temples. "I remember back to the briefing they gave after its discovery. It's terrible and we're the ones that put it into the wrong hands."

"Perhaps they need to sort out their security," Fisher said. "You'd think a place like that would take things more seriously. I could have taken anything."

Franklin opened his eyes and looked over at Harris, who hadn't spoken all this time. "It was easy for you," he said in a low voice as he continued to stare at Harris. "I can't stress how important it is to get this back. Especially considering the new information."

"What new information?" Fisher said, looking to Franklin and then to Harris when he didn't reply. "What new information?" he said again when no one answered.

"Did Harris tell you we found the mole?" Clark said after Franklin nodded his permission.

"Yes," Fisher replied with a glance towards her.

"He was a section leader with a high access level," Franklin said. "They'd initially bank-rolled him before turning to blackmail. Once we got his family safe, he talked."

Franklin gave a weary nod to Clark as if asking him to take over.

"He'd been working for a South American group linked to the liberation of the Falkland Islands. We've been aware of them for a short while, and suspect they're sponsored by the Argentinian state. They call themselves Fuerza Libertad de Malvinas or FLM, Force for the Liberation of the Malvinas, which is what the Argentines call the Falkland Islands."

Fisher furrowed his brow and leaned back in his seat as Clark continued to speak.

"Relations have soured with Argentina. Their government has always seen our sovereignty of the islands as a focus point that brings their people together. It helped them overlook the economic crisis gripping their country. The president has taken it as her personal crusade."

Fisher nodded, looking at Franklin.

"The weapon itself is dangerous on its own," Franklin said. "My primary concern is if they're able to reverse engineer it and make it into a ship or aircraft killer. We'll have no defence. They could walk onto the Falklands almost unopposed. Most weapons have some electronic components these days."

"They may not even stop at the Islands," Clark said as he nodded.

"Surely we have shielding? EMC issues have been around for years," Fisher said, remembering back to some of his university lectures on electronics.

Franklin shook his head. "The weapon is powerful for that reason. Defensive shielding is years away. The scientists haven't found a material or configuration it can't beat. They've poured hundreds of millions of pounds and tens of thousands of man hours into the search since it was first developed."

"That's why the weapon is sitting in a storeroom, not in mass production. We can't use it until we can defend against it," Clark added.

Franklin nodded before speaking. "And together, the

three of you gave it to our enemy."

The room stayed silent for a long moment before he turned and walked to the door.

"I need to have a tough conversation," he said before leaving.

51

Like chastised school children waiting for the teacher to come back from the headmaster, no one spoke. Fisher wondered if, like him, the others were mulling the choices that led them to giving an enemy of the state a weapon the allies had no defence against. A weapon that could change the course of combat forever.

Still no one had spoken by the time Franklin returned, expressionless. He didn't take a seat.

"We have our orders," he said with a nod. "We're to deploy our full capability to retrieve the weapon. That's your team," he said, looking at Harris. "With Mr Miller's assistance. In parallel, my colleagues at the MOD are preparing a task force for a pre-emptive strike to destroy the weapon. They'll be assembling a significant local task group, staged from the Falklands, to take it back by force.

"Despite knowing full well that a military offensive will cost the UK dearly, not only in reputation, it might even sway international opinion regarding our claim to the Falklands. It could cost us the island," he said, then seemed to hold his breath before speaking again. "I have assured those above me this will not be necessary. They have given us a deadline of sixty hours to complete the objective or they will intervene by any means they deem necessary. I have already passed the details to Miller."

Each head nodded, with Fisher breaking the silence.

"Not to sound like a school kid," he said, despite feeling the opposite. "But what about me? Surely you're not leaving me here until this is over? You know I can help."

"Yes," Franklin said, nodding. "But I don't want your help. You've proven that you're unable to follow orders."

It felt like a hole opened in Fisher's stomach and as he turned to Harris, who seemed about to say something, Franklin spoke again.

"However, against my better judgment, you're going as

well, but under the strict condition that you must seek authorisation prior to using your influence."

Silence followed as Fisher thought it through, knowing there could be situations where there wouldn't be time to make the call.

"Do you understand, Mr Fisher?" Franklin said as he glared over.

"I understand," Fisher replied. "If it means I get to help. Although I'm not sure how practical the restriction is."

Franklin's eyes widened as he turned side on, then moved his gaze to Harris. "Do you understand?"

"I understand, sir," she said without delay, then watched as he turned to Clark's image.

"I understand, too, sir," Clark said before Franklin could speak.

"Good. Agent Harris with me," he said as he turned and left the room.

When the door closed on the pair, Clark didn't waste time before giving Fisher a rundown of the history of the Falklands.

Britain had occupied the land from as far back as 1833 and the population considered themselves British. With the 1982 Argentinian invasion, the British Government was forced to make a choice to either defend the people of the island and their right to self-determination, or to let a foreign state walk over them.

The choice cost two hundred and fifty-five service personnel's lives, but the island was successfully returned to the islanders, leaving the British people passionate that the sacrifice should not be in vain.

Just as Clark seemed as if he was about to add something else, he paused at the dulled sound of Franklin's raised voice from the corridor.

As if to hide what Harris was going through, Clark raised his voice as he continued to speak, describing the fortifications installed since the war and the work the government had done to bolster defences, including upgrades to the port and improvements to the runway and facilities to handle large aircraft. Personnel from all armed services protected the island, along with a Royal Marine trained volunteer defence force.

When the door opened, Fisher glanced over to Harris. But even though he'd only known her for a short while, she showed no signs of what he thought might have happened. After leaving the door open and barely acknowledging Fisher as she retook her seat, before he could ask what had happened, Miller entered the room and closed the door behind him.

Miller's stiff expression was just the same as when he'd first met Fisher a few weeks before and helped put together the military operation to free his friend on the Caribbean island of Barbados. Fisher was sure he wore the same blue pin striped suit, marvelling for the second time at how he got his bulging muscles and thick neck inside.

"Good morning," Miller said, glancing around the room. Satisfied with what he saw, he stepped up to the table but paused as Fisher stood and held out his hand. Miller looked at the palm for a moment before a wide smile appeared and he shook with a firm grip.

"It's good to see you again, Mr Fisher. Harris. Clark," he said, nodding at each of them. "Another day, another situation. Thank you for keeping me in a job," he added with a hearty laugh, which decayed when no one joined in. "Very well," he said, clearing his throat with his fist at his mouth. "We have a deadline of sixty hours to retrieve the complete package. If it's left the country and we can't get our grubby mitts around it before then, the first tactical option, Alpha, is to lase the target for a cruise missile strike. However, if that is not workable, Beta comes into play, which is a full scale land invasion by task force. There is nothing off the table to remove this risk."

"Nothing?" Fisher said as he looked at Miller.

"Nothing," Miller replied with no delay.

Feeling rising bile, Fisher shook his head at the thought

they were on the brink of invading another country because of what he'd done. He glanced at Harris, but her blank expression gave away none of her thoughts. Could it be that she was used to dealing with this level of jeopardy?

"To make this clear," Harris said, her words startling Fisher out of his spiral. "We find Farid. If he still has the E-round, we can nip this in the bud, but if it's left the country, then their group becomes the focus."

Miller nodded, and Clark followed suit.

"I'll get the MET commander on the line," Clark said. "And I'll see what we can find out about the FLM."

No sooner than he'd finished speaking, the projected screen changed to a black and white Royal Crest.

"I've recalled troop Gamma from their training exercise," Miller said, pouring himself a coffee from the two small urns on the table Fisher had paid no attention to. "They'll be ready in four hours to execute what we come up with."

Just as Miller finished speaking, the image of the crest disappeared and the screen split down the middle with Clark's face on the left and a man's bald head on the other. He wore a crisp white shirt with a black tie. The silver crossed tipstaves inside a wreath on his epaulets confirmed his high rank.

"Ms White. Mr Green," the man said with confidence. Harris and Miller nodded in reply.

"This is Commander Neil Jackson of the MET," Clark said, using the common term for UK capital's police force. "He's the liaison for SIS."

"Oscar 99 couldn't get a fix on the target from the air, but we found the vehicle twenty minutes ago," Commander Jackson said, seeming unsurprised when no one introduced Fisher. "It was abandoned and burnt out, but the multiple bullet holes in the chassis confirmed we have the right vehicle. As requested, we have eighty percent of the shift looking for him, but I'd like more to go on."

Harris thanked the commander before reciting the address where Fisher had been staying.

"They're armed and dangerous," she added.

The commander nodded as Fisher sat back, surprised when he didn't ask questions.

"Before I forget," he said, his eyes narrowing. "Thank you for the tipoff on Daryl Grant. We picked him up half an hour ago at the place you mentioned. Can I ask how you knew of his location?"

Clark smiled and a moment later the commander's image disappeared, the Welshman's face taking up the entire screen again.

"How did you know?" Miller said, his expression mirroring that of the commander's.

"I sewed a tracker into his back," Fisher replied with a shrug.

***

Farid's red silk sheets were gone from the large double bed as, beside Harris, Fisher stepped across the room. Other than an empty, battered suitcase, there was no sign anyone had lived in the flat.

As a pair of heavy boots arrived at the doorway, Fisher turned to a police officer clad head to foot in tactical black. His eyes, through protective goggles, were the only visible part of him. With an MP5 dangling at his front and a Glock 17 holstered at his side, he held a matching handgun.

Slightly out of breath, the officer pulled down the tactical material covering his mouth.

"The place is clean apart from this," he said, holding the weapon by the barrel. "We'll get forensics to see what they can find," he added, his gaze fixed on Fisher, who walked close and took the weapon.

"No need. It's mine," he said, pulling back the slide to inspect the chambered round. The officer drew back, clenching his teeth as Fisher pushed the weapon into an empty holster under his arm.

"He never planned to come back. I should have paid

more attention," he said as the policeman turned and walked away. A tone signified an incoming call, which they both answered. It was Clark.

"Bukin wants to see you. He says he can help us out."

52

"I know what he's up to," Bukin said, stroking back invisible wisps of hair. After refusing to change into a grey tracksuit, he sat in the same expensive suit he'd worn the day a snatch squad pulled him from his house moments before it exploded.

Physically, he was in a small detention area in the bowels of Vauxhall, but legally was another matter.

"How?" Harris replied, Fisher at her side as they both sat opposite Bukin with a small wooden table between them.

"The same reason I hear most things. He was showing off," he said. "And had consumed a lot of alcohol."

Bukin laughed whilst Harris nodded.

"What exactly did he say?" Fisher said, leaning forward, his expression unmoved.

"He told me all about you," Bukin replied, tilting his head back.

"Details please. What did he tell you?" Fisher said, holding Bukin's gaze.

"All about his plan. The heist," he replied, nodding. "I guess it should have been obvious he would want me dead."

"Not really. I offered," Fisher said, and Bukin let out a hearty laugh as he rested his hands on his ample stomach.

"I think I like you, Mr Fisher, and I am grateful that you didn't go through with it."

"Technically speaking, I did."

Bukin rubbed his eyebrows and let his forehead wrinkle.

"In the eyes of the law, your ashes lay with the rest of the burnt rubble," Harris said. "Which presents you with a unique opportunity, Mr Bukin."

"Yes. I see, and for you too," Bukin replied.

"Indeed," Harris said, nodding. "But we haven't got much time, so I'll spell it out. You no longer exist. You are no one and no one is looking for you. You no longer have the baggage of your past to carry. It's a clean slate. How many people can say that?"

Bukin nodded just as Harris continued.

"Option one is to spill everything before we send you off on your merry way with a new start. Option two... well, option two is not so nice. It involves a journey east, and I don't mean Norwich."

The old Russian closed his eyes and ran his palm over the top of his head, wrinkling his forehead as he rubbed. "I'll tell you where to find Farid."

53

Yanking up the parking brake, Harris brought the Series One to a halt between two silver marked police cars parked at angles, blocking the road of the quiet industrial estate. Fisher jumped out as the wheels stopped, with Harris joining him at the open boot a second later.

After tapping her fingers on the square keypad set into the carpeted floor, Harris pulled open the checker plate metal hatch to reveal the deep aluminium attaché case. Lifting the central clasp, she pushed her thumb against the black pad, then with a swift slide of each of the rotating combinations, the lid clicked open.

Just as he had before, Fisher watched over her shoulder as she grabbed at objects from the first tray before handing him a magazine packed with brass, pushing the remaining two into her jacket pocket. Laying the first tray to the side, she plucked three small matt black pyramids from the layer below.

Fisher leaned closer when he realised he'd not seen those shapes before, paying attention to the tiny wire sprouting from where the three triangles met before she tucked them into her bomber jacket.

After grabbing a medical kit and a black canister covered with illegible white writing, she shut the boot and the pair ran along the pavement to where Commander Jackson had reported Farid was cornered.

The industrial estate was home to low-rise buildings, each a different age to its neighbours, with those in the eastern corner surrounded by hoarding and ready for demolition. As Fisher scanned the workshops, warehouses and trade counter outlets, he spotted a small crowd and a lone, fresh-faced police officer tasked with keeping the inquisitive public away from the action.

The crowd looked on wide eyed as if waiting for a TV drama to play out, collectively flinching when a gunshot rang through the air and the pigeons took to the sky.

"He's got a hostage," Harris said, keeping her voice low whilst gathering her strawberry blonde hair in a bunch and securing it at the back of her head.

Seeing their arrival, the copper moved those who'd renewed their efforts to get a look through the single missing sheet of wooden hoarding to the side, letting the pair rush through the gap as they scoured the weathered brick warehouses and metal-sided units. A second shot rang out and Harris cocked her head to the side.

"MP5," she said, before changing direction with Fisher at her heels as she faced the oldest of the buildings, crossing a patch of compacted brown scrub toward a black Range Rover with its bonnet concertinaed and buried in the side of the venerable warehouse.

All five doors were open wide, with steam and blue smoke spiralling from the hot engine. Harris pulled out her weapon and Fisher fumbled for his as she slowed, staring at a door hanging open by a single hinge, its peeling paint littering the surrounding ground alongside large chunks of the bullet-ridden frame.

Pushing her shoulder against the brickwork, and with the backwards glance to make sure Fisher did the same, she peered around the door and into an empty corridor, her gaze following a trail of blood dotting the concrete as it traced a path past doorways either side before disappearing around a corner.

Fisher followed her step inside, mirroring the sweep of her weapon across each opening before leaning against the far wall and cocking her head as if listening for activity. Hearing nothing, she peered around the bend with her pistol following, where the corridor continued a short distance before opening out into a warehouse littered with debris. A shot rattled the window as it echoed across the vast hall and a pained call followed before an agonised moan blotted out the sound.

Light on her feet, Harris pounced, rushing along the corridor stripped clean of all fixtures and fittings, leaving behind only rough cavities potting the walls. Fisher followed, coming to rest beside her as she stood by the wide opening and listened before turning and pointing at him, then at the ground beneath his feet.

Replying with a nod, understanding her meaning, his wide eyes couldn't conceal his concern for what she was about to do. Before Fisher could voice or make some other case, Harris pushed her Glock inside its holster, then retrieved one of the black pyramids from inside her coat pocket. With it upside down, she briefly fingered the base, then, with a powerful underarm throw, launched the object into the vast space.

Fisher pressed himself up to the wall and pushed his hands against his ears as he squeezed his eyes tight, but rather than a loud bang, he felt an urgent tap on his arm and opened his eyes to find Harris shaking her head before looking away and launching a second object into the warehouse.

Feeling more than a little embarrassed at being unable to recognise the difference between a grenade and whatever it was she was throwing, he realised it was time to submit himself to training.

The pop of a round ricocheting against the dusty warehouse walls wrenched him back from his thoughts. The shot did nothing to stop Harris from swiping at her communicator and after a few more taps, Fisher leaned into the view of the corridor and the warehouse. He looked up, his brow raising as he realised they were cameras she'd deployed.

With a slide of her finger across the screen, the images replaced with a dirty blank wall, before, with another swipe, the image changed to a police officer lying on their back amongst broken wood and shattered glass.

Drawing away, Fisher's eyes went wide when he saw blood soaked into their white shirt above an armoured vest. An automatic rifle lay at their side. Not lingering on the image, with another slide the screen went black before, with a few more clicks, they saw a wide view of the warehouse, its vast space filled with all manner of rubbish.

Pinching the screen, the view zoomed to the back wall where Farid stood, his drawn, pale face only just visible behind a young girl. Despite his arm wrapped around her mouth, Fisher saw the terror projected from her wide, tear-filled eyes, but before he could get a better look, Harris lowered the screen and pulled her Glock from its holster.

"Let me," Fisher whispered, moving his hand to touch her arm, but without looking up, she shook her head. "I'll tell them it's all okay," he said. "I'll get him to drop his weapon."

But instead of meeting his gaze, she shook her head and pointed to his right trousers pocket. A little confused, he pushed his Glock into the holster and reaching inside the pocket, he pulled out his communicator. Before he knew what was going on, Harris placed hers next to his and swiped the screen. A moment later, the camera feed appeared on his phone.

"Neat," Fisher couldn't help saying, then she leaned up to his ear, her breath warm on his skin as she whispered.

"There's no time to get permission," she said, pulling back, then tapped at her screen before raising it to her mouth. "Attention State Zero officers."

Fisher drew away as the words echoed around the warehouse as if she were shouting.

"AFO State Six. Hold your fire."

After repeating the message, she didn't wait for a reply and pushed the phone into her pocket before she pulled back her weapon's slide to check the chambered round. Satisfied, she turned to Fisher and, with a determination he'd seen before, she held her left hand in the air and raised and lowered five fingers twice.

Fisher nodded, hoping he understood as he started a countdown in his head.

One. Harris pointed at Fisher, then to the ground with a nod.

Two. She pressed a small packet into Fisher's hand, then split another apart before pushing bright orange earplugs into her ears.

Three. She turned to the warehouse and pulled the green metal canister from her coat pocket.

Four. Slipping the pin free without delay, she threw it underarm.

Five. She bounded three steps away.

Six. And arrived at the doorway.

Seven. Feeling the packet in his hand, Fisher frantically pushed his phone into his pocket and ripped at the plastic.

Eight. Screwing up his eyes, he hoped there was still time.

Nine. He forced the plugs into his ears.

Ten. Tensed.

Eleven. And waited.

Twelve…

About to open his eyes, a sharp explosion shoved against his chest as intense light overwhelmed his senses, forcing a wave of nausea as he pushed against the wall. Shaking his head and almost forgetting where he was, two gunshots echoed from the main hall.

54

The silence loomed heavy even though Fisher knew from everything he'd seen in the last few weeks, Harris would have already got the job done while he'd cowered from the explosion. Opening his eyes, he raised his hand to shield his face, but seeing nothing other than the corridor, and whilst taking care where he placed his feet, he stepped along the corridor and toward the last wisps of smoke rising from the green canister.

With the sound of his heart pounding in his ears, Fisher pulled the gun from the holster and, using the wall for cover, peered around the frameless entrance, his gaze rushing to a handgun spinning across the floor in a space between the debris.

Soon spotting Harris, he found her with Farid at her feet. Unsure if he was dead, raising himself tall, Fisher took a step into the wide space as he stared at the man he'd lived in fear of for the last few weeks. He looked so pitiful with his eyes closed and slumped with his head on the dusty concrete.

About to step toward them, Fisher's breath caught when he found the young woman Farid had been holding cast to the side with her back on the floor and her white shirt soaked in blood.

His gaze met Harris as she looked up, but despite all he knew of her, he was more than a little surprised when he saw no hint of compassion in her steeled expression. The girl's death would have been unavoidable, despite knowing her aim was almost perfect.

With his hand at his side, Fisher was about to speak when he watched Harris push her index finger to her mouth before raising her arm and circling it in front of her. Fisher hunched over as he lifted his weapon and looked around the dim space, understanding they weren't yet safe.

When a scream cut through the silence, his gaze darted back to Harris, and he found the same girl sitting up with her eyes so wide he thought she'd explode at any moment. As she stared at the blood drying across her fingers, a gunshot drowned out her noise and she ducked with her hand reaching out to point past Fisher.

Crouching, Fisher turned, following the girl's finger to a stack of crates blocking his view. He twisted back in time for Harris to fire two shots toward the same place before dropping. Waiting, Fisher held his breath as he stared at the faded crates, hoping for something to aim at.

When another shot came from the same direction, he flinched, but kept himself raised as the top of a bald head lurched into view. About to shout and lift his hands in hope whoever it was would comply, Fisher's thoughts ran to his orders and the dressing down Harris had taken on his behalf. Not yet knowing what he was now capable of, and unwilling to put Harris through what Franklin would dole out, he lifted the gun. The head had ducked before he could fire.

Instead, he stood tall, rushing forward to sidestep the crate and pushed the gun out. Rounding the corner, he pulled the trigger long before he saw the back of the crouching man with two more shots shocking the body as he found his target.

The dead man lay slumped to the side, the grotesque scar leering at him. Fisher's adrenaline drained away with the smoke from his weapon and before he knew it, Harris stood beside him, her aim following his gaze.

Watching as she holstered her gun and checked the guy's pulse, hearing sobs from the other end of the room, Harris guided Fisher away, leading them to pick through the rubbish and stooping over Farid as she held her hand out for the young woman.

"It's okay," Fisher said. "It's all over," he added as she stood, then froze, her eyes going wide with Farid's hand curled around her ankle.

Avoiding the grotesque halo of blood around the man's form, Fisher unpicked the fingers from the Arab's tight grip, and as the last finger released, she whimpered and ran, bounding the debris toward the doorway.

Fisher knelt and grabbed Farid by the shoulders before helping him sit upright and against the wall as blood oozed from the hole in the Arab's chest and shoulder, speeding then slowing again with each silent, shallow breath.

With a glance over his shoulder, Fisher found Harris not by his side, but instead crouching by the fallen police officer as the wail of sirens grew louder.

"I liked you, James," Farid said, his voice quiet and throaty.

Fisher looked him in the eye as a drop of blood rolled down his chin from the corner of his mouth.

"Where's Luana?" Fisher said, raising his brow.

Farid coughed and Fisher moved to the side to avoid the red spray, watching as Farid grimaced with a smile before looking down at his chest as the siren's echo stopped.

"I'm no doctor, but I think you'll be alright," Fisher lied.

Farid shook his head. "I'm a dead man."

"Seriously, it doesn't look that bad. Please, Farid, tell me where Luana is?"

"If I don't die now, they'll kill me anyway."

Fisher nodded. "Perhaps we can protect you. Just tell me who's in charge. Tell me why this all had to happen."

"So many questions," Farid said, coughing blood into the air.

"Where are the bullets?" Fisher asked as he knelt down at the man's side.

"Long gone. A motorbike picked them up before your friends found us."

"Where are they taking them?" Fisher asked as he held his attention to the man's gaze.

"I don't know," Farid replied, stopping himself from shaking his head. His eyes closed as his voice trailed off.

Fisher touched the side of Farid's head and tapped. "Wake up."

His eyes opened to slits. "Ask the boss," his breathy voice came back.

"Where is he?"

Farid raised his hand hanging limp at his side and made a motion across his face. "Over there," he said, pointing toward the faded crates.

"The handsome guy from the flat?"

Farid nodded, the movement shallow. "It wasn't meant to end this way."

Fisher raised his brow. "How was it meant to end?"

Farid coughed and Fisher turned away as blood pulsed from the chest wound.

"You were meant…" he said, interrupted by his cough. "You were meant to help us free them."

Fisher's eyebrows lowered, leaning in to catch the ever-reducing volume of his words. "Free who?"

Farid's eyes snapped wide as if with a shot of adrenaline. "Your parents…" he said, his voice trailing into silence as his eyes closed and his head slumped forward, the blood stopping its flow.

Pushing his limp head up with two fingers on Farid's forehead, it fell back down as he let go.

"You bastard. Don't fucking do that. Wake up," Fisher shouted and slapped him hard across the cheek, but when he didn't move, Fisher leaned closer and pushed his ear up to Farid's mouth.

Hearing no breath, Fisher looked over to Harris walking over, her hands covered in blood.

Lifting his chin, Fisher picked himself up to find the room swarming with armed police and paramedics.

"He's fucking with me," he said, nodding. "He must be," he added, speaking to no one in particular.

"What did he say?" Harris said, her words soft.

"He said my parents were alive," Fisher replied, sounding as if he was somewhere else, his eyes only focusing when he heard Franklin's gravelly voice.

55

"Braulio Armando Soria," Clark said from the speakers as Harris and Fisher watched the man's sickening image appear on the wall of the conference in Vauxhall. "His INTERPOL record reads like a renegade state's wet dream. We categorise him as a terrorist for hire. He's an Argentinian national, and although very patriotic, he's happy to follow the money. Trained in the disputed mountainous regions between Chile and Argentina, he's been linked with various causes and served a ten stretch in a Chilean prison when he failed to blow up a military base in the mountains."

"Known associates?" Harris asked, looking at a printed page in front of her.

"Various names come up, some of which have links to similar activities, but the ones that stick out are Juliana Padilla, Bruna Tolendo, Agustin Marino and Mateus Williams, all of which keep our American colleagues very busy. The team are running searches as we speak."

Fisher couldn't help wondering if amongst those names really was the man behind all he'd gone through. The man he would kill. "Is that all you've got?" he said, noticing Clark twitch sideways. "Anything more on Braulio?"

After glancing at the desk, Clark nodded.

"That's about it. Although he has a large Argentinian flag tattooed across his chest."

"How did he get the scar across his face?" Fisher asked.

"It could be a Chilean cell mate issuing payback for the attack on the country, but other sources show it as a sign of allegiance," Clark said, still reading.

"That's not a club I'm interested in joining!" Fisher said. "What about Luana? She came to the flat."

Clark's gaze seemed to turn to Harris, but soon went back to Fisher as his fingers tapped on his keyboard.

"The logs show thirty-eight different people in and out of the flat. Times that by ten, and that's the number we recorded outside. The team have so far verified half of them. Have you got a description and I'll look through myself?"

"Five foot nine. Around eighteen years old. Slim build. Brunette with a blonde streak," he said, his voice trailing off. "Trust me, you'll know when you see her."

"Anything on the motorbike Farid mentioned?" Harris said, pulling Fisher back from his thoughts whilst Clark tapped away at his keyboard again.

"We've backtracked Farid's Range Rover through CCTV and ANPR and there was a window of ten minutes and a quarter of a mile where the exchange could have taken place. The site isn't far from where the police cornered them.

"Twenty-three motorbikes passed ANPR within a small enough radius of the location, most of them on the busy Western Avenue. We've determined that four are registered to couriers. Two headed to the motorway and were seen westbound, whilst two went into central London."

"Embassies?" Fisher replied.

"It could mean a lot of things," Harris said, as she played a pen between her fingers.

"How easy would it be to get them out of the country?" Fisher directed to Clark.

"As you said, embassies would be the easiest route. If you have the connections. We have almost no way of stopping a diplomatic package," he replied.

Fisher nodded.

"If it arrived at an embassy, we have to assume it's out of the country," Harris said.

Clark's image shrank and moved to the left half of the screen with a map of central London appearing on the right portion. Green and red round markers scattered across the image.

"Widen the ANPR search to see if we can find out if any of the bikes went to an embassy," Harris said as she pushed a stray hair behind her ears.

"Yes," Clark replied as the pair stared at the image in silence.

"I want all hits from the twenty-three tracked," she soon added.

Clark nodded and Fisher sat back in his chair as an involuntary yawn overtook him.

Harris turned toward him. "It's been a long week."

Clark looked up from the desk. "For you both. You should get some sleep."

"Dinner first?" Fisher replied, his eyebrows rising as he turned to Harris.

"I'll leave you to it and I'll call when I get something," Clark said, but before he could close the feed, Harris raised her hand.

"Hold fire," she said before turning to Fisher. "Can you ask security to call us a cab and I'll meet you in reception?"

Hearing their muffled voices as he pushed the door shut, Fisher only made it to the end of the corridor before he heard Harris jogging to catch up.

"Sorry about that. I just had an operational issue to sort out," she said, coming alongside him. After dropping the documents in a secure locker, they walked from the back entrance to find the evening sun low on the horizon.

"Where do you fancy?" she said as the black cab driver waited.

"I rarely eat out. You choose," Fisher replied.

Harris raised an eyebrow. Smiling, she turned to the driver. "Park Lane, please."

Expecting a restaurant, within five minutes they'd arrived along the front drive of The Excelsior Hotel, a tingle of surprise rising through his stomach.

Without paying the cab driver and thanking him by name, Harris led Fisher underneath the burgundy canopy of the main entrance, where a doorman in a towering round hat welcomed them into the splendour of the vast reception.

Despite feeling a need to grab her hand and hold it tight as she led them across the plush carpet, a French Maitre'd soon left them at a table in a quiet spot where they'd chosen their meals without much word, Harris accepting the waiter's wine recommendation.

As he walked off with their menus, sitting opposite each other, Fisher racked his brain for what to say. Since they'd met, they'd barely spoken about anything but the task at hand and he was desperate for this to be a rare moment they would open up. But instead of saying the wrong thing, he kept quiet, taking solace in her company, away from the frantic beat of what they would soon get back to.

"So how was it, the last few days?" Harris said, looking him in the eye.

Fisher smiled, relaxing in his seat. "Hard work. He liked to party every night, drinking into the small hours. Every evening he'd bring in new women, and I'd be expected to do things I wouldn't normally do."

Harris looked down at the oak place mat and rubbed her finger on an imaginary blemish. "Sometimes you have to do things you'd rather not."

"I didn't," he replied with a shrug as she looked up. "I didn't do anything, but they thought I did," he added, feeling a warm glow inside as her cheeks dimpled.

With the wine tasted and poured, Harris told him she was surprised Lucky hadn't already pulled him aside based on the amount of swearing when he went through the flat's rubbish to find the broken razor signal.

Fisher laughed as she described the bulky sailor in an apron and yellow marigold gloves searching the bags each day at their makeshift command post.

The meal seemed to be over almost as it started and when the waiter took their plates, Harris picked up her glass and the bottle and she found a leather sofa in a secluded corner of the hotel lounge. Shoes off and with her feet curled underneath her, they sat close, facing each other as Fisher tried his best to keep her smiling so he could delight in the dimples he loved so much.

"Will you come to the funeral with me?" he asked before sipping his wine.

"Of course," she replied, her smile solemn. "If you want

me there."

"I do."

"Thank you," Fisher said, looking down at the table.

"How are you handling all that?" she said, the words seeming more awkward than normal.

"I'm not. I haven't processed anything yet."

Harris nodded and before long she shuffled up closer and Fisher moved his head toward hers. As their lips were about to touch, they pulled back.

"Hi, Clark," they said in unison after accepting the incoming conference call.

56

"Sorry to disturb your meal," Clark said as his image appeared on the conference room wall.

"It's fine. We were almost finished," Harris replied, sipping from a china mug.

"We were about to have dessert," Fisher said, holding back a smile.

When Harris shot him a look, he wasn't sure if he saw the corners of her mouth upturned. They both looked elsewhere when Clark cleared his throat.

"Sorry," Fisher said and took another sip of his coffee as Clark spoke.

"None of the four bikes gave us anything useful," he said and Fisher felt his mood dip as he watched Clark's image shrink on the screen before moving to the right-hand side of the wall with the left filling with a map of Greater London, the motorways and River Thames easy to pick out. Seconds after the map appeared, a series of lines, each a distinct colour, rendered on the screen. "The lines are the bike's routes," Clark said. "None of them go anywhere near locations we have any interest in."

Fisher turned to Harris. "A dead end then."

"At first look," Clark said, before either could comment further. Still watching the screen, all but one of the four courier bike's courses disappeared from the map. "Let's add in the other nineteen bikes." As he spoke, more lines spread out in a random mess like new growth sprouting from a seed. "If we take off all but two bikes and add in their journey from half an hour before…"

Two lines remained on the map, their courses tracking from opposite directions. A red line came from somewhere in South London, then went close to the pickup point before heading northwest for two miles. It then disappeared back up to South London again. The blue line came from Kent, south of Greater London, before passing on the outer radius of the original detection circle, then continued on its northwest course for two miles where it turned around and headed back on the exact route it had just taken.

"They used two couriers," Fisher said as the others nodded.

"Yes. A sensible precaution," Clark replied.

"Then what happened?" Fisher asked.

"The bike heads to Dover, stops at the port before disappearing from the camera network."

"Is it safe to assume the package ended up on a ferry to France?" Fisher said, hoping he'd read the situation correctly.

"Yes, and from there, who knows? We're asking for cooperation from DGSE, the French equivalent of SIS," Clark explained, "but it's uncertain we'll get it. I'm working on the assumption the package will make its way to a South American embassy in Paris. I've asked the DGSE to watch two in particular, but it may already be too late."

"When will we know?" Harris asked.

"I'm waiting on the call now," Clark replied.

"Why those two embassies?" Fisher said, glancing between them both.

"Because," Clark replied, raising his eyebrows, "after his prison time in Chile, Braulio continued to associate with an interesting man." The image of a mugshot replaced the map on the screen, an official-looking photo of a short grey-haired man with a deeply tanned face and the collar of a bright orange prison jumpsuit.

"You're looking at Agustin Marino, leader of the FLM."

Fisher stared wide-eyed at the screen as he considered if this man was as far as it went. Was he the man he should kill in Andrew's name?

"Plus," Clark said, raising a finger in the air with his eyes going wide. "Whilst we were digging into his background, we found out he is a former lover of CFK."

"Who is CFK?" Fisher said, shaking his head.

"Catalina Ferreyra de Kaminker. The president of Argentina," Harris replied.

Raising his brow, Clark watched Fisher's expression widen as the information sank in.

"It goes up that high?" Fisher said quietly, his words trailing off as Clark nodded, but his thoughts were interrupted by Clark looking to his side and taking what looked like a piece of paper from someone off camera.

"DGSE has confirmed a bike from the Calais ferry travelled directly to the Argentine embassy," Clark said, nodding.

"That's all we need, isn't it?" Fisher said, swapping his attention between the pair.

"Your flight is in four hours," Clark replied with a nod.

Clark looked up as they stood. "I almost forgot," he said before rifling around on his desk. "I found the woman. Luana. And you were right. She stood out like a sore thumb," he added, holding up a darkened image as if taken at night that showed Luana arriving at the apartment building's ground floor reception wearing the short skirt and crop top Fisher recognised from their one and only meeting.

Swapping the page, Clark held up a second shot. They'd taken the photo from the same place but in the daylight, and dressed in similar clothes, she turned from the camera as if to get in one of Farid's cars. The bulk of Benny's huge hand rested on her back.

"Luana Montez. She doesn't have her own file, but she's named in another."

"What does that mean?" Fisher said, turning to Harris.

"It could mean a lot of things," she replied, shaking her head. "She's probably a dependant or associate of someone of interest."

"Her name is the only detail," Clark said, his tone rising as if repeating the surprise he'd felt when he'd first found out.

"Explain," Harris said, leaning forward.

"Someone scrubbed the file about fifteen years ago," Clark said.

"Why would someone do that?" Fisher said, shaking his head.

"It's an SIS file, based on its age. I'd assume they cut a deal or let the original file's subject loose for their safety," Harris added.

"So how does it help?" Fisher said, looking back, not hiding his confusion.

Clark looked down at his desk. "All we know is the subject, an Alana Montez, is a Brazilian and British joint national. They naturalised her in 1988, so I'm guessing there was some sort of deal."

"That's it?" Fisher said, not hiding the growing frustration in his voice.

"I'm afraid so. What else do you need?" Clark said.

"Can you find out where Luana is now?" Fisher replied, pushing back in his seat.

Clark glanced down, picking through the pages before selecting one and turning back to the camera.

"She wasn't in the car when it came back about two hours later. I'm afraid she could be anywhere. We've accounted for most of the surviving crew, each having left the country via dubious destinations. My best guess is they'll all be together with the E-Bullet, at least for the next few days."

"So we have no choice," Fisher said.

"We have to strike without delay," Harris added, pushing back her chair.

57

"At least we've got a bit of time until the flight," Fisher said as Harris's One Series pulled through the armoured gates and into the traffic deadlock.

"It looks like it's going to rain," she said as she leaned forward and looked up at the grey sky.

"What is it?" Fisher said, watching her tapping on the steering wheel.

"Rain?" she replied, her attention never leaving the red of the double-decker bus filling the view in front of them.

"We both know small talk isn't our thing. Just say it," he said, turning toward her.

Glancing over, she wore a warm smile, then looking back to the road, she filled the bus's place as it moved forward.

"Did you identify your parent's bodies?" Harris said, not looking over.

Fisher fidgeted in his seat for a moment, then swallowing hard, he straightened his back.

"The police wouldn't let me," he said, staring at the bus. "They used dental records instead."

Harris pulled out her phone, rolling the car forward another couple of car lengths just as a horn sounded from somewhere beyond the bus.

"What's this all about?" Fisher said, trying to catch her eye, but she was busy looking at her iComm.

"It's just what Farid said before he died," she said, resting the phone on her lap and pulling the car forward, closer to the rattling rear of the bus.

"He was confused," Fisher said before turning to the side window. "I mean, TV shows aside, I'm not sure how coherent anyone would be in their last moments," he added, whilst paying no attention to the mass of grey cloud. "My parents have been dead for years. How could he know anything about them?"

"Perhaps," Harris replied, before letting the silence grow

for a moment. "But he didn't sound confused to me."

"They're dead," Fisher said with a shake of his head.

"I'm sorry," Harris replied. "But says who?"

Despite them both staring through the windscreen, neither of them seemed to have noticed the bus had moved forward.

"The police. Dental records. The death certificates," Fisher said, his voice almost a whisper. When a car horn rang out from behind, she pulled forward just as a single, large raindrop dashed itself on the windscreen.

"Did they test their DNA?" she said, glancing over as he shook his head. "I would have wanted to be sure."

Another raindrop joined the first before a torrent of water followed, battering the glass. As Harris turned on the wipers, peering out his window, Fisher watched the deluge engulf commuters hurrying for shelter or unfolding umbrellas.

"I closed off that part of my life a long while ago. I don't want to go there again," he said, watching water wash down his window and only turning to her as she reached over, placing her palm on his knee. "But if there's a chance, I guess I owe it to them to find out. How long will it take?"

"We have what we need. Your parent's sample was in the police file and we already have yours."

"How?" he said furrowing his brow, not noticing the rain ease.

"Your induction medical. You should pay attention to what you sign."

Fisher nodded, looking away as she made a call.

"Thirty minutes," Harris said after ending the other brief conversation.

His eyes widened and he looked over with his head thumping in his chest. "That's quick."

"I had them start in case you said yes."

Fisher's stare shifted from traffic to the clock when the call came in. They'd hardly moved, and had spoken even less in that time. With the rain a miserable drizzle, the one sided conversation gave nothing away.

"Whatever the results, just tell me," Fisher said as she ended the call.

"We should do this somewhere more appropriate," she said.

"I'll be fine. Just tell me," he replied, peering into the footwell.

"They're no match," she said, just as another horn blared from behind, but despite looking forward, she ignored the gap in the traffic.

"Neither of them?" he said as his heart pounded in his ears.

Harris shook her head.

"So my parents were never murdered?" Fisher said, his eyes lighting up. "They're out there somewhere?" he added as adrenaline coursed through his body.

"Hold on," Harris said. "The dental records weren't wrong."

"But…" he said, trying to make sense of what she was saying.

"I'm afraid it means the people who brought you up *are* dead," Harris said as she turned in her seat to look him in the eye.

Fisher shook his head. Not knowing where to look, his gaze roved over the inside of the car. "I… I… I can't get my head around this," he said, eventually looking back at her. The prolonged blast of a horn broadcast from behind, but neither of them paid it any attention.

"You're adopted. I can't think of any other reason. The people that brought you up were not your birth parents," she said. With a thump at her window, she bolted around in her seat to find a man in a stiff shirt and tie, anger wrinkling his bald head as he bared his teeth.

Pressing the switch, she dropped the window. "Sorry," she said, her voice soft.

"Sorry?" the man replied. "Are you taking the piss?" he added, his volume rising.

Harris closed her eyes as she drew a deep breath, then

opening them, she beckoned him closer. With a glance at the long line of traffic behind, then the clear road in front, he stepped forward on the damp tarmac before leaning up to the window. His eyes bulged as her hand shot out, grabbing his garish tie as she yanked his pink head through the window. "Learn some fucking patience," Harris snarled, her face almost touching his before pushing him away and sending him stumbling back.

"I don't believe it," Fisher said, ignorant of what had just happened as the car rushed along the empty lane. "I can't believe it. No... They would have told me."

"I can prove it to you," Harris said as the road split into two lanes. "Do you have your birth certificate?"

"Of course, but it says nothing about adoption," Fisher said, staring at the road.

"Where is it? I can show you."

"Buried in a box of family stuff at my flat, I guess," Fisher replied, not noticing as Harris glanced at the digital clock on the dashboard.

"We've got time," she said, the car lurching forward as she changed down a gear.

58

Kneeling at the foot of his bed, the thick, stale air hung around him, but ignoring the dust irritating his nose, Fisher reached an arm underneath for a box he'd pushed away many years ago. Touching the cardboard, his fingertips slipped, but rather than trying again, he paused and drew in a slow breath of dry air.

After a moment he crouched lower, pulling the cardboard from its hiding place.

The plain box had once held cartons of cereal whose brands were long gone from the shelves, but now held memories he'd pushed away, but were already spilling out as he brought the box to his kitchen table.

Harris didn't speak as she sat at his side, watching as still standing he pulled the top open in the middle, then took out great handfuls of the jumbled contents, spreading photos, some loose and others in frames mingled with papers of different shapes and weights. Leaning forward, he rifled through the contents, shaking his head as his pace increased, then he withdrew, grabbing the box by its sides and upending the contents onto the table.

Reaching her hand out to his, she watched as he swept photos and printed pages to the side, and sensed his desperation not to linger on anything he wasn't looking for. As her hand caught his, he looked over, but his head was elsewhere.

With a deep breath, he nodded and she let go, watching as his hand went to the pile, only to linger on a group dressed for a wedding.

A bride and groom stood in the centre of a photo with smiling guests in their best clothes stretched out on either side. Fisher's gaze drew to where his parents stood, the picture having looked back from the mantelpiece for so many years. It didn't look right without its sun-faded, thin wooden frame, and the cut to the corner reminded him of when the glass had smashed under his hand.

His gaze wandered to the left of the bride in the billowing white dress and to an aunt he'd not seen since the funeral, and his father standing tall, smiling with his arm around his mother with her bulging loose curls of hair. Between the pair was his own cheeky grin, a hand held either side.

Closing his eyes for a moment, he fought the need to run. Instead, he opened his eyes, taking time over each of the faces until their names came to him.

Placing the photo away from the sprawling pile, he looked over the mess, stopping when his degree certificate came into view. As he slung it back into the box, he spotted the yellowed page with the neat writing from a fountain pen.

"May I?" Harris said, raising her hand toward the document.

He nodded, watching her reach out and take it from the pile, uncovering another photograph from the same occasion. Five people filled the shot taken on faded grass with the bleached stone of a stately home as the backdrop.

Taking the photo with a light touch, he drew it close, then turned it around before squinting to make out the scrawled writing.

Aunt May and Uncle Terry's Wedding 1993.

Turning the stiff page over, he focused on his parent's wide smiles before concentrating on a baby and the tender face of the child's mother with a white flower in her short dark hair, the sun highlighting a streak of blonde.

With a glance to Harris, he felt a contentment, but the feeling fell away as Harris spoke, turning the certificate toward him.

"I'm sorry," she said, holding his gaze as he took the page. "The filing date is two years after you were born." When he replied with the furrow of his brow, she pointed at the date. "You're adopted, and someone tried to hide it."

Letting the photo fall from his hand, he nodded. "If Farid knew, then the others might, too."

59

Fisher's eyelids shot wide as the soft-voiced landing announcement came over the cabin's speakers. Turning to his side, he fumbled the illuminated control until with a gentle motion the seat rose, returning upright just as a smiling, white-toothed stewardess served a steaming cup of coffee.

Within half an hour, the wheels of the giant Boeing 777 screeched onto the baking Orlando runway, where, meeting Miller and Harris in the aisle, they joined the short queue of those first to disembark.

To Fisher's surprise, they left Miller to head alone following the crowd to passport control, whilst he went with Harris towards flight connections.

"The plan changed while you were asleep," was all she said as they headed down the quiet corridor and into the plush American Airways lounge, before being shown into overstuffed seats where an enthusiastic steward delivered a brown package.

After pulling apart the seals, Harris drew out a fold of purple Peso notes, a red Santander Rio credit card and two airline tickets. Taking five notes from the fold and handing them over to Fisher, she raised her brow.

"It's for emergencies. Not champagne," she said, her dimples shining through as she tried not to smile before turning to her communicator and using it to change the name on her passport to match the tickets. Taking Fisher's, she did the same. Within half an hour, they were back in first-class seats and en route to Buenos Aires, giving Fisher no time to get any meaningful conversation going.

At the end of another nine-hour flight, they boarded a bus bound for the city centre. After obtaining the tickets in what sounded like a fluent tongue, Harris explained the taxi companies were run by criminals and were routinely bugged by either the gangs or the security services.

The twenty-minute bus journey took them through the

busy streets lined with a diverse blend of gothic architecture before arriving at their destination. Amongst the tall buildings, they strode a short distance along the main road before heading down a side street to the door of an office building with mirrored windows. Without consulting a map or direction notes, it was clear she knew where she was going.

Fisher stood back as Harris climbed the few concrete steps, knocking on the wooden door before stepping back. Not saying a word when the dusty grey net curtain hanging in the window above the door twitched, Fisher watched for her reaction when a clank of metal came from behind the faded wood. She neither moved nor spoke as the door swung wide, saying nothing when no one showed themselves in the dim recess beyond.

It was only as a man in his thirties pushing something into the back of his waist band appeared, did Harris raise her chin. The guy was short and with a head of jet black hair even around his mouth. In a khaki polo shirt and jeans, he beamed over, opening his arms as Harris climbed the steps. Tight in an embrace, they both raced to speak, the Spanish incomprehensible to Fisher who only moved toward them when Harris pulled herself free and glanced over her shoulder.

"Ingles, por favor," Fisher said, using half of his foreign vocabulary all at once. Looking around Harris, the stranger smiled.

"My apologies," he said in a throaty mid-west American accent. "I was just explaining if we'd had more notice, we would have tidied up."

Harris smiled at Fisher. "No, they wouldn't."

Both still laughing, they headed further inside as Fisher followed up the rest of the steps and closed the door behind him.

"Sorry, Estefan. This is Phineas," Harris said, pointing open-handed to Fisher as he tried to not to let his surprise at his new handle show. "Phineas, this is Estefan," she repeated in reverse, pointing at the guy who'd let them in the building. After nodding and smiling in Fisher's direction, he unlocked a heavy wooden door at the top of four flights of steps, behind which an unfurnished office spread out. Empty of all trappings, even the floors were bare concrete.

What he found to his right would have been at home in a forest clearing. Three fabric chairs arranged around a stack of wooden pallets with their top covered in grease-soaked pizza boxes and crushed cola cans. On the floor at the improvised table's side stood a camping stove with steam licking from a metal kettle's spout.

A bearded man stood at the tinted window with his face buried in the viewfinder of a large camera resting on a tripod, its lens longer than Fisher's arm. Another man sat in a chair, with tanned skin and dark hair. Like the others, they looked native. Sipping from a white mug with a yellow and blue crest, he stared at an iPad resting on his lap and didn't look up.

Fisher glanced to Estefan, then back at Harris. "Maybe you *should* have phoned ahead," he said.

Estefan laughed, holding his hand to his heart. "We've had enough of cleaning up after Miss Trinity's visit last year."

Hearing her name summoned visions of the first day they'd met. An image of the nightdress that still visited Fisher in his dreams dissolved as the camera guy looked over.

"I don't want to think about what would have happened if she hadn't retrieved that satellite," he said, his accent deep Texan.

Fisher looked away when he felt himself staring at half his missing ear and a large white line contrasting against his olive skin as it ran down his throat. In jeans and a t-shirt, he wore much the same as the others, and opened his arms as he walked over.

Meeting him halfway, Harris accepted his embrace whilst Fisher watched the guy with the iPad stand and move to the camera.

"So you're here for Agustin Marino?" he said, glancing away from his view down the street.

Harris nodded as she stepped out of the other man's hold.

"We have questions," she said. "As I said in the cable, it's more than urgent."

"We're waiting for him to arrive," he said, turning to look through the viewfinder. "But you won't get anything out of him. He's spent almost a year in custody in the last ten and I know we haven't scratched the surface."

Harris smiled and glanced at Fisher. "That's why I've brought a specialist along."

As if only just noticing Fisher, they each turned toward him.

"Ah, yes," the guy at the camera said. "Well Mr?"

"Phineas," Fisher replied.

"Nice to meet you, Mr Phineas. You're indeed privileged to have such a beautiful travel companion. She usually insists on working alone," he said, stepping over as the other man swapped places at the window. "I'm Benjamin," he said as they shook hands. "And just so you know, I'm in charge here in this beautiful city, and we've worked this guy over so many times, I'm afraid you ain't getting anything out of him in a hurry."

"Does he speak English?" Harris said. Benjamin nodded. "Then it won't to be a problem."

Fisher drew in a slow breath as Benjamin's narrowed eyes looked at Harris before turning to him, his stare only breaking as a sudden crack of thunder filled the air.

Out of the window, Fisher found dark grey clouds smothering the sunlight, with the first few drops of rain sliding down the glass.

"So what's he been up to during the last six months?" Harris said, turning away from the window.

Benjamin opened his palm toward Estefan, who stepped from her side.

"Although we've only had him under close surveillance for a few days, there's been a big increase in activity in the last three months. His crew has been in and out of the country more than usual. Some of them haven't returned."

"Where'd they go?" Fisher asked.

"We don't know," he replied, turning his way. "They left

through surrogates."

"Surrogates?" Fisher asked, tilting his head.

Benjamin beamed a grin. "Have you got yourself a baby?" he said, his voice raising with surprise. "I never would have thought it," he added, looking at Harris as he held his mouth open in exaggerated shock.

Taking a single step towards him, Harris raised her right brow. "Stow it, Jackson. There's no time for playing."

Benjamin's eyes flashed wide before he took a step back and pushed his palms up in surrender.

"Surrogate country," Harris said, turning to Fisher. "They fly to a country we don't have a great relationship with, like Iran or Venezuela. Then, using a new ID, they fly on to their destination and they're almost impossible to trace."

Fisher nodded, glancing at Benjamin, who'd turned to the driving rain, as if no longer interested.

Estefan took a seat before reaching for a satchel underneath and pulling out a red cardboard folder.

"Apart from four members, much of his crew reappeared yesterday, but we think they've left the country again. By road this time," he said, sliding his hand under the folder's worn flap. Pulling out a stack of A4 colour photographs, he handed them over to Harris. Fisher moved to her shoulder, watching as she thumbed through the images. Each was of the front entrance of a red brick building. A doorman, dressed in a woollen overcoat and matching peaked cap held the glass door as people came and went. Despite the shots coming from some way down the street, Fisher thought he recognised people in the first few images, but he'd seen so many unfamiliar faces in the brief time he'd lived with Farid.

The second collection was of the target himself. The older man's skin was a darker brown, but looked more relaxed as he puffed on a giant cigar, rather than holding up a placard in police custody.

"They were taken yesterday afternoon," Benjamin said as he moved to her side, watching as Harris flicked through another set of images of people he recognised from the first photos. Some arrived on their own and others together.

"Wait," Fisher said, reaching out to place his hand on her arm. She stopped flicking through and handed over the lower half of the collection.

Concentrating on the image, Fisher studied two men, both in long sleeve coats. Then his gaze moved to focus on the two women following behind. The woman nearest the camera scowled, her plump frame filling a bright-blue raincoat as if to bursting point and her arm looped tight around that of a younger woman. Despite the white raincoat, he could tell her body took up much less room than her companion. A bubble of water, perhaps on the window, obscured her face.

"Who's the girl?" he said, pointing the photo toward Estefan, who pulled a pocketbook from his shorts and flicked through the last few pages.

"The fat one is Verónica Sanchez, sister of Braulio Soria. He's still AWOL."

"The other one," Fisher said, trying his best to temper the urgency in his voice as he watched Estefan flick through more pages before shaking his head.

"No idea. We only saw her that once. Well, once in, then back out again. Felipe?" he said, turning to the guy back at the camera, who picked up the iPad and tapped his fingers on the screen as Benjamin swapped places. Within a couple of seconds, he passed the tablet over to Fisher.

He stared at the photos. The ground was still wet but with the picture much lighter than before. It had stopped raining and he slid his finger across the screen, watching a procession of images of the same people heading in the opposite direction as one after the other they disappeared down the busy street, many flicking their heads either side, making him question if they knew they were being watched.

With each of them gone from the shot, the next few images showed the building entrance which, apart from the studious doorman standing upright, showed nothing of interest. Then, as if catching the cameraman napping, the next showed a large Chevrolet SUV parked outside and the sister's chubby hand on the young woman's head, pushing her into the car.

A spark rushed up Fisher's spine as a face he thought he'd never see again looked back.

60

"It's Luana," Fisher said out loud.

"Who is she?" Benjamin asked.

"I met her in Farid's flat in London," he added, regretting the words as Harris sighed and shook her head.

"Farid Nassar?" Felipe blurted out, turning from the camera. Benjamin's smile hung high on his face as he looked between Fisher and Harris.

"He's a right little gold mine. Isn't he?" he said, then as Harris glared, Fisher understood the second mistake he'd just made.

"Yes. The same," Harris replied.

"He's got quite the charisma, that Nassar," Benjamin added, watching Fisher nod. "What do you want with him?"

"Wanted," Harris replied. "He's how we got here," she added, with Fisher deciding to remain quiet.

"I hope you've locked him up in a damp dungeon on your little island somewhere. If you're taking requests, I'm sure my old station chief would happily fly over to spend an hour alone with him," Benjamin said, beaming.

"He didn't survive his arrest, I'm afraid," Harris said, almost with a sigh.

"Losing your touch?" Benjamin replied with a raised brow. Seeming to ignore the assertion, Harris turned her attention back to the screen where Fisher had pinch-zoomed in on Luana's face, nodding when he saw the streak of blonde confirming her identity.

"She's pretty," Benjamin said, peering down at the screen. "And perhaps she's not there of her own free will, according to what I'm seeing."

Fisher stared at the photo again, surprised when he felt the same attraction when he'd met her in London. With a redness to her cheeks and eyes, she looked like she'd been crying.

"Boss," Felipe said, not taking his eye from the

viewfinder. Each of them turned his way whilst Estefan grabbed the iPad, jamming in a cable trailing from the camera, the screen coming to life. To Fisher it felt as if the air in the room disappeared when he saw the man he'd been searching for since Andrew's death flanked by two flabby figures. Question after question raced through his head.

Did he know what happened to his parents? How was Luana involved in this mess?

When no answers followed, he felt an almost overwhelming need to grab a gun and fill the guy with lead. Instead, he stared at Agustin's squat, leathery face bobbing along the street until they disappeared into the neon of an American diner.

"His morning coffee," Estefan said to no one in particular.

"He's a creature of habit," added Felipe.

"He must know we're watching," Harris said and Fisher turned her way, expressionless as he spoke.

"We're about to find out."

From the outside of the building, it looked to Fisher that they could be in any American town. The pale blues and bright reds of the window dressing were so synonymous with a fifties-style diner that not even the flamboyant greens and yellows of the coffee shops and street bars either side could push the thought from his head.

Inside, a long chrome countertop stood the length of the narrow room, lined with shiny metal stools smoothed with bright red leather. Row upon row of glossy red leather booths ran along the opposite wall, the space filled with a buzz of South Americans eating double stack burgers and sipping tall milkshakes through colourful straws.

Stepping through the doorway, Fisher spotted the man sat alone, his bushy eyebrows plain to see over a copy of the Buenos Aires Herald and a frothy latte perched on the table in front of him. The minders sat apart, paying Fisher and Harris little regard from their booth by the entrance, as if the smartly dressed duo didn't fit the bill of who they needed to protect their charge from and did nothing to stop them from joining the eager customers already enjoying mustard-covered hot dogs and cheese-soaked pasta.

With his back to the counter whilst Harris ordered cappuccinos from the server dressed head to toe in candy-stripes, out of the corner of his eye he spotted the tabloid laid on the table with a hand beckoning him over.

Glancing at the moving hand, Fisher locked his gaze with the man in the photo, swearing under his breath when he realised he'd been stupid. Of course the man would recognise him.

Hearing Harris still busy paying the bill, Fisher slipped from the bar and across the tacky black-and-white tiles, drawing a slow breath before speaking softly to himself.

This is for you, Andrew. Enjoy, and slid across the leather.

61

Agustin raised his liver-spotted hand as Fisher paid attention to the skin hanging loose over skeletal fingers, barely covering bright blue veins, then looked up as the man's head dipped a shallow nod he guessed was to calm his minders. Knowing Harris would have his back, he didn't turn around to check.

"You came," the man said, showing off yellowed teeth.

Remaining silent, Fisher took in his features, unsure why his expression was so full of delight when he must have known why he'd taken the long journey.

"We thought we'd lost you," Agustin said, his voice accented and much lower than he'd expected.

"Lost?" Fisher said, the word carrying a hard edge.

Agustin's eyes narrowed and his shoulders hunched before coughing. "Why are you here, Mr Fisher?" he said, the sound rasping in his throat.

"I came to find out why," Fisher replied. Spotting Harris standing facing them from the bar, he did his best to ignore her glare.

"Mr Fisher, I don't have time for games."

"You killed my friend," Fisher quickly replied, desperate to gauge the man's reaction.

"Ah. Yes," he said, considering his words, his cheeks bunching in sympathy. "That was more than unfortunate and I couldn't be more sorry."

"Sorry?" Fisher replied, raising his voice and leaning forward. "Sorry for killing my friend? My brother? You need to come with me. There are some people you need to meet."

Agustin shook his head. "I have no care to meet with the Americans again. They cannot see further than the end of their nose. Mr Fisher, it was not me who ordered your capture, or what happened to your friend."

"Call it what it is. Murder," Fisher said, spitting out the words.

Agustin dipped his head for a moment before looking

Fisher in the eye. "No one gave those orders. They were the misplaced initiative of an associate and…" he said, rubbing his forehead, "unfortunately, a friend of mine."

"What the hell is going on?" Fisher said, shaking his head.

The old man closed his eyes. "It took me a long time to figure that out," he replied with a nod.

"And?" Fisher said, his tone rising, but Agustin kept quiet, staring across the table. "Enough," Fisher added before reaching out across the table.

Agustin snatched his arm away with surprising agility before pushing himself back into the red leather, a smile turning up the corners of his mouth.

"You can't forget her, can you?" he said, and although Fisher knew who he was talking about, his words only added to his confusion. Even now, with his heart racing, Luana was in the forefront of his mind.

Unable to stop himself, he glanced to Harris, who stared back, trying not to think of her beautiful curves that he craved so much. He had such different feelings for her. He wanted to be close to Harris. He wanted to get to know her, take her in his arms, and make love. With Luana it wasn't sexual, but still he couldn't stop thinking about her.

"I can see in your eyes. I'm right," Agustin said, raising his brow.

Fisher turned back to the old man with a nod. "How do you know?" he said, his voice much softer.

Agustin picked up the glass mug before taking a sip and wiping the foam from his top lip. "She's one of the more interesting ones," he said.

"The more interesting ones?" Fisher replied, furrowing his brow as the smile crept back onto the old man's features.

"Do you know what she is?"

"What do you mean?" Fisher replied, leaning on the table.

"She's a Locator."

Fisher hung on every matter-of-fact word, leaning closer still when Agustin's lack of expression implied no further explanation was needed. But seeing the question on Fisher's lowered brow, the old man's eyes wrinkled. "She can sense people like you. She's quite famous. Well, she had a famous mother. You might remember her?"

Fisher shook his head, but not just at his question. "What are you talking about?"

"Her mother was the first to locate you," Agustin said, his expression flat.

"Locate me?" Fisher replied, shaking his head as Agustin nodded. "None of this makes any sense. Let's go somewhere we can talk so you can tell me what the hell is going on."

"Here is fine for now," the old man replied, but Fisher barely heard the words for the thoughts racing inside his head.

"What has all this got to do with the Malvinas?" Fisher snapped.

"Oh, Mr Fisher," Agustin replied. "My past follows me around, but I'm afraid that's a bad conclusion. That was my old life. My eyes, my mind, my soul were closed. That petty dispute is inconsequential now."

Fisher leaned forward and stood, grabbing the old man's weathered arm in a tight grip.

"Cut the crap and stop talking in riddles. What the hell do you mean? Your eyes are open. She's one of the more interesting ones. One of what? Where are the things you stole? And if it's not about the Falklands, then what is it about?" he said, Harris stiffening at his side.

The old man raised a hand for his minders to sit. "There's a war going on and you need to pick a side. After all you've been told, I would have thought your choice was clear."

"Been told?," Fisher said, almost shouting. "What do you mean, been told? All I've heard is riddles." Fisher tightened his grip around Agustin's wrist.

"Braulio didn't tell you?" the old man said, rubbing his forehead as he looked between Fisher and where he held.

"I never spoke to him," Fisher said.

Agustin's eyes shot wide, his brow lowering a few moments later. "Reuben assured me they would do it my way. He never said anything to you?"

Fisher shook his head.

"Shit. In that case, we have much to talk about. But not here. It isn't safe. They're not going to like us meeting like this," Agustin said, his gaze flitting around.

Fisher let go and as he sat back in the seat, the large pane of glass at the front shattered just as Agustin's wrinkled forehead exploded, showering everything in a small radius with bone and brain.

Before Fisher could take a breath, the wind thumped out of him as Harris's weight pushed him into the leather.

62

Despite one ear sandwiched between his head and the leather seat and the rest of him covered with some unseen part of Harris, the muffled screams and her commands barked in Spanish still made it through. Watching the dark liquid drip under the table as the shouts subsided, he tried to remember how many shots he'd heard.

When all sound had gone and feeling the slow percussion of her heart through his back, he felt his own pace slow, taking comfort until her weight slipped away as she dropped underneath the table, leaving only a firm hand resting on his shoulder.

"Stay down," she said before she moved in front of the body slumped on the seat, and as Fisher angled his head for a better look at her rifling through the trouser pockets, he wished he hadn't moved. With half the head gone, he realised it was the missing parts that covered him.

The room remained quiet as Harris tugged a revolver from inside the blood-soaked jacket, followed by a leather wallet and phone. As she turned to Fisher with a deep burgundy streak of hair matted to her face, a familiar American voice called from the entrance.

"Trinity!"

Fisher's gaze locked to hers, her finger at her mouth as she held her bloody hand out to stop him from raising in his seat. With a nod, letting the revolver lead the way, she rolled out from her hiding place.

Steeling himself for the loud report, when no gunfire came, only a crack of thunder cutting through the air followed by the gush of rain pouring from the sky, Fisher couldn't tell how much time had passed before he raised his head when Harris called his name.

Pulling a sticky, dangling mess from his hair, his gaze fell to the table covered in clumps of grotesque debris as he lifted his head. Although he tried not to linger on the sight, he knew he'd never un-see the fragments of bone and the curve of what might be a nose nestling among the tall condiments, whilst a sheen of red covered the coffee foam in the mug.

Standing on unsteady legs, he kept his breathing shallow, trying to limit the metallic smell from entering his nostrils.

Fisher turned his attention to the door and found only Harris beckoning him over. Pulling himself out of the stall, he walked towards her, trying his best not to look at the minders slumped in the booth with coffee and blood pooled like an oil slick on the table.

***

The white flannel still came back pink as Fisher stood in front of the bathroom mirror scrubbing at his face, despite the long shower. The journey which had started with Estefan whisking them through the doors of a panel van whirled through his mind. They'd sat on the floor not saying a word, barely noticing the turns this way and that until around ten minutes later they were through the back door of a hotel, arriving a moment later where he stood.

Their hosts had watched from the street, spotting the sniper high on a roof but too late to stop the four shots on target.

Glancing to the screen of his communicator, he saw the message from Harris. She was outside the room with fresh clothes and, with a towel wrapped around his waist, he opened the door, inviting her in with a swing of his palm. She'd changed into a pair of tight blue jeans and underneath a black jacket she wore a white t-shirt that hugged her breasts. Another pair of jeans and a black t-shirt draped over her arm.

Stepping into the plush suite, she placed the clothes at the foot of the double bed, then stared, silent for a long moment before taking off her jacket and resting it beside the pile.

"You look a sorry state," she said, and with that Fisher headed back to the bathroom to stare at his bright-red reflection. After rinsing the flannel, he bent his arm around the back of his neck, then felt a soft hand take the cloth. Looking in the mirror, he watched as, with care, she worked at the skin on the back of his head, resting a warm hand on his shoulder.

After wringing the flannel several times more, her touch sent a spark down his spine as she traced his contours to the edge of the towel and around to the side.

Fisher turned around, catching her eye, the events of the day long gone as her hands hovered between them. Unable to resist, he moved his head forward, and she did the same until her shallow breath lapped at his face. As she closed her eyes, he did the same, but at the muffled sound of a rousing polyphonic arrangement of the Argentine National Anthem, they drew apart and looked back into the bedroom and at her jacket.

After chucking the flannel onto the counter, she reached for her coat, drawing out a clear plastic bag wrapped around the phone she'd taken from Agustin's body. With the screen alight, a streak of dried crimson covered half the digits, but without hesitation she ripped it free, scratching the gore from the screen whilst Fisher rushed over to the small wooden desk, almost tripping over his towel on the way to grab a pen as Harris dictated the number into her communicator and took a photo of the vibrating screen for good measure.

As the anthem began a bass-less repeat, the noise stopped, and she was already on a call, repeating the number back to Clark as she hurried into the corridor, letting the door shut behind her.

63

With the powerful midday sun pouring through the window of the fifth floor landing, Estefan's balled fist thumped on the wooden door, beside which Felipe stood, leaning on the flaking frame with Fisher and Harris a few steps behind, waiting by the wall. Scraping his boot across the bare concrete, Felipe watched as Estefan hammered a second time before turning to the spectators, raising his brow with a question. Harris nodded for him to try again.

Whilst he called out something urgent in Spanish, Harris pulled out her communicator and held it vertical as she moved it across the view.

"Get us inside," she said, completing the sweep before Fisher could see the screen.

Felipe looked at his colleague and shared a short but silent conversation that gave Fisher the impression that if it had been anyone else, they'd have ignored the request and given up. Instead, they disregarded the law of the land and with the deft application of a pick, the door clicked open as quickly as if they'd use the right key.

Handguns drawn and directed out in front, their hosts headed into the darkness. Fisher went to step forward, but Harris held him back with her arm outstretched as she moved to the side of the frame and peered around to watch the American's backs.

Over her shoulder he peered down a corridor, much of it dark before ten paces along where sunlight bathed the walls from somewhere unseen. To his left, a door stood ajar, the room beyond bright with light bouncing off white appliances. The Americans parted, Felipe stepping through a doorway, giving Fisher a view of a dining room and white plastic garden furniture arranged in a circle.

A feminine cry ripped through the silence as Felipe entered the light room, and despite not knowing the language, Fisher felt the urgent terror and he looked at Harris for permission. Glancing back, she held her palm up, then pointed to the ground with the familiar instruction before they both peered along the corridor to find their colleagues out of sight whilst both their weapons lay on the floor by the entrance.

Unable to understand why they'd dropped their guns and still with the background of unintelligible shouts from a high-pitched voice, Fisher went to speak but found Harris already stepping along the corridor, despite not having drawn a gun he hoped she'd secreted somewhere.

Despite the noise, he held still, until out of the corner of his eye he spotted the light from the far room on his left blocked out for a fleeting moment. Without pause he stepped into the flat, walking to where neither of them had gone, the darkness of the room soon engulfing him. Staring at the bright light from the ajar door, he halted at the silhouette of a shotgun's barrel.

The screams continued to fill the air, the light going in and out, disturbed by the figure as if they were pacing, their movement stilted with foreign screams and shouts raging.

With another step, and almost able to touch the ajar door, Fisher held still in the darkness, peering through the crack. Watching as the figure's movement settled into a rhythm, moving backwards and forwards across the door, a moment later the light blotted out. When they held there for a breath, Fisher rushed against the door, using his bulk to slam the wood into the short figure, sending them falling back and he realised it was a child.

Fisher's hands gripped the rising shotgun before pushing it down as he fell on top of the girl with the gun between them.

Settling on the floor, he felt the shotgun slip sideways from his grip, just as the slight figure struggled under his weight. Not wanting to hurt the kid, Fisher pushed his hand under her long brunette hair, gripping her neck as he tried to speak as softly as he could manage.

"We won't hurt you."

The girl convulsed, trying to wriggle free, but Fisher just

kept his grip. "Agustin sent us," he cried, feeling an almost instant relief as the squirming settled.

After holding back to make sure their pause wasn't a tactic, Fisher pulled himself up, then with a glance to his right he found the two Americans, their eyebrows raised and mouths gaping open in the room's corner. Harris stood to their side in the doorway, holding the shotgun, its length snapped open, exposing the brass of two round cartridges in the breach. He tried his best to ignore the deep frown, which said more of her disappointment than any words.

Forcing himself not to dwell on her expression, Fisher turned back and held out his hand to help the child from the floor, who before taking the offer, swept a hand across her olive brown face to reveal a wisp of hair on their upper lip proving she was in fact a boy.

Just as the realisation came to Fisher, Estefan appeared at his side, pulling thick plastic ties from his back pocket as he motioned for the boy to press his hands together.

"That won't be necessary," Harris said and, as if the chain of command had reversed, Estefan withdrew.

"English?" Fisher said, pulling up a plastic chair for the boy who stared back.

"Yes," came his calm reply as he lowered onto the seat. Fisher grabbed a chair for himself, sitting opposite.

"What's your name?" he asked, keeping his voice as calm as he leaned forward.

"Didn't Agi tell you?" the boy replied, his eyes narrowing as he watched the Americans leave, taking the weapons with them. Harris leaned against the door frame.

"He employed us to take you somewhere safe. There are some terrible people trying to find you," Fisher replied. "There wasn't time for him to tell us your name," he added, swallowing hard as he looked at the floor. "Before they killed him."

Looking up, Fisher found the adolescent's expression unchanged.

"You're not surprised?"

The boy shrugged, sending loose hair falling from his shoulders. "He let his guard down. That can be the only reason. He's..." he said, but held back, staring at a mark on his jeans before picking at it with his finger. "He was old."

"I'm sorry. He must have meant a lot to you," Fisher replied. The boy looked up, his eyes narrowing as he stared back. "I'm Phineas. What's your name?"

After a long moment, the boy's expression relaxed and he lifted his chin.

"Joseph Travolta, but people call me JT."

"Any relation?" Fisher said, raising his brow.

"My mother thought I am. Why are you asking me all these questions? What did Agi tell you?" he replied, narrowing his eyes again.

"Not much. Where are your parents?" Fisher said, watching as the boy shrugged.

"Padres?" Harris said over Fisher's shoulders.

The boy's eyebrows twitched before he shook his head.

"Guardian?" Fisher said, then twisted around to Harris.

"El Guardián?" Harris replied, mirroring the boy's slight smile.

"Rudy," he said with a nod.

"Where is Rudy?" Fisher asked, but the boy just shrugged again. "How old are you, JT?"

"Sixteen next week," he said, his cheeks bunching as he nodded.

"I think Agustin hired us because he thought something like this might happen. He wanted us to take you somewhere, but he couldn't tell us where," Fisher said, leaning closer.

"He's dead now," JT said, his voice low as he looked down at his trousers and fingered the same spot. "You can walk away."

"We had an agreement," Fisher replied. "And a reputation to uphold."

The boy nodded. "So, what did he tell you?"

"He said the safest place is with his other friends, but I don't know what that means," Fisher said, raising his brow as he shook his head.

"I know, but I don't understand. I was forbidden to go there and had to wait," JT replied, screwing up his face.

"Something must have changed," Harris said over his shoulder.

The boy looked at her. "It's why I was told to stay here."

"What changed?" Fisher asked, sitting back in his chair.

"When they came back two days ago, they only had half of what they'd hoped for," JT said, rubbing his forehead.

"What was missing?" Fisher said.

"A weapon, I think," JT replied and Fisher glanced back, catching Harris's eye.

"What was the other?" she said without acknowledging Fisher.

"I don't know," he replied, shaking his head. "When they came back, they were… uh… devastado."

Fisher turned back to Harris again.

"Devastated," she replied, and JT nodded.

"It flipped everything on its head. Everything they'd planned was gone, that's what they said."

"But they went anyway?" Fisher asked, despite his uncertainty at what they were really talking about.

"When you've spent five years of your life searching for something, training and building up to that point, even if it turns out to be a suicide mission, you're going to give it your best shot," JT said, still looking down as a tear formed a dark spot on his trousers. "We should find them."

"We will," Fisher replied. "Do you know where they are?"

JT shook his head. "I'm not even sure which continent they're on."

Harris stepped to their side and crouched beside Fisher. "Do you have a phone?" she said, her voice soft.

JT looked between them, then raised a little before reaching into his back pocket to retrieve an old model iPhone.

"Are their numbers in there?" she said, her voice softer still.

He nodded and tapped in a PIN, the screen coming to life

before scrolling along the contacts and stopping.

Wei.

Fisher read the number aloud before Harris turned and headed through the corridor, calling over her shoulder.

"Let's go. We have a busy day ahead."

64

Touching down in Orlando Airport, the trio left the American Airlines 747 with the rest of the cattle class. All it took was a reassuring touch to the back of JT's hand and Fisher's soft voice in his ear to push through the hesitation in the false chill of the terminal at the sight of a military uniform diverting them away from the well-trodden path to passport control.

Following Harris and with Fisher at his back, JT headed out through a side door and into the sticky heat of the airfield, where they climbed into the belly of a grey US Air Force Pave Hawk with its blades already a blur above their heads.

After twenty minutes in the air they were back on the ground, touching down a rotor's length from the wing tip of a C17 Globemaster, then stepping through the downdraft with the full scale of the giant air lifter filling their view. To Fisher it seemed impossibly large and as if it could fit the airliner they'd just stepped from inside, albeit with its wings cut off.

Climbing the steps at the side of the vast hulk, Fisher's brow raised when he saw a venerable Bell Huey helicopter made so famous by the Vietnam war, strapped to the floor inside.

"A successful trip?" Miller's voice echoed from the front as he shouted over the noise of the idling engines.

"We'll have to wait and see," Harris said as the three reached a single row of seven seats that wouldn't have looked out of place in an airliner rather than as an isolated group bolted to the floor in front of a fifty-year-old helicopter.

With a nod, she pointed JT to the middle leather seat and after watching him fumble with the straps, she took the place next to him then motioned for Fisher to sit the other side. Looking up, Miller had taken the position to the far right just as a man in Air Force uniform opened the door they faced and came down the steps, before handing Harris a tough-looking blue plastic wallet, the opening sealed with bright yellow tape and the words *Diplomatic Bag* repeated in a multitude of languages in bold black letters.

With the uniform's feet clanking on the metal floor as he headed into the cavern behind them, the engine's drone all but disappeared as she stashed the package down the side of her seat whilst JT gawked around the extensive fuselage.

After twenty minutes in the air and a Valium-laced cola later, with JT's head angled to the side and a string of dribble pooling on the sleek upholstery, Fisher watched Harris retrieve the package, ripping open the seals before emptying the contents onto her lap. All he saw through the clear plastic bag was the phone they'd taken from Agustin, still covered in his blood, and he looked away a moment before Harris recited the IMEI number to Clark back in Wales.

Listening to her voice, Fisher closed his eyes, letting his mind drift to the moments before that phone rang.

As his lips grew near to hers, the sound of footsteps opened his eyes and he watched Miller climb to the cockpit. Realising they were alone again, he turned, looking over the sleeping boy to Harris as she did the same, but like a teenager himself, he didn't know what to say despite his desperation to find out what the moment had meant to her.

"Benjamin called," Harris said, the first to break the silence. Fisher nodded. "They didn't catch the shooter. Although they have a lead, he wouldn't give me any details."

"Who would want Agustin dead?" Fisher said, the words reminding him of Harris's pressing weight as blood ran down his face.

"They think it's an inside job, but there are too many uncertainties. We need to find where his group's vanished to. He also gave me some info about Reuben Vega," Harris said, watching as Fisher's eyes narrowed. "He was Agustin's prodigy for years and with Agustin getting older, there were rumours he was the one running the show."

"Do we call off the task force? It's not about the Falklands now," Fisher said after a moment.

"I'm not so sure that's true," she said.

Fisher slowly nodded as he thought about everything he'd been told.

"Clark should have a better idea from the phone by the time we land," Harris said.

Fisher nodded again, looking away at the sound of Miller's feet on the steps and let the low drone of the engines punctuated with Harris's taps on a laptop send him into a kind of trance. With his eyes closed and head bobbing as he drifted in and out of sleep, silent images of Harris, sometimes Trinity, washed in and out as a montage of their time together. Mingled in between were thoughts of Luana from their only encounter. He pictured her head laying on his pillow as they talked long into the night.

As time went on, in his dreams she stood and walked towards him whilst not getting any closer, and with every step her skin wrinkled and the blonde streak whitened. Just as she seemed to have made progress and reached out, Andrew's face sprang into his head, his eyes open with the bullet hole punctuating his forehead.

Fisher bolted upright, tensing with a sharp intake of breath, surprised to find himself back on the plane with Harris peering across the seats.

"Are you okay?" she mouthed, eyes narrowed and full of concern. With Miller's seat empty, they were alone again.

"Just a bad dream," Fisher replied, running his hands down his face.

"Have you seen this woman before?" Harris said as she picked up her laptop and angled the screen toward him. His chest tightened and his breath held when he saw an image of the older version of Luana he'd just dreamed about.

"Where did you...?" Fisher replied, stumbling over the words as he focused on the white streak. "How did you...?"

"Alana Montez. She's Luana's mother."

A deep breath drew in without Fisher's asking, and his eyebrows rose as he nodded. *Her mother, of course*, he replied, but only in his head. The dream wasn't of the future. He hadn't watched the woman age. It was the past, which meant he knew her.

"How did you…?" he said, unable to get the words out.

"I just dug a little deeper than Clark," Harris said.

"I have seen her before," Fisher replied, remembering back to his flat. Harris looked on, giving him time. "The wedding, with my parents, or whatever I need to call them now. She had a different hair style, but it's her. I'm sure."

"Hang on," Harris said as she turned to the door. Fisher followed her gaze, but looked back when she spoke again. "The baby. It's Luana. The timings are right. She's eighteen now and that photo was taken in 1993."

Fisher stared over, unable to process what she was saying. "I don't understand. She was a friend of my parents? Does that mean she betrayed them? Does it mean she betrayed me?"

Harris shook her head and although it looked like she was about to unclip her belt and come over, she didn't. "We don't know yet. We need to find Luana."

He didn't reply, instead looked to where she'd just turned away from.

"Does this fit with what Agustin said about locators?" he asked, looking at her shrug. "Do you think a person could be drawn to another?" he added, screwing his eyes up.

"I believe in what you can do," she said with a raise of her eyebrows. "So why not?"

Fisher took a moment before nodding. "Then what the hell could they be looking for?"

"Don't you mean who? Agustin said they sensed people like you. But either way, our priority has to be the E-Bullet. We have to stop the assault. I have to undo my mistakes," she said, fidgeting in her seat and turning back down to the computer screen.

"Carrie," Fisher said, his voice soft, and she looked up, her expression full of surprise. "I wanted to talk to you about…" He stopped talking as Miller's boots clanked on the metal steps.

"About what?" Harris said after nodding to Miller, who held two cardboard cups in his hands.

"It's not important," Fisher said, shaking his head.

Miller handed them each a cup of coffee and, after thanking him, Fisher slumped back into his seat. The boredom soon overcame the caffeine, sending him drifting back between the dreams.

"We got 'em."

Fisher's eyelids shot wide at the sound of Harris's voice and found her face alive with excitement as she looked over. "Clark cross-checked Agustin's phone and the number in JT's. We've got a triangulated last location. And," she added, raising her finger in the air, "he's matched it to intelligence Chile was more than willing to hand out. Their location is a known FLM property and routine eyes over the area confirm activity in the last twenty-four hours."

On the other side of Harris, Miller pushed his communicator to his ear.

"Be ready within thirty minutes of our touchdown."

65

Blue sky poured in as the huge side door opened to reveal the airfield cut through a craggy landscape. Harris was the first out, leading Fisher holding JT with a light grip by the arm to keep him steady down the metal steps as tanker trucks and utility vehicles swarmed around the mammoth aircraft.

Pausing as he stepped to the tarmac, Fisher couldn't help but stare out at the undulating land punctuated with large swathes of long grass reflecting bright green with the powerful sun. Despite knowing where they were, it felt as if they'd just arrived in the harsh emptiness of the Brecon Beacons. Guiding JT along, he soon followed Harris around the aircraft to find a sea of low dark green buildings grouped across the horizon, which were just one of the telltale signs they'd landed at a military base and not a tourist airport.

Glancing back to where he'd just walked from, he followed movement out of the corner of his eye, spotting a Typhoon fighter jet rolling from a white domed hanger to taxi along the runway.

As a drop of water landed on Fisher's head, he looked up at dense, grey clouds which hadn't been there a moment earlier. Turning back, he jogged to catch up to the others, heading towards a tall sign with bold white lettering.

Mount Pleasant.

Shown to a room by a man in RAF uniform, they dropped their black holdalls in a room buzzing with a familiar banter. Hotwire stood at the centre of a circle, holding one leg by the ankle as he hopped on the other. As the door slammed at their backs, all eyes turned their way, focusing on the boy. It didn't take long for the dance to resume, along with the volume.

Only Biggy left the circle, an arm outstretched as he showed the trio to a bare side room save for tables loaded with kit bags and a long cardboard tube.

"I thought you would appreciate a bit of space," he said and Harris smiled before reaching out to Fisher's arm.

"There's a briefing in thirty minutes," she said, before moving to the table and setting the piled bags on the floor. Then she took the tube, removing the white stopper from the end before smoothing out a large sheet of paper to reveal a green and brown satellite image of forests and hills.

Fisher stepped forward, keen to look, soon finding two crooked paths from the north and what appeared to be the only man-made features as they swept the south-eastern corner.

"See if you recognise anything," Harris said, pointing to the page before turning to JT, who stared back, blinking as if in a daze.

"Look," Fisher said, beckoning him over before his gaze followed Harris's index finger, motioning a large circle in the centre.

As JT stepped forward, Harris moved away, then grabbed two kit bags and left the room, leaving Fisher with the boy resting his elbows on the table. It wasn't long before she returned in combat blacks matching those in the next room.

"It all looks the same from above," JT said, then Harris turned around, calling for Biggy through the open door.

Wearing an optimistic grin that dropped when he saw the boy shaking his head, Biggy moved his hand to stroke a non-existent beard as he turned to Harris.

"So it's plan B?"

She nodded, looking at Fisher. "Get kitted up. We're all going for the ride," she said, then left with Biggy following as Fisher tried to ignore the spark of excitement tingling through his body.

To the background of the muffled briefing in full flow in the adjacent room, Fisher zipped up his black combat jacket as JT sat on a plastic chair, gawking over.

"This seems a lot of effort just to deliver me to Rudy?" he eventually said, lowering his brow.

"Agustin had friends in high places and he paid us well," Fisher replied, before crouching in front of JT and placing his palm on his hand. "We're going to take you to Rudy," he said as he nodded. "Remember, we're your friends and you're safe with us. We don't mean any of them harm."

JT remained still, only nodding with a slight movement when Fisher stopped speaking. As Fisher stood, the door opened and Hotwire poked his head through, motioning them out before he disappeared.

The troop were filing out as Fisher stepped over the threshold, each of them dressed head to foot in the familiar black tactical combat uniform with no markings or designations, small kit bags hung over one shoulder and various weapons slung over the other.

Biggy, Hotwire, Miller & Lucky carried the HKs Fisher had already seen in action. Bayne carried a long uncomplicated shotgun and Boots held his trusty sharpshooter rifle.

Harris waited inside the room, holding out a Glock which Fisher took and pushed into a holster on his hip, then they pressed in earpieces and fitted black combat helmets before following two aircrew into the bright sun and across the tarmac where Fisher spotted the painted orange and yellow band around the green tail of the Huey they walked towards, the word 'Ejercito' stencilled in white alongside.

After Fisher settled JT in the helicopter's belly, Harris pulled him to the side just as the engine's whine increased.

"She'll take us to the border with Chile where we think their base is," she said, her voice rising as the rotors started spinning. "Although it's painted Argentine Army colours, we'll have to turn off the transponder. It tells other traffic and radar who we are," she added in response to the dip of Fisher's brow. "Which means when they spot us on their screens they'll launch fast jets to intercept," she said. "But that shouldn't be a problem because we have teams heading to the coastal radar stations to punch a hole in their coverage."

Fisher nodded, but not giving him time to speak, she continued.

"We'll rendezvous with HMS Dragon on the edge of international waters to top up with fuel." Her voice grew louder as the engine noise peaked.

"Not everything inside the helicopter is from the seventies," she said, pulling him by the arm as she moved her mouth close to his ear. "You'll see orange stickers in places and if anything happens and we have to ditch, we have to recover them. You won't have to do anything, but I'm telling you just in case."

Fisher nodded, the move exaggerated by the weight of the helmet. "I get it. They'll identify us from the equipment."

Harris pulled back, nodded and replied with a thin smile before ushering him over to the chopper where he climbed up, squeezing himself in the middle of the worn fabric bench seat with JT on one side and Harris on his other.

As Bayne pressed up to JT's other side. Boots crammed up against Harris, with Lucky beside the other sliding door. Biggy and Miller sat where the door guns would mount, and with Hotwire in the co-pilots seat, Fisher congratulated himself on the best view out of the windscreen for the journey ahead.

As they lifted, he wasn't sure if having a clear view was a benefit.

66

Listening to the pilot's voice over the radio, Fisher looked away from the orange stickers which seemed to be on almost every surface. With the rotors thumping their way through the air, he watched the mountainous land shrink out of view. Instead, as he peered across the row he spotted lonely, colourful houses on top of hills dotted with specks of dirty white wool. A rough blue green sea soon took the land's place, and he glanced to Harris, squeezed in beside him.

"Won't they be suspicious about Dragon on the edge of their waters?" he said as she caught his eye.

She grinned back as her voice came through his earphones. "All they'll see is a fishing boat going about its business."

Her words reminded him of what he'd been told when he'd last been on one of the Royal Navy's newest ships, which were designed with stealth technology to give them a much smaller radar footprint.

After a few moments with no land in sight, Fisher felt the Huey swoop lower and, gripping the round edge of the bench, he hoped the pilot would pull up before they hit the cold Atlantic. His hands ached when they eventually levelled out and he told himself there was no chance they were as close to the turbulent sea as it looked, despite the potent smell of the briny water.

He'd watched the clock for over an hour before Fisher focused on an almost invisible speck floating in the middle of his view.

"What if they don't shut the radar down?" Fisher said, leaning to his side, unable to stop himself from voicing the thought.

Hotwire turned to glance over his shoulder from the co-pilot's seat. Fisher followed his gloved finger as he tapped on a metal box with an orange sticker and four unlit LEDs. Three on the left were green, whilst the final one was red.

"Then a couple of French-built fighter jets will track us down and blow us out of the sky," he said, starting a murmur of laughter across the cabin.

Fisher swallowed hard, unsure if he'd ever get used to their humour, just as Hotwire glanced over again and tapped the box once more.

"This here do-hickey detects active radar. If all three green lights are on, you can bet they know where we are and that's when my buddy sitting next to me earns his bonus."

Fisher glanced to the back of the pilot's helmet, then to Hotwire before settling on the four lights.

"What's the red light for?" Fisher said.

Hotwire caught his eye again, his face contorted with a grimace. "It's for secondary radar."

"What's secondary radar?" Fisher asked, but before Hotwire could speak, Bayne's voice came over the headset as the big man leaned around JT.

"It's what they call a radar lock in the movies. A missile's guidance system," he said, then puffed his cheeks. "Boom." His hands spread, his arms arcing out into the cabin with the headset erupting with laughter.

By the time their noise had died back, Fisher was already concentrating on the imposing sphere topping off the large triangular mast which dominated the ship getting bigger on the horizon. Whilst feeling the aircraft slow, the pilot kept in near continual contact with another voice Fisher couldn't hear and they were soon lowering onto the back of the destroyer.

No sooner had they touched down than the hanger doors rolled open with a procession of sailors pulling along a hose, and a silver suited fireman dragging a huge, wheeled extinguisher behind him. Still with the twin rotors slicing through the air, after five minutes the sailors withdrew along with their equipment and as soon as the hangar doors closed, the pilot pulled back the collective and they were back in the air.

That was it, Fisher thought to himself. *The next time we touch down, it'll be on enemy soil.*

The mood in the aircraft seemed calm and he'd soon grown used to skimming the sea again as those in the cabin kept quiet, listening to a woman giving updates, most of which were jumbled acronyms. Depending on what she said, the pilot corrected left or right, as over the next hour, the sea seemed to climb higher with each crash of the waves.

Despite the occasional buffeting from the turbulent air, the mood remained unchanged, with even JT keeping his cool, perhaps still under the influence of the Valium. Fisher couldn't help but watch the hypnotic crashing of the waves and his eyelids grew heavier.

It was only when a high-pitched tone rang from somewhere in the cockpit that Fisher's eyes sprang open. His gaze landed on a single green light blinking on the radar detector, which sent the cockpit into action. Hotwire leaned to his right, pressing a small red button on the lower edge of the unit, which silenced the piercing alarm and the green light stopped blinking, instead staying solid as his voice came over the headset.

"We're just about in the outer detection zone. Delta team should be on target about now."

Fisher felt the wave of interest from those around subside as he settled back in his seat, but he soon leaned forward, noticing a line of green mountains on the horizon just as the tone returned, seeming more urgent than the first with the second light blinking.

As he'd done before, Hotwire pushed the button and the aircraft slowed just a little.

"Any moment now," he said, staring at the panel just as the two green lights went dark.

Fisher let himself smile as he relaxed, watching their approach as their speed built, the noise in the cabin rising as they climbed, going faster each moment until yellow sandy beaches flashed out of view, turning to the greens and browns of grasses and scrubland.

Closing his eyes, Fisher pulled in a slow breath, hoping no one would see the nerves of someone who only a month ago had been content as a tree surgeon's labourer, not a veteran of combat that knew if they didn't get their job done right innocents would die.

Each moment that passed, Fisher felt his muscles tense. As his breathing sped, a panic rose. Forcing himself to think about something else, his mind wandered to the hotel room. Whether it was yesterday or the day before, he wasn't sure. He'd travelled across so many time zones, his biological clock felt shot to pieces.

With a slight shake of his head, he pushed away the semantic and was in the bathroom feeling her breath on his face as their heads moved closer, but about to touch lips, the hotel fire alarm rang.

Realising that wasn't how it happened, he opened his eyes to three lights blinking on the detector. His hands rushed to grip the front bar of the seat as they dived to lose altitude.

With Hotwire silencing the high-pitched squeal, Fisher held his breath, waiting for someone to make a joke over the headphones, or the three lamps that seemed so bright in Fisher's eyes to blink out. When neither happened, he overheard Biggy in the gunner's seat trying to raise the other team, the ones who should have kept the shrieking alarm at bay.

Levelling just above the carpet of trees, it felt like a lifetime before Biggy's voice caused Fisher to turn his attention from their lightning pace.

Delta team were out of the picture. Compromised was the word he'd used. They'd abandoned their mission, but were on their way to safety. They were alone in their task now, although he didn't say that part.

No one commented or reacted in any other way, and much to Fisher's surprise, the pilot didn't twist the stick to turn them around, only raising their altitude enough to stop the skids from striking the trees as the hills climbed in front of them.

If Hotwire had been right, and Fisher had no reason to think it had been a joke, the Mirages would be in the air and they'd soon catch up.

They were still alive fifteen long minutes later. No fast jets had arrived and the red light hadn't signalled the launch of missiles. Either growing in confidence or weary of the concentration, the pilot pulled the aircraft a few more feet into the air which allowed Fisher to release the seat's steel bar to flex his fingers and rub the pain from his hands.

The lull soon ended as Hotwire's voice came through his headset. "Fifteen minutes to target."

As if they'd forgotten all worry, without conversation or committee, those in the back came to life. Bayne and Lucky cocked their rifles before reaching for their Glock side arms. Harris checked hers, Fisher following her example, and he knew the others were doing the same, but the thoughts fell to the side as a crystal-clear tone rang in his head. Knowing it would only be Clark, he answered and as he did, a different sound told him Harris had also connected.

"I'll keep this short because I know you're going to be busy soon, but I thought you'd like to know. We've gone over the details of everything we've gathered so far from Alan, Bukin and Farid and we've found more than one link."

Fisher turned to Harris, watching her stare at the back of Hotwire's seat.

"Go on," she said.

"We recovered a phone in Farid's flat and it had both Alan and Bukin's phone numbers programmed. It was so well hidden they must have forgotten to take it with them."

Fisher glanced over to see Harris checking her watch.

"Both Bukin and Farid attended appointments with the same psychologist," Clark said. "A Dr Stein."

Fisher lifted his head. "Alan went there too. He's a hypnotherapist." Harris turned to look at him with her brow raised.

"There's more," Clark continued. "We visited, and it didn't take too long to confirm they were all given the same treatment."

"What sort of treatment?" Fisher blurted out.

"He called it building up the mind's natural defences against suggestion."

Harris turned to her side window whilst Fisher glanced at JT when he heard his low voice.

"We'll have to follow that one up when we're done here. Thanks, Clark," Harris said.

"There's more," he interrupted. "We asked him why we struggled to get in contact."

"Go on," Fisher replied with a scowl, urging Clark to get to the point.

"He said he was on a business trip in Argentina," Clark said, but just as Fisher heard the words he glanced to his right to another sound, his eyes going wide when he saw JT holding Bayne's Glock still tethered by a cord, his finger on the trigger and aimed at the pilot as he raised his voice.

"Humanity will survive on its own."

With the boy's words only just heard, without thought Fisher pushed out his hand, grasping at the weapon. A shot went off, sending heat searing across his palm. Out of the corner of his eye, Bayne smashed his fist down to release his restraints and was on JT just as a second shot exploded, sending the aircraft lurching to the right with a pain-fuelled scream lighting up their headsets.

67

The helicopter corrected with a sharp roll to the left as JT's shout overtook the scream, his words ringing in Fisher's ears. "They're not animals for your profit."

Ignoring the words and despite the heat in his hand, Fisher tightened his grip on JT's fingers, still on the gun, forcing against the teenager's surprising strength as he tried to push the aim away from the two front seats.

Making some progress, Bayne was out of his seat and pounding the kid in the chest. As Fisher pushed further still, with a sickening snap, JT's grip released, his arm falling limp to his side as Fisher pulled the gun free.

Pinning the teenager against the seat, Bayne forced his full weight against his chest as Fisher watched JT go pale before his eyes rolled back in their sockets and his lids closed.

His hand throbbing, Fisher released the magazine and pulled back the slide to send the chambered round onto the floor before handing it back to Bayne. They shared a look, the big man saying nothing, pulling back from the unconscious boy whilst Fisher got first sight of his injured hand.

Despite the swelling on his palm, the pain was already easing as Bayne undid the boy's seatbelt before bundling him to the floor, where he zip-tied his hands and feet together.

Taking comfort when he realised they were flying straight and level, the feeling fell away when he found Miller leaning between the two front seats, his hands busy around the pilot as Lucky squeezed down the other side.

Hotwire came over the comm, a hint of excitement in his voice. "I've got the controls," he called out. "If you don't need to move around, please sit down. Biggy, you have five minutes to give me a go, no go before we're committed."

Fisher turned to Biggy, watching his brow lower as he replied. "Understood. Give me a sit-rep on the pilot."

The silence that followed felt like a lifetime.

"Through and through," Miller eventually said, without

looking away. "Along his thigh. We're trying to stop the bleeding, Luck…" the voice tailed off into the whine of the engine and the thumping of the blades above them.

Feeling so helpless, Fisher watched Miller's back, seeing only Lucky's lower half as a chilling scream filled the cabin.

"Hotwire. Sit rep on the airframe," Biggy said a moment later.

"She's fine," he replied as he moved his head as if to check again. "It smashed some glass, but these beauties can take a fair beating."

"Make room," Miller said, but before Fisher could react, the man in charge stepped back. The air punctuated with a scream as he strained against the pilot's weight. Dragging him from his seat, they pulled him across the centre console and into the back, where Harris pressed against Fisher to get out of the way.

With Lucky holding the pilot's legs to place him on the fabric bench seat, Harris bunched up to Fisher's side as the medic and Miller knelt at the injured man's side, wasting no time in ripping the soaked flight suit from his leg.

Wishing he'd turned away, Fisher leaned in as Lucky mopped blood from the two wounds with a dressing as it overflowed like tomato soup boiling over from a hot pan, before Miller jammed a dressing near the pilot's hip and then a second on the hole by his knee.

Lucky pulled out a clear Ziplock bag from the pilot's top left pocket, and ignoring the nylon zip, ripped the top half clean off before taking out a miniature box shaped like a coffin. Snapping it open, he pressed a compact syringe against the pilot's leg.

As Miller moved the top dressing, Lucky sprinkled a white powder and despite the agonising screams, he repeated the same on the other side before Miller pushed on fresh bandages.

With everyone in the back staring, the pilot's breath soon slowed and the pair who'd crouched at his side pulled back, wiping their hands on their trousers.

"The blood's already clotting," Lucky said, looking over at Biggy. "He should be okay."

Biggy glanced at Harris, who nodded in reply.

"Hotwire, are you okay with taking us in?" Biggy asked.

"Yes, sir," came the immediate reply.

"Okay. Give us ten minutes, then take us down. When we hit the ground, Hotwire you stay with the airframe. Harris, you're in Hotwire's place."

Fisher watched her nod out of the corner of his eye as she leaned forward to take Hotwire's HK, which he passed over from the front seat.

"Mr Smith, you'll have to keep yourself out of trouble. Bring the kid. We may still need him. If he gives you any crap, can you handle it?"

"Yes, sir," Fisher replied, the words coming out of instinct. The comms went quiet as Fisher stared out of the window. While they'd been fighting a life and death battle in the air, the landscape had changed to a sea of dark green trees, beautiful against the sun beating down through a clear sky.

A moment later, his throbbing hand and Biggy's voice brought his attention back to the cabin.

"Let's double time so we can get our man home, but," he said, looking at each of them, "safety remains our priority. We have no body bags, so remember your drills. We'll be hot in five."

A collective "Yes, sir" rang across the headsets and Fisher turned back to the treetops so close to the window.

With the aircraft slowing, turbulent air poured in as Lucky and Biggy slid open the doors. After binding JT's good arm to the limp one, and immobilising him with bandages which replaced the zip ties, Bayne positioned the boy with his feet dangling into the fresh air whilst gripping the back of his belt loop to stop him from falling. Pumped full of morphine, the boy put up no fight.

With the sea of trees relenting for a small farm in the centre, a white house and a group of barns stood amongst wild and coarse green plants in the fields. Patched with dark green grass and a tangle of weeds, it hadn't been tended in a long while. Still, in Fisher's eyes at least, it appeared to be the best landing spot for miles.

As if Hotwire agreed, their landing felt heavier than Fisher expected, but with little time to crush the grass, the cabin emptied and those in black fanned out, crouching to cover their angles. Fisher followed Bayne, who dragged JT beyond the treeline and into darkness before the helicopter lifted, its noise soon receding.

With JT dumped at Fisher's feet, without a word Bayne ran back to the others, leaving behind Fisher in a lull to listen to his own breath as the comms clicked to signal the timing for the assault.

His vision soon adjusted to the shade, and he watched JT laying on the rough grass, the teenager's eyes hooded as he stared at the trees, his mouth hanging slack.

Fisher hadn't noticed when the clicks in his ear had stopped, and despite straining, all he heard was the leaves rustling in the breeze. Swapping his attention between the kid and the treeline behind him, he couldn't help but wonder how long their assault would take and what he should do if he heard gunfire. If he left JT and rushed to the house, how could he help the super soldiers?

Glancing back to JT's closed eyes, with his good shoulder the boy stroked his face as if on the verge of sleep.

"Are you alright?" Fisher said, his voice quiet, but when the boy didn't reply, he turned back to where they'd landed.

After taking a step, he glanced at the kid still on the floor. With his eyes still closed, Fisher took another step before glancing over his shoulder when he heard a gentle snore. With another few steps JT hadn't moved, but still Fisher went back and prodded him with his foot. Giving no response other than a slight pause in his breath, he showed none of the concerning signs Lucky had warned him to look out for.

Back at the treeline, Fisher peered along at the house in the distance, surprised to see no black figures stalking the field and no trucks full of mercenaries arriving to spring a trap. The comm clicked and Fisher held his step.

"No, no, Mr Smith."

Fisher smiled at Boots' words and stepped back into the shade. Turning, his eyes took a second to adjust as he blinked when he couldn't quite believe there was a space where JT had been laying.

Rushing forward then spinning on the spot, Fisher searched, hoping he'd just forgotten where he'd left him, but hearing a rustle of leaves, he glanced over but saw nothing.

Still he ran, bounding around a thick trunk and through knee-high ferns before catching sight of a branch pinging back.

Pushing himself to run faster, his attention fixed out in front, Fisher's foot caught something out of sight amongst the leaves, sending him off balance. Reaching out to grab a tree limb, pain shot up his leg as his knee jarred and he dropped. Catching the snap of twigs to his right, he gritted his teeth and, not wanting to let the team down, he picked himself up, pushing through the pain as he ran towards the sound.

Taking out his iComm, he double-pressed the home button, then sliding the screen to the right, he selected the radar icon. The screen turned green as white concentric circles radiated from the centre and a single red icon pressed up against his bright blue dot.

After the split-second it took him to realise what it meant, he twisted around, but all he saw was the bark of a tree filling his vision as it rushed towards him.

68

With the wind silently blowing the branches high above and light shining through the leaves like stars twinkling in the night, only the pressure of his forehead forcing against his helmet halted Fisher's dream-like marvelling.

Raising his hand towards the hurt, he held back at the sight of an unfamiliar jagged shape getting slowly larger.

"Sector three clear," Harris said in his ear, her tone bringing everything back to full speed just in time to knock the branch away, its weight thumping instead against the ground at his side.

The wind blew hard, rustling the leaves as Fisher's head pulsed, but knowing he had no choice but to move, he rolled. Peering along the tunnel in his vision, a branch rushing his way was enough to send him feinting to the right before turning his back to the attack and rising unsteadily to his feet.

"Sector two clear," Bayne's voice called out as a blow thumped across Fisher's back, but when it lacked any power, he felt his resolve galvanise. Despite feeling like his forehead had split open and fighting a wave of nausea, he turned to find the teenage boy with bronze skin, his right arm bandaged to his body and another length of cloth hanging free from his wrist as he held a long thick lump of tree.

The boy leapt forward, lifting the branch, but feeling like he could pass out at any moment, Fisher ripped out the Glock from his holster and fired.

Staring at the boy crumpled on the leaf-covered ground, it was only as Lucky and Bayne arrived, both barely panting, that he looked away.

"You okay?" Bayne said, leaning closer to look at Fisher's deformed head. "What happened?"

Not wanting to nod for fear of the pain, Fisher raised his palm, glancing at Lucky kneeling by the boy before lifting his limp form and carrying him out into the clearing.

"He was pretending to be asleep. What'd you find?"

Fisher asked as they followed the medic out from the tree cover.

"They're still searching, but it's unoccupied. There were people here at least a day ago," Bayne replied as they walked.

Regretting the slight movement of his head, Fisher stared at the cottage that wouldn't look out of place in the UK.

A large tin bath and the rusty skeleton of a mangle lay discarded in the rough grass beside the main building. Two barns stood further along, their doors fallen and on the hard baked mud that separated the buildings. Deep wide tyre tracks crisscrossed the yard, but he had yet to see any vehicles.

Catching sight of Fisher, Biggy beckoned him toward the house and into the kitchen where faded pictures of the farm from days gone by hung on wooden panelled walls. With no modern appliances under the heavy block counters, the room focused a thick porcelain sink with wide steel taps arching out of the wall.

Twisting a chair around from a small wooden table, Fisher enjoyed the easing pressure in his head as he sat, then unclipped his helmet's strap from under his chin.

"Woah," came Lucky's call and Fisher pulled his fingers back as he looked up to the medic standing at the sink, the plumbing groaning as water flowed over his blood-soaked hands. After drying them on a white towel at the side, Lucky walked over and, after shining a bright light in Fisher's eyes, he produced a small bottle of pills from a camouflaged pouch.

"Take two of these, then give it a few minutes before you take that off," he said. Lucky didn't wait for a response before he left.

With the pain almost gone five minutes later, it was back with avengeance as he pulled off the helmet, only to fall away as the pressure eased. Resting the helmet on the kitchen table, but leaving the digital earplugs in place to hear the chatter, Fisher stood. Taking care with every step, he walked into the adjacent room.

"How's the head?" Harris said, standing in a dining room where the only furniture was a wooden table with its leaves folded down and tucked up against a wall, besides which was a tall, dark wooden unit, its shelves stacked with dusty crockery. A bright orange and red rug stretched across the floor in the centre.

Standing at the unit, Harris sifted through the drawers, but it was the close fit of the combat trousers around her butt that kept Fisher's attention. As if sensing his stare, Harris glanced over, causing Fisher to regret the quick turn of his head.

"It's fine," Fisher said, remembering her question. It was true, as long as he kept very still.

With a nod, Harris went back to the open drawer as Fisher took careful steps over to the table, his gaze following the tracks in the dust across the folded wood. "Bayne said you haven't found anything yet."

"Nothing," she said, not pulling her head out of the cupboard as she rose on tiptoes.

"Have we got the right place?" Fisher replied as he walked around the room.

"I don't know," Harris replied, upending loose change from a blue ceramic vase as Biggy appeared in the doorway.

"Hotwire called in two frog fighters doing a high level pass. We need to be gone within ten minutes," he said, looking at Harris still moving crockery, then leaving before she responded.

"Grab this," she said, holding out a stack of plates. Taking long steps, Fisher walked across the room, the floorboards creaking as he stepped across the bright rug. After taking the heavy plates, he retraced his noisy steps before setting them down on the thin part of the table. Turning back, he found her holding an envelope.

"Shit," she said as she tossed the yellowed folded papers into the cupboard and looking around the room. After taking a step forward, Fisher glanced down at the rug before lifting his leg and retracing his step to recreate the sound.

"Secret basement?" he said, eyeing Harris with a smile, the pain in his head all but gone.

"No more pills for you," she said, raising her brow as he repeated the move. "Only in the movies," she added before heading into the kitchen.

Taking care, Fisher looked up at the yellowed ceiling, listening to the boards groan as he moved.

"You never know," he said to himself as he stepped to the edge of the rug, his head swimming as he bent over. Changing his mind, he lowered at the knee before grabbing the edge of the material and stepping backwards. When he found no out-of-place lines on the boards, or no handles or keyway in the wood, he took a breath of the dust he'd unsettled.

When a sneeze leapt from his mouth, sending a throb across the front of his head, the room span as he opened his eyes. Stepping forward to reach for something to hold on to but finding nothing, he lowered to his knees before he could fall. As he leaned his hand to the floor for balance, a board pivoted toward him.

Staring in disbelief, he called out.

"Harris."

"You okay?" she said, her voice distant.

"I found it," Fisher replied, and a moment later the light through the kitchen door vanished as she joined him. He hadn't taken his gaze from the raised board as she pulled it free and rested it at the side. He couldn't help but smile as Harris crouched down over the dark space.

"It's just earth," she said, reaching below before pulling her hand up and rubbing the grit from between her fingers.

Frowning, Fisher leaned forward and peered down. Not willing to believe the loose board was just a coincidence, he reached to take a handful of the earth, but instead felt cloth underneath.

Turning to Harris, he pulled the material up and out came a large square of fabric the texture of mud.

Wide-eyed, Harris looked on as Fisher discarded the fabric to the side to reveal wood much lighter than the dark, dry boards above. With his pain all but forgotten and still kneeling, he grabbed at the adjacent dark board, pulling it free to reveal more of the same underneath, along with the glint of a brass hinge.

"Biggy. On me," Harris said, touching at the radio's switch around her neck.

69

"All clear," Harris said pushing her iComm back into her pocket after completing a scan through the wood. Then he watched as Biggy and Bayne, both standing beside each other, swung their rifles around to rest on their straps, each pulling out torches and pointing them to the brass handle recess pressing into the nearest edge of the exposed hatch the size of two people stood side by side.

It was Bayne who bent down to grasp at the metal handle first, whilst Biggy swapped his rifle for his Glock, resting it alongside his light and pointing them both into the darkness before moving down the wooden steps revealed with the hatch open.

"Bingo," he called, when with a flick of an unseen switch, light came from below.

About to follow Harris down the steps, Fisher turned to Lucky, who'd joined them in the dining room, pushing an empty syringe into a pocket at the front of his body armour.

"How's JT?" Fisher said.

"Full of morphine and away with the fairies," Lucky said, distracted as he stepped closer to the opening.

"Is he going to make it?" Fisher asked.

"He's stable enough," he replied, still preoccupied despite looking past Fisher down to the space between the floorboards.

"What's wrong?" Fisher asked.

Lucky shook his head, then looked up and caught Fisher's eye. "He keeps mumbling something."

"Mumbling what?" Fisher said.

"A name. Something like James, but I couldn't quite catch it," he said. Before he could say anything else, Fisher rushed out to the yard where he found JT with a thick bandage wrapped around his shoulder and sitting with his left hand cuffed to the black metal drainpipe. He peered up at the sky, rocking back and forth.

He heard his name before kneeling on the ground at the boy's side.

"Who is James Fisher?" Fisher asked, peering into the teenager's tiny pupils, but when it seemed as if he hadn't noticed him, Fisher waved his hand in front of the boy's face. "Who is he?"

"A let down," JT said, still staring up.

Fisher stood, concentrating on the faraway expression.

"What do you mean, a letdown?" he said.

The kid laughed before his expression hardened. "He should have been everything. He was the one who'd change it all. But it turned out he was nothing, just like those before him," he said, sitting against the drainpipe and knocking against it with his head. "Have you found what you wanted?" JT said with a slight slur as he made eye contact.

"We found the basement," Fisher replied, watching as the boy smiled.

"You should go help them search. You never know what treasures you might find," he said, closing his eyes.

"What do you mean, he turned out to be nothing?" Fisher said.

JT let out a long sigh. "They're going to need your help in there," the boy said.

"I'll go when you tell me what you meant," Fisher replied, trying his best to keep his voice low.

The kid opened his eyes wide, meeting Fisher's gaze as he looked up.

"They wasted so much time trying to find him and bring him along, but somehow you got to him first. He betrayed all of it," JT said, turning his attention to the ground.

"Maybe if you told me what it was you were doing, then I would have been willing to help," Fisher said as he stood, anger welling in his chest.

JT lifted his head, his eyes narrowing as he looked up.

"James?" the boy said, furiously blinking. "Is that you?"

After nodding, Fisher glanced to the house, then back to the boy.

"Why wouldn't you help?" JT added, shaking his head with his brow furrowed.

Fisher leaned down and clenched his fists at his sides. "They tried to kidnap me and killed my best friend. They made me do terrible things, but not once did they ask me to help. Not once did they explain what it was all about."

JT's eyes narrowed as he continued to shake his head. "I don't understand."

Fisher turned, but about to walk back to the door, JT's voice was urgent.

"Where are you going?"

"To help my team," Fisher replied without looking over his shoulder.

"Would you have helped us?" the boy said, impatient.

Fisher stopped and turned, looking off into the distance as he considered the question. "Maybe if I knew what the hell was going on," he said, then turned, taking another step toward the door.

"Shit. Don't go," JT said with a sudden brightness in his eyes. "Who are these people if they're not with the corporation?"

"The Corporation? What are you talking about?" Fisher said, stopping before shaking his head and turning to walk away.

"Don't go in there," JT shouted, his voice high just as Lucky came through the doorway wearing a wide smile.

"They've found the mother-load," the medic called over.

Despite JT's renewed calls, Fisher bounded into the house, rushing into the dining room but finding no-one there. Biggy's raised voice came from where light rose from the floor.

"Oh shit. Clear the building."

Before Fisher could react, Harris appeared clutching a pile of papers as she rushed up the steps with Bayne and Biggy in her wake. Biggy screamed into his radio.

"Take cover!"

Bayne and Biggy hooked their arms under Fisher's

armpits, dragging him off his feet and into the sunlight a split second before an almighty explosion smashed him to the ground, sending shrapnel raining all around.

70

With the last of the debris thumping against the ground, Fisher raised his pounding head to the sway of the surrounding trees, then squinting through the cloud of dust as it settled, he found Biggy at arm's length pushing himself up onto his palms. When a moment later, Boots' urgent voice came into his ears, he felt gratitude for the digiplug's protection.

"This is Alpha Four. Sound off," the sniper said.

"Alpha One. All okay," Biggy said after a tense wait as he brushed himself down.

"What's going on down there?" Hotwire said as Fisher's gaze caught Bayne pulling himself up to his feet.

"Alpha Three okay," he said, his voice deep and dry as Biggy reached down and helped Fisher to his feet. "They'd rigged the cottage."

"Alpha Six. Dusty, but fine," said Miller, as Fisher found him emerging from a pile of shattered wooden planks a few steps in front of him.

"Charlie Two accounted for," Biggy said as he patted Fisher on the shoulder. "Lucky. Harris. Sound off."

When only silence replied, Fisher twisted around to a jumble of shattered timbers where the house had once been and his heart leapt when he heard the transmission as he scoured for movement in the chaos.

"Alpha Five. I'm okay," Lucky said before coughing into the radio, just as a tin bath lifted next to a jagged tree stump beside the remains of a metal drainpipe. "Charlie Three's down," the medic said as he emerged, peering to his feet as he stood.

"Harris?" Fisher said, watching Lucky look up with a shake of his head.

Drawing a breath he hadn't realised he'd held, the relief was short-lived.

"Harris," he shouted and turned on the spot, his gaze

darting across the desolation.

"Charlie One. Sound off," Biggy called on the radio, joining Fisher at his side as they manhandled great lengths of smoking timber from their path, wood that had once been the walls and furniture, pausing only when in the corner of his vision they saw the rubble shift.

Dodging wooden spears and smashed crockery, Fisher picked his way toward where a plume of dust rose. His focus held, then with his path blocked, he threw wood either side, ignoring the sharp jabs in his skin. Pausing for breath whilst he tried to pick the next place to step, he heard a sound, a muffled cry perhaps, coming from what looked like the toppled remains of the dining room sideboard.

Spotting the pages she carried when he last saw her, his feet slipped, teetering on the uneven mess as he rushed over.

"Here," he called out.

Bayne soon arrived and together they grabbed the dark bulk of what remained, toppling backwards and out of the way to find Harris on her back, blinking at the sky.

Dropping to his knees, Fisher ran his hands over her arms in search of injury. "Are you okay?" he said, rushing out the words.

Harris closed one eye and squinted out of the other, only opening them both as Fisher moved to block the sun.

"I'm fine," she said, rolling to her side, before taking Fisher's hand and getting to her knees.

"You shouldn't move," Fisher said, shaking his head.

"I said I'm fine," she said, before rising to her feet and letting go of his hand as she dusted herself off, then bending at her knees to gather the paperwork laying where she'd fallen.

"She's fine," Lucky pronounced after checking her over after they'd made it out of the debris field a few moments later.

"I told you," Harris replied with a glance at Fisher.

"That was a damn lucky escape," Lucky said before turning to the stubby remains of the drainpipe that JT had been attached to. "For most of us."

"What the fuck happened?" Fisher said, looking between Harris and Biggy.

"They're covering their tracks," Harris said.

"Leave this to the debrief. We're still on a time limit," Biggy interrupted, looking up from his watch. "If they didn't know where we are, they will now."

"Get the chopper on the ground," Harris said to Biggy, who nodded. "It'll buy us more time. Everyone in the barn," she added, already striding toward the outbuilding.

Within five minutes, the thump of the rotors filled the air as Miller, Biggy, Fisher and Harris huddled around the first of three large black and white maps spread across a battered work bench. The lines drawn across the paper showed the South Australia and Queensland border. An unnamed lake in the east and a handful of lines with Australian sounding names were the only features, and with no title block or other label, nothing else helped to pinpoint their location.

"It's west of Lake Yamma Yamma. I'd know it anywhere," Harris announced.

Fisher decided not to ask how she could be so certain; instead, he pointed to a hand-drawn red circle between the border and the solitary road.

"What's this?"

"No idea," Harris replied, and looked each of them in the eye before removing the map from the workbench and revealing another underneath.

The second was drawn in the same way, with no title block or clue of its origin. The location was much different to the first and with sparse and faded Cyrillic writing, he guessed it showed Russia, or somewhere close. The same red pen circled a space in the top north-east corner of the large page.

When their expressions remained blank, Harris pulled out the last map, not needing to look up to know their interest when they saw two marks on the plan, one in red, the other a bold black circle marking their current location.

71

Fisher tracked the portrayals of forests and farms before crossing a line denoting the Chilean border, nodding to himself as in his head he climbed the tree-laden mountain to a red circle highlighting a plateau halfway up the peak.

Looking up from the map, he found Harris had turned away. Not quite able to make out what she was saying, she turned around and caught Fisher's eye before reaching into her combats and handing over a silver attaché case.

"You found them," Fisher said, his eyes going wide with recognition. Whilst she was still in quiet conversation with someone else, he wasted no time in pulling open the latch and shrank with disappointment when he found spaces in the foam where he'd hoped for the electronic bullets.

After saying goodbye to whoever she was speaking to, Harris reached inside the opposite pocket and pulled out a red USB stick.

"I found this too," she said. "But I've got nothing to read it."

Pushing it back into her pocket, Harris turned her attention down to her phone screen, but unable to see what she was engrossed in, he stepped out into the open air to find Bayne and Lucky shovelling earth from a mound. Before he could step closer, he turned back as Harris called him to the makeshift table just as a tone rang in his head.

With his gaze fixed on her finger held at her mouth, he answered the call, understanding when an American male voice spoke as if in mid conversation.

"...Take much looking. I saw it on the TV and I've got two sources who verify the information."

"So what have you got?" Harris said, holding Fisher's gaze.

"Juan Carlos Maldonado," replied the man's voice.

"Our old friend," Harris said, nodding.

"Yeah. It was about time he got caught with his fingers in

the till. They've indicted him on corruption charges, but we've seen the file and there's no chance he'll get his day in court."

"House fire or heart attack?" Harris replied.

"Based on the size of his waistline, I think they'd choose the latter. He's linked to the FMJ, but behind the scenes I'm hearing they've had their day. What with the current political climate, there's no need for an underground organisation. For all intents and purposes, they've disbanded," the American man said. Fisher was sure it was Benjamin.

"What was he doing?" Harris said, turning away and running her finger along the open map.

"Leaking surveillance files, military intelligence," he replied.

"Maps?" Harris said, cutting in.

"Yeah, that sort of thing."

"Okay. Thanks, Ben," Harris said, but before she could hang up, he spoke again.

"There's something else. It might be unconnected, but knowing you... How secure is this line?" Benjamin asked.

"All the way," she replied with a nod, staring at Fisher.

"I got a tip from a friend on high. He told me not to travel down country or to cross the border into Chile, for the next few hours at least. They're expecting a strike against a major drug trafficking organisation."

"Thanks again, Ben," Harris said.

"You owe me dinner when you're next in town," he replied, and she looked away from Fisher for the first time.

"You owe me more," she said and ended the call before glancing at her watch and back to Fisher. "That gives us only four hours."

Fisher followed as she walked to the back of the shed.

"It's not about the Falklands..." she said, her words confusing Fisher at first until from her tone he realised she was on another call. "We don't know... Yes, we're on the right track."

Hearing the thump of heavy feet behind him, Fisher turned to find Biggy jogging over.

"We've got hostiles inbound. ETA twenty minutes," he said.

Fisher turned to Harris, watching as she nodded without looking over.

"Yes, sir," Harris said. "Yes, he's fine... No, sir, he hasn't."

With a shake of her head as she turned to face them both, he realised she was off the call.

"Franklin's not interested in what we've found," she said, walking towards Miller, calling for everyone to form up. "He doesn't care that it's not the Falklands. He just wants the E-Bullets back."

"We have our orders," Miller said, pointing a long stick at a map laying on the ground. "We're to assault the mountain base to recover our objective, but we're pretty blind as to what's up there.

"The only evidence of civilisation is a Chilean Army outpost about a mile before the objective. Day plus one images show a chopper but no heavy vehicles and what looks like maybe thirty troops. Their readiness seems low, so we don't think there's any connection with our objective. However, we need to go in quietly. We'll fly in low around the edge of the camp and avoid all contact with these guys if possible." As he spoke, he circled the stick in an arc away from the base marked with a small, polished rock. "From here, we'll tab the last mile. Questions?"

"What's the activity like at the target?" Biggy said.

"Nothing on the last flyover, but the brains are rolling back the tapes to see what they can find. Any questions?" Miller replied, looking around the scrum of faces. "Mount up then," he added when none came, then he turned to Lucky. "How's our pilot doing?"

"Stable, but I've given him some light sedation to make him comfortable," the medic replied.

"Dragon's still tracking three slow movers on an intercept course," Miller said as he glanced at his watch. "Due in fifteen minutes. We need to be gone in five."

The men dispersed, finding their packs and pulling them open before stepping into what Fisher recognised as climbing harnesses. As they shouldered the weight and jogged the short distance to the aircraft sitting in the field, Harris held out a black harness, already wearing her own.

"Biggy wants the option to repel out of the aircraft if we can't land," she said.

Fisher nodded before climbing into the gear, but with no time to contemplate how the snug fit reminded him of his past life, they joined the others at the chopper where Biggy waited in the co-pilot's seat and the injured pilot lay across the floor at their feet. Unable to replace his helmet over his swollen forehead, Fisher climbed onto the bench as the rotors turned, the dust swirling as he heard the chirp of a call from Harris.

Clark spoke, his tone matter-of-fact as he answered.

"We've delved through the previous ten satellite flyovers covering the last twelve months and activity is sporadic. There is a tanker delivery around once a month, and we have three visits of the same civilian four by four at that time."

"Tankers?" Fisher said, his stomach lurching as they took off.

"The type used for transporting liquids. Perhaps foodstuffs or chemicals."

Unsure what it could mean, he glanced over to Harris who, like the rest of the team, rested her pack on her lap.

"Each fly past covers an hour and the tanker hooks up a hose. Within half an hour it's gone. The four by four brings more people than leave, but our coverage is sporadic, so anything could have happened in between."

"Any more on who owns the place?" Harris said.

"It appears to be Chilean Government, but only by default. Based on government records, the buildings don't exist," Clark replied.

Fisher turned to the window. Then, not wanting to linger on how close they were to the treetops, he turned his gaze to the two blinking green lights on the dashboard, only then realising Clark hadn't spoken in a while.

"What about the outpost?" Fisher said, regretting a glance out of the window where it seemed they were even closer.

"It's Chilean Army, but that's all we know," he replied.

"Thanks, Clark," Harris said, and the line went dead.

Not wanting to look at the lights any longer, he watched Hotwire move the collective to the right, and the Huey pitched in the same direction. Seeing one light blink off, Hotwire straightened up their course and nodded over to Biggy, staring at the radar detector.

"Right," Biggy said over the radio as he turned in his seat, locking eyes with Fisher, whose dread in the pit of his stomach grew. "We don't know what we're going into," he added. "So when we land, stay with me. If we can't land, we'll have to rappel. Have you done that before?"

"I've abseiled a bit," Fisher replied, his thoughts flashing back to his old life where he'd strap himself into a harness to climb into the trees daily.

"Great. It's much the same thing, but we do it at speed," Biggy said.

Fisher raised his thumb, but by Biggy's growing grin he knew he'd failed to stop his nerves reaching his expression. As Biggy turned away, Fisher's attention went to the dash just as the second light came back on, this time with no alarm.

"We got a choice to make," Hotwire called out. "The radar signal is strong on our intended southerly course, but it's weaker closer to the outpost."

"Do what you need to do to keep us in the dark," Miller replied. "I'd rather avoid the Sidewinders, if you don't mind." With no delay, the aircraft banked to the right before correcting the other way. The last light blinked out.

Feeling the relief they were out of radar cover, Fisher stared out to the sky above the sea of unbroken green. Seeing nothing out of the ordinary, he turned down to the pilot whose head rested near his feet, watching him mumble with his eyes closed before he turned his attention to Hotwire's hands as they played over a series of switches.

"I'm getting Spanish over the radio on the short range,"

Hotwire said. "Anyone got a clue what they're saying?"

"Let me hear it," Harris replied and a moment later each of their custom moulded earpieces came alive with Latino voices speaking Spanish.

"Helicóptero encontrado en distancia," a male voice said.

"Argentinian dialect, not Chilean. They've spotted a chopper in the distance." Harris paused as the radio went quiet.

"How far to target?" Biggy asked.

"Ten clicks," Hotwire said without delay, as the high-pitched voice spoke again before a slower, much deeper voice replied.

"Argentine, el ejército."

"Lejos cómo?"

"They're close enough to know it's an Argentine Army bird, but their voices don't show any concern. They're trying to figure out how close we are, but I didn't catch their reply."

"Nine clicks," Hotwire added.

"Hotwire, divert left," Harris said. "Let's see if we can work out where they are, but make it look as natural as possible."

Hotwire let the stick drift to the left, stopping only as a second light flickered on and the voices came back.

"Lejos el giro, derecho."

"Okay. They're close, and somewhere to our right. Take her back and higher," Harris said.

"Eight clicks to target," Hotwire said with a nod.

"They've got us in their sights now from multiple locations. I don't think we can avoid them," Harris said, turning to Miller as Fisher looked on.

"They must be spotters. We'd pick something up on the equipment if it was radar," Miller replied.

"Take her down lower," Harris said.

"Seven clicks," Hotwire replied as they lowered.

"Permiso para atacar." The youthful voice was back on, more high-pitched than before.

Harris looked back at Miller with her head tilted to one

side.

"Uh, they're asking for permission to attack," she said, but her voice betrayed no concern.

Miller shook his head. "We're too low for an effective RPG strike," he said, his tone remaining businesslike.

"Six clicks," Hotwire butted in.

"What if…" Fisher said, then Harris locked eyes with him.

"They have the E-Bullet," she replied with no discernible change in her voice.

"Take her up," Miller barked. "Take her out of small arms range," he added, his tone rising for the first time.

Yanking back the collective, Hotwire didn't speak as those inside pinned back in their seats.

"Five clicks," he called out as they angled skyward with the engines whining, his voice strained as they continued to climb.

"Seguir adelante."

"They've got their permission. Brace," Harris shouted.

With pressure building inside his head and adrenaline coursing through his veins, Fisher grabbed the seat in front as they levelled out and a calm seemed to descend, but as it did, the third light on the dash blinked on, followed by a short thud of something hitting their metal skin.

Before Fisher could blink, he let go of the seat, rushing his hands to his ears as a high-pitched squeal rippled through the cabin and the lights inside the aircraft went dark.

The rotors still pounded above their head, but despite only seeing him from the side, he knew Hotwire was shouting. Fisher glanced to Harris, watching as she dug out her digi-plugs from her ears and he did the same, surprised at the whine of the slowing engine.

"We've lost all power," Hotwire kept shouting, then just as if they'd reached what felt like a rollercoaster's peak, the aircraft tipped forward and sped downward.

"Mayday. Mayday. Mayday. This is Tricky Four Nine. Tricky Four Nine. Six miles south east of Natales. Sudden loss of power. Attempting a forced, unpowered landing. Mayday. Mayday. Mayday. Tricky Four Nine. Tricky Four Nine."

As he halted his call, he balled his fist, hitting out at a black box with an orange sticker mounted on top of the instrument cluster, then turned his head to the cabin, shouting over the whine.

"All electrics out, even the radio. We're going down. Brace. Brace. Brace."

With a glance around before Fisher pushed his head between his knees, those beside him secured their weapons before gripping their packs tight to their laps, but without a helmet he felt so vulnerable as they careered toward the ground.

72

Still with his head between his legs, Fisher forgot the rush of air from their sharp descent when with a thunderous crack, something hit against the helicopter's skin, sending them lurching from side to side, only to come to a sudden stop but without the great impact Fisher had expected. Instead, facing toward the ground, they swung, still strapped tight inside the noiseless cabin.

Expecting the sensation not to last, Fisher's eyes bolted wide. Jerking upright against his own weight, he stared through the side window to find it filled with leaves, but it was only as he looked down through where the plexiglass windscreen should have been that he saw the forest floor and realised they were balanced high in the tree canopy.

Hearing movement to his right, he turned, his frantic look pausing on a thick tree branch, its surface pale and raw, shredded of all leaves and bark as it hung like an accusing finger through the spider-web-patterned side window.

Looking away, his stomach flipped as the airframe lurched to one side, pivoting around the wooden finger, which was all that kept them tumbling down.

Grabbing on to the seat's steel frame, he saw the others do the same as he listened to the slow crack of the glass and the menacing scrape of wooden claws against the aluminium skin as they swayed.

Afraid to move, out of the corner of his eye he watched heads turn to look around the cabin.

As if fearing the pressure of their voices could be enough to send them on their final journey, no one spoke for what felt like a long time. It was Miller who broke the tension, rummaging with considered movement through his pack he'd somehow kept hold of during the descent. When he drew out a long length of rope and the airframe hadn't shifted, Fisher watched him shuffle in his seat before reaching out and tying off one end of the black coil to the top of the doorframe. At the sound of movement from the co-pilot's seat, Fisher found Biggy following suit.

"How far it is?" Harris said to no one in particular as she peered at the ground, loose strands of hair hanging on either side of her face.

"Thirty feet. Give or take," Biggy said from the front, just as Miller finished feeding the rope through his harness and dropping the other end, which only just reached the ground. Biggy let his go a second later. "We'll lower first," he added, with Miller nodding.

"Once we're down, secure the pilot," Miller said, pointing to a coil of rope Fisher hadn't seen Bayne take from his pack. "Get a pulley system going."

"We've got to be quick," Biggy added to the metallic click of his restraints unclipping.

With a huff of air, Fisher watched as, taking hold of the rope in one gloved hand, Miller released his restraints, holding onto the rope and swinging through ninety degrees. Fisher gripped tight against his restraints as the fingers of wood scratched along the airframe. Before he knew it, Miller slid away at such a speed as if he'd barely held the rope.

Shaking his head as Miller landed on the ground beside Biggy, Fisher didn't know if he could bring himself to unclip his restraints and repeat the same feat.

Bayne was the next to move and, pushing his feet out against the seat in front, he released his seatbelt, then bent his knees to crouch on the back of the co-pilot's seat. Unsecured and with nothing to keep him from falling if the aircraft shifted again, Fisher watched as Bayne looped the rope under the pilot's arms before tying a knot around his torso. Standing as tall as he could, about two-thirds of his full height, he looped the other end of the rope around the bench seat's steel. Pulling the slack through, he handed the loose end to Fisher, who then passed it to Harris to feed it on to Lucky and Boots.

With nothing more than a nod along the line to those still strapped in the back, each pulled the rope, taking the pilot's weight whilst Bayne guided the man, his features bunched against the discomfort, between the seats before slowly lowering him.

Relieved when on the ground, Miller and Biggy took the pilot's weight, but when Bayne let go of the rope, Fisher realised it wasn't how he would get down. He'd have a more active role. Soon distracted by Hotwire pulling orange-stickered equipment from around where he sat, a voice caused him to turn.

"You can do this," Harris said.

With a deep breath, Fisher nodded.

"But you go first," he said, then held himself, still in fear any movement could upset their balance.

Without reply, Harris reached over and grabbed the rope Miller had left behind, then clipped herself in. As if not giving it a second thought, she released from the seat and glided to the ground before Hotwire dropped the destroyed electronics after her.

"You know what to do?" Boots called over, and Fisher nodded before he looked over to Hotwire, who'd unclipped himself and stood, straddling either side of the windscreen as he reached around the area for the rest of the equipment they were under orders to remove.

Boots slid out of view, rushing to the ground as if this was something they did every week. Then again, it might have been.

With just the three of them left and Miller's rope waiting for Fisher, Lucky climbed around the cabin, still unconnected and reaching out to grab a black box with a sticker from above Fisher's head that he hadn't noticed.

"Lucky. Hotwire. Clip yourself in. I'm not carrying your remains in a bag over my shoulder," Biggy called up as they watched him moving about with nothing to protect him.

Lucky paused then pulled the rope towards himself, but Hotwire, the only one of them to not be wearing a harness, pulled up half the length of Biggy's rope from the ground, before he tied it around his middle.

"Don't worry," Hotwire whispered. "I won't leave you,"

he said, realising from Fisher's expression he knew what was going through his head.

Before Fisher could reply, Lucky stretched out to reach another box marked with a sticker, and just as he did, their entire world lurched as the branch, and the only thing holding them up, gave way.

73

Gripping tight to the straps at his shoulders, Fisher watched as Lucky slipped, his hands scrabbling out to his sides but unable to get purchase. Before the medic could fall, he grabbed the back of the seat just as Hotwire dropped.

Filled with despair, Fisher called out, but the call did nothing, the aircraft shifting with a jolt when the rope around Hotwire's waist caught. The sharp movement sent Lucky off balance, sending him falling past the missing windscreen with the rope rushing through his harness.

It seemed to take Lucky forever to react, but eventually he clamped his hands down on the rope running out of control. It was only as he rushed past Hotwire dangling in the air, and with smoke coming from his gloves, he slowed his plummet. Bending his knees as he met the ground, rather than moving out of the path of the helicopter that could fall through at any minute, he stood, looking up, staring back at Fisher's wide, petrified stare.

"Oh shit," Fisher said, watching Hotwire's failing attempts to pull himself up the rope.

"Cut it," Biggy called up, no emotion in his voice.

Hotwire stopped trying to get a grip to drag himself high, then seemed to go slack in his self-made harness before reaching into a pocket and pulling out a large combat knife, not waiting to slice through the rope.

Unable to believe what he'd just done, Fisher stared transfixed as Hotwire fell, then bent his knees as he hit the ground before rolling to the side and out of his view.

Voices percolated from below, but not loud enough for Fisher to hear. He looked around the cabin, finding no orange stickers other than on the equipment Hotwire had piled in the pilot's footwell. Failing to block out the scratch of the branches along the helicopter's skin, he eyed Miller's rope and for the first time realised he'd have to release himself from his restraints before he could reach it, knowing that as soon as he opened the clasp he'd fall and hit the co-pilot's seat. If the impact didn't send the surrounding metal plummeting, he'd have to find his way across the cabin.

Steeling himself, he went through the motions in his head, imagining what would happen when he released the clasp, but with his fear growing every second, he knew if he left it much longer he'd lose his bottle.

Pulling the clasp open, the fall took much longer than he'd imagined, and as his chest hit the back of the seat, despite the complaint of the metal and creak of the branch, the airframe stayed where he needed it to. Holding tight, he heard Biggy call up.

"Careful."

Not able to hide a smile that he'd do anything different, Fisher pulled himself up to his hands and knees, then craned over to where the rope dangled just out of reach. With the scratch of the branches punctuating his every move, he twisted around until he perched on his behind and took a breath.

Leaning across the space with an ease that surprised himself, he grabbed the rope and clipped himself in, then revelled at the relative security it gave before slipping off the seat to let the harness take his weight. Growing in confidence with every move, he lowered level with the footwell.

"Watch out," he said, then with a glance to make sure the ground below was clear, he reached and pulled what looked like a car radio from the footwell before letting it drop. He did the same with four metallic boxes, listening to their satisfying clatter as they landed.

"That's it," Fisher called, his heart racing at the realisation he'd soon be on the ground.

"There's one missing," Biggy called up, sending Fisher's heart pulsing even harder as, wide-eyed, he scanned the cockpit. About to call out that they must have made a mistake when he couldn't see any more orange stickers, his gaze fell on the far corner of the rear of the cabin where he'd been sitting, settling on an innocuous brushed-grey metal box with an unlit green LED and a bright orange sticker.

"Bollocks," Fisher called out.

With a huff of breath, he raised his leg to the edge of the windscreen, then whilst pulling against the rope, he lifted himself to stand between the two pilot's seats as the creak of the structure reminded him of his precarious situation.

Soon, standing on the backs of the seats, he had the box pulled off its sticky mounts before letting it drop.

"Are you sure there's no more?" Fisher called, his voice echoing as the metal clattered to the ground.

"That's it," came Biggy's reply and just as it did, an almighty crack came from his side and Fisher felt the aircraft slip along the bare branch.

Looking across, he found the wood at a sharp angle to the ground and every time he opened his eyes from a frantic blink, it had moved further before giving way all too soon, with the rush of acceleration charging through his chest.

With no time to think and even less to panic, hearing the calls from below over the scratching branches, Fisher did the only thing he could and jumped, despite knowing the rope still held in his harness.

Falling just as fast as the surrounding metal, for a moment he saw himself high on a suburban street and surrounded by his former workmates, each holding chainsaws as they worked away, but the pull of the harness around his groin tugged him out of the memory.

With air huffing from his lungs, the pilot's seat back hit against his arm as the metal around him crunched and groaned.

Battered from every side, hitting branches as together they fell, Fisher realised they'd slowed and this was his chance, however small. Pulling up the rope he'd held down around his middle, he raised his hand high, letting the cord slip through and watching as his surroundings changed from inside the fated helicopter to the dark space below the canopy.

But as his feet touched the ground, he knew it was still too late and he looked up to the airframe crashing over him.

74

Panting, Fisher still felt alive. But with no pain as he squeezed his eyes closed, he thought perhaps it was his time to answer the universal question. When his breathing slowed and the creak of metal around him stopped, opening his eyes, he realised he wasn't dead.

Still inside the helicopter, he stood with his head almost reaching where he'd sat. Peering around, he found the metal had crashed nose-first, with the scrape of branches slowing it enough to stop it from breaking up, but the building acrid smoke told him he might not be breathing for much longer.

To shouts and calls all around, Fisher fumbled to free the rope from the harness.

Finally free, he scrambled to the remains of the side door, finding Hotwire reaching through the tangled metal.

"That was close," he said, pulling Fisher free.

"Are you hurt?" Harris asked, grabbing his free hand and helping him to the ground before pulling him away from the smoking metal to a huddle of gawking faces.

"You should buy a lottery ticket," Biggy said, as his gaze moved from Fisher to the helicopter's remains.

Fisher stopped and glanced back, his mouth falling open when he saw the smoking mess he'd walked out unscathed from, then looked up to see the hole in the canopy and the branches stripped bare up so high it made him feel unsteady.

"I'm glad you're not mince meat," Biggy called out. "But the time for cuddling is over. Get your shit together. We're moving."

Forcing his mouth closed, Fisher glanced around, watching as each of the dark figures bent over packs, picking through the contents against the background of tall tree trunks and rambling foliage.

"Check your equipment. See if any of it's still working," Biggy called out.

Fisher continued to look around, but saw no sign of his

pack so instead delved into his pocket and pulled out his iComm. Finding it wouldn't turn on, Lucky called out.

"GPS. NVGs. All screwed."

Fisher glanced at each of the group shaking their heads, then turned to Hotwire who held a radio above his head. "Check your short-waves. Mine's working," he called.

"Mine, too," Boots said, his voice low.

"What now?" Fisher said at Biggy's side.

"We get the job done," he replied. "There's no rescue party."

Fisher turned away and swallowed hard, his gaze catching Harris twisting the stubby knob on her radio before throwing the handset back in her pack.

"Boots, go do your thing. Hotwire, you're on point," Biggy called. The pair didn't hesitate and Boots, with his long rifle slung over his back, was soon out of sight.

Fisher followed Harris's lead, forming up behind Hotwire, holding a HK at the ready as he found a path between the foliage. Bayne and Lucky took up the rear with the pilot slung between them, suspended on a fabric olive-green stretcher.

Despite Hotwire's best efforts, the going was hard, with thorns catching against their legs on almost every other step, the ground uneven and covered in roots, ready to trip them at every moment. Fisher tried his best to think of anything but what he might step on, or what could slither out of its hiding place.

Thankful for his hard-wearing footwear, it must have been half an hour before they stopped with Boot's near whisper through the radio Biggy clutched.

"I'm at the Army post, but someone got there first. It's a massacre."

75

The acrid stench of burning plastic hit Fisher as he stepped from the vegetation's cover, his stare fixing across the mud and gravel road before centring on the crumpled red and white barrier discarded to its side.

Figures in camouflage clothes, the green and black pattern so different to what he'd seen before, lay in the mud, grouped around the two stumpy concrete buildings forming the outpost. When his gaze fell on the anguish contorting a bloodied face, he turned away. Despite regretting the detail, he'd seen enough to know they'd not had time to draw their shouldered weapons.

Harris hadn't slowed to take it all in. Instead, she stepped toward a stricken soldier. Bending over the teenager, she pressed the back of her hand against his face before shaking her head as she glanced over. Raising the kid's arm to a sharp angle, she let it drop.

"Still warm and no sign of rigor," she called over as Biggy joined at her side.

"Boots reports their perimeter detection system is out. They had no warning," he said with a shake of his head.

Hearing a low voice from the radio, Fisher watched the pair duck before hurrying to the treeline.

"Two o'clock. Half a click. Chopper on the ground," came Boot's low voice and without delay Biggy took a detached optical sight from his pocket and used it to peer into the distance.

"Got it," he soon said, and Fisher leaned forward, squinting where Biggy looked.

"Eyes on a single X-ray in jeans and a t-shirt around the aircraft. Confirm," Biggy said, his voice low.

"Roger. One X-ray only. Shall I take him out?" Boots replied.

"What's he carrying? Your optics are better than mine," Biggy said, without moving his focus.

"Nothing, but there's an AK on the co-pilot seat."

"I see the door open and the weapon is in easy reach," Biggy said. "Take the shot."

Without delay, a dull pop echoed across the clearing.

"Confirmed," Biggy said, before stuffing the sight back into his pocket. "Hotwire, can you handle that bird?"

Hotwire stepped beside him and peered down the iron sights of his rifle before turning to Biggy with a wide grin.

"A Super Puma. She's a beauty. I want my hands all over her. She'll have a radio, too."

Biggy nodded without moving his gaze. "Take Bayne and secure it. Stay alert. These guys are animals, so don't give them any opportunity. Contact us on channel one-two when you're secure."

Within a few moments, the pair nodded at each other, then bent over before moving with care across the mud, their pace rising as they arrived at the buildings, where they sprinted to cover the open ground with Fisher squinting to keep them in sight.

Five minutes later, the radio clicked.

"I'm in love," Hotwire said, not trying to hide the smile in his voice, despite Bayne's groan in the background. "The controls are in Spanish, but I could fly this bad boy with my eyes poked out."

Within another ten minutes, Lucky and Miller had stretched the pilot to the helicopter and returned empty-handed, joining the remaining three to hike along the edge of the gravel track. Miller and Lucky took point whilst Harris and Fisher walked side by side with Biggy bringing up the rear, each leaving five paces between them.

With her machine gun straddling her chest, Harris moved closer to Fisher whilst taking care to keep to the grass beside the gravel.

"He knows how you got to Barbados," she said, her voice hushed.

Fisher turned her way, his eyes wide.

"Franklin knows you influenced him," she added and

Fisher stopped walking, only moving as she urged him on with a touch of his arm. "He understands why you did it, but he's got his concerns."

"I didn't," Fisher said with a shake of his head.

Harris raised her brow. "Well, he thought you were going to, and that's just as bad," she replied, her brow low and lips straight.

"He saved me the trouble," Fisher replied.

"It's the same result. Do you understand?" she said.

Fisher nodded. "And now he thinks it's how I'll get my way?"

It was her turn to nod. "And he's concerned about your new skills. He worries you can't be..." she paused as if taking great care with her words. "... Managed."

"What happens if he thinks I can't be managed?" Fisher replied, struggling to keep his voice low.

"From what you've seen already, I'm sure you know the deal," Harris said, her eyebrows raised. "But we're a long way from that," she added.

Fisher looked ahead, unsure if she'd just made that part up to keep him calm, but before he could think about it anymore, she spoke.

"There are rumours others are attempting to track you down."

"Who?" Fisher said, raising a brow.

"Franklin thinks it might be other states."

"Other states?" Fisher replied, narrowing his eyes.

"Middle Eastern, or perhaps the Chinese. Russia maybe," she said, her voice still low.

"But *you* don't?" he asked, unsure if he'd heard an uncertainty in her tone.

She shook her head.

"Who then?" Fisher replied.

"I think they might be closer to home."

Before Fisher could question what she meant, the faint crackle of the radio coincided with a sweep of Miller's hand, directing them into the trees. With the going much slower, they continued to walk in silence until Miller raised his hand for them to stop at the sight of a concrete structure beyond the leaves.

As they crept forward, taking care where they placed their feet, their view of the pale grey walls formed a building with no windows, its featureless angles bringing Fisher thoughts of an Armageddon retreat. The walls slanted into a depression in the centre of where they peered, but where Fisher had expected a door was no lock or handle or lines in the concrete hinting at an opening.

The gravel road ended in a wide circle with a dark green, mud-splattered army truck parked at the furthest point. In the centre of the turning circle stood a pile of neatly stacked logs with a green jerry can propped at its side.

Boot's soft voice soon pointed out the red and white paint scratched into the bull bars at the front of the truck.

"I can't find any visible light fittings or cameras," he added. "And no X-Rays, but check out the middle of the depression."

They each took another step, leaning closer as one to get a better look at the faint concentric circles halfway up the wall.

"The E-bullet," Fisher said, almost under his breath, his heart pounding in his chest. "This is it," he added in a whisper.

Feeling a hand on his upper arm, he turned to Harris, her expression grave.

"Remember, we're not here for revenge," she said, just as Fisher drew out his Glock from inside his jacket.

"We're here for justice," he replied, nodding. "And for answers."

"And to set things right," she said, her eyes boring into his.

"To undo our mistakes," Fisher added.

Harris nodded with a weak smile.

Biggy was the first to step from cover, taking care where he placed his feet on the crushed stone with the butt of his assault rifle pressed into his shoulder as he headed towards what they hoped was a hidden entrance. Miller left the safety of the trees next, taking equal care as he crossed to the building's right-hand corner, whilst Lucky detoured to the truck and pulled off his glove, pressing his hand onto the matt paint of the engine cover before turning to Biggy looking over.

"Warm," Lucky mouthed with a nod before moving to the other corner of the building.

Harris held her open palm out in her usual signal for Fisher to stay put, then she pointed to the ground to make sure he understood before peering down the sight of her HK. Together they watched Biggy press a hand against the wall in the centre of the depression.

Letting out a breath when nothing happened, Fisher held his gaze, watching Biggy sweep his hand to the right, pushing again before repeating the gesture on the other side. When the wall moved inwards, pivoting against the right edge, Biggy looked over his shoulder, locking eyes with Harris.

Not taking her eye from her sight, Harris tugged at Fisher's arm and he followed, moving slowly at first as she led him over the crushed stone and around the dry piled wood creaking in the heat of the sun. With her weapon still aimed at the concrete, Biggy pushed the opening wide to reveal a long, straight downward slope and a dark corridor beyond.

Stepping closer still, Fisher smelt strong disinfectant and with the door wide, sunlight bounced off the far end of the corridor.

Beckoning Lucky and Miller, Biggy stepped back before sending the medic into the treeline to provide cover, then moved up to the opening, with Miller following. As Fisher came alongside Harris, she leaned in.

"Remember our objective," she whispered, before turning to the others to make sure they'd heard.

Fisher took the rear, following the line of three and finding the floor rubber like, his feet almost bouncing with every step which brought the alcoholic sting of disinfectant. Lifting his hand to his nose in the hope it would slow the assault, he stared along the seamless corridor of concrete, disappearing into the ever-decreasing light.

Passing through the doorway, Fisher looked back, but finding no mechanism or lock to pick, he realised their need for the E-Bullet.

Miller had waited beside the door, and as Fisher passed by, Miller pushed the heavy concrete back into its place and silently shut out the light.

After a thin metallic click, followed by a short rasp of grinding metal, the orange glow of a flame from Biggy's Zippo lit the room, riddling it with shadows dancing across the walls as each of them searched for features.

Finding nothing of interest in the space, all eyes turned along the corridor to a large metal door Fisher was thankful included a handle.

Biggy stepped toward it, pushing the flickering flame close, then tipped his head for Harris to try the handle.

With his eyes adjusting to the eerie pale light, Fisher watched as she swung her assault rifle onto her back, then after replacing it with her Glock, without hesitation or backwards look, Biggy's Zippo clinked closed to the slight rush of air as the door opened.

With no light coming through from the other side, Fisher held his breath, feeling the hot lighter pushed into his hands. His chest tightened when a soft female voice he recognised penetrated the silence.

"James?"

76

Stunned into inaction at the call of his name, and despite the worsening sting of antiseptic, Fisher stared wide-eyed into the darkness, blinking only when the sweet voice repeated. With a flip of the lighter's lid and a flick of his thumb, the flame sprang to life. Not pausing on the shadows dancing across the rough grey walls, he squeezed between Biggy and Harris, rushing through the doorway to find a pale face squinting up from the corner behind the door.

Making way for the others following with their weapons pointed out, Fisher's mouth hung open as he gawked at Luana's wide-eyed expression, showing no hint of surprise.

Holding back his words, he beckoned her to stand, but rather than rising from where she crouched, she looked down to her right where Fisher's gaze followed along the blue sleeveless summer dress. Unable to see where she stared, he dropped to his knees and pushed the flame out until its orange glow glinted off a grey metal manacle binding her wrist to an eye bolt welded against the metal skirting.

After lifting the lighter, he took in the rest of the room, following the line of evenly-spaced eyebolts with empty manacles along the edge of the floor. Hearing a hint of her voice, Fisher pressed his finger gently to her warm lips, then pulled away before making a fist and miming the turn of a key.

Scattering fresh tears, she shook her head as another dull light warmed the room.

I'll be back, Fisher mouthed as he stepped away, but not before seeing her silent reply.

I know.

Joining the others, he peered over Harris's shoulder, watching Miller hold up another lighter to examine the new door, but before he took in the sight, Miller pressed down the handle and pulled. Bright light burst through the gap, but not waiting for his eyes to adjust, Miller peered in. Within a second, darkness fell as he closed it up again.

Each of them stepped back then watched the older man point to his eyes before holding up his index fingers and crossing them over. When Biggy nodded his understanding, Miller held out each of his palms, then together pushed them forward before squeezing his eyes closed and shaking his head.

Unsure if he'd understood, Fisher guessed there were two X-rays beyond the door and that despite the corridor continuing, it was too bright to see any detail. Before he could think over what he should do next, a high-pitched squeal Fisher knew so well caused the group to flinch and take a step back, raising their rifles towards the door as the lighters extinguished.

Fisher pressed himself against the wall behind the door with a pressure wave pushing against his chest and, as his hearing recovered from the assault, he heard muffled English and Spanish voices.

A sob at his side reminded him why he'd come to this place and, with a deep breath as the broken conversation continued, he told himself it was time for justice. When a long, agonising scream cut through his thoughts, he pulled the Glock from the holster.

"Hold," Biggy whispered as Fisher imagined his fist in the air, his voice sounding so loud in the renewed silence, broken only as a high-pitched voice followed.

"Please, no. Please, don't. No."

"We have to…" Fisher whispered, his words cut short by a gunshot's echo and when a hand rested on his arm, he realised he was shaking.

The muffled voices grew louder and soon they could make out the accompanying beat of footsteps rattling a metal grated floor. Luana sobbed as the sounds clarified. When the touch fell away, he felt the sudden loss along with a desperation to light the flame and reassure Luana that everything would be okay.

With the steps so loud, bodies pressed against both his sides and about to move for comfort, the light burst on, slamming his eyes closed. With the brightness came a renewed antiseptic sting, and knowing nothing good would come from his blindness, Fisher forced his streaming eyes wide, finding a figure walking across his blurred view.

As the view clarified with every rapid blink, he saw they held something out behind them.

"Show some respect," came a deep Spanish voice as another figure walked through the doorway. But despite Fisher's fear, the new arrivals paid no attention in their direction.

"Vee, get on the other end. You too, Mano," came the same voice over Luana's sobs.

With Fisher able to see their lanky frame, their rugby ball-shaped head had dark hair on the lower part of his face but with nothing growing on top. Another man, who other than his grey hair was indistinct from behind, rushed beside him to take the weight.

Fisher spotted pistols stuffed into their rear waistbands.

"Stop crying, you devious bitch," the one in front said, spitting the words with a glance towards Luana. "Just think yourself lucky you've got a use."

Luana quietened, covering her face with her free hand.

Between them they carried a body in a hospital gown, an arm hanging down at their side, the wrist thin and skin gaunt as it dragged along the floor.

With his thoughts turning to Andrew's last moment, the vision fell away when Fisher saw the long scar down the arm of the man they carried, the red raw edges of the wound clumped together and held with thick staples.

Knowing it was Harris who held her arm across his front when behind a pudgy woman followed, Fisher still leaned forward as she passed through the doorway, letting the door close behind her to plunge them into darkness.

"We're taking lights with us to the Congo," the man at the front said. The other voices murmured before a moment later, the middle door opened with a suck of air.

"Stop fucking crying," the round woman said between

sniffs as if her nose were running. "Hold the fucking door, bitch. We need to let some air in."

The delicate arm pressed across Fisher's chest, holding him back as light soon poured from the main entrance. Despite squinting at the brightness filling the space, he saw Luana leaning along the wall, her free arm stretched out to hold the door open.

About to let out a relieved breath, Fisher's heart sunk when a click echoed out from Biggy's radio and the pudgy woman span around on the spot.

77

Miller and Biggy didn't wait, rushing toward the light and digging their stocks into their shoulders before Fisher's head reeled from the rattle of gunfire.

With the wall blocking the view of where they'd aimed, he imagined hands had rushed to the guns pressed against their backs, but knew they'd had no time to grip the metal before they collapsed. At Luana's howl, Harris let her arm drop and Fisher followed her, stepping to get a better look as Miller and Biggy screamed commands to the unresponsive bodies blocking the corridor.

Harris surged with the pair whilst Fisher stayed back, watching the trio kick weapons out of limp hands before pressing fingers against necks. As his eyes adjusted to the light, he saw Lucky rush from the trees as Luana's pained calls subsided.

"Are you hurt?" Fisher said, positioning himself in a crouch in front of her and holding the door open as his gaze roved her body for signs of injuries before catching the shake of her head and tears rolling down her red cheeks.

"Try to calm down," he said, just when his gaze fell on the red raw skin around her wrist. "I need your help," he added, trying his best not to grimace. Looking up, her eyes went wide as he motioned the Glock toward the inner door. "Are there any others inside?"

"I don't know. Are they all dead?" she said, shaking her head with her attention not moving from his face.

"It's okay," he said, glancing at the door. "Where's the key?"

Bursting into tears once more, she dipped her head.

"They can't hurt you now?" Fisher replied, placing a hand on her shoulder.

"I don't know," she said, before pulling a deep breath as she tried to stop the emotion from taking over. "I didn't see a key."

Fisher stood and slid the gun into the holster, then struck the Zippo's wheel. Using the flame, which added little to the light already streaming in, he scoured the walls until he found a stainless steel panel by the first door. In the centre, a keyhole waited beside a black and white numbered keypad. A blank electronic readout didn't respond as he jabbed the buttons.

"Please, James. Get me out," Luana mumbled between the tears.

"I will," he said, before pocketing the lighter. "And I'll be back. I promise," he added as he followed the trails of blood, letting the door close out Luana's sobs as he rushed into the humid air.

Feeling instant relief as he pulled in deep breaths, he found the bodies laid out in a line beside the piled firewood. Lucky and Harris knelt over the older man, whose eyes were closed as his chest strained against a blood-soaked, salmon short-sleeve shirt. Lucky pressed a white field dressing against his chest whilst Harris held his arm at the wrist as she searched his pockets.

Despite knowing the key had to be his priority, as the pain in his eyes calmed, Fisher felt a desperate need to pay the man a visit. But after a deep breath, he instead jogged over to the first of the dead, a man laying on his back with his skeletal hands turned up on the gravel. Dressed in the gown, he was the one they'd carried between them and in the sunlight's warmth his skin seemed so tight against the thin muscle and bone, reminding him of those found in Second World War concentration camps.

Arriving at his side, Fisher's gaze ran over the scar, causing a lump in his throat, the thick staples glinting in the sunlight before he looked along pronounced blue veins running to a cannula crusted with dried blood just above his wrist. Accepting his own cowardice, he turned away, hoping to keep Andrew's image at bay.

The two bodies at his side were twins, each tall and awkward with long faces rounding in the middle. Their eyebrows were pitch-black, matching what covered their chins. The only difference between the pair seemed to be where the fatal wounds had punched through their sweat-soaked white shirts.

Bile rose in his throat as he turned to the woman he'd seen in the pictures, her figure almost the opposite of the men, overfilled and with much of her muscle tension gone, the excess flab hung down her face to pronounce a bone structure she wouldn't have seen since she was a teen. Blood tracked like a dried-up river from the wound in her left cheek, filling a crevice in her face before drying down to her second and third chins, then falling into the folds of her neck where it pooled in the dusty gravel.

Stooping, Fisher patted her jeans pockets, but stood as someone stepped to his side.

"What you looking for?" Miller said.

"A key. There's some sort of panel I think will unlock the girl," Fisher replied, before stooping again as Miller spoke.

"Harris has their stuff."

Standing, Fisher rushed back to where she still held the older guy's hand whilst Lucky continued to work on the guy's chest.

"Any keys?" he said, hurrying the words.

"No," she replied. "But I'm still searching."

Fisher looked away, eyeing the twins.

"Got it," Harris called out, not hiding her delight, and Fisher turned to find her beaming at what looked like an E-bullet between her thumb and forefinger. "Biggy. We're done here," she called out, before slipping her hand back into the pocket. "Five E-bullets and the chica had the gun," she added, nodding over to the dead woman. "We'll get the girl out whilst you guys package this one ready for transport, then figure out how the hell we're going to get the news home so we can turn World War Three into a training exercise."

Biggy nodded as he grabbed the radio from his belt. "Alpha Two, this is Alpha One, over.

"Alpha Two received, over," Hotwire replied.

"We've got the package and need to phone home. Is the

chopper's radio powerful enough to contact Dragon?"

"That's a negative, Alpha One. All the equipment in the compound is trashed. I'll get Alpha Three to see what he can do."

"The quicker the better. I don't know how long it will be before the locals figure out there's something going on," Biggy said, turning to Harris to make sure she'd heard.

"It would have been for nothing if we can't get a message out," Harris said, standing and beckoning Fisher towards the bunker's opening. With the lighter struck, he showed Harris the panel.

"She's a whizz with electronics. You'll be out in a minute," Fisher said, pushing his cheeks high with a smile.

Luana half-heartedly tried to mirror his expression.

Hearing her sob, he handed the lighter to Harris and crouched in front of Luana. "London to Chile, eh? How'd that happen?"

Sucking in a breath, she held it for a moment, then spoke. "After we spent the night together," she said, her voice low, "I went to the hostel where I got a call. I was so excited to see you again."

"Luana," Fisher said before coughing lightly into his fist. "You know we didn't…" he continued, but stopped himself when he couldn't find the words.

"I know," she said with a gentle laugh. "That's not what I meant. I know what you did for those women, and it's very sweet," she added, reaching out and pressing her hand into Fisher's. "It was one of the guys from the night before. He told me you wanted to see me again, but when I arrived, this guy stopped me in the car park and shoved me in a big car. The Arab from the flat was there."

"Farid?" Fisher asked, but she shrugged.

"As we drove off, he talked about stuff I didn't understand. Like my attraction to people like you."

Fisher's eyes narrowed despite the renewed sting.

"And then we stopped at a block of flats. That's where I met Verónica," she said, tipping her head toward the doorway.

Fisher nodded and leaned a little closer.

"They took away all my things and locked me in a room."

"Did they hurt you?" Fisher asked, relieved when she shook her head.

"They just kept asking questions," Luana said, looking down.

"What sort of questions?" Fisher asked as he bent lower, trying to make eye contact.

"They asked about a number I had in my bag. Did you put it there?" she said.

Fisher nodded.

"When I told them I didn't know how it got there, they asked about people I could feel when they were close. When I couldn't answer she seemed to flip, calling me a mutant, but then a few moments later she apologised and said I was special. It was as if she was two different people.

"In the end, all I could do was laugh at the absurd things they were saying. They said you were special, too, but that your talent was dangerous if you mixed with the wrong people."

Fisher's eyes narrowed as he thought back to what he'd done for Farid.

"They said they were worried about you and kept asking me what I knew. They didn't believe me when I said we'd only just met."

"How did you find me?" Fisher said, unable to take his eyes from her.

"Like I told them, I was just drawn to you. It's like a sensation I feel all over. It's like a comfort whenever I'm getting closer, but the opposite as I move further away. They said my mother was the same, and she was the one to first find you."

"Your mother?" Harris said.

Fisher glanced over, forgetting she stood at the panel.

Luana nodded as he looked back. "They said she'd been working with the British Government when she found you."

"The partial file," Harris said, almost in a whisper.

Luana looked at the rubber floor again. "When I couldn't

tell them anything new, they took pride in telling me it hadn't taken much to get details removed from her file. A well-placed death meant the promotion of someone with a different outlook to fill the space," she said, and her expression darkened. "James," she said, looking him in the eye. "Did you know the government was watching you for years until these people took over?"

Fisher nodded, thinking back to Alan's diaries.

"They took so much delight in telling me how they'd set you up so long ago," Luana said, staring up.

"What exactly did they say?" Harris asked as she went back to examining the panel.

Fisher nodded when Luana didn't speak, as if waiting for permission.

"They weren't sure what you were capable of, only that you were special. At first, all they did was keep an eye on you, but when there was little to show what you could do, they gave you a push."

"A push?" Fisher said, lowering his brow and leaning a little closer.

She shrugged. "They took something from you," she said, tilting her head.

Fisher stood and glanced over at Harris's silhouette beside him. "My parents," he said, the words breathy. "Or whoever they were," he added as he shook his head.

"When you didn't react, their attention turned elsewhere, but Verónica said it was her decision to keep tabs on you. She loved it when you proved her right and when you left the country, they knew it was time to act. Does any of this make any sense?" Luana said, craning her neck to keep Fisher's gaze.

Fisher nodded slowly and closed his eyes, but when the thoughts raced, he twisted around to Harris. "How's that lock coming along?"

She shook her head. "It's dead. We'll have to cut her out," she said. "I'll see what Hotwire can find back at the compound," she added, before leaving Fisher to catch and hold the door to keep the room lit. The lighter was too hot to hold much longer.

"They wanted me to work for them," Luana said, and Fisher turned to face her, unsure whether he was ready to hear more. "They wanted me to help find other special people so they could keep them safe. After a while I believed them, but they'd been lying all along."

"What happened?" Fisher asked, still standing.

"They drove me around London. We spent two hours just cruising the streets. All the while they kept asking me how I felt," Luana said. "After what seemed like a long time, I got the same feeling I always did when I was close to you. Following the feeling, I directed them until it got to where I knew who it was. I pointed them out."

"Then what happened?" Fisher said, crouching.

"We just drove away and they started treating me with some respect. They gave me a proper room," she said, her voice trailing off.

Fisher nodded and gave her a moment to collect her thoughts.

"Then one evening a few days later, I saw the man I'd pointed out to them on the news. He'd fallen under a tube train."

Fisher stood but didn't speak.

Luana closed her eyes, then dipped her face toward the ground.

"The next day, they handed me a British passport and told me we were leaving, but they wouldn't tell me where we were going. I only knew we'd landed in Argentina when I saw the signs, but rather than leaving the airport, we got on a much smaller plane. It was tiny. They flew me out to the borders, tracing circles in the air until I found this place."

"How did you know it was here?" Fisher said as she looked up.

"The same way I found you. I don't know how I can describe it any better," she said.

"It's fine," Fisher replied, just as Miller's head appeared around the door, his gaze searching out Fisher with an urgency in his expression.

"The old guy's come around."

Fisher let the door slip from his grip as without a word he rushed from the space, following Miller to Harris crouching over the pale old man with Lucky at her side, still pressing a bandage onto the man's heaving chest.

Harris spoke, her voice too soft for Fisher to hear any detail, even as he crouched at the man's side and reached to take Lucky's place.

"Apply plenty of pressure," Lucky said, pulling his blood-sodden hands away and standing. Staring into the man's barely open eyes, Fisher did as asked, pressing the sticky dressing which sent up a wave of sweet copper tang he tasted.

"Reuben Vega," Fisher said, watching the man's eyelids flitter. "The man behind all this pain."

Reuben drew a sharp breath, wincing with the effort as he tried to lift his head.

"You've misplaced your compliment," Reuben said, his Spanish accent strong despite panting the words. "We're a movement, not a single man."

"What's a collection of killers called?" Fisher said, spitting out the words.

"We're not killers. We're protecting the Human Race y de su miseria," Reuben replied, his breathing faltering as he spoke.

"Protecting us from what?" Fisher said, leaning closer.

"Not you, desde usted," Reuben said, grimacing, and his skin seemed to pale even more.

Fisher looked up at Harris, watching her head shake.

"He'll be dead soon," she replied, her expression blank as she looked him in the eye.

"They think they can explotar por dinero as weapons or whatever sickness they have planned," Reuben said, his gaze fixed off in the distance.

Fisher forced himself to laugh, then leaned closer still.

"Stop rambling. If I were you, I'd make your last words count. Just tell me what this is all about? Tell me why you've made my life into a façade. You put my friend through weeks of pain," Fisher said, his volume growing with every word. "You killed my parents and then my best friend."

Clenching his teeth, Fisher pushed harder on the dressing as warm blood surrounded his fingers with Reuben's breath becoming more shallow.

Glaring into Reuben's red eyes, Fisher smiled. "Just tell me why you killed my parents," he said, then closed his eyes, opening them to Reuben's laughter.

"We didn't kill them. You must know they weren't your parents by now? You freaks pass on your mutant genes."

Fisher looked up, but when Harris returned his stare, he turned back to Reuben.

"Those people you called your parents were human. You..." he said, scowling, the words halted by a wet cough. "You're an aberration, just like your mother and the rest of her spawn."

"My mother worked for you," Fisher said, pressing against the dressing harder still.

"Forget what you think you know. Alana never worked for us. She's how we got to you, yes, and we protected you for years. We kept you safe."

"You tortured, not protected. What kind of sick bastards are you?" Fisher said, spitting out the words.

"We were testing you. Pushing you harder, but you were just a disappointment," Reuben replied, gritting his teeth.

Fisher closed his eyes and shook his head. "I can't do this."

"We're out of time," Harris said, her voice soft. "Lucky, bundle him up as best we can and let's get out of here."

"He's not coming with us," Fisher snapped, not looking away from Reuben's ashen face. "He won't make it."

"We're not who you should fight," the old man said, his breathing laboured. "It's those that built this place you should be after."

Fisher turned away, but despite glancing at the concrete bunker, he paid it no attention. "He's killed so many people and is never going to give us a straight answer."

"We're not here for revenge," Harris said, her voice still soft.

"If someone else had taken this stand, my parents and Andrew would still be around. But they aren't and I owe them their right to vengeance."

"It's your vengeance, not theirs. Remember that," Harris said, standing, but didn't move Fisher away.

He shook his head, then lifted his chin before he stood, pulling off the bandage as he did and dropping it to the mud before grinding it into the dust.

Staring into Reuben's wide eyes, blood gulped out of the hole in his chest and sprayed from his mouth as he coughed.

78

"Please don't leave me again," Luana said as Fisher knelt in front of her. Without speaking, he took her hand. "What did he say?" she added as she held him tight.

"Nothing but riddles," Fisher replied.

"I mean, tell me exactly what he said," Luana said, her voice sharp, all softness gone.

"It was nonsense. Stuff about my parents," Fisher replied, closing his eyes.

"Did he say if they're alive?" she asked.

Fisher let go of her hand.

"I didn't think…" Fisher replied, the thought having not crossed his mind that his biological parents might not be dead. "He can't tell us anything now," he finally said as he pushed the corner of his mouth up. When the thought bought him no joy, he opened his eyes to Luana's screwed up expression.

"Why did you let him die? He could have told us everything. Now we'll have to start again," she shouted, glancing at her captive hand as she tugged at the restraint.

"Luana?" Fisher replied, surprised at the outburst.

"I'm sorry," she replied, the softness back in her tone. "I… I… I… Oh, don't worry. Please, just get me out of here."

"Let me," Harris said, her voice taking them both by surprise as she knelt at Fisher's side to look at the manacle.

"We will," Fisher replied. "They're looking for something to cut you out." He stood to give Harris more room, heading to the door they'd carried the gaunt man through. "What the hell is this place?" he said to no one in particular as he stared at the tall steel door. Pressing down the handle, he was surprised to find it locked. Turning back to the corner of the room, Luana frowned back.

"You know something," Fisher said, reading her expression, but it took her a long moment before she shook her head. "What do you know?" he said as he took a step closer.

"It's nothing," she replied with a shake of her head. "It's a fantasy."

"Like what we can do?" Fisher replied when she looked away.

"Renan kept talking about the Panchrest," she eventually said, and Fisher watched as Harris pulled back from Luana's side and stood, tilting her head down to the other woman. "He'd joke about what he'd do with it. It made little sense. Like much of what they said."

Fisher's gaze fell to Harris in the half-light as she shook her head.

"Which one is Renan?" Fisher turning back to Luana.

"Dungarees and short, mousey hair," she said. Fisher glanced at the entrance, but was too distracted to place the description.

"Have you heard of a Panchrest?" he asked as he turned back to Harris.

"It's mythology, nothing more," Harris replied, looking away.

"But what is it?" he said, moving closer as if urging her to make eye contact.

"It's science fiction," she said, standing up straight. "The stuff religious people have searched for across the millennia."

"You're talking like that dead man. Please don't," Fisher replied, fighting to keep his tone neutral.

Harris nodded. "It goes under many names. Panacea. The universal remedy. The Elixir of Life. You know, drink from the cup for eternal youth, that kind of thing."

"Oh," Fisher said, raising a brow, unsure how he should feel. "Like in Indiana Jones?"

"Exactly," Harris said with a nod. "These guys were deluded."

"Are you saying they went through all this for some magic potion?" Fisher replied, swapping glances between Harris and Luana, who were both looking over. "And I assume you found nothing on them that could have been this miracle?"

Harris shook her head. "Of course not," she said, turning

back toward the door.

After a moment of silence, Fisher stood. "I don't remember seeing this Renan."

"Me either," Harris said. As Fisher scowled back, Harris left the room.

"I'll be back," he said. Following, he found Biggy's bulk blocking out much of the light, but he moved to let them pass.

"What is it?" Fisher said out in the heat, watching the army truck rolling away with Miller jumping from the cab moments before it crashed into the trees.

"We're clearing space for the chopper to land," Biggy said, looking between the pair. "I don't know how, but Hotwire's contacted Dragon. The Americans have pushed the button on a thermobaric missile. They're wiping this place clean."

"But we've got the E-Bullet," Fisher said, his tone high.

"They won't abort," Biggy replied, shaking his head. "We've got twenty minutes before it's barbecue time, and we need to be long gone when it hits."

Fisher had already turned away, his gaze swapping between the bodies. "He's not here," he said, looking to Harris.

"We have an X-ray unaccounted for," she near-shouted to Biggy as she drew her Glock in time with Fisher, but before she could turn back to the bunker, a shot rang off from in the darkness.

Fisher rushed away with Harris following, but being closer to the building he arrived through the opening first, bounding in with his gun raised and pulling the trigger when he saw the stubby silhouette backlit from the open door he'd found locked only moments earlier.

Even as the figure dropped onto the sloping floor, they both ran, the door behind the figure held open.

With a few more steps, a scream echoed just as Fisher saw the same man raise his arm holding a pistol. Another shot went off, a muzzle close to the floor flashing bright.

Fisher fired and the arm dropped, shooting again before

he was right on him, kicking away the gun despite finding he'd blown the right side of the man's skull away.

Fisher's eyes stung with a renewed onslaught, but despite the antiseptic, he couldn't help but stare at the corridor beyond the door, his gaze following the open grid as it sloped off into the distance. On either side, the walls were glass framed with what looked like stainless steel panels. Both surfaces reflected the lights from overhead as they vanished to a point where they lost all detail.

The first three lights clinging to the low ceiling were dark, with the fourth flickering in time with the beat of Fisher's heart. Every so often, it would skip a beat. Below the strobe hung a whiteboard with black lines up, down, and sideways, forming a grid.

Barely noticing the blood he stepped in, climbing over the broad body dressed in blue overalls, Fisher leaned for a better look at movement beyond the glass a little way down the corridor. About to take another slow step as intrigue pulled him into the room, a high feminine scream felt like an ice cold dagger through his heart.

"Medic," Biggy boomed and, holding his breath, Fisher span around with his feet slipping as he palmed at the wall for balance until his gaze fell on Luana, before staring open-mouthed toward where Harris slumped.

79

Stumbling, Fisher fell to his knees as his hands rushed to Harris's once unblemished neck to stem the blood spurting from just above her protective vest.

Still calling out, Biggy dropped, his giant palms pressing on top of Fisher's as he shouted again.

"Medic," he continued to bellow, despite the thud of the rotors pushing the sound back.

Fisher joined the call and about to jump up and run to find Lucky, he saw the medic running towards them.

Dropping to their side, he wrenched their hands away and placed a thick bandage for Biggy to press down.

"No. No. No," Luana called out, rocking back and forth as Fisher's mouth hung agape, unable to look anywhere but Lucky's fingers rushing to pull open Harris's vest.

"We've got to go," Miller called over the din, but only Lucky moved, leaning over to check her vitals before rummaging around in his kit.

"James." The woman's sharp voice sounded distant.

"James," the voice said again, but only on the third call did he look up, his mouth still hanging open when he saw Luana's lips form his name in slow motion.

"She'll die if we move her."

It was Lucky who'd said the words that ripped away all hope whilst he stared at Luana, her lips still moving in slow motion.

"It's her only chance," she said.

Somehow he heard this time and realised what she was talking about. Feeling disconnected from his body, he glanced back to Harris, but unable to see past Lucky's frantic activity and struggling against his own weight, he stood, stumbling as he turned around, his hands slipping on the wall. Leaving smears of blood as he groped to stay upright, without looking over his shoulder he called out.

"Get everyone out."

Not waiting for a response, he stepped into the light. Despite holding his hand to his forehead against the brightness, even the pungent vapour did nothing to take away the smell of her blood. With his feet clattering on the metal grid as he walked, his steps were uneven, as if he had no control, but he stopped when his gaze fell to the floor and a word stamped into every metal section.

ExEvO.

With every shallow breath, he felt himself back in the moment as his gaze searched for what could help. Staring at the whiteboard, each box was numbered in the top left corner from one to a ninety-nine. All but a few were unmarked. Those numbered three, six, and eighty through to eighty-nine showed letters drawn with a red pen. The sequence meant nothing to him.

Leaving behind Luana's sobs, heated calls from the men punctuated by the thump of helicopter blades outside, Fisher buried his mouth in the pit of his elbow to slow the sting in his throat as light flickered over his head.

Looking to the right, he held his gaze when he found the walls were not just glass. Instead, beyond was a small room with a single door at the back. In the centre stood a stainless steel block the length and the width of a bed, with a slight indentation in the middle. At each corner was a cream cotton clamp held together with thick leather-like stitches.

In the left-hand corner of the glass wall stood a tall etched number two and at the stainless steel edge about waist height, a seam traced out a rectangular panel. With a glance over his shoulder, he found a mirror image of the space except for the number one in the corner.

His boots felt heavy as he squinted against the flickering light above, but he soon forgot their pull when he found the transparent front of the next room missing and as he got closer, rather than it not there, he found it had lowered through the floor, leaving just a section protruding as high as his ankle.

The space was just as empty as the others he'd passed, but

the bounds looked damp with sweat and tide-marked white. A thin brown liquid welled in the steel table's indentation. A translucent tube lay discarded on the floor, its inside spotted with the remnants of a deep red, a puddle of which formed a slick on the floor as it dripped from the open end, whilst the rest snaked across the room before disappearing into the wall just below a plain black square embedded into the metal.

Letting his arm relax from his mouth, Fisher barely noticed the burn in his throat as he took a breath, his focus instead on the corridor as he walked, where he soon brought his arm back at the first hint of a fetid odour pressing against his tonsils.

Despite finding the next cell empty, he steeled himself as he turned around, flinching when he found a naked man laying on his side and facing him from the slab. Perfect skin covered bulbous muscles and a washboard stomach, his face insulated with tight curls as long hair flowed down the side of the steel table. Along with the bounds at his ankles, another pair of fabric manacles, one just under his armpit and the other below the elbow, held his left arm out to the side and hovering over the edge of the metal bed where a cannula pressed into his skin with the end connected to a clear tube snaking away.

Thankful he still held his mouth in the crook of his arm, Fisher gagged, his stomach retching when his gaze fell to decaying lumps of flesh and bone, fingernails easy to spot in the mess as they gathered in a fetid pile underneath the suspended arm.

Fisher cocked his head at the sound of a dull hum from somewhere close as it rose above the helicopter's drone, but as he searched for the source, it was the man's eyes blinking wide that sent him stumbling back into the glass. Holding his gaze and afraid to move from his blank expression, his attention only fell away as the tube from his wrist turned burgundy.

Unable to draw himself away, Fisher watched the liquid follow the tube's snaking path as it went from the table before trailing across the floor where it rose to the left-hand wall before disappearing halfway up. Just as his attention shot back to the staring man, Fisher glanced to his side to find the top half of the dark panel lit with the four bright zeros of an LED display.

With the rising hum of the miniature pump, the right number changed to a nine. Fisher turned back to the naked man and found his eyelids fluttering as he rocked on his side. His hair swished back and forth and his eyes widened, mouth opening as he shook his head before letting out a scream Fisher could barely hear.

Panic rose as Fisher tried to figure out what was happening, then movement from the top of the glass cage pulled his attention from the man's screwed-up eyes to stare at a lowering mechanical strut driven by a thin piston.

His mind still racing, Fisher stepped forward and banged his fist on the thick glass. When it didn't deflect, he grabbed his Glock, but it still didn't give way as he smashed against it with the stock. Still staring at the arm, he backed away when a gleaming metal cleaver unfolded from the lowering strut.

With one swift movement he'd have missed if he'd blinked, the blade fell through the air, swinging down, shearing off the clamped hand and sending it slapping onto the putrid pile with blood spurting from the stump as the mechanical arm raised out of sight.

Holding his hand over his mouth, Fisher stumbled, unable to look away from the gulping blood and the face twisted with pain. Feeling like the time had passed in an instant and at the same time perhaps hours had gone by, Fisher's feet fixed to the spot with the pain draining from the man's expression as every moment passed.

Movement from the digital display caused Fisher to turn to the numbers counting up, having risen to twenty as he watched. Looking back at the stump, despite already regretting the move, he was surprised to see the blood had stopped flowing in the tube, replaced instead with a foam, a creamy shade of pink dripping to the severed hand.

The blood flowing in the cannula lightened and was soon the same sickly colour which had oozed from the wound but was now drying a dark colour with each moment. Again, Fisher traced the liquid as the pink wound its way around the tube and into the wall, where the digits raced higher still.

By the time Fisher looked away, the wound had formed an orangey, red scab, still darkening. As he continued to watch, it shrivelled, drying to a crisp, and fell in a matter of seconds. As the scab drifted onto the wretched pile, Fisher moved to the side, unsure he was seeing right when underneath he saw the skin, pink and fresh as it bulged.

"We're leaving," Biggy's voice boomed from the entrance. "With or without you."

His words did little to break the spell. Fisher's gaze instead locked on the man's face, his eyes peering down as if to follow the tube, the contents of which were crimson again.

Like an electric shock, Luana's words jumped into his head.

Pushing the pistol back into the holster, Fisher rushed in front of the readout and, reaching out, he tapped at the shiny metal where the numbers fell to zero.

"No," he bellowed when nothing happened, but as he did, his eyes went wide, his gaze landing on the lowest gap in the steel's outline. Finding it wider than the rest, he pressed his palms against the top edge and it moved a little and emitted a click.

Letting go, the panel fell towards him, pivoting on the bottom edge to reveal the end of the tube as it wound its way around a pump before ending at a stainless steel manifold. With too many connections for Fisher to count, his attention fell instead to a stubby glass bottle brimming with the soapy pink liquid.

Reaching in, Fisher took the warm glass and batted away water from his eyes. He mouthed a thank you to the staring man, then ran back along the corridor, knowing he had no choice but to leave him behind.

With the liquid spilling from side to side, he ran. Despite

the acrid antiseptic sting, it smelt divine, its sweetness tinged with a copper tang.

Almost at the first door, movement to his right caught his eye and he spotted a man in white overalls behind the glass that he didn't notice on his way in. The front of the fabric was splattered with blood from a long gash across his forehead. The man blinked as he stared.

Not slowing, rather than looking him in the eye, Fisher concentrated on the writing scrawled across the glass in blood that wasn't there before.

IT'S TOXIC. THEY WILL DIE.

Before he could take in what he saw, his foot caught on the grate. With the glass slick in his hands, it slipped from his grip, crashing to the metal floor and sending a column of pink foam into the air.

Thankful the glass hadn't broken and at least half of the contents remained inside, hearing his name screamed from the head of the corridor, he wiped his hands on his combats then picked up the container, holding it close to his chest as he rushed forward.

Nothing had changed as he appeared at the opening. The man in dungarees lay motionless in the way. With dirt and dust whirling in the air beyond the last door and the drone of the helicopter fighting for his attention, Luana still sobbed as Miller crouched beside her, drawing a hacksaw back and forth.

Harris lay cradled in Biggy's arms, limp and pale.

"Put her down," Fisher screamed.

"We've got to go," Biggy replied. "Or we're all dead, too."

"Put her down," he called again, rushing over. Biggy shook his head, watching as Fisher reached out. "Don't make me…"

Biggy narrowed his eyes then stooped, laying Harris gently on the floor whilst holding eye contact with Fisher. A moment later, he shook his head, then jogged the other way.

"I can't get her out," Miller screamed, his voice barely registered by Fisher as he dropped to his knees beside Harris.

"Just cut it off," Luana screamed through a broad smile

as she stared at the glass Fisher held to his chest.

"There's no time," Miller replied over the din.

"Cut my fucking hand off," she screamed before gritting her teeth and looking away.

With a heavy breath, Miller nodded, then leaned forward, holding the hacksaw out. Hardly noticing any of this, Fisher peered at Harris, her body limp as he leaned down to her face, kissing her gently on the lips and not bothering to fight against his tears.

"I'm sorry," he whispered, and then sat up straight before pulling off the sodden bandage from around the hole in her neck, pouring where blood welled, the pink liquid settling across the curve of her exposed skin.

Luana let out a blood-curdling scream, but as Fisher looked up, her call cut off and she went limp.

The engine noise grew more ferocious and Miller threw the bloody hacksaw into the corner of the room, glancing at Harris, still lifeless, before he gathered up his own casualty.

Fisher cradled Harris close to his chest as he pumped his legs for all he was worth, only just able to keep up with Miller holding Luana just as tight. Biggy sat at the open chopper door, beckoning them forward as it took its weight from its wheels.

Miller's older but conditioned legs pulled him ahead, and Biggy soon heaved Luana aboard, followed by the old soldier. With several paces still left for Fisher to push through, he stumbled, his gaze catching Hotwire's eye in the pilot seat and when Fisher only just held himself and his load from falling, the chopper swooped closer so Biggy could scoop Harris inside.

Despite the shouts from inside the cabin, the moment Biggy's hand connected with Fisher's, they sped and were above the trees with Fisher never fearing the grip would fail.

Soon he leaned over Harris's body, staring at the pink foam collected around the wound.

"Hold on to your balls. It was nice knowing you," Hotwire shouted, the call barely heard over the engine's scream a moment before blistering heat rocked the aircraft just as Harris coughed.

80

James grabbed a handful of dirt from the box offered by the priest, letting it slip through his fingers as he held his hand over the grave. With her arm curled around his, Carrie did the same before he watched Susie, then George and the rest of the mourners follow the gesture.

As the ceremony concluded, James looked across the crowd, his gaze falling on Alan's sorrowful expression. Watching him stand next to Doctor Devlin, James hadn't been sure if Alan could come and despite the nerves of how he'd feel, he felt no anger towards his old friend. Some of the emotion had transferred elsewhere. The rest had gone with what he'd gone through, its place taken by confusion along with uncertainty about his past and what the future might hold.

After the hugs and goodbye kisses were done, he walked beside Carrie toward her car in the distance.

"I'm sorry we've had little time to talk," she said, squeezing his arm.

"It's okay. You've been recuperating," James replied.

"Not really. I feel amazing, but I wanted to give you time with your friends."

"Thank you. It's been great, but I missed you," James said and as he turned to her, she swallowed, replying with a smile, a dimple forming on her cheek.

"When does your training start?" she said, her voice soft.

"Two weeks," he replied with a nod.

Carrie's smile grew. "I'm signed off for another two myself. But I can't sit still," she said, letting go of him before pushing her hand inside her jacket and pulling out a thick wad of folded paper he recognised as the maps they'd found in the mountains.

"What did Franklin say about that place?" James asked.

"He denied all knowledge and said the decision to blow it away was above his pay grade."

James let out a sigh.

"How are you really doing?" she said.

"I thought I would feel okay by now. We got the weapon back. We averted a world war and saved Luana in one go, and all without dying. Even though you gave it a good go. But still I feel like I've opened a can of worms. I regret nothing, but I can't decide. Were they the bad guys?" he said, then paused, looking off into the distance. "And if it's not them, then who is?"

"It's all about perspective," Carrie replied, nodding.

"And mine keeps changing," he added with the same gesture.

"Have you spoken with Luana since we got back?" she asked.

James shook his head. "She discharged herself from the hospital and I don't have a clue where she's gone."

"She'll come round. It's not your fault they couldn't save the hand," Carrie said, taking her gaze from his.

James turned around and watched Doctor Devlin walk over, holding a large brown envelope. There was no sign of Alan as he tipped his head towards James when he arrived.

"I'm sorry for your loss," the doctor said, his voice low.

"Thank you. And for bringing Alan. You didn't have to," James replied.

"It's part of his healing process, too," the doctor said with a nod as he pushed the envelope out but not offering it to either of them in particular. "Which one of you wants this?"

Carrie took the package. As she did, Devlin turned, drifting back to where he'd come from.

"I… I ordered some extra tests. Do you want to know?" she said, fingering the paper flap.

"I think I've already guessed, but it won't hurt to see it in black and white," he replied, then took a deep breath, staring at her hands as she pulled out a single piece of paper. Resting it on top of the bundle she already held, she looked it over from top to bottom.

James felt his heart rate rising as she continued to

concentrate on the words.

"You can't leave me hanging like this," he said, his skin flushing hot at her silence. "She's my mother, isn't she?"

Carrie nodded, but still hadn't looked up. James looked to the horizon, thoughts of what it could mean racing through his head. "So I've got a sister," he said, turning back, but Carrie continued to read. Then, as if only just realising what he'd said, she looked up with a shake of her head.

"She's not your sister. Alana is your mother, but Luana isn't related to either of you," she said, her brow lowered.

"What the hell?" James replied, taking the page as Carrie offered it, then shook his head when all he saw were a table of numbers besides acronyms he didn't understand. He turned the page, but found only more of the same.

"Did you ever see her use any sort of ability?" Carrie said, watching as James lowered the paper, narrowing his eyes.

"No," he replied a moment later, shaking his head.

"And it was her who told us about the Panacea?" she asked.

James nodded, his eyes widening as he took in a sharp intake of breath. "When you were out cold, she changed. Everyone said her whole demeanour flipped. I put it down to the pressure, but she was suddenly certain the Panchrest was beyond the door and it would save you," James said. "Oh my god. Maybe she meant for me to get it for her, not you…"

He looked up from the sheet again and locked his gaze with hers.

"And the guy who shot me? He was wearing a uniform?" she asked.

"Kind of," he replied.

"If she already knew about the place, it would have been easy to trick Reuben into believing she'd found it with some sort of extra sense," Carrie said, watching as James nodded and took shallow breaths. "We didn't even ask why she was cuffed. Maybe they figured it out before us."

"I think there's a good chance she worked for whoever built that place," James replied.

"Those *places*," Carrie added, waving the thick folded maps through the air.

"And now she's vanished," James replied with his eyebrows raised.

"I can guess where she's gone," Carrie said. "What would you do if you'd lost a hand and knew there was a way to grow it back?"

"I'd find that way."

The pair nodded and turned along the road.

"I take it you didn't mention the other maps to Franklin?" James said, the first to speak in what seemed like a long moment.

Harris shook her head and Fisher replied with a wry smile, pulling his passport from his jacket pocket.

To be continued…

James Fisher Book 3

Out 2024

The adventure continues 2024.

Agent Carrie Harris Action Thriller Series

If you like high-stakes thrills, strong female heroes, and action-packed adventures, then you won't be able to put down these intriguing novels.

In The End Zombie Apocalypse Series

In The End is a fast-paced post-apocalyptic zombie thriller. If you like nightmarish settings, reluctant heroes, and action-packed adventures, then you'll love these spine-chilling novels.

Visit my website for more details, an episode guide and for free books!

www.gjstevens.com

All my books are available from Amazon on Kindle, paperback & audio.

Search 'GJ Stevens'

Printed in Great Britain
by Amazon